A BEAUTIFUL PLACE TO DIE

Malla Nunn

ISIS
LARGE PRINT
Oxford

First published in Great Britain 2009
by
Picador
an imprint of Pan Macmillan Ltd.

Published in Large Print 2009 by ISIS Publishing Ltd.,
7 Centremead, Osney Mead, Oxford OX2 0ES
by arrangement with
Pan Macmillan Ltd.

British Library Cataloguing in Publication Data
Nunn, Malla.
   A beautiful place to die.
   1. Police - - South Africa - - Fiction.
   2. Police murders - - South Africa - - Fiction.
   3. Apartheid - - South Africa - - Fiction.
   4. South Africa - - History - - 1909–1961 - - Fiction.
   5. Detective and mystery stories.
   6. Large type books.
   I. Title
   823.9'2–dc22

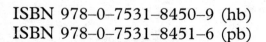

ISBN 978-0-7531-8450-9 (hb)
ISBN 978-0-7531-8451-6 (pb)

Printed and bound in Great Britain by
T. J. International Ltd., Padstow, Cornwall

For the ancestors

Acknowledgements

If it takes a village to raise a child, it takes two villages to raise a family and write a novel. These are the people of my village to whom I owe thanks.

Imkulunkulu the great, great one. The ancestors. My parents Patricia and Courtney Nunn for love, hope and faith. Penny, Jan and Byron, my siblings and fellow travellers on the dusty road from rural Swaziland to Australia.

My children Sisana and Elijah, lovely beyond compare. My husband, Mark Lazarus, who gave me time, space and the use of his impeccable eye for story. You are the roof and the walls of my little hut. Many thanks also to Dr Audrey Jakubowski-Lazarus and Dr Gerald Lazarus for their generosity and support.

Literary agents Siobhan Hannan of the Cameron Creswell Agency and Catherine Drayton of InkWell Management who bridge the gap between my writing desk and the world with focus and enthusiasm. I could not be in better hands.

For historical and cultural help I send special thanks to: Terence King, author, police and military researcher and historian; Gordon Bickley, military historian; Audrey Portman of Rhino Research, South Africa; Susie Lorentz for Afrikaans help and her honesty. Aunty Lizzie Thomas for Zulu help. Any errors or omissions are entirely my own.

Thanks also to members of the Nunn and Whitfield clans for stories and memories, both light and dark, of life in southern Africa.

To the Randwick "Gals" (Cass, Tash, Julia, Julie W, Una, Ilsa, Mary and Julie N) and the Kingsgrove "Gals" (Angie, Julie I and Jodie) for being a great posse of women with whom to ride out the transition into motherhood. Kerrie McGovan for introducing me to the mysteries of the intrawebs and delicious restaurant-quality meals. Loretta Walder, Maryla Rose and Brian Hunt who lit the path on the darkest nights.

Members of the "Blind Faith Club", an invaluable group of friends who, in the absence of proof, believed I would finish the book and that it would be published. They are Penny Nunn, the terrific Turks Yusuf and Burcak Muraben, Tony McNamara, Steve Worland, Georgie Parker and Paula McNamara.

Double thanks to Pan Macmillan for giving my book an international home. Maria Rejt in London. Rod Morrison and James Fraser in Sydney. You have re-invigorated my belief in lucky stars. Editors Kylie Mason and Anna Valdinger who simply made the book better. To all the Pan Macmillan staff for their warm welcome and hard work.

Ngiyabonga. Thank you all.

CHAPTER
ONE

South Africa, September 1952

Detective Sergeant Emmanuel Cooper switched off the engine and looked out through the dirty windscreen. He was in deep country. To get deeper he'd have to travel back in time to the Zulu wars. Two Ford pick-up trucks, a white Mercedes and a police van parked to his right placed him in the twentieth century. Ahead of him a group of black farmworkers stood along a rise with their backs towards him. The hard line of their shoulders obscured what lay ahead.

In the crease of a hot green hill a jumpy herd boy with fifteen skinny cows stared at the unusual scattering of people in the middle of nowhere. The farm was a genuine crime scene after all — not a hoax as district headquarters had thought. Emmanuel got out of the car and lifted his hat to a group of women and children sitting in the shade of a wild fig tree. A few of them politely nodded back, silent and fearful. Emmanuel checked for his notebook, his pen and his handgun, mentally preparing for the job.

An old black man in tattered overalls stepped out from the band of shade cast by the police van. He approached with his cloth cap in his hand.

"You the *baas* from Jo'burg?" he asked.

"That's me," Emmanuel said. He locked the car and dropped the keys into his jacket pocket.

"Policeman says to go to the river." The old man pointed a bony finger in the direction of the farmworkers standing along the ridge. "You must come with me, please, *ma'baas*."

The old man led the way. Emmanuel followed and the farmworkers turned at his approach. He drew closer to them and scanned the row of faces to try and gauge the mood. Beneath their silence he sensed fear.

"You must go there, *ma'baas*." The old man indicated a narrow path that snaked through tall grass to the banks of a wide, shining river.

Emmanuel nodded his thanks and walked down the dirt trail. A breeze rustled the underbrush and a pair of bullfinches flew up. He smelled damp earth and crushed grass. He wondered what waited for him.

At the bottom of the path he came to the edge of the river and looked across to the far side. A stretch of low veldt shimmered under clear skies. In the distance a mountain range broke the horizon into jagged blue peaks. Pure Africa. Just like the photos in English magazines that talked up the benefits of migration.

Emmanuel began a slow walk of the riverbank. Ten paces along he saw the body.

Within reach of the river's edge a man floated face down with his arms spread out like a parachute diver in

2

free fall. Emmanuel clocked the police uniform instantly. A captain. Wide-shouldered and big-boned with blond hair cut close to the skull. Small silver fish danced around what looked like a bullet wound in the head and another gash torn into the middle of the man's broad back. A thicket of reeds held the body fast against the current.

A blood-stiffened blanket and an overturned lantern with a burnt-out wick marked a fishing spot. Bait worms had spilled from a jam can and dried on the coarse sand.

Emmanuel's heart hammered in his rib cage. He'd been sent out solo on the murder of a white police captain.

"You the detective?" The question, in Afrikaans, had the tone of a surly boy addressing the new schoolmaster.

Emmanuel turned to face a lanky teenager in a police uniform. A thick leather belt anchored the blue cotton pants and jacket to the boy's narrow hips. Wisps of downy hair grew along his jawline. The National Party policy of hiring Afrikaners into public service had reached the countryside.

"I'm Detective Sergeant Emmanuel Cooper." He held out his hand. "Are you the policeman in charge of this case?"

The boy flushed. "*Ja*, I'm Constable Hansie Hepple. Lieutenant Uys is on holiday in Mozambique for two more days and Captain Pretorius . . . well . . . he's . . . he's gone."

3

They looked over at the captain, swimming in the waters of eternity. A dead white hand waved at them from the shallows.

"Did you find the body, Constable Hepple?" Emmanuel asked.

"No." The Afrikaner youth teared up. "Some kaffir boys from the location found the captain this morning . . . he's been out here all night."

Emmanuel waited until Hansie got control of himself. "Did you call the detective branch in?"

"I couldn't get a phone line to district headquarters," the boy policeman explained. "I told my sister to try till she got through. I didn't want to leave the captain by himself."

A knot of three white men stood farther up the river-bank and took turns drinking from a battered silver flask. They were big and meaty, the kind of men who would pull their own wagons across the veldt long after the oxen were dead.

Emmanuel motioned towards the group. "Who are they?"

"Three of the captain's sons."

"How many sons does the captain have?" Emmanuel imagined the mother, a wide-hipped woman who gave birth between baking bread and hanging up the laundry.

"Five sons. They're a good family. True *volk*."

The young policeman dug his hands into his pockets and kicked a stone across the bank with his steel-capped boot. Eight years after the beaches of Normandy and the ruins of Berlin, there was still talk of folk-spirit and race purity out on the African plains.

4

Emmanuel studied the murdered captain's sons. They were true Afrikaners, all right. Muscled blonds plucked straight from the victory at the battle of Blood River and glorified on the walls of the Voortrekker Monument. The captain's boys broke from their huddle and walked towards him.

Images from Emmanuel's childhood flickered to life: boys with skin white as mother's milk from the neck down and the elbow up; noses skewed from fights with friends, the Indians, the English, or the coloured boys cheeky enough to challenge their place at the top.

The brothers came within shoving distance of Emmanuel and stopped. Boss Man, the largest of the brothers, stood in front. The Enforcer stood to his right with his jaw clenched. Half a step behind, the third brother stood ready to take orders from up the chain of command.

"Where's the rest of the squad?" Boss Man demanded in rough-edged English. "Where are your men?"

"I'm it," Emmanuel said. "There is no — one else."

"You joking me?" The Enforcer added finger pointing to the exchange. "A police captain is murdered and detective branch send out one lousy detective?"

"I shouldn't be out here alone," Emmanuel conceded. A dead white man demanded a team of detectives. A dead white policeman: a whole division. "The information headquarters received was unclear. There was no mention of the victim's race, sex, or occupation."

The Enforcer cut across the explanation. "You have to do better than that."

Emmanuel chose to focus on the Boss Man.

5

"I was working the Preston murder case. The white couple shot in their general store," he said. "We tracked the killer to his parents' farm, an hour west of here, and made an arrest. Major van Niekerk called and asked me to check a possible homicide —"

"Possible homicide?" The Enforcer wasn't about to be sidelined. "What the hell does that mean?"

"It means the operator who logged the call got one useful piece of information from the caller — the name of the town, Jacob's Rest. That was all we had to work with."

He didn't mention the word hoax.

"If that's true," the Enforcer said, "how did you get here? This isn't Jacob's Rest, it's Old Voster's Farm."

"An African man waved me off the main road, then another one showed me to the river," Emmanuel explained and the brothers shared a puzzled look. They had no idea what he was talking about.

"Can't be." The Boss Man spoke directly to the boy constable. "You told them a police captain had been murdered, hey, Hansie?"

The teenager scuttled behind Emmanuel. His breathing was ragged in the sudden quiet.

"Hansie . . ." The Enforcer smelled blood. "What did you tell them?"

"I . . ." The boy's voice was muffled. "I told Gertie she must say everything. She must explain how it was."

"Gertie . . . Your twelve-year-old sister made the call?"

"I couldn't get a line," Hansie complained. "I tried . . ."

"*Domkop.*" The Boss Man stepped to the side, in order to get a clear swing at Hansie. "You really that stupid?"

6

The brothers moved forwards in a hard line, cabbage-sized fists at the ready. The constable grabbed a handful of Emmanuel's jacket and burrowed close to his shoulder.

Emmanuel stood his ground and kept eye contact with the head brother. "Giving Constable Hepple a smack or two will make you feel better but you can't do it here. This is a crime scene and I need to start work."

The Pretorius boys stopped. Their focus shifted to the body of their father floating in the clear water of the river.

Emmanuel stepped into the silence and held out his hand. "Detective Sergeant Emmanuel Cooper. I'm sorry for the loss of your father."

"Henrick," the Boss Man said and Emmanuel felt his hand disappear into a fleshy paw. "This here is Johannes and Erich, my brothers."

The younger brothers nodded a greeting, wary of the city detective in the pressed suit and green-striped tie. In Jo'burg he looked smart and professional. On the veldt with men who smelled of dirt and diesel fuel he was out of place.

"Constable Hepple says there are five of you." He returned the brothers' stares and noticed the areas of redness around their eyes and noses.

"Louis is at home with our ma. He's too young to see this." Henrick took a swig from the flask and turned away to hide his tears.

Erich, the Enforcer, stepped forwards. "The army is letting Paul out on compassionate leave. He'll be home tomorrow or the day after."

"What unit is he in?" Emmanuel asked, curious in spite of himself. Six years out of service and his own trousers and shirtsleeves were still ironed sharp enough to please a sergeant major. The army had discharged him, but it hadn't let him go.

"Paul's in intelligence," Henrick said, now flushed pink from the brandy.

Emmanuel calculated the odds that brother Paul belonged to the old guard of the intelligence corps — the one that broke fingers and smashed heads to extract information. Exactly the kind you didn't want hanging around an orderly murder investigation.

He checked the brothers' posture, the slack shoulders and unclenched hands, and decided to take control of the situation while he had a moment to do so. He was on his own with no backup and there was a murder to solve. He started with the classic opener guaranteed to raise a response from idiots and geniuses alike:

"Can you think of anyone who would do this to your father?"

"No. No-one," Henrick answered with absolute certainty. "My father was a good man."

"Even good men have enemies. Especially a police captain."

"Pa might have got on the wrong side of some people, but nothing serious," Erich insisted. "People respected him. No-one who knew him could do this."

"An outsider, is your guess?"

"Smugglers use this stretch of river to go in and out of Mozambique," Henrick said. "Weapons, liquor, even

8

Commie pamphlets, they all come into the country when no-one is looking."

Johannes spoke for the first time. "We think Pa maybe surprised some criminal crossing over into SA."

"A lowlife bringing in cigarettes or whisky stolen off the docks in Lourenço Marques." Erich took the flask from Henrick. "Some kaffir with nothing to lose."

"That casts the net pretty wide," Emmanuel said and studied the full length of the riverbank. Farther upstream, an older black man in a heavy wool coat and khaki uniform sat in the patchy shade of an indoni tree. Two frightened black boys nestled close to him.

"Who's that?" he asked.

"Shabalala," Henrick answered. "He's a policeman, too. He's half-Zulu, half-Shangaan. Pa said the Shangaan part could track any animal, and the Zulu part was sure to kill it."

The Pretorius brothers smiled at the captain's old explanation.

Hansie stepped up eagerly. "Those are the boys who found the body. They told Shabalala and he rode into town and told us."

"I'd like to hear what they have to say."

Hansie pulled a whistle from his breast pocket and blew a shrill note. "Constable Shabalala. Bring the boys. Make it fast."

Shabalala rose slowly to his full height, over six feet, and made his way towards them. The boys followed in the shadow he cast. Emmanuel watched Shabalala approach and instantly realised that he must have been the policeman who'd set up the series of native men to guide him to the crime scene.

"Quick, man!" Hansie called out. "You see that, Detective Sergeant? You tell them to hurry and this is what you get."

Emmanuel pressed his fingers into the ridge of bone above his left eye socket where a headache stirred. The country light, free from industrial haze, was bright as a blowtorch on his retina.

"Detective Sergeant Cooper, this is Constable Samuel Shabalala." Hansie performed the introductions in his best grown-up voice. "Shabalala, this detective has come all the way from Jo'burg to help us find out who killed the captain. You must tell him everything you know like a good man, okay?"

Shabalala, a few heads taller and a decade or two older than any of the white men in front of him, nodded and shook Emmanuel's outstretched hand. His face, calm as a lake, gave nothing away. Emmanuel made eye contact, and saw nothing but his own reflection in the dark brown eyes.

"The detective is an Englishman." Henrick spoke directly to Shabalala. "You must use English, okay?"

Emmanuel turned to the brothers, who stood in a semicircle behind him. "You need to move back twenty paces while I question the boys," he said. "I'll call you when we're ready to move your pa."

Henrick grunted and the brothers moved away. Emmanuel waited until they re-formed their huddle before continuing.

10

He crouched down to the boys' level. "*Uno bani wena?*" he asked Shabalala.

Shabalala's eyes widened in surprise, then he joined Emmanuel at child height and gently touched each boy on the shoulder in turn. Continuing in Zulu, he answered Emmanuel's question. "This one is Vusi and this one is Butana, the little brother."

The boys looked about eleven and nine years old, with close-shaven heads and enormous brown eyes. Their rounded stomachs pushed out their frayed shirts.

"I'm Emmanuel. I'm a policeman from Jo'burg. You are brave boys. Can you tell me what happened?"

Butana held his hand up and waited to be called on.

"*Yebo?*" Emmanuel prompted.

"Please, *baas.*" Butana's finger twisted through a hole at the front of his shirt. "We came here fishing."

"Where did you come from?"

"Our mother's house at the location," the older boy said. "We came when it was just light because *baas* Voster doesn't like us to fish at this place."

"Voster says the natives steal the fish," Hansie said and crouched down to join the action.

Emmanuel ignored him. "How did you get to the river?" he asked.

"We came down from that path there." Vusi pointed past the blanket and lantern that lay on the sand to a narrow pathway that disappeared into the lush veldt.

"We came to here and I saw there was a white man in the water," Butana said. "It was Captain Pretorius. Dead."

"What did you do?" Emmanuel asked.

"We ran." Vusi rubbed one palm against the other to made a swishing sound. "Fast, fast. No stopping."

"You went home?"

"No, *baas*," Vusi said and shook his head. "We came to the policeman's house and told what we saw."

"What time?" Emmanuel asked Shabalala.

"It was past six o'clock in the morning," the black policeman said.

"They just know what time it is," Hansie supplied helpfully. "They don't need clocks the way we do."

Blacks in South Africa needed so little. A little less every day was the general rule. The job of detective was one of the few not subject to policies forbidding contact between different races. Detectives uncovered the facts, presented the brief and gave evidence in court to support the case. White, black, coloured, or Indian, murder was a capital offence no matter what race the offender belonged to.

Emmanuel spoke to the older boy. "Did you see or hear anything strange when you came down to the river this morning?"

"The unusual thing was the body of the captain in the water," said Vusi.

"What about you?" Emmanuel asked the smaller boy. "You notice anything different? Besides the captain in the water?"

"Nothing," the little brother said.

"When you saw the body did you think of anyone you know who could have hurt Captain Pretorius?"

The boys considered the question for a moment, their brown eyes wide with concentration.

12

Vusi shook his head. "No. I thought only that today was not a good day to go fishing."

Emmanuel smiled.

"You both did a very good thing by telling Constable Shabalala what you saw. You will make fine policemen one day."

Vusi's chest puffed out with pride, but his little brother's eyes filled with tears.

"What's the matter?" Emmanuel asked.

"I do not want to be a policeman, *nkosana*," the small boy said. "I want to be a schoolteacher."

The terror that came with discovering the body had finally surfaced in the little witness. Shabalala laid a hand on the crying boy's shoulder and waited for the signal to dismiss the boys. Emmanuel nodded.

"To be a schoolteacher, first you must go to school," the black policeman said and waved to one of the farmworkers standing on the ridge. "Musa will take you home."

Shabalala walked the boys past the Pretorius brothers to a man standing at the top of the path. The man waved the boys up towards him.

Emmanuel studied the riverbank. The green spring veldt and wide sky filled his vision. He pulled out his notebook and wrote the word "pleasing" because it was the first thing to come to his mind when he examined the wider elements of the scene.

There would have been a moment just after the blanket was spread and the lantern turned to full light when the captain would have looked out over the river and felt a sense of joy at this place. He might even have been smiling when the bullet struck.

"Well?" It was Erich, still put out by being moved away from the questioning. "Did you get anything?"

"No," Emmanuel said. "Nothing."

"The only reason we haven't taken Pa home," Henrick said, "is because he would have wanted us to follow the rules . . ."

"But if you're not getting anything —" Erich said, his short fuse lit "— there's no reason for us to stand here like ant hills when we could be helping Pa."

The wait for the big city detective to work the scene had taken a toll on the brothers. Emmanuel knew that they were battling the urge to turn the captain face up so he could get some air.

"I'll take a look at the blanket, then we'll take your father back to town straight after," Emmanuel said when Shabalala rejoined the group. "Hepple and Shabalala, you're with me."

They leaned in close to the blood-stained blanket. The material was coarse grey, scratchy, and comfortable as a sheet of corrugated iron to sit on. Every outdoor event, farm truck, and *braai* came with blankets just like this one.

Blood had dried rust-brown on the fabric and spilled over the blanket's edge into the sand. Deep lines, broken at irregular intervals, led from the blanket to the river's edge. The captain had been shot, then dragged to the water and dumped. No mean feat.

"What do you make of this?" Emmanuel said and pointed to the blood-stiffened material.

"Let's see." Hansie came forwards. "The captain came fishing, the way he did every week, and someone shot him."

"Yes, Hepple, those are the facts." Emmanuel glanced at Shabalala. If the captain was right, the Shangaan part of the silent black man would see more than the obvious. "Well?"

The black policeman hesitated.

"Tell me what you think happened," Emmanuel said, aware of Shabalala's reluctance to show up Hansie's poor grasp of the situation.

"The captain was shot here on the blanket, then pulled over the sand to the water. But the killer, he's not strong."

"How's that?"

"He had to rest many times." Shabalala pointed to the shallow indentations that broke the line as it ran from the blanket to the water. "This is the mark of the captain's boots. Here is where his body was put down. Here was his head."

In the hollow lay a dried pool of blood and a matted tuft of blond hair. The indentations appeared closer and closer together, the pools of blood larger, as the killer stopped to catch his breath more often.

"Somebody wanted to make sure the captain wasn't coming back," Emmanuel muttered. "Are you sure he didn't have any enemies?"

"None," Hansie answered without hesitation. "Captain got on good with everyone, even the natives, hey, Shabalala?"

"*Yebo*," the black constable said. He stared at the evidence, which said otherwise.

"Some places have trouble between the groups. Not here," Hansie insisted. "A stranger must have done this. Someone from outside."

There wasn't much to go on yet. If it had been a crime of passion, the murderer might have made mistakes: no alibi; murder weapon hidden in an obvious place; blood left to dry on shoelaces . . . If the murder was premeditated, then only careful police work would catch the killer. Outsider or insider, it took guts to kill a white police captain.

"Comb the riverbank," he instructed Hansie. "Walk as far as the path where the boys climbed up. Go slowly. If you find anything out of the ordinary, don't touch it. Call me."

"Yes, sir." Hansie set off like a labrador.

Emmanuel scoped the scene. The captain's killer had dragged the body to the water without dropping a thing.

"Did he have enemies?" he asked Shabalala.

"The bad people did not like him, but the good people did." The black man's face betrayed nothing.

"What do you really think happened here?"

"It rained this morning. Many of the marks have been washed away."

Emmanuel wasn't buying. "Tell me anyway."

"Captain was kneeling and facing this way." Shabalala pointed in the direction Hansie had gone. "A man's boot prints come here from behind. One bullet in the head, captain fell. Then a second bullet in the back."

A boot print with deep, straight grooves was pressed into the sand.

"How the hell did the killer manage a clean shot in the dark?" Emmanuel asked.

"It was a full moon last night and bright. The lantern was also burning."

"How many people can take a shot like that even in broad daylight?"

"Many," the black policeman said. "The white men learn to shoot guns at their club. Captain Pretorius and his sons have won many trophies." Shabalala thought for a moment. "Mrs Pretorius has also won many."

Emmanuel again pressed his left eye socket where the headache was beginning. He'd landed in a town of sharp-shooting inbred Afrikaner farmers.

"Where did the killer go after dumping the body?"

"The river." Shabalala walked to the edge of the water and pointed to where the captain's heel marks and the killer's footprints disappeared into the flow.

A clump of bulrushes with the stems snapped back lay on the opposite bank. A narrow path trailed off into the bush lands.

"The killer came out there?" He pointed to the trampled rushes.

"I think so."

"Whose farm is that?" Emmanuel asked and felt a familiar surge of adrenaline — the excitement of the first lead in a new case. They could track the killer to his door and finish this today. With luck he'd be back in Jo'burg for the weekend.

"No farm," came the reply. "Mozambique."

"You sure, man?"

"*Yebo*. Mo. Zam. Bique." Shabalala repeated the name, long and slow, so there was no mistake. The syllables emphasised that across the river was another country with its own laws and its own police force.

Emmanuel and Shabalala stood side by side and looked across the water for a long while. Five minutes on the opposite shore might give up a clue that could break open the case. Emmanuel did a quick calculation. If he was caught across the border he'd spend the next two years checking ID passes at whites-only public toilets. Even Major van Niekerk, a canny political animal with connections to burn, couldn't fix up a bungled visit across the border.

He turned to face South Africa and concentrated on the evidence in front of him. The neatness of the scene and the sniper-like targeting of the victim's head and spine indicated a cool and methodical hand. The location of the body was also a deliberate choice. Why take the time to drag it to the water when it could have been left on the sand?

The brothers' smuggler theory didn't hold water, either. Why wouldn't he cross farther upstream and avoid all that attention and trouble? Not only that, why would he compromise his path between borders by murdering a white man?

"Did the killer come out of the river?" Emmanuel asked.

The Zulu policeman shook his head. "When I came here the herd boys and their oxen had been to the river to drink. If the tracks were here, they are gone now."

"Detective Sergeant," Hansie said, walking towards them, pink skin flushed with exertion.

"Anything?"

"Nothing but sand, Detective Sergeant."

The dead man floated in the river. A spring rain, gentle as mist, began to fall.

"Let's get the captain," Emmanuel said.

"*Yebo*."

Sadness flickered across the black man's face for a moment and then it was gone.

CHAPTER
TWO

The coffee was hot and black and spiked with enough brandy to dull the ache in Emmanuel's muscles. A full hour after going in to retrieve the captain, the men from the riverbank were back at the cars, shoulders and legs twitching with fatigue. Extracting the body from the crime scene proved to be only slightly easier than pulling a Sherman tank out of the mud.

"*Koeksister*?" asked Old Voster's wife, a toad-faced woman with thinning grey hair.

"Thank you." Emmanuel took a sticky pastry and leaned back against the Packard. He looked around at the gathering of people and vehicles. Two black maids poured fresh coffee and handed out dry towels while a group of farmworkers tended the fire for the hot water and milk. The wheelchair-bound Voster and his family, a son and two daughters, were deep in conversation with the Pretorius brothers while a pack of sinewy Rhodesian ridgebacks sniffed the ground at their feet. Black and white children ran zigzag together between the cars in a noisy game of hide and seek. The captain lay in the back of the police van wrapped in clean white sheets.

Emmanuel drained his coffee and approached the Pretorius brothers. The investigation needed to move forwards fast. All they had so far was a dead body and a killer walking free in Mozambique.

"Time to go," Emmanuel said. "We'll take the captain to hospital, get the doctor to look him over."

"We're taking him home," Henrick stated flatly. "My ma's waited long enough to see him."

Emmanuel felt the force of the brothers as they turned their gaze on him. He held their stare and absorbed the tension and rage, now doubly fuelled by alcohol and fatigue.

"We need a medical opinion on the time and the cause of death. And a signed death certificate. It's standard police procedure."

"Are you blind as well as fucking deaf?" Erich said. "You need a doctor to tell you he was shot? What kind of detective are you, Detective?"

"I'm the kind of detective that solves cases, Erich. That's why Major van Niekerk sent me. Would you rather we left it to him?" He motioned to the fire where Hansie sat cross-legged, a plate of *koeksisters* on his knees. The thin sound of his humming carried through the air as he selected another sweet pastry.

"We won't agree to a doctor cutting him up like a beast," Henrick said. "He's God's creature, even if his spirit has departed his body. Pa would never have agreed to it and we won't either."

True Afrikaners and religious with it. Wars started with less fuel. The Pretorius boys were ready to take up arms for their beliefs. Time to tread carefully. He was

21

out on his own with no backup and no partner. Some access to the body was better than none at all.

"No autopsy," Emmanuel said. "Just an examination to determine time and cause of death. The captain would have agreed to that much, I'm sure."

"*Ja*, okay," Erich said and the aggression drained from him.

"Tell your ma we'll get him home as soon as possible. Constable Shabalala and I will take care of him."

Henrick handed over the keys to the police van, which he'd found in the captain's pocket when they hauled him out of the river.

"Hansie and Shabalala will show you the way to the hospital and then to our parents' place. Take too long and my brothers and I will come looking for you, Detective."

Emmanuel checked the rearview mirror of the police van and saw Hansie following in the Packard with Shabalala's bike lashed to the roof. The boy was good behind the wheel; tight and confident. If the killer was a race car driver, Emmanuel noted, Hansie might get a chance to earn his pay packet on the police force, possibly for the first time.

The vehicles entered the town of Jacob's Rest on Piet Retief Street, the town's only tarred road. A little way down, they turned onto a dirt road and drove past a series of low-slung buildings grouped together under a haze of purple jacaranda trees. Shabalala directed Emmanuel into a circular drive lined with whitewashed stones. He parked at the front entrance to the Grace of God Hospital.

Crude icon images of Christ on the Cross were carved into the two front doors. Emmanuel and Shabalala slipped out of the police van and stood either side of the filthy bonnet. Mud-splattered and sweat-stained, they carried the smell of bad news about them.

"What now?" Emmanuel asked Shabalala. It was almost noon and the captain was doing a slow roast in the back of the police van.

The doors of the hospital swung open and a large steam engine of a black woman in a nun's habit appeared on the top stair. Another nun, pale-skinned and tiny as a bantam hen, stepped up beside her. The sisters stared out from the shade cast by their headdresses.

"Sisters." Emmanuel lifted his hat, like a hobo practising good manners. "I'm Detective Sergeant Emmanuel Cooper. You know the other policemen, I'm sure."

"Of course, of course." The tiny white nun fluttered down the stairs, followed by her solid black shadow. "I'm Sister Bernadette and this is Sister Angelina. Please forgive our surprise. How may we be of service, Detective Cooper?"

"We have Captain Pretorius in the van —"

The sisters' gasp broke the flow of his words. He started again, aiming for a gentler tone.

"The captain is —"

"Dead," Hansie blubbered. "He's been murdered. Someone shot him in the head and the back . . . there's a hole . . ."

23

"Constable . . ." Emmanuel put the full weight of his hand on the boy's shoulder. No need for specific information about the case to be sprayed around so early. It was a small town. Everyone would know the bloody details soon enough.

"Lord rest his soul," said Sister Bernadette.

"May God have mercy on his soul," Sister Angelina intoned.

Emmanuel waited until the sisters crossed themselves before pushing ahead.

"We need the doctor to examine Captain Pretorius to determine cause and time of death, and to issue the death certificate."

"Oh dear, oh dear, oh dear . . ." Sister Bernadette muttered quietly, her Irish brogue now thick. "I'm afraid we can't help you, Detective Cooper. Doctor left on his rounds this morning."

"When will he be back?" Emmanuel figured he had four hours at most before the Pretorius brothers showed up to claim the body.

"Two, maybe three days," Sister Bernadette said. "There's been an outbreak of bilharzia at a boarding school near Bremer. Depending on the number of cases, he might be longer. I'm so sorry."

Days, not hours. Country time was too slow for his liking.

"What would you do if Captain Pretorius was badly injured, but still alive?" he asked.

"Send you on to Mooihoek. There's a doctor at the hospital full time."

24

He didn't get his hopes up. The situation was fubar, as the Yank soldiers were fond of saying. Fucked up beyond all recognition. He tried anyway.

"How long?"

"If the road is in good shape, just under two hours." Sister Bernadette delivered the good news with a weak smile, then cast about for a friendlier face, one that understood geography. "Isn't that so, Constable Shabalala?"

Shabalala nodded. "That is the time, if the road is good."

"And is the road good?" Emmanuel asked. The headache suddenly pulsed red and white behind his left eye socket. He waited for someone to answer the question.

"Good until ver Maak's farm." Shabalala spoke up when it became obvious no-one else was going to. "Ver Maak told captain there was a *donga* in the road, but he drove around it to come to town."

The collapse in the road was passable, but it would add time onto the journey to Mooihoek. He didn't want to risk breaking the case open like this. A police van with a dead police captain was sure to get noticed, especially in Mooihoek, where a phone call would bring the press swarming down on them in no time.

"Detective Cooper." Sister Bernadette touched the silver cross around her neck and felt the comforting sharpness of Jesus's ribs against her fingers. "There is Mr Zweigman."

"Who is Mr Zweigman?"

"The old Jew," Hansie said quickly. "He runs a dry goods store down by the bus stop. Kaffirs and coloureds go there."

Emmanuel kept his gaze steady on Sister Bernadette; God's black-robed pigeon ready to take flight at the smallest sound. "What about Mr Zweigman?"

Sister Bernadette released a pent-up breath. "A native boy was run over a few months ago and Mr Zweigman treated him at the scene. The boy came here later and you could see . . . he was fixed up by someone qualified."

Emmanuel checked Shabalala. Shabalala nodded. The story was true.

"Is he a doctor?"

"He says he was a medic in the refugee camps in Germany but . . ." Sister Bernadette gripped the silver cross tightly and asked the Lord's forgiveness for the confidence she was about to betray. "We have had Mr Zweigman look at one or two cases while Dr Kruger has been away. Not officially, you see. No, no. A quick look, that's all. We'd rather doctor didn't find out."

"The old Jew isn't a doctor," Hansie said, bristling. "Dr Kruger is the only doctor in the district. Everybody knows that. What kind of rubbish are you talking?"

Sister Angelina stepped forwards with an angelic smile. She could have crushed Hansie in her enormous black fist, yet she chose to appear small in front of the puffed-up boy policeman. "Yes, of course," she said in a warm voice. "Dr Kruger is the only proper doctor, that's correct, Constable. Mr Zweigman is only for us natives who don't need such good medicine. For the natives only."

Emmanuel found himself no closer to knowing if the old Jew was a doctor or a shopkeeper with a first aid certificate.

"Shabalala." He motioned the policeman to the back of the police van, and out of earshot. "What do you know about this?"

"The captain told me, if you are sick you must go to the old Jew. He will fix you better than Dr Kruger."

Better, not worse. That was the captain's opinion and this was his town. Emmanuel fished the Packard keys from his pocket.

"Here." Shabalala pointed to a row of shops pressed close together under sheets of rusting corrugated iron. A pitted footpath added to the derelict appearance of the businesses, each with its doors thrown open to the street. Khan's Emporium was pungent with spices. Next stood a "Fine Liquor Merchant" manned by two bored mixed-race boys playing cards out the front. After that sat Poppies General Store, which looked in danger of sliding off its wooden foundations and into the vacant lot adjoining it.

Across the road, there was a burned-out garage with a charred petrol pump and piles of blistered tyres. A lanky walnut-coloured man patiently worked his way through the rubble, picking up bricks and pieces of twisted metal and throwing them into a wheelbarrow.

A black native woman ambled by with a baby tied to her back and a mixed-race "coloured" boy pushed a toy car made of wire along the footpath. No English or Afrikaners. Emmanuel and Shabalala had slipped out of white Africa.

"The last one is the old Jew's place." Shabalala pointed to Poppies General Store. Emmanuel switched off the engine and put his optimism on ice. A broken-down shop on the wrong side of the colour line was no place for a qualified doctor unless he was crazy or had been struck off the medical register.

Poppies was crammed with hessian sacks of corn, cans of jam, and corned meat. The air smelled of raw cotton and bolts of plain and patterned material leaned against the far edge of a long wooden counter. Behind the counter stood a slight man with wire-rimmed glasses and a shock of brilliant white hair that flew up from his skull like an exclamation point.

A crackpot, Emmanuel judged quickly, and "the old Jew" wasn't as old as he'd imagined. Zweigman was still on the right side of fifty, despite his hair and stooped shoulders. His brown eyes were bright as a crow's as he took in the sight of the mud-spattered pair without reaction.

"How can I help you, officer?" Zweigman asked in an accent Emmanuel knew well. Educated German transplanted into a rough and charmless English.

"Get your medical kit and your licence. We need you at the hospital." He made sure Zweigman saw the police ID he slapped onto the counter.

"A moment, please," Zweigman answered politely and disappeared into a back room separated from the main shop by a yellow-and-white-striped curtain. The mechanical whir of sewing machines filtered out, then stopped abruptly. There was the sound of voices, low and urgent, before the shopkeeper reappeared with his medical bag. A dark-haired woman in an elegant blue satin dress tailored to fit the generous curves of her body followed close behind Zweigman.

The old Jew and the woman were as different as a gumboot and a ball gown. Zweigman could have been any old man serving behind any dusty counter in South Africa, but the woman belonged to a cool climate place with Persian carpets and a grand piano tucked into the corner.

The word *"liebchen"* tripped from the woman's mouth in a repetitive loop that stopped only when Zweigman gently placed his fingers to her lips. They stood close together, surrounded by a sadness that forced Emmanuel onto his back foot.

The headache had returned, glowing hot behind the socket. He pressed his palm over his eye to clear the blur. An image of Angela, his own wife, imprinted over his retina. Pale-skinned and ephemeral, she called to him from a corner of the past. Had they ever stood together as intimately as the old Jew and his anxious wife did just now?

"Let's go," Emmanuel said and headed for the door.

Outside, the light was soft and white and shot through with fine dust particles. The coloured boys in front of the liquor store looked up, then quickly returned to their game. Better to have a policeman walk by than stop and ask questions.

Emmanuel got into the driver's seat, cranked the engine, and waited. Zweigman slid in next to him with his medical bag balanced on his knees. No-one spoke as the car eased away from the kerb and started back towards the hospital.

"Where did you get your medical degree?" he asked. All the boxes had to be ticked before Zweigman was allowed to work on the captain's body.

"Charité Universitätsmedizin in Berlin."

"Are you qualified to practise in South Africa?" He couldn't imagine German qualifications being denied by the National Party, even if the person holding them was Jewish.

Zweigman tapped a finger against the hard leather of his medical bag and appeared to give the question some thought.

They swung off Piet Retief Street with its white-owned businesses, and headed up General Kruger Road. Every street in Jacob's Rest was the answer to an exam question on Afrikaner history.

"Are you qualified?" Emmanuel asked again.

The shopkeeper waved the question away with a flick of his hand. "I no longer feel qualified to practise medicine in any country."

Emmanuel eased off the accelerator and prepared to swing a U-turn back in the direction of Poppies General Store.

"Ever been struck off the register in Germany or South Africa for any reason, Dr Zweigman?" he asked.

"Never," the shopkeeper said. "And I don't answer to doctor, anymore. Please call me the old Jew like everyone else."

"I would," Emmanuel pulled the car up in front of the Grace of God Hospital and switched off the engine, "but you're not that old."

"Ahhhh . . ." The sound was dry as parchment. "Don't be fooled by my youthful appearance, Detective. Under this skin, I am actually the *ancient Jew*."

Strange turns of phrase were one possible reason the oddball Kraut was sitting next to him, and not in some swank medical suite in Cape Town or Jo'burg.

"I think I'll call you the peculiar Jew. It suits you better. Now let's see your papers." Friendship with a man crazy enough to choose shopkeeper above physician was not on his list of things to do. He just wanted to verify the qualifications, then get relief for the pounding in his head.

Sunlight caught the rim of Zweigman's glasses when he leaned forwards, so Emmanuel wasn't sure if he'd seen a spark of laughter in the doctor's brown eyes. Zweigman handed him the papers, the first of which were in German.

"You read Deutsch, Detective?"

"Only beer hall menus." He flipped to the South African qualifications written in English and read the information slowly, then read it again. A surgeon, with membership in the Royal College of Surgeons. It was like finding a gold coin in a dirty sock.

Emmanuel looked hard at Zweigman, who returned his stare without blinking. There had to be a simple explanation for the white-haired German being in Jacob's Rest. Deep country was the ideal place to bury a surgeon with shaky hands. Did the good doctor have a fondness for alcohol?

"No, Detective Sergeant." Zweigman read his thoughts. "I do not hit the bottle at any time."

Emmanuel handed the papers back with a shrug. Zweigman was more than qualified to do what was asked of him. That was all the case needed.

Far enough from the main buildings to create a buffer zone between the living and the dead, a round mud-brick hut worked double time as the hospital's morgue and hardware storeroom.

Emmanuel paused under the shade of a jacaranda tree and allowed Shabalala and Zweigman to get ahead of him. The stooped doctor and the towering black man moved towards the morgue on a carpet of the jacaranda's spent flowers. At the path's end, Sister Angelina and Sister Bernadette administered spoonfuls of cod liver oil to a row of ragged children while Hansie slept the dense sleep of the village idiot, with his head propped against the morgue door.

My team, Emmanuel thought. He stepped out of the shade and the headache hit him again. The thatched roof of the hut bled into the sky and the grass merged with the white walls of the buildings so that everything resembled a child's watercolour. He pressed his palm hard over his eye socket, but the blur and the pain remained. By nightfall the headache would be a sharp splinter of hot light that shut down the eye completely. After the examination of the captain's body was set up, he'd get a triple dose of aspirin from the sisters. A double dose for now and a single one he could chase with a shot of whisky before bed. At least he knew where the liquor store was.

"Asleep on duty." Emmanuel gave Hansie a sharp tap on the shoulder. "I could write you up for that, Hepple."

Hansie jumped to attention to prove his alertness. "I wasn't sleeping. I was resting my eyes," he said, then caught sight of Zweigman. "What's he doing here? I thought you went to fetch the Pretorious brothers."

"We got lost." Emmanuel sidestepped Hansie and pushed the door to the morgue open. It was cool and dark inside. He looked over his shoulder and saw Zweigman walk over to the sisters, who were flushed and uncomfortable in front of the man whose confidence they'd betrayed.

"Sister Angelina and Sister Bernadette." The white-haired German gave no indication he'd been co-opted by the police. "Will you please assist me?"

"Yes, Doctor," Sister Bernadette said. "Excuse us while we prepare the necessary things."

The sisters marched the children towards the main building, where black and brown faces pressed up against the glass windows. The whites-only wing was empty. This afternoon the non-whites would have something to tell their visitors. "The captain — ma big boss man Pretorius — he's dead!"

"Doctor?" Hansie was fully awake and glaring at Zweigman. "That's the old Jew. He's not a doctor. He sells beans to kaffirs and coloureds."

"He's qualified to look at natives, coloureds and dead people," Emmanuel said and took refuge inside the darkened morgue. The pulsing behind his eye eased off a fraction but not enough. He switched on the examination light. Hansie and Shabalala stepped in and took up position against the wall. When the sisters got back he'd ask for the painkillers right away. There was no way he'd make it through the examination with the harsh white light in the stifling mortuary.

He pulled the sheet back to reveal the captain's uniformed body. Zweigman looked ready to deposit the contents of his stomach onto the concrete floor. His knuckles strained white against the leather handle of his medical bag.

"Were you friends with the captain?" Emmanuel asked.

"We were known to each other." Zweigman's voice was half its normal strength, the guttural accent more pronounced than before. "An acquaintance that, it appears, has come to a most abrupt end."

Zweigman regained his colour and started to clear a side counter with robotic precision. Was there the smallest hint of satisfaction in Zweigman's comment about an abrupt end?

"Not friends, then," Emmanuel said.

"There are few whites in this town that would claim me as a friend," Zweigman said without turning around. He calmly rolled up his sleeves to his elbows and snapped open his medical kit.

"Why's that?"

"I did not come here on the first Trekboer wagons and I do not understand how or even why one would play the game of rugby."

34

Emmanuel shaded his eyes against the naked light to get a clearer look at Zweigman. His headache pounded behind his eyeball. Zweigman had gone from shock to calm in the blink of an eye.

"Where to, Doctor?" Sister Angelina entered the morgue with a huge bowl of hot water in her muscular arms. A starched white apron covered her nun's habit, reaching to her knees.

Zweigman pointed to the cleared counter. Sister Bernadette shuffled in under a load of towels and washcloths. They set up in silence, moving like dancers in a well-rehearsed ballet. Zweigman scrubbed his hands and forearms, then dried himself with a small towel.

"Doctor?" Sister Bernadette held out a white surgical robe with the name "Kruger" embroidered on the pocket in dark blue. Zweigman slid into the robe and allowed Sister Bernadette to knot the ties along the back. It was obvious they'd worked together before.

"What do you want from me?" Zweigman asked.

"Time of death. Cause of death and a signed death certificate. No autopsy."

Emmanuel pulled out his notepad, but his headache blurred his writing into dark smudge marks.

"Detective?"

Emmanuel refocused and saw Sister Angelina in front of him with a glass of water in one hand and four white pills in the upturned palm of the other.

"Doctor says to take these right away."

He swallowed the tablets and chased them down with the water. Double the dose, the way he always took it when the blurring wouldn't go away. Perhaps "the clever Jew" was a better name for Zweigman.

"Thanks."

"No need." Zweigman turned to the body. The ghostly face shone white under the glow of the naked light bulb. "Let us begin with the clothes."

Sister Angelina picked up a pair of pruning shears, sliced along the stiff line of buttons that ran from neck to waist, then flicked the material out like the skin of a fruit to reveal the pale flesh of the captain's bloated torso.

Emmanuel stepped closer. Until the blurring lifted, he needed to take it slowly and write all the information down in large slabs. Obvious details needed to marry to a one- or two-word description in the notebook — at least until he could see straight.

"Big" was the first word. The Pretorius brothers had inherited their height and strength from their father. The captain was six-foot-plus with a body built by physical labour.

"Captain still play sport?" Emmanuel asked no-one in particular. The captain's nose, broken and then crudely reset in the face, was probably the result of time spent on the muddy playing fields dotted throughout Afrikanerdom.

"He coached the rugby team," Hansie said.

"And he ran," Sister Bernadette continued. "He ran all over town and into the countryside sometimes."

"Same time every day?"

"Every day except Sunday, because that was the Lord's day." Sister Bernadette sounded full of admiration. "Sometimes he ran in the morning and sometimes we'd see him run by well after dark."

That would explain why the captain hadn't piled on the fat like so many senior officers on the force. It was practically against police procedure to remain at normal weight after more than ten years' service.

"Yes." Zweigman pulled a bootlace free from its knot. "Early morning or late at night. There was no way to tell when the captain would run by. Or when he'd stop for a friendly talk."

Emmanuel wrote "Zweigman vs Captain?" in his notebook. He sensed a sting behind the doctor's words. He'd sniff out the details later.

"Oh, yes." Sister Bernadette sighed. "The captain always stopped when he had the time. He knew all our little orphans by name."

"Trousers." Zweigman moved aside and Sister Angelina sliced each trouser leg open with her pruning shears. The top buttons of the trouser fly were undone and the buckle of the leather belt had twisted open in the rough river current.

"Sister Bernadette," Zweigman said. "Please remove the trousers while we lift."

Zweigman moved to position himself at the captain's shoulders.

"Doctor, please." Sister Angelina waved him aside and single-handedly pushed the captain's dead weight into a sitting position while her miniature Irish partner pulled the dirty uniform free and threw it onto the floor. They repeated the action with the trousers, leaving the captain naked and pale on the gurney. Sister

Angelina discreetly draped a towel over the exposed genitals.

"Poor Captain Pretorius." Sister Bernadette placed the dangling arms back onto the gurney. "No matter what condition the body was in, I'd still know it was him."

There were no identifying marks. Was there something about the naked captain only the little nun could identify?

Sister Bernadette lifted a dead hand. "There wasn't a time I didn't see this watch on him. Captain wore it always."

"He never took it off." Hansie's eyes were reddening. "Mrs Pretorius gave it to him for his fortieth birthday. The strap is real crocodile skin."

Even under layers of dirt it was easy to see the quality of the watch. It was dull gold with a textured wristband. Elegant. Not a word that kept easy company with the meaty captain or his sons. Emmanuel lifted the hand up. Fresh bruises stained the flesh along the knuckle ridge. Captain Pretorius had recently hit something with force. He made a quick note in his pad, then turned the hand over. A small collection of calluses was scattered across the tray-sized palm.

"What kind of physical work did the captain do?"

"He liked to work on engines with Louis. They were fixing up an old motorbike together," Hansie sniffled.

"No," Emmanuel said. Some of the calluses had the soft, broken edges of newly minted blisters. This was the hand of a labourer who hauled and lifted right until the day he died. "I mean heavy work. Work that makes you sweat."

38

"Sometimes he helped Henrick out on the farm," Hansie said softly. "If it was cattle dipping or branding time, he liked to be there to watch because he grew up on a farm and he missed the life . . ."

Shabalala said nothing and kept his gaze directed at the concrete floor where the captain's uniform lay, torn and disregarded. If the black policeman knew the answer, he wasn't inclined to share it.

Emmanuel turned the cold hand palm down and stepped back. Perhaps the sons had an answer. He wrote "heavy work/blistered hands" on the pad. The black lines held steady on the page — the medication had kicked in.

Zweigman began a sweep of the body. "Severe trauma to the head. Appears to be the entry wound from a gunshot. Bruising to the shoulders, upper arm and underarm area . . ."

From dragging the body, Emmanuel thought. The killer had to hold on tight and pull hard as a mule to get to the water. Why bother? Why not shoot and run off into the night?

Zweigman continued down the body, paying meticulous attention to every detail. "Severe trauma to the spine. Appears to be the entry wound from another gunshot. Bruising along the knuckles. Blistering on the palms . . ."

The German surgeon was completely focused on the task, his face lit by something close to contentment. Why, with all his obvious expertise, was he serving behind the counter of a decrepit general store?

"Let's wash him down," Zweigman said.

Sister Angelina wrung warm water out of a hand towel and began wiping the pale skin down with the no-nonsense touch of nannies throughout English and Afrikaner homes across South Africa. Forty-something years on, the captain was leaving life as he'd entered it, in the hands of a black woman.

"No, no, no." Hansie rushed forwards, breathing hard. "Captain wouldn't like it."

"Like what, Hepple?" Emmanuel said.

"A kaffir woman touching him down there. He was against that sort of thing."

There was a tense silence, coloured by the ugly tide of recent history. The Immorality Act banning sexual contact between whites and non-whites was now law, with offenders subjected to public humiliation and jail time.

"Go out and get some air," Emmanuel said. "I'll call you when I need you."

"Please. I want to help, Detective Sergeant."

"You have helped. Now it's time for you to take a break. Go out and get some fresh air."

"*Ja.*" Hansie headed for the exit with hunched shoulders. It would take a while for the image of the captain, naked and molested by a black woman, to clear from his mind.

Emmanuel waited for the door to close before he spoke to Sister Angelina and Zweigman, both of whom had stepped back from the body during the young policeman's outburst. A white teenager with a uniform and badge clearly outranked a foreign Jew and a black nun.

40

"Carry on," he said, trying to move past an acute feeling of embarrassment. The Afrikaners had voted the National Party in. Racial segregation belonged to people like Captain Pretorius and his sons. A detective didn't have to adhere to the new laws. Murder didn't have a colour.

"It is just as well," Zweigman said after he'd murmured a low instruction to the sisters, who unfolded a white sheet and held it across the front of the captain's body to shield it from view. Zweigman reached for the internal thermometer, hesitated, then cast Shabalala a concerned glance.

"You can leave now, if you'd like," Emmanuel said to the Zulu constable.

"No." Shabalala didn't move a muscle. "I will stay here with him."

Zweigman nodded, then continued with the grim task of extracting information from the dead. He checked the results of the internal thermometer, rechecked the milky film masking the captain's eyes, and then examined the cleaned body for a second time.

"Cause of death was trauma to the head and spine caused by a bullet. The trauma to these areas is so specific and severe I believe the victim was most likely dead before reaching the water. I have not gone into the lungs to confirm, but that is my opinion."

"How do you know he was found in water?" Emmanuel was sure he hadn't mentioned the fact to Zweigman.

"Sediment on his wet clothes and in his hair. Captain Pretorius smells of the river."

Emmanuel's shoes were covered in mud and decaying leaves. Both he and Shabalala looked as if they'd been dredged in the river and then hung out to dry.

"Time of death?" he asked.

"Hard to tell. The captain's lack of body fat and the cool water in which his body was found make calculations difficult. Somewhere between eight pm and midnight last night is my best guess." The white-haired grocer handed the internal thermometer to Sister Bernadette and peeled off his gloves.

The sliced police uniform was heaped on the floor. The buttons still shone.

"Shabalala, did the captain always go fishing in his uniform?"

"Sometimes, when it was late, he went straight from the station to fish. He didn't like to disturb madam after dinner."

"Or maybe," Zweigman pulled off the untied surgical gown and dumped it onto the side counter, "he just liked to wear the uniform."

Emmanuel flicked back in his notebook and placed a tick next to "Zweigman vs Captain?". The uniform statement was harmless enough, but there was an edge to it. Had Pretorius used his position to come down on the shopkeeper for some minor infraction? Every year the National Party introduced a dozen new ways to break the law. Zweigman wouldn't be the first to get caught.

"If you'll excuse me, I will fill in the death certificate and be on my way. Here is a supply of painkillers for your head." Zweigman handed over a full bottle. "No offence, Detective, but I hope not to see you again."

"Can you think of anyone who could have done this?" Emmanuel pocketed the pills and opened the morgue door for the physician.

"I'm the old Jew who sells dry goods to natives and coloureds. Nobody comes to me with their secrets, Detective."

"An educated guess, then?"

"He didn't have any enemies that I know of. If the killer is from this town, then he has kept his feelings well hidden."

"So you think the murder was planned and personal?"

Zweigman lifted an eyebrow. "That I cannot say, as I was not privy to any discussions leading up to the captain's unfortunate demise. Will that be all, Detective?"

"For now."

There were few certainties this early in a case but one was already clear: he'd be seeing the old Jew again and not to buy lentils.

"Constable Hepple!" Emmanuel called.

The boy policeman scuttled over. "Get the Pretorius brothers. Tell them their father is ready to go home."

CHAPTER
THREE

The front office of the Jacob's Rest police station consisted of one large room with two wooden desks, five chairs, and a metal filing cabinet pushed against the back wall. Grey lines worn into the polished concrete floor made a map of each policeman's daily journey from door to desk to cabinet. A doorway at one side led to the cells and another in the back wall to a separate office. Shabalala was nowhere to be seen.

Emmanuel entered the back office. Captain Pretorius's desk was larger and neater than the others and had a black telephone in one corner. He picked up the receiver and dialled district headquarters.

"Congratulations." Major van Niekerk's cultured voice crackled down the line after the operator's third attempt to connect them.

"What for, sir?"

"Uniting the country. Once the story gets out, the native, English and Afrikaans press will finally have something to agree on — that the detective branch is understaffed, ill-informed and losing the battle against crime. One detective to cover the murder of a white police officer — the newspapers will have to run extra editions."

Emmanuel felt a jolt. "You know about the case, sir?"

"Just got a call from the National Party boys." The statement was overlaid with a casual indifference that didn't ring true. "The Security Branch, no less. They think Pretorius's murder may be political."

"The Security Branch?" Emmanuel tensed. "How did they get to hear about it so fast?"

"They didn't get the information from me, Cooper. Someone at your end must have tipped them off."

There was no way Hansie Hepple or Shabalala were hooked up to such heavy hitters. The Security Branch wasn't a regional body monitoring rainfall and crop production. They were entrusted with matters of national security and had the power to pull the rug from under anyone — including Major van Niekerk and the whole detective branch. Did the Pretorius brothers have those kinds of connections?

"What do they mean by political?" Emmanuel asked.

"The defiance campaign's got them spooked. They think the murder may be the beginning of a communist-style revolt by the natives."

"How did they come up with that?" The revolution idea would be funny if anyone but the Security Branch had flagged it. "The defiance campaign protesters prefer burning their ID passes and marching to the town hall after curfew. They want the National Party segregation laws repealed. Killing policemen isn't their style."

"Maybe the Security Branch knows something we don't. Either way, they made sure I knew they were taking an interest in the case and they expect to be informed of any developments as they occur."

"Is taking an interest as far as it goes?" Even members of the foot section of the police knew "taking an interest" was code for taking control.

There was a long pause. "My guess is, if the defiance campaign dies down, they'll step back. If it doesn't, there's no telling what they'll do. We're in different times now, Cooper."

The defiance campaign showed no signs of dying down. Prime Minister Malan and the National Party had begun to enact their plan as soon as they'd taken office. The new segregation laws divided people into race groups, told them where they could live and told them where they could work. The Immorality Act went so far as to tell people who they could sleep with and love. The growth of the defiance campaign meant that the Security Branch, or Special Branch as it was tagged on the street, would walk right into Emmanuel's investigation and call the shots.

"When can you get more men onto the case, sir?"

"Twenty-four hours," van Niekerk said. "Everyone here is focused on a body found by the railway line. She's white, thank God. That means the press will keep running with the story. I'll get a day to pull some men from headquarters and load them onto your case on the quiet."

Major van Niekerk, the product of a high-bred English mother and a rich Dutch father, liked to keep a clear line of sight between himself and his ultimate prize: commissioner of police. His present rank of

46

major wasn't high enough for him. His motto was simple. What's good for me is good for South Africa. Sending out a single detective on a crank call that turned out to be an actual homicide wasn't something he was keen to make public.

"And the Security Branch?" Emmanuel asked.

"I'll handle them." Van Niekerk made it sound easy, but it was going to be more like taking a knife from a gypsy. "Meanwhile, you've got a chance to treat this like an ordinary murder, not a test case for the soundness of the new racial segregation laws. Consider yourself —"

Static swallowed up the rest of the sentence and left an industrial hiss breathing down the line.

"Major?"

The singsong *beep, beep, beep* signalled a disconnected line. Emmanuel hung up. Lucky? Was that the major's last word? Consider yourself lucky?

Emmanuel tipped the contents of the captain's drawer onto the desktop and began sorting through them. Booking forms, paperclips, pencils and rubber bands got placed to one side. That left a small box of ammunition and a weekold newspaper. The box revealed rows of gold bullets. The newspaper stories he'd read last Wednesday. No luck there.

"Detective Sergeant?"

Shabalala stood in the doorway, a steaming mug of tea in hand. For such a large man, he moved with alarming quiet. He'd stripped down to his undershirt and his trousers were damp from where he'd washed the material in an attempt to clean it. The black location, five miles to the north of town, was too far to ride his bicycle for the sake of a change of clothes.

"Thank you, Constable." Emmanuel took the tea aware of the crisp lines of the shirt he'd changed into half an hour earlier. The Protea Guesthouse, the boarding house where he'd thrown down his bag, then washed and changed, was in the heart of town surrounded by other white-owned homes. Shabalala would have to wait for nighttime to wash the smell of the dead captain from his skin.

"Where's your desk?" The front office, like the one at district headquarters, was reserved for European policemen.

"In here." Shabalala stepped back and allowed him entry through the side door to a room that included two jail cells and a narrow space with a desk and chair. A row of hooks above the desk held the keys to the cells and a whip made of rhino hide called a *shambok*, the deadly South African version of an English bobby's truncheon. A window looked out to the backyard, and underneath it sat a small table with a box of *rooibos* tea, a teapot, and some mismatched porcelain mugs. Tin plates, mugs and spoons for the native policeman rested on a separate shelf.

"What's out there?"

Shabalala swung the back door open and politely motioned him out first. Emmanuel picked the black man's tea up off the table and handed the tin mug to him. The police station yard was a dusty patch of land. A huge avocado tree dominated the far end and cast a skirt of shade around its trunk. Closer in, a small fire glowed in a circle of stones. Shabalala's coat and jacket, wiped down from filthy to dirty by a wet cloth, hung over some chairs crowded around the outdoor hearth. A small sniff of the air and it was possible to imagine the smell of the police station's Friday night *braai* and fresh jugs of beer.

"Did you know the captain a long time?" Emmanuel's tea was milky and sweet, the way he guessed Pretorius must have liked it.

The black man shifted uncomfortably. "Since before."

Emmanuel switched to Zulu. "You grew up together?"

"*Yebo.*"

Silence breathed between them as they stood drinking their tea. Emmanuel noted the tension in Shabalala's neck and shoulders. There was something on his mind. He let Shabalala make the first move.

"The captain . . ." Shabalala stared across the yard. "He was not like the other Dutchmen . . ."

Emmanuel made a sound of understanding, but didn't say anything. He was afraid of breaking the fragile bond he felt between himself and the native constable.

"He was . . ."

Emmanuel waited. Nothing came. Shabalala's face wore the curious blank look he'd noticed at the crime scene. It was as if the Zulu — Shangaan man had flicked a switch somewhere deep inside himself and unplugged the power. The connection was broken.

Whatever Shabalala had on his mind, he'd decided to keep it there under lock and key.

Emmanuel, however, needed to know why the Security Branch was sniffing around this homicide.

"What clubs did the captain belong to?" he asked Shabalala.

"He went always to the Dutch people's church on Sunday, and also the sports club where he and his sons played games."

If the captain had been a member of a secret Boer organisation like the Broederbond, Shabalala would be the last to know. He had to find a simpler way to track down the Security Branch connection.

"Is there another phone in town besides the one here at the station?"

"The hospital, the old Jew, the garage, and the hotel have phones," Shabalala said. "The post office has a machine for telegraphs."

Emmanuel swallowed the remainder of his tea. Two phone calls that he knew of had gone out regarding the murder. One to van Niekerk, who'd sooner eat horse shit than call in the Security Branch, the other to Paul Pretorius of army intelligence. It was time to go direct to the source, the family home, and find out what information it yielded.

"I'll go and pay my respects to the widow," Emmanuel said. "Is the captain's house far from here?"

"No." Shabalala opened the back door and allowed him to enter first. "You must walk to the petrol station and then go right onto van Riebeeck Street. It is the white house with many flowers."

50

Emmanuel pictured a fence made from wagon wheels and a wrought-iron gate decorated with migrating springbok. The house itself probably had a name like *Die Groot Trek* — the Greak Trek — spelled out above the doorway. True Boers didn't need good taste; they had God on their side.

The late afternoon sun began to wane and blue shadows fell across the flat strip of the main street. The handful of shops sustained themselves with a trickle of holidaymakers on their way to the beaches of Mozambique and the wilds of the Kruger National Park. There was OK Bazaar for floral dresses, plain shirts and school uniforms, all in sensible cotton. Donny's All Goods, for everything from single cigarettes to Lady Fair sewing patterns. Kloppers for Bata shoes and farm boots. Moira's Hairstyles, closed for the day. Then, on the corner, stood Pretorius Farm Supplies behind a wire fence.

A handwritten sign was tied to the mesh: CLOSED DUE TO UNFORESEEN CIRCUMSTANCES. Unforeseen. That was probably the simplest way to get a handle on the murder of your father. Inside the compound a black watchman paced the front of the large supply warehouse while an Alsatian dog, chained to a spike in the ground, ran restless circles of its territory.

Across a small side street was the garage Shabalala had told him about. The sign above the three petrol pumps read PRETORIUS PETROL AND GARAGE. It was open, manned by an old coloured man in grease-covered overalls, probably called in at short notice to supervise the black teenagers operating the pumps. Why wasn't the town called Pretoriusburg? The family owned a big enough slice of it.

Emmanuel turned right into van Riebeeck Street. The neat country houses with manicured beds of aloe and flowering protea had a deserted air. Garden boys, now usually finishing up for the day, were nowhere in sight. Dried laundry flapped on backyard lines. No maids. No "missus" or "baas" either.

The news was out, he guessed. A quick glance down van Riebeeck confirmed it. A group of the captain's neighbours was gathered in front of a house at the end of the street. Housemaids and garden boys, many of them grey-haired despite the title, stood in a group two dwellings down: close enough to look on yet far enough to show respect.

A woman's sob floated out into the afternoon. Emmanuel approached a wide gravel driveway choked with cars. An elegant Cape Dutch — style house, nestled in an established garden. A dark thatched roof perched over graceful gables and gleaming whitewashed walls. Wooden shutters, the exact shade of the thatch, were shut against the world. A long veranda, decorated with flowerpots, ran the length of the house. There wasn't a wagon wheel in sight.

Like the captain's hand-tooled watch, the house was a surprise. Where was the bleached antelope skull he expected to find nailed over the doorway? He stepped past the front bumper of a dusty Mercedes and into the garden.

52

"Hey! Who you?" A hand settled on his shoulder and stayed there. A skinny white man with watery blue eyes stared him down. The crowd turned to examine the interloper.

"I'm Detective Sergeant Emmanuel Cooper." He flicked his ID open and held it uncomfortably close to the man's face. "I'm the investigating officer in this case. Are you a family member?"

The hand dropped. "No. Just making sure we all act decent towards Captain Pretorius and his family."

Emmanuel returned his ID to his pocket and smiled to show there were no hard feelings.

"He's okay, Athol. Let him by." Hansie stood on the veranda in his filthy uniform, cheeks glowing an eggshell pink. Exercising his authority in public agreed with him.

"This way, Detective Sergeant." Hansie waved him across the garden flushed with early spring colour, and up the stairs that led to the imposing front door. Emmanuel took off his hat.

"I've come to pay my respects to Mrs Pretorius. The family all here?"

"Everyone except Paul." Hansie opened the front door and ushered him in. "Mrs Pretorius and her daughters-in-law are seeing to the captain. The rest are out on the back veranda."

They entered a small receiving area that led farther along to a series of closed doors, most likely the bedrooms. Hansie walked left into a large room dominated by heavy wooden furniture, the kind built to withstand generations of pounding by unruly boys and leather-skinned men. The polished-tile floor was smooth as snakeskin under the yellow light of the glass-faced lanterns. An enormous sideboard covered in trophies and framed photos ran along one side of the room.

The photographs covered several generations of the Pretorius clan. There was a girl in ponytails playing in the snow, then a dour-faced clergyman surrounded by an army of equally humourless children. The next photo showed a young Captain Pretorius and a pretty woman in her twenties seated on a park bench. Then an image stopped Emmanuel in his tracks. The Pretorius boys, ranging in age from five to fifteen, stood shoulder to shoulder in their Voortrekker Scout uniforms. It was night and their faces and uniforms gleamed in the light of the flaming torches held high in their hands. Their eyes stared out at him, hard with Afrikaner pride. Emmanuel thought of Nuremberg: all those rosy-cheeked German boys marching towards defeat.

"The great trek celebration," Hansie said. "Captain and Mrs Pretorius took us Voortrekker Scouts on a trip to Pretoria for the ceremony. We got to throw the torches into a huge fire."

Emmanuel remembered his own trip to the same celebration well. He remembered the heat of the flames breathing onto his face and the uncomfortable feeling that he was outside the circle of those selected by God to be pure.

"I read about it in the papers," he said and moved on to the next photo. Paul, as big and thick-necked as his brothers, in army uniform, then a Pretorius family portrait no more than a year or two old. He focused on the youngest son, who was finer-boned than his brothers, with a sensitive mouth and messy blond hair that fell over his forehead. The captain and his wife had run out of brawn by the time it came to making Louis.

"An Englishman came through town with his camera and charged one pound to take a photo. We have one in our house showing me with my ma and sisters."

They went through to the kitchen where two black maids laid cold meat and slabs of bread onto a giant platter. A third maid, white-haired and ancient, sat at the small table and sobbed in quiet bursts.

"That's Aggie," Hansie whispered. "She's been with the family since Henrick was a baby. She's not so good anymore, but the captain wouldn't let her go."

They passed a dining room, dominated by a wooden table and chairs that carried a whiff of the Bavarian forest. Large windows looked out onto the vine-covered back veranda where a group of older men, rough farmers in khaki, stood together in a tight bunch.

"The fathers-in-law," Hansie explained. They stepped out of the house and onto the veranda. Six children, from knee to shoulder height, played with a wooden spinning top that wobbled and bounced between them. A young black girl rocked a fat white baby on her knee. The Pretorius brothers held their own council out on the garden lawn. All except Louis.

Emmanuel approached them. Erich started straight in.

"Hansie here says it was the old Jew who looked Pa over. How's that?"

"Checked his papers myself. Everything was in order. He was qualified to conduct the examination."

He waited for angry denials, but none came. The brothers stared back at him, expressions unchanged.

"Pa was right." Henrick's speech was a beat too slow, thanks to an afternoon of steady drinking. "He always said the old Jew had something to hide."

"Shifty," Erich threw in. "Who else but the old Jew would lie about something like that, hey? Probably doesn't know how to tell the truth. No practice."

The Pretorius brothers were halfway to being wrecked, and in no hurry to slow the ride.

"Did your father and the old Jew have a disagreement lately?"

"Not for a while," Henrick said. "Pa went to see him a couple of times this past year just to talk to him about how things work here in Jacob's Rest. Give him guidelines, like. To keep him clear of trouble."

"Good of him," Emmanuel said mildly, recalling Zweigman's comment about the captain dropping in for a "friendly chat". "You think the old Jew resented your father's help?"

Henrick shrugged. "Maybe."

"Enough to kill him over?" Emmanuel ploughed ahead, exploiting the brothers' relaxed state of mind. Sober, it was hard to find a wedge into them.

Erich snorted. "Him, kill my pa?"

"The old Jew's scared of guns," Henrick explained. "Won't touch them. Won't even sell bullets from his shop."

56

"He couldn't strangle a chicken without help," Johannes said.

"Couldn't piss on a fire without his wife aiming it for him," Erich added with a mean-spirited giggle that set the brothers laughing.

Emmanuel let the laughter subside. In a few hours, when the whisky bravado had worn off, they'd feel the full weight of their father's murder, and remember that the killer still walked free among them.

"Pa, look! Look, see." A boy of about ten called out from the veranda as the spinning top wobbled down the stairs and rolled onto the grass. The children followed in a rush of high-pitched squeals.

Henrick grabbed a tiny girl and threw her into the air. The other children crowded around, begging for a turn. Emmanuel wondered whereabouts the youngest brother was hiding himself. "Where's Louis?"

"In the shed," Henrick said. "He's been in there all day working on that bloody bike."

"*Ja.*" Erich ruffled the hair of a child in front of him. "Go see if you can get him out, Hansie. Ma will need his help soon."

Hansie turned to the far end of the garden, where a small shed stood flush against the back fence. Behind the corrugated iron structure, flat-topped trees threw their shaggy branches up against wide-open sky.

"I'll come with you." Emmanuel broke from the family group and fell into step with Hansie. A man's shed was a good place to start feeling out the man himself. Something about the captain had marked him out for a violent death, and something about his death had caught the attention of the Security Branch. No time like the present to try and find out why.

Hansie knocked on the shed door. "Louis. It's me."

"Come." The door swung open and Louis, a boy of about nineteen, stepped back to allow them entry. With a featherweight's build, the captain's youngest son was more finely drawn than the photo in the house suggested. If the other brothers were rock, Louis was paper.

"Louis, this here is the policeman from Jo'burg." Hansie performed the introductions in a rush, embarrassed about taking an adult role in front of his teenage friend.

"Detective Sergeant Emmanuel Cooper," Emmanuel said and shook Louis's hand. There was strength in the boy's grip that belied the softness of his appearance.

"Detective Sergeant Emmanuel Cooper." Louis repeated the title as if he was memorising it, then saw the grease stains on Emmanuel's hand. "I'm sorry, Detective. I've made a mess of you."

"It's nothing." Emmanuel wiped his hands clean with his handkerchief and Louis moved back towards a pile of engine parts laid out on an old rug. The restored body of a black Indian motorcycle rested up on blocks close to the rear door.

Louis kneeled down and continued cleaning pieces of metal with a rag. His whole body shook with the effort he expended. "I've been cleaning parts all day and I forgot . . ."

"What's this?" Hansie squatted down next to his friend. "I thought you finished the engine already."

58

Louis shook his head. "Have to wait on a part to come from Jo'burg. Do you know much about engines, Detective?"

"Not much," Emmanuel answered truthfully. The righthand side of the shed was the hunting area. A pair of giant Kudu horns hung above a gun rack holding three sighted rifles. Below the guns was a beautiful Zulu *assegai*, a warrior's spear, complete with lion-hide bindings. Under the spear was a wooden desk with two drawers. To the left side of the shed engine parts and tools surrounded the Indian motorcycle. Diagrams and calculations were stuck to the wall under a manufacturer's illustration of the dismantled motorbike in its prime. The organisation of the shed indicated a clear and methodical mind. The back door was propped open with a brick to let in the afternoon breeze and it wasn't hard to imagine the captain happily at work here.

"You know a lot about engines." Emmanuel stepped over the spare parts and headed for the hunting desk.

"Oh, no," Louis said. "Pa is the one who knows all about fixing things."

There was an awkward silence, then the loud clank of metal on metal made by Louis sorting through a pile of spanners with shaking hands.

"You can finish the bike, hey, Louis?" Hansie pumped enthusiasm into his voice. "Get that coloured mechanic to help and you'll have it going in no time."

"Maybe," Louis said quietly, then began sorting the cleaned screws and bolts into neat piles on the floor. Emmanuel watched the compulsive behaviour for a moment, then moved deeper into the shed. Grief made people act in strange ways; it could rip them open or close them right down.

A check of the guns found them clean and unused. Inside the desk, Emmanuel found newspaper articles on rural pursuits like the art of *biltong* making and the proper care of hunting knives. He kneeled down and peered into the empty drawer cavity.

"Looking for dirty magazines, Detective?" Louis asked.

Emmanuel caught the hard edge of the boy's stare.

"You want to show me where he hid the magazines, Louis?" he asked casually, aware it was a clumsy attempt to catch the boy out, but worth a try.

Louis flushed pink and began sorting through the spanner box again. "No, because there aren't any. My pa was very clean that way. If you knew him you'd understand."

"That's right." Hansie took up the fight on Louis's behalf and threw Emmanuel a look of disgust.

"I wasn't the one who mentioned dirty magazines," he pointed out. Did the captain have a secret stash somewhere? Or was Louis worried about a dog-eared magazine hidden in his own bedroom?

Two maids and a garden boy hurried past the back entrance to the shed without slowing pace or looking in. The three figures disappeared into the darkening veldt.

"What's this?" Emmanuel pointed to the grass pathway the servants had taken.

"A kaffir path. The kaffirs use them to get around," Hansie said. "They run all through the town and join up near the location. It's quicker than using the main roads."

"People don't mind?"

"No. Nobody uses the paths in town after eight-thirty. There's big trouble if a kaffir is caught walking along here between then and sunrise."

"You ever use them?"

"They're kaffir paths. For kaffirs." Hansie had the dumbstruck look of an idiot asked to explain the facts of life to an imbecile. "Coloureds use them sometimes, but we never do."

"Then how do you know they're not used at night?" Emmanuel stepped out of the shed and onto the path.

"The captain," Hansie replied. "He ran along these paths three or four times a week. Sometimes in the morning and sometimes at night. Shabalala took care of the paths near the location."

Emmanuel moved deeper into the veldt as a second group of house servants, determined to clear the white part of town before curfew, jogged by singing. Emmanuel knew the song:

"*Shosholoza, shosholoza . . . Kulezontaba . . .* "

The song translated roughly to "Move faster, you are meandering on those mountains. The train is from South Africa". The sound of the word "*shosholoza*" was like the hiss of a steam train itself.

The servants' rhythmic chant drifted back and he felt the African night warm on his skin and hair. The voices of the servants grew softer and he turned towards the captain's house.

"How often did you and Lieutenant Uys patrol?"

"We patrolled when the captain asked," Hansie said. "Once we went out every night for a week, then not again for a long time. It wasn't a regular type thing."

"Random," Emmanuel said, aware of the simple genius underpinning the captain's system. Zweigman was aware of the close scrutiny of the patrols and didn't like it. How much did the captain see and hear as he criss-crossed the town at constant but irregular intervals? Had he uncovered a secret someone was willing to kill to protect?

Emmanuel re-entered the shed, where Louis packed the last of his tools into a red metal box. The boy appeared engrossed in his task, but there was a tightness in his shoulders that suggested an alert and mindful presence.

"Hey, Louis." The shed door swung open and Henrick stepped in. "Get yourself cleaned up, it's time for supper and Ma needs you."

"*Ja*." Louis ducked out past his elder brother and made his way quickly towards the house. He scuttled up the stairs and across the veranda like a crab racing for safety on a rock ledge.

"Ma will see you now, Detective," Henrick said. "She's not doing so well, so make it quick."

"Of course," Emmanuel said. Henrick's boss man act was starting to get on his nerves.

Lamplight flickered over a group of young women in mourning clothes who were gathered around a small blonde woman in an oversized armchair. Her pale face, lined with grief, was all cheekbones and wide mouth. It was still possible to see vestiges of the young beauty who had married a hulking policeman and produced five sons to swell the ranks of the Voortrekker Scouts and the Dutch Reformed Church.

"Who is this?" she asked. Emmanuel felt her blue eyes focus on him for the first time. "Who is this person?"

"The detective," Henrick explained from the doorway. The room was now a female space that he did not want to enter. "Detective Sergeant Cooper has come from Jo'burg to lead the investigation. He's going to help find out who did this to Pa."

Mrs Pretorius sat forwards like a sleepwalker awakened. "What are you doing here? You should be out there, arresting whoever did this evil thing."

"I need your help. I know it's hard, but there are some things only you can tell me about your husband."

"Willem." It was the first time the captain's name had been spoken. "My Willem is gone . . ."

The tiny woman howled in anguish, her body swaying back and forth like a marionette on broken strings. Emmanuel sat down, breathed deeply and allowed himself to observe but not connect. Disconnection. That was the trickiest part of the job, the one in which he excelled.

"Shhh. Ma. Shhh . . ." Louis slipped into the room and kneeled beside his mother. He kissed her on the cheek and mother and son held on to each other for a long moment. There was a startling resemblance between the youngest Pretorius boy and the fragile woman who held him in her arms.

Out of his grease-covered overalls, Louis was comfortable in the room full of women. He was blonder and finer-boned than the sisters-in-law, buxom farm girls built to outlast famine on the veldt.

Emmanuel glanced over at Henrick and caught a flicker of discomfort. How had the captain felt about the soft boy who bore no resemblance to the hard-edged Pretorius men?

"It's okay," Louis whispered. "I'll take care of you, Ma. I promise."

Emmanuel waited until mother and son loosened their grip on each other. The daughters-in-law murmured comforting words.

"Mrs Pretorius . . ." Emmanuel knew he was about to make himself unpopular. "May I talk to you alone? I have a few questions I need answered and it would be better if we had some privacy."

"Not Louis," Mrs Pretorius said. "Louis stays."

The daughters-in-law glared at him and walked out of the room to join the family groups congregated on the back *stoep*. He waited until the sound of their whispers faded, then said, "Mrs Pretorius, when was the last time you saw your husband alive?"

She held on to Louis's hand. "Yesterday morning. We had breakfast together before he went to work."

"Did he say he was going anywhere unusual or meeting anyone in particular?"

"No. He said he was going fishing after work and that he'd see me in the morning."

"You were normally asleep when he came home from fishing?"

"Yes. Willem used the spare room so he wouldn't disturb me." She squeezed Louis's hand tighter. "I had no idea he wasn't home until Hansie came . . ."

She began to cry and Henrick stepped into the room. Emmanuel held his hand up like a traffic policeman and Henrick stopped in his tracks.

"Can you think of anyone who would do this to your husband, Mrs Pretorius? Anything he told you would help." Emmanuel kept his voice soft and urgent.

"Come, Ma," Louis said. "Tell the detective what you know."

The blonde woman took a deep breath. When she looked up her eyes were hard as uncut diamonds.

"The old Jew," she stated flatly. "Willem said he caught him hanging around the coloured area at night. He was up to some funny business."

"Did your husband catch him doing something?" That would explain Zweigman's resentment.

"No. You know how clever Jews are. Willem saw him going in and out of different coloured girls' houses after sunset. It was obvious what he was up to so Willem gave him a warning."

"Did he tell you how Zweigman reacted?"

"He didn't like it, I know that. Willem had to see him a few times before he was sure Zweigman had stopped."

"Did Captain Pretorius have problems with anyone else?"

She was ahead of him, ready with the answer. "That pervert Donny Rooke. Willem sent him to jail for taking

65

dirty pictures of the du Toit girls. He's been back in Jacob's Rest four or five months."

"He lives out past the coloureds," Henrick said from the doorway. "He doesn't come into town unless he has to. His brother runs the shop now."

Emmanuel remembered Donny's All Goods on the main street. "He was angry with the captain for sending him to jail?"

"Of course. The worst sinners don't believe they should be punished for their sins." There was no mistaking the contempt in her for the morally weak. "Willem helped guide this town and now he has been struck down. I pray to God for swift retribution upon the killer."

"Amen," said Louis.

Emmanuel shifted in his seat, unnerved by the intensity of the woman in front of him. There was no room in her for forgiveness.

"Anyone else?"

Mrs Pretorius sighed. "There was always trouble with the coloureds, drinking and fighting, that sort of thing. They find it hard to control their emotions no matter how much white blood they have in them. Willem understood that, and tried not to be too hard on them."

Emmanuel flicked his notebook to a clean page. He'd heard every race theory in South Africa. None of them surprised him anymore. "Can you remember any specific names?"

"No. Lieutenant Uys will know all the coloured cases. Shabalala will know the native cases. They were a good team, Willem and Shabalala. Everyone respected them. Everyone . . ."

The tears came again and Emmanuel stood up before Henrick had a chance to kick him out. He flicked his notebook closed and put it in his pocket. "Thank you for your time, Mrs Pretorius. Please accept my condolences on the loss of your husband."

Louis sprang up and made it to the front entrance ahead of him. He swung the door open and leaned a shoulder against the wood frame. "You'll catch the killer, won't you, Detective?"

"I'll try." Emmanuel stepped out onto the veranda. "I can't promise you any more than that, Louis."

"My grandfather was Frikkie van Brandenburg and Pa was a police captain. Your boss sent the best detective out, didn't he?"

Stuck in the shed all day, Louis had no idea about little sister Gertie's botched call to headquarters. As far as the boy was concerned, the police department had hand-picked him to break the case open.

Emmanuel let him down easy. "I've solved quite a few cases and I'll do everything I can to solve this one. Goodnight, Louis."

"Goodnight, Detective." Louis's voice followed him as he crossed the veranda and walked down the stairs to the garden. He made his way back to the police station.

Emmanuel paused at the corner of van Riebeeck and Piet Retief Streets, and felt himself pulled in the direction of the liquor store. Instead, he turned towards the station and Constable Shabalala.

Now he understood: Frikkie van Brandenburg was the reason the Security Branch was involved. Captain Pretorius was son-in-law to one of the mighty lions of Afrikaner nationhood, a man who preached the sacred history of white civilisation like an Old Testament prophet. No wonder the Pretorius brothers hated Zweigman. Jacob's Rest was too small to contain two tribes claiming to be God's chosen people.

The main street was empty. Lights from the garage made a yellow circle in the darkness. A fragment of memory flickered to life: he was running barefoot down a small dirt lane with the smell of wood fires all around him. He ran fast towards a light. The memory grew stronger, and Emmanuel pushed it aside. Then he disconnected it.

CHAPTER
FOUR

"Down there."

Shabalala pointed to a corrugated iron shack anchored to the ground by rocks and pieces of rope: Donny Rooke's house since his fall from grace. Emmanuel pulled the sedan into the patch of dirt that was the front yard. The early morning light did nothing to soften the hard edge of poverty.

He exited the car and the first stone, sharp and small, hit him on the cheek and drew blood. The second and third stones hit, full force, into his chest and leg. The stones hit hard, and he lost count of them as he ran behind the car to take shelter. He crouched next to Shabalala, who calmly wiped blood from a small cut in his own neck.

"The girls." Shabalala raised his voice over the torrent of sound made by the pebbles hitting the roof of the car.

"What girls?" Emmanuel shouted back.

Shabalala motioned to the front of the car. Emmanuel followed and risked a quick look out. Two girls, skinny as stray dogs, stood at the side of the shack, a pile of rocks in front of them. Behind them a man with blazing red hair took off across the veldt.

"Go after him," the black policeman said and filled his pockets with stones. "I will get the girls."

Emmanuel nodded and sprinted full speed across the dirt yard. A stone knocked his hat to the ground, another skimmed past his shoulder, but he kept the pace up, eyes on the redheaded man running into open country.

"Ooowww!" There was a high-pitched squeal, then the sound of yelping. Shabalala walked calmly towards the girls, his stones hitting their target with sniper-like accuracy. The girls scuttled into the shack, seeking shelter.

Emmanuel cleared the side of the dilapidated vegetable patch and ran hard. The gap closed. Donny slowed to catch his breath, his hands resting on his knees. A minute more and Emmanuel body-slammed Donny, who toppled over with a groan. He held the man's face in the dirt for longer than he needed to, and heard the dust fill his mouth. The dents in his Packard meant he'd have to write a detailed damage report. He pressed down harder.

"Where you going, Donny?" He flipped the choking man over and looked down at his dirty face.

"I didn't do it. Please God, I didn't do anything to the captain."

He pushed a knee into Donny's chest. "What makes you think I'm here about Captain Pretorius?"

Donny started to cry and Emmanuel pulled him up with a jerk. "What makes you think I'm here to talk about Captain Pretorius?"

"Everyone knows." The words came out between broken sobs. "It was him that put me in jail. He forced me to live out here like a kaffir."

Emmanuel pushed Donny towards the shack. His cheek stung from where the stone had broken the skin and his suit was covered in dust. All in pursuit of a man with less sense than a chicken.

"There's your army." He shoved Donny between the shoulder blades and forced him to acknowledge the girls, now crouched in the dirt next to Shabalala. They were hard faced and thin from living rough.

"Inside," Emmanuel said. "We're all going to have a talk."

The girls clambered up and slipped in through the rusting door. Emmanuel followed with Shabalala and Donny.

"Nice place," Emmanuel said. There wasn't a piece of furniture not propped up by a brick or held together with strips of rag. Even the air inside the shack was inadequate.

"I used to have a good home," Donny said from the edge of the broken sofa. "I was a businessman. Owned my own place."

"What happened?"

"I was —" Donny started, and then bent over with a groan. His right arm hung limp by his side.

"You hurt him," the oldest girl said. "You got no right to hurt him. He didn't do nothing wrong."

Emmanuel pulled Donny into a sitting position. He'd been rough with him, but no more. This pain was something else.

71

"Take your shirt off," he said calmly.

"No. I'm okay. Honest."

"Now." The faded shirt was unbuttoned to reveal a collection of dark bruises spread out across Donny's stomach and chest.

"What happened?"

"Fell off my bicycle, landed on some rocks."

Emmanuel checked the tear-streaked face; saw the swelling at the corner of the weak mouth. "A rock hit you in the mouth as well?"

"*Ja*, almost broke my teeth."

Emmanuel glanced at Shabalala, who shrugged his wide shoulders. If Donny had taken a beating, he knew nothing about it.

"You were telling me about your business."

"Donny's All Goods. That was my shop."

"What happened?"

Donny pulled at an earlobe. "Border gate police told Captain Pretorius about some photos I brought in from Mozambique. He didn't like them and had me sent off to prison."

"What kind of photos?"

"Art pictures."

"Why didn't the captain like them?"

"Because he was married to that old piece of *biltong* and me here with two women of my own."

"He was jealous?"

"He didn't like anyone having more than him. Always top of the tree. Always putting his nose into everyone else's business."

"You didn't like him?"

"He didn't like me." Donny was in full steam now. "He stole my photos and my camera, then put me in jail. Now look at me. Skint as a kaffir. He should have been the one in jail. Not me."

"Where were you last night, Donny?"

Donny blinked, caught off guard. His tongue worked the corner of his bruised mouth.

"We was here all night with Donny," the older girl stated. "We was with him all the time."

Emmanuel looked from one hard-faced girl to the other. Their combined age couldn't have been more than thirty. They stared back, used to violent confrontation and worse. He turned to Donny.

"Where were you?"

The girl had given him time to collect himself. "I was here all day and all night with my wife and her sister. As God is my witness."

"Why did you run?" Emmanuel asked quietly.

"I was scared." The tears were back, turning Donny's face into a mud puddle. "I knew they'd try to pin it on me. I ran because I thought you'd do whatever they asked you to."

"We was here with him all the time," the child-wife insisted. "You have to leave him alone now. We's his witness."

"You sure you were here, Donny?"

"One hundred per cent. Here is where I was, Detective."

Emmanuel took in the sordid ruin that was Donny Rooke's life. The man was a pervert and a liar who'd scraped together a flimsy alibi, but he wasn't going anywhere.

"Don't leave town," he said, "I'd hate to chase you again."

The air outside Donny's squalid home smelled of rain and wild grass.

"Detective." Donny scuttled after them with Emmanuel's filthy hat as an offering. "I'd like my camera back when you find it. It was expensive and I'd like it back. Thanks, Detective."

Emmanuel threw his hat into the car and turned to face the scrawny redheaded man. "Just so you know, Donny. Those are girls, not women."

He slid into the sedan and gunned the engine, anxious to leave the shack behind. The car wheels bumped over the potholed road and threw up a thin dust serpent in their wake.

"Where are the parents?" he asked Shabalala.

"The mother is dead. The father, du Toit, likes drink more than he likes his daughters. He gave the big one as wife, the small one as little wife."

They rode the rest of the way in silence.

The mechanical whir of sewing machines filled Poppies General Store as Emmanuel and Shabalala walked in for the second time. Zweigman was behind the counter, serving an elderly black woman. Who pocketed her change and left with a parcel of material tucked under her arm. Zweigman followed and shut the doors behind her. He flipped the sign to "Closed", then turned to face his visitors.

74

"There's a sitting room through this way," Zweigman said and disappeared into the back. Emmanuel followed. For a man about to be questioned in connection with a homicide, Zweigman was cool to the point of chilly. He'd obviously been expecting them.

The back room was a small work area set up with five sewing machines and dressmaker's dummies draped in lengths of material. The coloured women manning the machines looked up nervously at the police intrusion.

"Ladies." Zweigman smiled. "This is Detective Sergeant Emmanuel Cooper from Johannesburg. Constable Shabalala you already know."

"Please introduce us," Emmanuel insisted politely. He wanted to get a good look at the seamstresses. Maybe there was something to Mrs Pretorius's poisonous accusations. Zweigman did have access to five mixed-race women under the age of forty.

Zweigman's smile froze. "Of course. There's Betty, then Sally, Angie, Tottie, and Davida."

Emmanuel nodded at the women and kept a tight focus on their faces. He ticked them off with crude markers. Betty: pockmarked and cheerful. Sally: skinny and nervous. Angie: older and out of humour. Tottie: born to make grown men cry. Davida: a shy brown mouse.

If he had to lay money on Zweigman's fancy he'd bet the farm on Tottie. Light-skinned and luscious, she was the kind of woman vice cops used as bait in immorality law stings, then took home for a little after-hours R&R.

"Gentlemen." Zweigman opened a second curtain and led them into a small room furnished with a table and chairs. The dark-haired woman, so nervous yesterday, now poured tea into three mugs with a steady hand.

"This is my wife, Lilliana."

"Detective Sergeant Cooper," she responded politely and waved him and Shabalala over to the table which was already set with tea and a small plate of biscuits. Emmanuel sat down, senses on full alert. With a few hours' notice, the old Jew and his wife had rebuilt their defences and nailed all the windows closed.

"Which one of those women are you *ficken*?" he asked conversationally, using German slang to sharpen the impact.

Zweigman flushed pink and his wife dropped the plate of biscuits onto the table with a loud crack. There was a drawnout silence while she collected the pastries and rearranged them.

"Please," Zweigman said quietly. "This is not the kind of talk for a man to have in front of his wife."

"She doesn't need to be here," Emmanuel answered. "We'll question her later."

"Take the ladies out for a walk, *liebchen*. The air will do you good."

The elegant woman left the room quickly. Emmanuel sipped his tea and waited till the front door closed. He turned to Zweigman, who looked suddenly stooped and worn down by life. There were tired circles under his brown eyes.

"That was cruel and unnecessary," Zweigman said. "I did not expect it of you."

"This town brings out the worst in me," Emmanuel answered. "Now, which one of those women is the lucky one?"

"None of them. Though I'm sure if you had your choice you'd pick Tottie. I saw how you looked at her."

Emmanuel shrugged. "Looking was still legal the last time I checked the list of punishable offences. Captain Pretorius thought you'd done a lot more than that."

"He was mistaken." The answer was clipped. "I walked the ladies home after dark because there was . . ." he struggled to find the right word in English, "a peeping man in the area. It was purely a safety measure."

"Really?"

"Constable Shabalala, please tell your colleague that I did not make the peeping man up."

Shabalala stared at the floor, uncomfortable at being included in the questioning. He cleared his throat. "There was a man. The captain looked, but did not find anyone."

"No arrests?"

"No," Shabalala answered.

"The man would have been found if it was European women being harassed," Zweigman said. "The activity stopped and it was never mentioned again."

"Did you have occasion to comfort the scared women? It's easy for emotions to get heated up when there's an element of danger."

"Ah . . ." Zweigman had regained his composure. "How your mind works: always looking for the dirty secret. I will repeat. I am not and never was '*ficken*', as you so gently put it, any of the women in my wife's employ."

"Captain Pretorius came to see you a couple of times this year. What for?"

"To give me advice. Don't be seen with women other than my wife after dark. Don't let my employees become too friendly. Don't go to social get-togethers with coloureds or blacks. Don't forget you are a white man and not one of them. Would you like me to go on?"

"You didn't like him."

"That is correct."

"Did you kill him?"

"I did not." Zweigman took off his glasses and wiped them down on the front of his shirt. "I do not own a gun or know how to use one. Anton the mechanic across the road and my wife Lilliana will both tell you that I was here in the shop until after ten trying, unsuccessfully, to balance the store accounts."

Emmanuel wrote the witnesses' names down. He had no doubt they'd supply Zweigman with gold-plated alibis. Two suspects both accounted for during the hours Captain Pretorius was shot. His thin list was washed out on the first full day of the investigation. It was time to join Hansie in the door to door. He had to turn over some rocks and see what spiders crawled out from underneath.

★　★　★

Emmanuel sat upright in bed, mouth open, gasping for breath. He was in darkness and sweat beaded on his skin. Deep in his stomach he felt the familiar ache of fear. He slid a hand over his body, to check for injuries. The bullet wound on his shoulder had long since healed and the cut on his cheek from Donny's insane girl blitzkrieg was only a nick. No knife, no blood.

He swung his legs over the side of the bed. The dreams came and went, but never with the woman. She was new. No way to know who she was. The cellar in his dream was in darkness, always. The pattern of events the same: a bombed-out town. The patrol moving on foot from one ruin to the next, checking and double checking for the enemy. A routine sweep of a wine cellar. He turns to leave. The blade slices deep into his flesh and he falls forwards into darkness and pain.

That was the dream, played out in an eternal loop. Every door to door he conducted as a detective brought up memories from the bottom of the well. Things weren't so bad now. He didn't scream anymore, or reach for a light to bring himself back to reality.

Emmanuel breathed deeply, closed his eyes, and imagined the corner of the cellar again. The smell of the woman fills the space. His ex-wife? No, her scent was English tea rose and iced water. Angela, so polite and restrained, would never claw and lick and bite. Sex was for the half-hour before bedtime. Primal cellar fucking was not her thing. Fucking was not her thing.

He lay back down. The woman was no-one he knew from his waking life. Surely he'd remember if she was.

Why hadn't the dream ended with them falling, naked and warm, into a black morphine sleep?

The sound when it came was crisp and distinct. A footstep on the gravel pathway leading to his door. He held still. This was not a dream. This was Jacob's Rest and the crunch of gravel was close and getting closer. He slid off the bed and moved in the darkness towards the door. Moonlight spilled in from a crack in the curtain. He crouched close to the handle. The screen door opened, then closed just as quickly. Then the sound of something heavy pressed against the mesh, and the footsteps grew fainter.

Emmanuel pulled the door open hard. Across the yard, a figure moved quickly into the shadow of a sprawling jacaranda tree and slipped into the night. Emmanuel charged at the screen door, ready to fly. The door jammed, held closed by the weight of a whitewashed stone borrowed from the garden edging. He pushed again, and the door gave way.

"You! Stop!"

Emmanuel sprinted out into the moonlit night. The sound of the intruder's footsteps running hard across open ground drove him on. He felt the brush of tall grass and tree branches against his body. Dark houses disappeared behind him. He was on a kaffir path heading out to who knows where. He sped up and glimpsed the figure rounding a bend just ahead. After the bend the path split into two. He sprinted to the left and pressed on, full throttle, until he realised he was alone and running blind into the moonlit veldt.

A wave of nausea hit and he doubled over. His lungs were on fire, the bile rose up in his throat. Four years in the detective branch and he'd never been outrun. Down alleyways and over fences he was the fastest in the department. Whoever led him on this barefoot marathon across sand and stone had not let up or slowed down. Emmanuel sucked in a mouthful of cool night air. He was beaten clean and clear by a country mile.

He closed his eyes and, without warning, there she was. The woman in the cellar, lit just enough for him to see her brown-skinned arms reaching up to him. Definitely not a European. One of the women from Zweigman's shop: the delectable Tottie with her juicy mouth and grab-onto hips? Or could it have been Betty, pockmarked and eager to please?

You have to get out, get laid, he thought. Call the brunette who works the tie and hat counter at Belmont Menswear. She was perfect. Attractive, willing, and most important, white. Black and brown women were for vice cops with carnal appetites and no ambition. Mrs Pretorius would have him hanged for being sinful enough to have the dream.

"Move and I'll blast you, mister."

Emmanuel felt the heat of a spotlight on his bare back and heard the click of the safety releasing. He froze.

"Put your hands up where I can see them, and turn around to face me. Slow like."

Emmanuel did as he was told and the glare of the spotlight shone in his face. He squinted out and saw two dark figures standing side by side.

"Who you?" the man with the gun demanded.

Emmanuel kept his hands held high, palms spread open like flags of truce. He was a barefoot stranger in pyjama pants caught panting in the darkness. If they shot him now, a jury would move to acquit.

"I'm Detective Sergeant Emmanuel Cooper. I'm here to investigate Captain Pretorius's murder. My ID is back at the boarding house." He concentrated on sounding sane.

"My fat behind." The man with the torch spat onto the ground. "Even white men can't be policemen if they're crazy."

"The Protea Guesthouse." Emmanuel stuck to familiar things. The men were local and coloured by the sound of it. "I was at Zweigman's shop this afternoon. Ask anyone who works there. They'll tell you who —"

"Shut it, mister." The man with the light stepped closer. "You people think now Captain's gone you can come back and interfere with our women?"

"That's not —"

"Get down on your knees or I'll get my man here to shoot you for the fun of it."

Emmanuel turned his head away from the white glare of the light and slowly sank to his knees. The men stepped closer and he sucked in his breath, ready for the kicking he knew was coming. Heat from the spotlight burned his face.

"Who you got?" The question was shouted across the veldt. Another coloured man come to join the hunting party.

"Crazy white man," the gunslinger called back. "Says he's a policeman."

The third man picked up pace until he was running hard towards them.

"Jesus Christ, Tiny." The third man gasped for breath. "That's him. That's the detective from Jo'burg."

"You kidding me? Look at him."

"Truth's faith." The new arrival swore an oath. "That's the detective. He came to my place this afternoon with Shabalala."

Emmanuel placed the voice. It belonged to the coloured mechanic who'd alibied Zweigman. A lanky man with dark brown skin and a gold filling set into his front tooth.

"Anton Samuels," Emmanuel said, still on his knees. "Number one mechanic in Jacob's Rest. That's what Constable Shabalala told me."

"I will be as soon as my shop is up and running again," Anton said and stepped forwards to offer Emmanuel his hand. "I've got a month or so to go before I rebuild, but I'll get there."

The safety was back on the gun and the spotlight aimed at the ground by the time Anton pulled him to his feet. There was a tense silence. The men waited for a cue. Assault of a white police officer meant jail time. An assault carried out by armed coloured men meant jail time with hard labour and regular beatings thrown in. Shooting him and slipping away was probably their best option.

"Sorry about this," Emmanuel apologised. "I must have given you a fright, running around like a lunatic in the middle of the night. I'm lucky you didn't shoot me right off."

"Lucky for all of us, Detective," Tiny said. He was a small man with a few wisps of coarse hair combed in a grand sweep across his skull. What he lacked in height and hair he made up for in girth. His stomach curved in front of him and strained against the buttons at the front of his shirt.

"I'm Tiny Hanson." He cleared his throat to minimise the quaver in his voice. "This here is my son, Theo."

"A half-naked white man out on a kaffir path," Theo said. He was a half-foot taller than his father but already beginning to run to fat. "That's something I never thought I'd see. You do this sort of thing in Jo'burg, Detective?"

The men laughed nervously, aware of how much still lay in the balance. One wrong move could send them plunging over a precipice, with no hope of a rescue mission to pull them out.

"I thought you were used to white policemen on these paths. Didn't the captain run on them all the time?"

"*Ja*, but he had clothes on."

"Good point." Emmanuel smiled. "Where did you guys come from, anyway?"

"Liquor store," Anton replied. "Tiny and Theo are back from Lourenço Marques tonight. We were having a card game out the back when we heard you run by."

Emmanuel glimpsed a pale window of light to his left. He had no idea where he was. Off the grid of main streets, there was no way to orient himself. The kaffir paths put him on the outside looking in.

"Will you take a drink, Detective?" Tiny offered politely. "Theo will show you back after."

Under usual circumstances the invitation was breaking all the rules. Coloured men and white police officers were not natural drinking partners.

"Okay," Emmanuel said. Sleep was a long way off, the dreams waited for him to return to his bed. "It'll help wash the dust from my mouth."

"I own the liquor store," Tiny said proudly and moved towards the light. "I have enough to wash the dust from your throat and your stomach, too. I got new stock in from Mozambique. Port. Whisky. Gin. You name it."

"Did you bring it in through the border post or across the river?"

"I do everything legal. The captain knew that and I never had no trouble. A bottle or two to those at the border post. A keg of beer to the police station. I make sure everyone gets their share."

Tiny pushed open a wooden gate and led the party into a small courtyard at the rear of the liquor store. Three kerosene lanterns hung from hooks in the rafters of a lean-to built up against the back door.

"Well, my share is a glass of whisky," Emmanuel said. A card table was set up in the middle of the lean-to. "What's your game?"

"Poker." Theo poured a triple measure into a clean glass and slid it across the table. "You play?"

"Used to," Emmanuel said. "Where's your other player?"

"Harry," Theo called into a darkened corner. "You can come out, it's just the detective from Jo'burg."

A sunken-chested old man with a waxed moustache shuffled out of the corner and slid into the vacant seat. His skeletal frame was weighed down by an army issue greatcoat decorated with service medals and faded ribbons from the Great War.

Emmanuel took the seat next to the old soldier, who'd no doubt been dumped into the back blocks of the Empire with a warm coat to keep out the memories of gas and gunshots. There but for the grace of God . . . Emmanuel thought.

"Relax, Harry," Anton said kindly. "It's just past midnight. You've got another hour before you get in trouble. I'll make sure you get back on time."

"Harry here is married to Angie, who works for the old Jew's wife," Tiny explained. "She's very strict with the poor fellow. Isn't she, Harry?"

"Tough. Tough," the man muttered to himself. "Tough on everything."

Emmanuel remembered Angie. Older and out of humour was how he'd labelled her. Right on the money, as it turned out.

"You in, Detective?" Anton asked.

Emmanuel took a mouthful of whisky. Staying was foolish. It would put the whites off side if they found out and make the investigation more difficult than it needed to be.

"Deal me in," he said. "What's the ante?"

"Five matchsticks," Tiny informed him seriously. "You sure you can afford it? I hear they don't pay police so well these days."

"I can handle it," Emmanuel answered with equal gravity. "Someone will have to stand me. I've got nothing on me."

Theo slid the matchsticks across the table. "Look at you, man. You've got a body like a *tsotsi*. How'd you get like that?"

"Scratches from my little run tonight. The bullet wound from the war."

"My grandfather was German," Tiny said and topped up the glasses. "From Dusseldorf, he said."

"Mine, too," Harry muttered. "Mine, too."

"No, man," Theo corrected him. "Your grandfather was the Scottish preacher who drank like a fish. Ask Granny Mariah, she'll tell you."

"Who are your people?"

It took Emmanuel a moment to realise that the question was addressed to him. He took a deep swallow of his drink before he answered. There was no shame at this table in being a product of the Empire: impure and resilient.

"English mother. Afrikaner father." He had no idea why he told the truth. He didn't speak about his parents often and in the last four years, on van Niekerk's instruction, not at all. They were one of the things he kept at the bottom of the well.

"Ah." Anton laid his cards down with a flourish. "So, you're mixed race just like us. Imagine that."

The laughter was loose and natural, greased by the whisky and the dark blanket of night. South Africa, with its laws, each more punishing than the last, was a long way from the backyard of Hanson's Fine Liquor Merchants. The unreal truce would hold until tomorrow.

"Hope it wasn't one of my relatives that did that to you, Detective." Tiny gestured at the bullet wound. "We aren't all bloodthirsty like the English say."

"Could have fooled me," Emmanuel said. "You almost finished me off tonight. Must be the Kraut in you."

"No! Honest," Tiny protested over the easy laughter. "We thought you was the pervert. With captain gone, who knows what will happen?"

"They never caught the guy?"

"Not that we know of," Anton said. "The old Jew kicked up a fuss, but the police said to forget about it. Go home. It's over."

Tiny swallowed his tumbler in one hit. "That's why I don't mind serving Donny Rooke in my shop. The white hotel banned him, but I say he's served his time and done the right thing by the girls. I don't like what he done, but I know about it. The whole town knows."

"You should have seen Donny when the captain came into the store the other night," Theo said. "So scared he almost kaked himself. The man who molested our women should be the same way, instead he's walking around free as a lark."

"What night was that?" Emmanuel asked. Theo and Tiny were out of town when the door to door happened. Their information wasn't on file yet.

88

"Wednesday." Tiny threw his losing hand down with a grunt. "The night the captain passed."

"What time?"

"Some time after six. Donny was running late and I opened the store especially for him. He's fonder of the bottle than he used to be, is Donny."

"The captain came by?"

"*Ja*, once a month he'd come by for a little bottle. Just a tot."

"Donny saw him?"

"Heard him," Theo snorted. "He was hiding behind the counter like an old woman."

"Pretorius know he was there?"

"No. The captain didn't stay long. Had to go to old Lionel's place to get bait worms, so he took off. Donny stayed another half-hour or so, till he was sure the captain had cleared town."

Emmanuel threw his cards in and noticed the casual way his own hands performed their task. Donny was back on the list with time, opportunity, and motive next to his name.

"Well, that's me done for. Got to get some sleep before the big day."

"All of us," Tiny agreed. "Got to look respectable for a funeral, that's one thing I remember from mission school."

Anton tapped Harry on the shoulder. "Time to make a move, my man, if you don't want a fry pan to the head like last week."

"Home." Harry sank the last of his drink. "Home."

"I'll see you back, Detective," Anton offered when they stepped out onto the kaffir path. "I've got to walk Harry to his house, and he lives just on the edge of the Dutch area."

Emmanuel waved goodnight and started down the path behind Anton and Harry. First thing tomorrow morning he and Shabalala would pay Donny another visit, and this time he and his child bride were going to tell the truth. He was going to give Donny a good reason to cry.

"The Protea Guesthouse is down there to the right." Anton aimed his torch at a narrow path wedged between two houses. "It would be better if you went alone. That part of town is off limits for us at night."

"Thanks." Emmanuel shook Anton's hand and watched him slip away into the veldt with Harry trailing behind. The old soldier's voice drifted back in a thin and broken rendition of "It's a Long Way to Tipperary".

Emmanuel followed the path and emerged into the gardens of the Protea Guesthouse. The coloured mechanic had saved him from a beating and worse. Donny wouldn't be so lucky. The screen door groaned, and then a flash of white at the corner of his eye. A torn piece of paper was wedged between the frame and the mesh. He pulled it free. His latenight visitor had left him a present. Moonlight hit the page. Two words in black ink: "Elliott King".

CHAPTER
FIVE

The sheet of corrugated iron gave way and Emmanuel was in, crouched in the dim interior of the shack. Donny Rooke was sandwiched between his wives, head thrown back like a walrus bull protecting his harem with rumbling snores. Emmanuel crossed the room before Donny opened his eyes. He grabbed him by the throat and lifted him from the squalid bed. The smell of unwashed bodies wafted from under the blankets and he heard the cry of the girls as he swung Donny out and pinned him naked against the wall.

"You lied to me, Donny."

"Leave him!" The older girl was on the attack. Emmanuel felt the sting of her fists across his back, then the sound of her flailing and kicking in midair. Shabalala had the furious girl off the floor. Emmanuel kept his focus on Donny.

"You lied to me," Emmanuel repeated calmly and eased his hold on Donny's neck a fraction. "Why did you lie?"

"Scared —" Donny gasped for breath.

"That was your excuse for running yesterday. You have to come up with something a lot better or I'll give you good reason to be scared. You understand me, Donny?"

"Please —"

"You. Englisher." It was the older girl. "Tell the kaffir to get off me. He can't touch me. It's against the law."

Emmanuel pushed Donny into a chair and turned to the girl sitting naked on the sofa. Shabalala was behind her, a hand resting firmly on her head, his gaze directed at the floor. The strange, paternal scene was undercut by the grotesque angle of the girl's hips, which tilted upward to offer a full view of everything between her thighs.

"Close your legs." Emmanuel picked up a thin sheet from the floor where it had fallen and threw it over the girl's lap before turning back to Donny. "You ready to tell me the truth or do you need me to help you remember?"

"No." Donny cowered in the chair. "I was too scared to tell you yesterday. Honest to God."

"Why?"

"I knew it would look bad. Me being the last person to see Captain Pretorius in town."

"At the liquor store?"

"No," Donny insisted. "On the kaffir path that goes behind the coloured houses."

Emmanuel pulled up a chair opposite Donny. The chair tilted to the side and came to rest at a crooked angle, like everything else in Donny Rooke's life. He picked up a discarded shirt from the floor and handed it to the naked man.

"On Wednesday?" Emmanuel prompted.

"*Ja.* I go in once a week to pick up supplies. This day I was running late and it was getting dark when I got to Tiny's shop." Donny stopped to pull the shirt over his bruised body. He didn't bother with the buttons. "While I was picking up my bottles Captain Pretorius came in and I hid behind the counter. I didn't want him to see me. I thought he'd take the bottles off me."

"Go on."

"Captain left and I stayed behind. I thought I'd give him long enough to get his worms and head out fishing. I went out on the kaffir path. The sun was down so I took it slow. I came around the bend heading towards the hospital and saw the police van parked behind a tree. I hid myself and waited for him to leave." Donny pulled his shirt tight around himself. "I wasn't spying. I was waiting for him to leave. That was all. I swear it."

"Then?"

"I heard footsteps. I looked up and he's standing there with his torch pointing right at me. 'You spying on me, Donny?' he says. I say, 'No, Captain, I'd never do nothing like that. Never.' He laughed and I almost wet myself. There was something . . ." Donny struggled with his poor vocabulary. "Something like a stone about him. Hard like. He didn't raise his voice, nothing like that. I said, 'Listen, Captain —' and bam."

Donny swung his head round to indicate a slap to the face. "He hits me like this, then he lays into me with his fists. He beat me down to the ground, then he grabs my hair and says, 'This is just a taste of what you'll get if I catch you spying on me again.' I wasn't spying but I says, 'Yes, Captain.' He pulled me up and brushed some dirt from my shirt, like I'd fallen all by myself. Then he picks up my bottles and gives them to me. 'Don't forget these. You're going to need them tonight,' he says. My hands was shaking, I was so scared. 'Thank you, Captain,' I said and limped away as fast as I could."

"What time you get home?"

"I don't know," Donny cried. "He beat me like a dog. There was pain all over my body. I got no idea how long it took me to get back from town."

"You own a clock?"

"It's broken."

"You own a gun?"

"*Ja*, of course." Donny pointed to a ledge behind the kitchen sink. Emmanuel got up and removed the gun. He slid the bolt back and wasn't surprised when the whole piece fell to the floor.

"Own any other guns?"

"No." Donny motioned to the girl on the couch. "She's good with a slingshot . . ."

Emmanuel returned the rifle to its stand and sat down in the tilting chair. The sight of Donny, naked but for the shirt yawning open at the front, was unsettling. He pressed his palms against his eyes as Donny began a quick slide off the suspects list. The killer was patient and careful. The crime scene was neat and controlled. Donny Rooke was a shambles. Body, mind and shack: all in disarray. He was the sort to leave a flask engraved with his name and address next to the corpse.

"You were angry at Captain Pretorius for handing you a beating. You wanted to get him back, get revenge." Emmanuel kept down the path.

94

"I wanted to get as far away from him as I could. There was something . . ." again a struggle for words ". . . wrong about him. Different."

"Did you follow him?"

"And get more of the same? No dice. I came straight home and pushed the furniture against the door."

Emmanuel looked over at the eldest girl. She was tougher than most of the gangsters he ran into in Jo'burg. He turned to the younger sister; a silent figure huddled under the weight of a tattered patchwork quilt. She was his best bet. He approached slowly and squatted by the side of the bed.

"I'm Detective Cooper," he said. "What's your name?"

"Marta." The voice was barely audible.

"Did Donny tell you how he got hurt, Marta?"

"*Ja.*"

"How's that?"

The adolescent chewed on her bottom lip before answering. "Said Captain Pretorius kicked the *kak* out of him. Belted him black and blue for no reason."

"What did Donny do when he got home on Wednesday?"

"Got into bed and cried. In the finish we give him a second bottle to put him to sleep he was making so much noise."

"He didn't leave again?"

"No, he was too drunk to stand up."

"I was hurt." Donny rushed to defend himself. "My arm still don't work properly from where he punched me. Look."

He struggled to raise his right arm above shoulder level. There was no doubt he'd been worked over thoroughly and that Captain Pretorius's hands with their bruised knuckles were the perfect fit for the assault.

"Why didn't you say this yesterday? You have the injuries, and you have witnesses to back up your story."

Donny's laugh was a thin, bitter sound. "Who was going to believe he beat me for no reason? A 'good man' like him. Never smoked or swore in front of women. Always friendly like. And me here with nothing. The whole town would laugh at me. Call me a liar."

"Are you lying?"

"No, if you'd seen Captain Pretorius that night you'd understand." Donny went down on his knees, his shirt thrown off to highlight his dire circumstance. "I left him on the kaffir path and came straight home. I didn't know nothing else till a coloured boy told Marta he was dead. As God is my witness."

Emmanuel doubted that God and Donny were on speaking terms, but his own gut reaction was now a solid feeling. The pathetic man kneeling in front of him was, in all likelihood, not the killer.

"Constable Shabalala. What do you think? Is our friend here telling the truth?"

Shabalala spoke with deep pity. "I think this man could not kill the captain. This man is not strong enough to do this thing."

"That's right. Look at me." Donny jumped up and used his skinny body as an exhibit. "Look. I hardly got any muscles. No way I could handle someone as big as Captain Pretorius."

"Put your clothes back on, Donny. That's not what Shabalala is talking about."

The killer wasn't physically strong: both he and Shabalala knew that. It was mental strength Shabalala was talking about, a toughness of the mind. Emmanuel wondered about the tight-lipped constable. He never volunteered information and didn't comment unless specifically asked to. There was resistance there, a stubborn refusal to get involved.

"Hey, you." It was the older girl, peeved at not being included in the conversation. "Is it true what they say about Englishmen? That they like it with boys?"

"You shut it, you hear?" Donny rushed towards his wife, fists clenched with violent intent. The girl stared him down.

"Sit," Emmanuel instructed Donny quietly. The shack and its inhabitants were beginning to seep into his skin. He picked up a cotton dress, discarded on the floor, and handed it to the older girl. She stood up and allowed him to get a good look at her. The flat stomach and small high breasts, the thatch of strawberry blonde hair covering her mons. And most arresting of all, the defiant sexual invitation glittering in the dark brown eyes.

"We have to get to the funeral," he said to Shabalala. Brassy young girls did nothing for his libido.

"*Yebo*," the black policeman answered with relief. The squalor of the shack was beginning to get to him, too.

"If I have to come back here again," Emmanuel said to Donny, "you're going to get a double dose of what Captain Pretorius gave you. That's a promise."

"*Ja*, of course, Detective." Donny was giddy with relief. "Everything I said is true as the Bible. I swear on my mother's grave."

The older girl flashed Emmanuel a look of disgust when he passed by. "Scrotum licker," she said coolly in Afrikaans, certain that the English detective had no taste for girls. Emmanuel made his way out to the sunlight.

Donny followed them to the car, shirt open like a tent flap. "Detective, if you find my camera —"

Emmanuel slammed the car door behind him and flicked the key. "I'll make sure to bring it to you." Emmanuel eased the car into first gear. He gave it some juice. Donny and his sad dirt yard were soon behind them.

"Did Captain Pretorius get rough with people?"

"No," Shabalala answered firmly.

"Why Donny?"

"That one —" Shabalala motioned in the direction of Donny's receding figure "— he came to the station and asked Captain Pretorius for his camera. The captain said he did not have such a thing and Rooke called him a liar and a thief."

"Captain Pretorius give him a tap or two?"

"No, but I think maybe Captain remembered what this man said to him."

Emmanuel turned onto the main road leading back to Jacob's Rest. The image of Pretorius's bruised knuckles was clear in his mind, as were the faces of the townsfolk when they talked about their murdered police captain. Righteous and upstanding were two words that came up frequently. That was the problem. The righteous also believed in punishment and retribution.

"Up here," Emmanuel instructed a puffy-eyed Hansie, who jumped onto the car's mudguard. "Tell me when you see him."

Hansie rubbed his swollen lids and squinted at the mass of people pouring out of the graveyard of the Dutch Reformed church. First came the blacks who had been on the outer rim of mourners, then the coloureds, then the inner core of whites. The whole district had turned out for the funeral. Every inch of space on the street leading to the church was taken up by bicycles, cars, and tractors driven in from outlying farms. Many more blacks from the location had come into town on foot. The captain's death had turned Jacob's Rest into a bustling metropolis.

"Well?" Emmanuel prompted. Shabalala had been invited into the Pretorius family's honour guard, which left Hansie as his only source of local intelligence. The phrase almost made him laugh.

"I can't see him," Hansie said. "Maybe he didn't come."

"If he's alive, he's here. Keep looking."

"I am." Hansie sulked as the crowd pressed out of the church grounds.

A curvy brunette made her way towards the street. "Is that Elliott King with the brown hair and the big breasts?" Emmanuel said.

"No." The young policeman hiccupped in surprise. "Mr King has light hair."

Emmanuel thought Hansie was joking, but there was no spark in the dense blue eyes, just a teenaged yearning to be close to the sweetie jar. A powerful mix of sadness and longing had sucked the last spark of energy from a brain that had no backup generator.

"Go," Emmanuel said. It was time to cut his losses and find an alternate source of local knowledge. Hansie was as much use to him as a blind parrot. "I'll see you back at the police station later this afternoon."

Hansie was down and pushing his way through the crowd before the sentence was finished. The brunette was still in the church grounds when the most senior police official in Jacob's Rest, eighteen-year-old Hansie Hepple, laid a hand on her shoulder.

At least he feels something, Emmanuel thought. In a small crush of coloured people he caught sight of Anton, the levelheaded mechanic who'd saved him from a beating. He motioned him over.

"Elliott King," he said, after they'd exchanged greetings. "Can you tell me where he is without pointing him out?"

Anton's brown eyes flickered over the gathering with quick intelligence. "Under the tree to your left, paying his respects to the family. Fair-haired, wearing a safari suit."

100

Emmanuel spotted him right off. He exuded the kind of casual ease that comes from sitting on a pot of family gold. The tailored khaki suit was a nice touch. It imparted a rural man-of-the-people charm without diminishing his superior status.

"Money?"

"Sugar mills and now game farms."

Elliott King proceeded down the line of family members, shaking hands as he went. The chill from the Pretorius men reversed the midday heat by a few degrees. Even Louis managed a look of disdain.

"What's up?" Emmanuel asked.

"Captain Pretorius sold the old family farm to King a year or so ago. They think King cheated the captain on the price."

"Did he?"

Anton shrugged. "Captain never complained about the money, only the sons."

"Anything come of it?"

"Just a lot of hot air. Silly talk from the brothers about King being a swindler, but King is too big for them to mess with. The Pretorius boys don't like it when they don't get their way."

"You know what it's like to be on the wrong side of them?"

"Everyone in Jacob's Rest has had a taste. I'm no different."

Emmanuel was about to ask for more details when two newcomers to the family group caught his attention. The men, crewcut commando types, were squeezed into the cheap cotton suits worn for court appearances and interrogation cell duties. Both were drawn from the "rough justice" section of the training manual. Neither appeared capable of playing the soft man, versed in worming confessions out of prisoners using empathy and skill. They were the Security Branch.

"Friends of yours?" Anton asked.

Emmanuel jumped off the mudguard and pulled Anton down after him. The crowd washed around them like a black sea, momentarily blotting out the presence of sharks in the water. Emmanuel took a deep breath. Two days. Just long enough to select personnel for the assignment, brief them, and arrange transport. The Security Branch had no intention of taking a back seat. They were in on the investigation from the start. "Taking an interest" was just the bullshit they'd thrown van Niekerk's way to keep things calm while they marshalled their forces.

"Don't know them," Emmanuel replied. "But I've got a feeling they'll introduce themselves to all of us soon enough."

Anton swallowed. "Should I be worried, Detective?"

"Are you a political man? Do you belong to the Communist Party or a union that disagrees with the National Party laws?"

"No," the coloured man replied quickly. "Can't say I like what's going on, but I've never done anything about it."

"Are all your identification papers in order?"

"Far as I know."

"Then keep it that way," Emmanuel said. "The Security Branch is here to look for political activists and whatever the Security Branch looks for they find."

"So I've heard," Anton answered quietly. If the Security Branch had the power to spook a white detective, what chance did a coloured man have?

"You know how to play the game, Anton. Just keep playing it."

"You a strange man," Anton said lightly. "What do you know about the game, anyway?"

"I was born here. Everyone in SA has to know their place. Some of us are pawns and some of us —" he stopped and motioned in the direction of Elliott King, who was walking towards a canvas-topped Land Rover parked on the street "— are kings. I'll see you later."

Emmanuel pressed through a gathering of white farmers and drew parallel with the dapper peacock of a man just as he reached his car. The door to the Land Rover was held open by an older native in a green game ranger's outfit with the words "Bayete Lodge" embroidered over the breast pocket.

"Mr King." Emmanuel stepped into the space in front of the door and held his hand out in greeting. "I'm Detective Sergeant Emmanuel Cooper. Could I have a moment of your time?"

"Certainly, Detective Sergeant." The smile was cool, the handshake brief and firm. "How can I help?"

In the churchyard, the Security Branch goons were deep in conversation with Paul Pretorius. They'd be down at the police station this afternoon, pissing in all the corners to make sure everyone knew the investigation was theirs.

"I'd like to ask you a few questions about Captain Pretorius. Would it suit you to talk at your house? Town is crowded, and I think it would be better if we had some privacy."

"Am I a suspect, Detective Sergeant?"

"It's just an informal chat," Emmanuel said, aware of the thinning crowd and the risk of exposing his leads to the National Party muscle men. "A favour to the investigation."

"In that case I'll be happy to see you at my farm in an hour or so." King slid into the Land Rover. "As you're coming out my way, do go to the old Jew's place and pick up my housekeeper and her daughter, there's a good fellow. It will save Matthew here a trip back into town. They'll be ready to come out to the farm in about an hour."

The door slammed shut before Emmanuel had a chance to reply. His reflection blurred in the dusty car window. Elliott King had given an order and he expected it to be obeyed.

Emmanuel gave a mock salute and the car pulled away from the kerb and headed out to the main road. He'd met every form of arrogant Englishman on the battlefield but at least this one, in his tailored khaki suit and new Land Rover, didn't have the power to order him over a hill littered with landmines. He'd play the lackey for as long as it took him to figure out why Elliott King's name had been given to him as a clue in the dead of night.

"When's my backup getting here, sir?" Emmanuel asked. He'd reached Major van Niekerk at home: a redbrick Victorian mansion nestled on vast grounds in the posh northern suburbs of Johannesburg. "I can't run this investigation on my own."

"No backup," van Niekerk replied over the sound of a whistling kettle. "The commissioner has told me to step away. The Security Branch is in control now."

"Where does that leave me?"

"Alone," the major replied. "The Security Branch wants you replaced but I've convinced the commissioner to keep you on. That means you'll be a very unpopular addition to the team."

"Why not replace me?" Emmanuel asked.

"You're not a Security Branch stooge," van Niekerk informed him. "You'll make sure the right person hangs for the crime."

Despite what he said, van Niekerk wasn't big on the pure justice element of policing. The ambitious major was making sure that a detective loyal to him was on the ground to represent his best interests. Van Niekerk wasn't going to hand over the headline-making murder of a white police captain to the Security Branch without a fight. Fine, Emmanuel thought, except for the fact that van Niekerk was in Jo'burg sipping tea while he was about to go toe to toe with the hard men of law enforcement.

"What are they like?" van Niekerk asked with mild curiosity.

"They look like they can beat a confession out of a can of paint."

"Good. That means you can turn the whole thing around on them."

"How do I do that?" Emmanuel asked dryly.

"Find the killer," van Niekerk said. "Find him before they do."

Outside the captain's office the Security Branch officers rifled through the contents of the police station's file cabinet. Their faces made two sides of an ugly coin. They turned to him and Emmanuel felt their hostility radiate outwards. Unwelcome addition to the team? Major van Niekerk had a talent for understatment.

"We can relax, Dickie," the older, leaner officer instructed his hefty colleague, his smile a bare stretch of his lips over yellowing teeth. "God is with us. Finally."

"You must be the smart one," Emmanuel said and threw his hat onto Sarel Uys's vacant desk. He waited for the second salvo. The Security Branch boys were going to give him a kicking just to let him know who was in charge.

"God?" Dickie's brain was straining to keep up.

"Emmanuel," the senior officer said. "That's what his name means. 'God is with us'. According to Major van Niekerk, Detective Sergeant Cooper here can walk on water. He's a real miracle worker."

Emmanuel let the comment ride. If the Security Branch wanted a fight they'd have to land a few more solid punches.

"Where are you off to, Cooper?"

"I report to Major van Niekerk," Emmanuel said. "No-one else."

"That was yesterday. From today you report to me, Lieutenant Piet Lapping of the Security Branch. Your major was informed of that fact by my colonel." He paused to let the full weight of the information sink in. "Now, where are you off to, Cooper?"

"A farm," Emmanuel said.

"You sure you want to do that?" Lapping asked. "Farms are dirty places. You might get cow shit on your shoes."

Dickie, the muscle of the outfit, rested his beer-fed rump against the edge of Hansie's desk. "That's what we heard, hey, Lieutenant? That Manny here likes to keep himself neat and tidy. Always with the ironed shirts and polished shoes."

Piet lit a cigarette and threw the packet over to his sergeant, Dickie Heyns. "That's probably why his friend, Major van Niekerk, promoted him so quickly. Neat bachelors like to stick together."

"Truly?" Dickie asked conversationally.

"Ja." Piet blew a cloud of smoke out from between bulbous lips. "They meet in secret and starch each other's underpants till they're good and stiff."

Emmanuel ignored the urge to shove Piet, head first, into the rubbish bin. Security Branch intelligence was becoming legendary, but pockmarked Piet and his partner had only a few days' worth of it to draw on. They knew he'd been promoted quickly: too quickly for some senior detectives' liking. His personal hygiene habits and the ugly liaison rumour came from deep inside the district detective branch. Somebody had talked.

"Where does a man learn such unnatural things?" Dickie's hippo-sized head tilted to one side as they continued their routine.

"The British army," Piet replied. "That's probably why Manny here did so well during the war. Foot soldier to major in a few years, plus all those shiny medals to pin onto his pretty uniform."

Emmanuel sifted through the ranks of his detractors and came up with a name. Head Constable Oliver Sparks: a bitter twig of a man due to be pensioned off the force after twenty years of indifferent service. The homosexual liaison rumour was his doing, payback for van Niekerk's refusal to offer up the high-profile cases.

"How is Head Constable Sparks?" Emmanuel asked. "Still planting evidence and drinking on the job?"

The porridge flesh on Piet's face tensed noticeably and he took a long drag of his cigarette and exhaled. Emmanuel knew he'd scored a hit with Sparks's name. The lieutenant's pinprick eyes darkened.

"Whose farm are you going to?" Lapping continued the previous conversation and Emmanuel felt a rising uneasiness. Lieutenant Piet Lapping and his sidekick were not the "hard man/hard man" combination he'd picked them for at the funeral. Beneath the lumpy facial mask and the concrete-reinforced body, Piet had a brain that worked at above average capacity.

"Elliott King's farm," Emmanuel said. "I'm following up a rumour that King cheated Captain Pretorius on a financial transaction. There might have been bad blood between the two."

"You're chasing the personal angle?" Lapping made it sound like a fool's errand.

"Is there another?" Emmanuel asked.

"None that I can discuss with you." Lapping waved a hand towards the front door. "Go off to your farm visit and report to me immediately you get back to town. I am in charge of all aspects of this case. Understand?"

Emmanuel got the feeling that the Security Branch was way ahead of him. They were searching for specific information. "The personal angle", as the lieutenant put it, was at the bottom of their list of motives.

"Back again so soon, Detective?" Zweigman was wrapping a parcel in a length of brown paper. "Are you perhaps interested in our special on apricot jam? Top quality. You won't find better. Not even in Jo'burg."

"The funeral's put you in a good mood," Emmanuel said. "Planning a party for later?"

"Just a quiet drink with my wife," came the deadpan reply.

"I thought you never hit the bottle, Doctor."

"Only on special occasions." Zweigman tied the parcel up neatly and laid it with a pile of others on the counter. "Do you plan to join the funeral reception at the Standard Hotel, Detective? I hear Henrick Pretorius is serving up half-price drinks until sunset."

Emmanuel imagined the Pretorius brothers and their Boer brethren singing Afrikaner folk songs late into the night. Someone might even pull out a squeezebox for good measure. His blood ran cold.

"Not my thing," he said. "I'm supposed to give King's housekeeper and her daughter a lift to his farm. He said they'd be here."

Zweigman stilled. "Mr King has a driver."

"I know that, but as I'm going out to King's farm he thought I'd be a 'good fellow' and do him the favour of driving his staff back: 'Saves Matthew making two trips.'"

"I see." Zweigman busied himself picking pieces of string off the countertop.

"Well, are they here?"

"Of course." The German shopkeeper collected himself. "I will go out to the back and inform them that you will be providing them with transport."

"Thank you," Emmanuel said and strolled over to the window that fronted the street. A throng of white men passed across the corner of van Riebeeck on their way to the half-price drinks at the Standard Hotel. Groups of blacks drifted onto the kaffir paths that headed out to the location. The town was emptying.

He turned and found Zweigman at the counter with Davida, the shy brown mouse, and a graceful woman dressed in a dark cotton dress teamed with a row of fake Indian shop pearls.

"This is Mrs Ellis and her daughter, Davida, whom you have already met." Zweigman performed the introductions as though the task itself was distasteful to him.

"Mrs Ellis. Detective Sergeant Emmanuel Cooper."

"Detective." King's housekeeper gave a deferential bow, the kind reserved for white men in power. She was green-eyed and brown-skinned, her lips full enough to hold the weight of a weary man's head. Davida stayed in the background with her head bowed like a novice about to take orders. The tiger had given birth to a lamb.

"Pleased to meet you, Mrs Ellis," Emmanuel said and fished out the car keys. "I'm afraid we have to get going."

"Of course." Mrs Ellis hurried to the counter and Zweigman shooed her away while he and the shy brown mouse divided the parcels between them.

Emmanuel stepped outside. A skinny mixed-race woman with coarse yellow hair walked a chubby toddler past the burned-out shell of Anton's garage. The wreckage reminded him of any one of a thousand French towns flattened in the march towards peace.

A cloudbank passed overhead and a dark shadow crossed the street, followed by the blinding light of the sun as the clouds moved on towards the veldt. Emmanuel blinked hard in the changing light. Mrs Ellis stood on the store veranda, and Davida and Zweigman stood face to face on the bottom stair. They were so close Emmanuel could almost feel the breath move between them. White glare reflected off the car's bonnet, then died away to a soft shimmer.

"Headache bothering you again, Detective?"

"No, it's just the sun," Emmanuel said. He checked Mrs Ellis for a reaction. She gave no indication that her daughter's honour might have been compromised in any way.

Emmanuel opened the car door and slid into the driver's seat. He didn't put much store in Mrs Pretorius's lecherous Shylock story: her world was populated with crafty Jews, drunken coloureds and primitive blacks. It was the standard National Party bullshit that poor Afrikaners swore by and educated Englishmen loved to mock while their own servants clipped the lawn.

The passenger doors closed and he switched on the engine. What he'd seen, so briefly, between Zweigman and the mute girl was not an offence under the Immorality Act. Had he imagined it?

"Where to?" he asked Mrs Ellis, who was perched at the edge of the seat, as if she was afraid her weight might offend the springs.

"Take Piet Retief Street to Botha Drive, then turn left at the Standard Hotel and head out to the main road. Bayete Lodge is about thirty or so miles west."

"Is there any way out of town that doesn't take us past the Standard?" Emmanuel asked.

Every white man in the district would be there, the Pretorius brothers included. Driving by with two brown women in the back seat when he could be attending the formal reception was the quickest way to get doors slammed in his face.

"There's only one way in and out of town," the older woman pointed out. "We have to go past the Standard."

Emmanuel turned onto Piet Retief Street and slowed down. He glanced in the rearview mirror, uncomfortable. "I need to ask you both a favour."

"Yes," Mrs Ellis said, her hands played nervously with the fake pearls around her neck. White men asking favours spelled bad news for non-white women.

"I'd like the two of you to lie down in the back before we get to the Standard. It would be better for the investigation if no-one saw you." He said it all at once, without stopping: he'd never ask a respectable white woman and her daughter to do the same. "You can get back up once we clear town."

"Oh." Mrs Ellis twisted the pink-tinted pearls tighter. "I suppose that would be okay. Hey, Davida?"

Davida smiled at her mother and slowly laid her head down on the back seat, like a child playing a game she already knew the rules to. Mrs Ellis copied the movement and lay next to her daughter.

Up ahead, groups of men stood on the pavement in front of the Standard Hotel. It was early afternoon and the crowd hadn't spilled out onto the street yet. Another hour or two and traffic would have to negotiate a slow crawl through the crush of mourners.

Emmanuel checked faces on the drive past the hotel. His luck held good. No-one from the Pretorius family camp was in the roadside throng. He took the left turn and gave the accelerator a tap. Soon he was out past the town boundary and heading west on the main road.

He slowed almost to a stop and looked over his shoulder at the women hidden on the back seat. Davida lay with her cheek against the warm leather, her arm thrown across the top half of her face. She breathed slow and deep, her mouth held open slightly. For a moment he thought she was asleep.

"We're clear," he said and turned his attention back to the road. The veldt rolled out either side of them in a tangle of wild fig trees and acacia bushes. Against the blur of the landscape he recalled the image of the girl fallen and fragile in the back seat of his car.

CHAPTER
SIX

"What do you think?" Elliott King pointed to the half-finished construction perched above a riverbank.

Emmanuel knew there was only one correct answer to the question. "Very impressive," he said.

"This is going to be the finest game camp in the southern part of Africa. Five luxury lodges with views to the waterhole, top-level trackers and rangers, private game drives on tap. The best food, the best wine, the biggest variety of animals. I have spent an absolute fucking fortune stocking this place, but then again people will pay a fortune to stay here, so it's only fair."

Emmanuel heard pride in the Englishman's voice; he was filled with the joy that comes from being supreme ruler of your own piece of Africa.

"This used to be the Pretorius farm," Emmanuel said, thinking of the captain's family, who also owned a giant slice of the Transvaal.

"Yes." King reached over and rang a small silver bell on the low table next to him. "Captain Pretorius sold it to me about a year ago when he realised Paul and Louis weren't going to take up farming."

"I hear there was some trouble over the sale."

"Oh, that." King smiled. "The problem was between Pretorius and his sons. They don't have their father's business acumen . . . he was an intelligent man."

"Mr King?" It was Mrs Ellis responding to the bell. She had changed out of her black mourning clothes and was now wearing the lodge uniform, a tailored green shift with the words "Bayete Lodge" embroidered over the pocket. She still managed to look elegant.

"Tea," King said. "And some cakes, please."

"Right away." Mrs Ellis dropped a half-curtsy and disappeared into the cool interior of the house. Being in Elliott King's company was like slipping into the pages of an old-fashioned English novel. Any moment now they'd hear the beating of drums and a frantic call to defend the house against a native uprising.

"Intelligent?" Emmanuel repeated the word. They were talking about an Afrikaner police captain with a neck the size of a tree trunk.

"I know," King said and smiled. "He looked the part of a dumb Boer, but under all that he was a complex human being."

"How so?"

"Come with me." King stood up and entered the house, talking as he went. "Yes, this was the Pretorius family farm. The captain was the third generation to live out here. He only left when he got married and moved to town."

Emmanuel followed King into the house. The main living area contained soft, wide-backed sofas and animal skin rugs. Paintings of the English countryside teamed with family photographs on the whitewashed

116

walls — Mrs Ellis kept it all in impeccable order. Tribal masks, shields, and *assegai* spears added just enough of a primitive edge to place the room in South Africa instead of Surrey.

"Look at this." King pulled open a drawer in the office and took out a stack of yellowed envelopes. There was writing on each envelope, faint but still visible. "Read them and tell me what you make of them."

"*Full moon fertility. Sprinkle across mouth of* kraal *after midnight,*" Emmanuel read aloud.

"Keep going." King was obviously delighted by his find.

"*Spring rain creator. Dig into topmost field first day after seeding.*"

Emmanuel flicked through the rest in quick order. All the labels had a mystical element to them. "They're black magic potions of some kind. The natives swear by them."

"Not just natives. We found these when we cleared the house. They belonged to old man Pretorius, the captain's father."

"White Police Captain Dabbles in Black Magic": the English papers would have a field day.

"When I found these, I asked my driver Matthew about Pretorius the Elder." King threw the envelopes in the drawer and started back towards the veranda. "He was widowed early and lived out here alone with his son. The other Boers thought he was insane and apparently steered clear of him. He believed the whole Boer white tribe in Africa story without reservation."

"Lots of people do," Emmanuel said. Two-thirds of the present government, in fact.

"True, but how many of those people partner their son with a black companion so they can learn the ways of the natives? How many make their sons undertake the training of a Zulu *amabutho* between the ages of fourteen and eighteen, and endure the pain that goes with it?"

"Pretorius did that?"

"He and Shabalala would apparently run barefoot from one end of the farm to the other five or six times without stopping, without drinking. Matthew says they were quite a sight. It brought tears to the eyes of those who remembered the old days. The sound of Zulu warriors, the *impi*, thundering across the veldt." King sat down in his chair with a nostalgic sigh. The expanse of sky and gentle hills, once native homeland, was now part of the man's fiefdom. What was it about the British and their love of nations they'd conquered in battle?

"Constable Shabalala was his companion?"

"Yes. Shabalala's father was a Zulu. He trained them."

"Why did the captain's father do it?" Emmanuel asked. Most whites were happy to claim higher status as a birthright.

"This is the crackpot element." King obviously relished talking about the eccentricities of the Boers. "Old man Pretorius thought that white men should be able to prove themselves equal to or better than the natives in all things. He brought his son up to be a white *induna*, a chief, in every sense of the word."

Mrs Ellis carried out a tea tray and placed it on the table between them. Her movements were sparse and economical, the body language of someone born into the service of others. She handed King his tea. Why the high-toned Englishman talked as if the days of the white chiefs were over was beyond Emmanuel.

Mrs Ellis, the perfect servant, vanished indoors.

"You know, Captain Pretorius could name every plant and tree on the veldt," King continued. "He spoke all the dialects, knew all the customs. Unlike the Dutchmen around here, he didn't need some paper shuffler in Pretoria to legislate his superior status."

"You knew him well?" Emmanuel asked. It was obvious the aristocratic Englishman believed that Captain Pretorius occupied the same "born to rule" category as himself. The rest of humanity, including police detectives, were mere servants.

"I got to know him a little while we were negotiating the sale and much better once he started building." King paused to select a cake from the tray. "As I said, he was actually very complex and intelligent, for a Boer."

"Building?" Emmanuel put his tea down. This was the reason he'd been given the note. He was sure of it.

"Nothing grand. Just a little stone hut on the allotment he kept for himself."

"He has a house out here?"

"More of a shack than a house," King said and bit into his cake. He took his time chewing. "It looks like something out of the kaffir location, but he seemed to like it."

"Did he spend a lot of time here?" No-one, not Shabalala or the Pretorius brothers, had mentioned a secondary residence of any kind.

"Not that I know of. He came out a few times during hunting season and then at odd times after that. It all seemed a bit random, but it was his land and his shack."

Captain Pretorius appeared to be a man of quiet habit and routine. Fishing on Wednesday, coach of the rugby team on Thursday, church every Sunday, and yet the word random kept coming up in connection with him.

"Where is the shack?" The weight of the car keys and the piece of paper with King's name scribbled on it suddenly became heavy against his thigh. Afternoon tea time was over.

"Ten or so miles back towards the main road. There's a giant witgatboom tree right at the turn-off. You passed it on your way in."

The witgatboom tree was a good signpost with its branches flung out to support a wide flat top. It was a quintessentially African sight.

"I'll need to go out there," Emmanuel said.

"It's not my place to give or deny permission. I have no say over that piece of land, so feel free to do as you wish."

Emmanuel stopped at the top of the veranda stairs. "I thought you bought this farm from Captain Pretorius."

"Most of it," King corrected. "He kept a small parcel. That's what his sons couldn't understand. The sale wasn't about money. Their father just wanted a piece of his old life back."

Emmanuel felt in his bones that the Pretorius brothers had no idea about the shack or their father's plans to resume his life as a white *induna*.

"I'll head straight back to the station after looking over the place," Emmanuel said. "Thank you for your help, Mr King, and for the tea."

"Pleasure," King said as a red two-door sports car with rounded haunches and curved silver headlights pulled into the gravel driveway and stopped inches from the Packard's back bumper. The driver's door swung open and a man in his twenties eased out of the scooped leather seat. Emmanuel caught the flash of his perfect white teeth.

"Winston . . ." Elliott King called out a greeting to the handsome boy making for the stairs. "I wasn't expecting you till tomorrow. Meet Detective Sergeant Emmanuel Cooper. He was just on his way out."

"An officer of the law." Winston smiled and shook hands. "Have you finally been able to bring charges against my uncle, Detective Sergeant?"

The King men laughed; the law was a servant to whom they did not have to answer.

The sleek sports car and the beachside tan irritated Emmanuel beyond reason, as did the simple elephant hair bracelet worn by Winston to authenticate his "African-ness".

"Routine questioning," Emmanuel said.

"What happened?"

"Captain Pretorius." King went back to his seat and sat down. "He was murdered Wednesday night. Shot twice."

"Jesus . . ." Winston leaned against the railing. "Are you a suspect?"

"Of course not." King took a sip of tea. "I provided the detective with some background information. As a favour to the investigation."

Emmanuel edged towards the top stair. Stuck between King and his linen-clad nephew was the last place he wanted to be. The secret hut beckoned to him.

"What made you think my uncle knew anything about Captain Pretorius?" Winston asked.

Although half the size of the Pretorius boys, Winston shared with them an uncomplicated sense of entitlement. Emmanuel took the first stair.

"Routine questioning." He took the second and third stairs then turned to Winston. "Do *you* know anything about the murder?"

"Me?"

"Yes. You."

"How would I? I just found out about it now."

"Of course." Emmanuel paused to enjoy Winston's moment of discomfort. "Thanks again for your help, Mr King."

He walked past Winston's Jaguar to the Packard, which looked wide and lumbering next to its expensive English cousin. No maps or discarded drink cans on the passenger seat. All Winston King needed for his travels was a fast car, a fat wallet and a smile. Emmanuel's dislike rose again and he pushed it aside.

122

He eased the Packard into first gear and piloted it out of the circular drive. Winston disappeared into the house and his uncle poured himself another cup of tea.

Elliott King carefully selected a piece of cake and watched the detective drive away. He rang the silver bell.

"Mr King?" The housekeeper stepped out onto the veranda.

"Bring Davida here," he said. "I want to speak to her."

A fence made of tall sticks lashed together with twine and strips of bark stood at the end of the red clay road. The construction was identical to those encircling the native *kraals* that nestled into the landscape like giant mushrooms.

Emmanuel got out of the car and checked the perimeter. The entrance, a small opening half the size of an average man, was located at the back, away from the road. Casual visitors were obviously not encouraged. He crouched down and entered the compound like a supplicant and there, directly in front of him, was a stone rondavel, a round hut, with a thatched roof and a pale blue door.

"Lair of the white *induna*," Emmanuel said and took in his surroundings. The entrance to the stone hut was deliberately aligned with the hole in the fence so that all visitors came and went under the watchful eye of the headman. Even here, miles away from the town, security and surveillance were taken into account.

A river, close by, filled the air with the hum and gurgle of water moving over rock. Emmanuel felt a deep satisfaction. The shed in Jacob's Rest was a front. A place to display the things acceptable to friends and family. This *kraal*, lying under a clear spring sky, was where the captain let himself out to play.

Emmanuel crossed the compound to a pile of stones heaped against the fence. What did King say? "When he started building . . ." That would explain the blistered hands and the sinewy muscles noted during the examination of the body. Pretorius had put the hut up himself: stone by stone.

Emmanuel pushed the pale blue door and it swung inward. He squinted into the dim interior. There were two windows, each with its curtains drawn. He left the door open to get more light. Cowhide rugs crackled under foot as he pulled the curtains open and looked around. As male bolt-holes went, it was embarrassing. Everything was in order: the bed made, dishes washed and resting on the sideboard, the small table wiped clean. Aunt Milly would be happy to spend an afternoon here.

"Come on," Emmanuel said. There had to be something. A man didn't build a secret hut, then use it to practise housekeeping skills.

Nothing in the room stood out as aberrant or unusual, but then it never did where the captain was concerned. Everything *appeared* normal until you got close enough to press your nose against the dirty window. The vicious beating handed out to Donny under the cover of night; the relentless surveillance of the town disguised as daily exercise; the building of a hut no-one in his family knew about. There was a reason this modest stone rondavel was a secret.

Emmanuel stripped the bed and checked the pillow, mattress and sheets, which were made of fine cotton weave. Nice. For a woman? Or did the captain have sensitive skin? Next came the chest of drawers, then the small cupboard holding cutlery and crockery. He looked over, under, on top of and behind every item until he arrived back at the front door, empty-handed.

He crouched low in the doorway. The room stared back at him with its scrubbed and innocent face. He'd missed something. But what? Everything had been checked, except the ceiling and the floor.

How many bizarre hiding places had the platoon come across during their sweep of villages in France and Germany? Cupboards with fake backs. Trapdoors cut into ceilings. Even a hollow staircase designed to hold a whole family. The captain, with his fondness for façades, would have the good stuff hidden.

Emmanuel grabbed the edge of the cowhide and pulled it towards him.

The opening, a small square with a wooden top, was craftily hidden. A woven loop of rope, finger-sized, was the only indication that the surface of the compacted earth floor had been violated. Emmanuel shuffled forwards on his knees and tugged at the rope. The trapdoor swung open easily, its hinges oiled in anticipation of frequent use. He reached in, expecting the usual bundle of frayed pornographic magazines.

125

The National Party crackdown on immoral publications had slowed the trade but not stopped it. His hand touched on soft leather, a strap of some sort. He pulled it up towards him and felt the weight at its end.

"My God . . ."

It was Donny Rooke's camera with his name proudly stamped into the hard leather casing in gold letters; he'd even included the J, his middle initial. Emmanuel flicked up the clips and examined the beautiful instrument. What had Donny said? The camera was expensive and the captain had stolen it from him — and the pictures of the du Toit girls with it.

"Even a broken clock is right twice a day," Emmanuel muttered and shut the case. He reached into the hole, and fished out a thick brown paper envelope. If Donny's story held, the "art" pictures of his wives would be inside. Did the captain have a taste for underage flesh? He flipped the envelope over and something cast a shadow from the doorway.

Emmanuel turned in time to see the hard line of a *knobkerrie* moving towards him. The Zulu club generated its own breeze as it arched downward and made contact with the side of his head.

Whack.

The sound exploded in his eardrums like a mortar round. He fell forwards and tasted dirt and blood in his mouth. There was a bright fizz of sheer white pain behind his eyelids and the club fell a second time. He heard his own laboured breath and smelled ammonia. A blue shadow flickered and then the distant sound of a mechanical rattle.

CHAPTER
SEVEN

"*You lazy bastard. How long are you going to lie there, humping the floor?*" It was the sergeant major from basic training, his voice thick with the coal and filth of the Edinburgh slum he'd crawled out of. Emmanuel felt the sergeant major's breath on his neck.

"*Call yourself a soldier? All you're fit for is fucking German whores. Is that why you joined up? You hopeless piece of African shit. Get up now or I'll shoot you myself. Get to your feet or get the fuck out of my army.*"

"Detective?"

Emmanuel shook his head. The dark blue shadow hung over him.

"*You going to let that Kraut piss all over you? What did I teach you? If you have to go, take one out with you.*"

"You okay?"

Emmanuel pushed himself off the ground, wheeled full circle, and jumped on the source of the voice. He felt neck muscles tense under his fingers; heard the slam of the body as it hit the ground; then he was straddling the flailing mass, gaining supremacy. There was the quiet hiss of air leaving lungs.

"De-tec-tive . . ." The sound drained away to nothing.

Detective. He'd heard that title recently. The memory of a police ID card fought its way past the hot shower of pain snaking down from his scalp to his jaw. He eased his grip and felt the body beneath him, small and surrendering: a boy soldier called to defend the fatherland against hopeless odds.

"Go home," Emmanuel said and released his grip. His hands were stiffened into the shape of animal talons. "*Ghet du zuruck nach ihre mutter.* Go home to your mother."

A relentless *boom, boom, boom* pounded the side of his skull with grim military precision. Piss and blood, the classic smell of the battleground, clouded the air.

"Detective. Please."

He focused beyond his hands and recognised the shy brown mouse, Davida, lying under him, a red mark slashed across her throat.

"You can speak," he said.

"Yes."

"What are you doing here?"

"Where do you think we are?" She lay still, afraid of startling him.

Emmanuel glanced around. Through the haze, shapes began to appear. A table, a chair, a bed stripped of its linen. The *boom, boom, boom* continued loud as a kettledrum. It was impossible to think.

"Where is that smell coming from?" he demanded. "The room is so clean."

128

"The smell's from you, Detective." There was a slight tremor in her voice, which was only slightly accented, as if she'd learned English from someone who demanded correct pronunciation and usage. "It's on your clothes."

The jacket and shirt, crisp and clean a few hours ago, were crusted in dried blood and urine. Emmanuel jumped up, hands feeling frantically at the crotch of his pants. The material was crumpled but dry.

"It's mainly here." She rose unsteadily to her feet. "Where my head was."

They looked at the dark pool, still damp and reeking. Emmanuel felt for his crotch again. Dry. He pulled off his jacket and sniffed at the material like a dog. Urinal odours rose up in an ammonia cloud. Someone — some fucking inbred country Dutchman — took a piss on him.

"Goddamn it." He threw the jacket from him in disgust. "What is it about this place? A man can't wear a suit two days in a row."

The jacket landed at the edge of the captain's homebuilt safe, and slithered inside. Images, each crisper than the last, flashed through his head until they made a seamless run of film: the camera; the envelope; the blue shadow; then the club crashing down against his skull.

Emmanuel dropped to his knees and scrambled towards the hiding place. The dirt floor threw up puffs of dust and sand as he frantically searched for Donny Rooke's camera and the brown paper envelope.

"Fuck." He widened his radius, hoping something had been knocked under the chair or the bed when he fell forwards. His hands patted the surface like a drunk in a minefield and came back with nothing but the dirt under his fingernails.

"Gone." He slammed the wooden lid shut and the hinges buckled.

"What's gone?" It was Davida; so quiet he'd forgotten she was there.

"Evidence," he said. "Someone took the camera and the photos."

Adrenaline stiffened the muscles of his neck, got his heart rate up to machine-gun speed. Who knew he was here besides King? One of those sanctimonious farmers with a Bible under his armpit? Or was it the Security Branch guard dogs?

His fist swung down hard onto the wooden lid. Never keep your back to the door: it was the most basic rule of selfdefence. Even Hansie would know that. Blood leaked from the slit on his knuckles. The *boom, boom, boom* continued with the intensity of artillery fire in his head and the world tilted to one side.

"Sit down." Hands pulled him up and a chair was pushed in behind him. "I'm going to find something for you. Sit. Don't move."

He heard the clang and scrape of drawers and cupboards being searched, then she was by the chair again.

"Open your mouth."

He did as he was told and a fine powder coated his tongue with the taste of bitter lemon mixed with salt.

"Now swallow this." There was the smell of whisky then the hot taste of it filled his mouth and washed the powder down a fire trail to his stomach.

"Stay here, Detective. I'll come right back."

"Wait." He grabbed her wrist harder than he intended and felt her delicate bones under his fingers.

"You're shaking," he said.

"I . . . I'm . . ."

"What?"

". . . not used to being touched," she looked out towards the open door, ". . . by one of your kind."

"My kind?" He repeated the words in a slightly comical tone. What did she mean?

She lifted her captured hand and held it at eye level. His fingers were white as pear flesh against the dark skin of her wrist. He let her go. The National Party and its Boer supporters weren't the only ones who believed SA was divided into different "kinds", each separate and unchangeable.

"Where are you going?" Emmanuel flexed his hand. Touching her was a mistake. Everything he did from now on was a potential source of ammunition for the Security Branch. Physical contact across the colour line was a no go.

"To get some water from the river."

Emmanuel watched her stop and pick up a bucket from near the doorway. She was still shaking. The bucket did a jiggling dance against her leg as she moved fast towards the breach in the fence.

She's scared of me, he thought. Scared of the crazy white man who tackled her to the ground, then almost snapped her wrist without once saying sorry. He closed his eyes and ignored the tightness gathering in his chest. He'd been beaten unconscious and what did he have to show for it? No suspects, no real leads, the evidence gone before he had a chance to examine it. The Security Branch would have a field day if they found out about the stolen evidence. It was all the excuse they needed to kick him off the investigation completely.

The slosh of water lapping over the bucket rim told him that she was back. He opened his eyes and took a good look at her.

"No wonder I thought you were a boy," he said once the bucket was placed in front of him. She was dressed in loose-fitting men's clothes, a faded blue shirt and a pair of widelegged pants that hid the natural outline of her body. Black hair, cut short and close to the scalp, glistened with moisture from a quick wash in the river.

She touched her wet curls. "I like it this way."

"Then why do you keep it covered?" The plain cotton scarf she normally wore lay on the dirt floor where it had fallen during their struggle.

"It makes people stare."

"Like I'm doing?" Emmanuel asked. Her eyes were the most unusual shade of grey. Davida had her mother's mouth, full and soft.

"You should wash your face, Detective," she said, and moved behind the chair and out of his view. Some questions had no correct answer, especially when white people asked them.

132

Emmanuel wiped the grime and blood from his skin and heard her shallow breath, amplified in the stillness of the hut.

"I'm not going to hurt you," he said. "Is that what you're afraid of?"

She studied the tip of her battered leather boots. "No. Mr King will be angry when he finds out I've been in here."

"Why?"

"This is the captain's place. Nobody's allowed but the captain."

"Why did you come?" She must have seen the sedan and known that one of his "kind" was inside. He could see her quickening pulse under the smooth brown skin at the base of her throat.

"You left Mr King's house a long time ago. I was riding by and I thought maybe your car was broken."

Emmanuel leaned forwards and splashed his face and neck with the cool river water. Something didn't feel right. Natives and coloureds shied away from white people's business, especially when the law was involved. Yet she was here in the hut with her shaking hands and uneven breath.

"You ever been inside before?"

"No." The word was sharp. "What would I be doing in Captain Pretorius's private place?"

"I don't know," Emmanuel answered dryly. "Cleaning?" The neatness of the hut was another thing that didn't sit right. "Your mother ever tidy up for the captain?"

Her hands were behind her now, held out of sight. "I told you. Only Captain Pretorius was allowed."

"Who knows about this place?"

"Those at Bayete Lodge. Mr King said not to tell people in town. He made everyone promise. The hut was going to be a surprise for the captain's sons at Christmas."

"You ever tell anyone about it?" Emmanuel studied his bruised knuckles, now eerily like the dead captain's.

"Never." The word was emphatic.

"How many people work at Bayete Lodge?" Clarity and focus, both bruised by the wooden club's bloody kiss, were slowly making a comeback. The first thing to do was narrow the field, concentrate on those who knew about the hut.

"About twenty," Davida said. "Most of them are back at the location for the weekend. Mr King gave them two days off because of the funeral."

That narrowed the field of suspects for the attack down to a small footprint. "Who's at the lodge now?"

"My mother, Matthew the driver, Mr King, Winston King, and Jabulani, the night watchman."

"Six, including you," Emmanuel said. The field narrowed to the head of a pin: large enough for angels to dance on but not thieves or murder suspects. "Any of those people leave the house?"

"Only me."

"You sure?"

Her gaze flickered up for a moment. "Everyone was there when I left."

134

He considered her for a moment, then turned towards the open door. The shy brown mouse was barely able to hold her own head up, let alone swing a club with enough force to knock out a grown man. Still, there was something about her being in the hut that niggled him. He moved on.

"You hear or see anything when you came near the hut?"

"Well . . ." She thought for a moment. "There was something . . ."

"What?"

"A sound. It was a machine."

"A mechanical rattle like an engine." The memory, still hazy and clouded, pressed forwards into the light. He'd heard the sound, just before passing out. "I remember now."

The pin-sized field of suspects collapsed into a black hole. His assailant had come to the hut with his own transport, a wooden club, and a full bladder. None of the workers at the lodge was likely to own anything more mechanical than a bicycle. That left the Dutchmen who'd ridden into town on tractors, motorbikes, cars, and pick-up trucks. Did one of them slip away and follow him to the hut? There was no way to know.

Emmanuel crossed to the safe and pulled open the buckled lid. He'd report to Lieutenant Piet Lapping and tell him the truth: that he had nothing to show from the visit to King's farm. He put his hand into the safe to retrieve his filthy jacket. His fingers touched on the crumpled material and something else.

135

135

"Jesus . . ."

"What is it?"

He threw his jacket to one side and studied the square piece of cardboard — a wall calendar with the months stapled to the front in easy pull-off sections. Red ink circled the dates August 14 to 18; 18 was heavily ringed.

"Two days before he was murdered," Emmanuel said and quickly flicked through the remaining months. It was the same on every page. Five to seven days marked in red ink, the last day marked out as special. He looked over the dates again. The pattern was clear, but the heavily circled day could mean anything.

"*Carlos Fernandez Photography Studio, Lourençco Marques*," Emmanuel read aloud from the calendar. The name was printed below a photograph of happy natives selling trinkets to whites on the beach. There was no street name or address: a low-profile business. Donny Rooke had been caught smuggling pornography across the border from Mozambique. Did the captain take over Donny's flesh and photo trade?

"Captain Pretorius go to LM a lot?" he asked.

"Everyone does," she answered. "Even my people."

"How far is it?"

"Less than three hours by car."

The circled days could be pickup or delivery dates for some other form of contraband. Being a policeman meant easy passage across the border. Wading across a river was for criminals and natives. A high-ranking officer could smuggle goods in comfort.

136

"How often did the captain visit? Once a month or so?"

"I don't know," she replied. "What the Dutchmen do is their business. You must ask Mrs Pretorius or her sons."

Emmanuel rubbed his bruised knuckles. The red-marked days glowed with hypnotic brightness. Was he willing to hand over this vital information to Lieutenant Piet Lapping, who made it clear that the "personal angle" was not something he was interested in? The calendar might just end up at the bottom of a drawer because it didn't fit the political angle the Security Branch was working.

"Can you keep a secret, Davida?"

"Uhh . . ." Her voice quivered with fearful anticipation. The skin of her throat and face flushed and made her dark skin glow. Passing for white was never going to be an option for the shy brown mouse.

"Not that kind of secret," he said. "You mustn't tell anyone about today. Not about me, the hiding place, or the calendar. Understand?"

She nodded.

"You have to look at me and promise not to tell anyone."

She lifted her head and made brief eye contact. "I promise."

"Not even your mother, hey, Davida?"

"Not even my mother." She repeated the phrase like a dutiful child instructed in the dark secrets of the house.

"Good," he said, and wondered how many white men had exacted the same promise once the sweat was dry and the shadow of the police loomed overhead. Even the use of her name, Davida, made him feel he'd crossed a line.

Emmanuel closed the safe and returned the cowhide rug to its original position before re-making the bed. He wondered about the sheets again. He folded the calendar and put it in the pocket of his jacket. Davida was the perfect accomplice. If he decided to keep the calendar to himself the Security Branch would never approach her as a person of interest. He ducked through the low opening, and followed Davida out of the compound.

A black horse with thoroughbred leanings was tethered to the fence next to his Packard sedan. The stallion, all rippling muscle and glossy coat, was not destined for the glue factory any time soon.

"Yours?" Emmanuel said.

"No." She blushed. "I ride him for Mr King."

"Ahh." That explained the unlikely teaming. In King's world the tedious upkeep of animals and property was a job for the servants. The habits of rich men duplicated themselves the world over.

Emmanuel pulled the car keys out of his jacket pocket. "You'll remember what we talked about?"

"Yes, of course." She made direct eye contact, let him feel the power he had over her. "I won't tell anyone, Detective Sergeant. I promise."

The urge to stroke her damp hair and say "good girl" was so strong he turned and rushed to the car without another word. If he wasn't careful he'd turn into a grown version of Constable Hansie Hepple: a puffed-up bully drunk on the extraordinary power handed to white policemen by the National Party.

Emmanuel sat back and closed his eyes. He needed a moment to get things clear in his head before driving back to Jacob's Rest and reporting in to the lieutenant.

"*It felt good, didn't it?*" It was the sergeant major again. Out of nowhere. "*A man could get used to it. Learn to love it even.*"

Emmanuel opened his eyes. Through the mud-flecked windscreen the dirt road unfurled in a soft red ribbon towards the horizon. Dark clouds gathered overhead, poised to feed the rivers and wildflowers with spring rain. He concentrated on the landscape; felt the dip and curve of it inside him.

"*It won't work, boyo. Nobody ignores me, you know that.*"

"Go away," Emmanuel said and switched on the engine to drown the voice out. He drove to the dirt road cutting across King's farm and swung left towards the tarred road. God knows what was in the powder he'd swallowed back in the hut.

"*I don't need a pissy medicine to get to you, soldier. You'll have to cut off your head to get rid of me, because that's where I live. Up in there.*"

"What do you want?" He couldn't believe he'd answered. The sergeant major, all six-foot-two of him, was probably trussed up in a dingy Scottish retirement home for ex-military tyrants.

"*To talk*," the sergeant major said. "*You know what I like about being out here? The open space. Enough space for a man to find out who he really is. You know what I'm saying, don't you?*"

He didn't answer. The army psych test passed him clean. "Healed and ready to return to active duty," that's what the hospital discharge papers said.

"*Her trembling brown hands. The feeling in your chest, tight and burning.*"

Emmanuel slowed the car, afraid of crashing.

"*You know what that was, don't you, Emmanuel, perfect soldier, natural-born leader, clever little detective?*" The sergeant major continued his assault. "*You want to think it was shame, but we know the truth, you and I.*"

"Fuck off."

"*It's been so long since you felt anything.*"

"I don't know what you're talking about."

"*Yes, you do,*" the sergeant major said. "*It gave you pleasure to hurt her and not say sorry. Felt good, didn't it, soldier boy?*"

Emmanuel stopped the car and took deep, even breaths. It was daylight, hours yet before the war veteran's disease crept up on him in the form of sweaty nightmares.

He tore at the buttons of his shirt and threw it onto the back seat with the jacket. The smell of the clothes had dragged buried memories to the surface. That's all it was. There was no truth in the sergeant major's bizarre accusations.

If the Security Branch caught even a whiff of the daylight hallucinations, he'd be off the case and in a sanatorium by week's end. Van Niekerk couldn't help him. He'd be suspended pending psychiatric evaluation and there was every chance he'd fail the test.

"You finished?" Emmanuel asked.

"*Don't worry,*" the sergeant major purred. "*I won't make a habit of visiting you. If there's something important to say, I'll drop by and let you know. It's my job to keep you alive, remember?*"

CHAPTER
EIGHT

Lieutenant Piet Lapping and Sergeant Dickie Heyns huddled over a decade's worth of files. A row of empty beer bottles sat on top of the filing cabinet. After an afternoon of steady drinking and mind-numbing file checking, the Security Branch boys would be in a foul mood, ready to jump on anything new. Emmanuel pushed the door open and stepped into the room.

"Where the fuck have you been?" Lapping snapped and lit a cigarette.

"Taking a bath," Emmanuel said. "You were right. Being a field detective is dirty work."

"I thought I smelled lavender," Dickie said.

Piet ignored his partner. "How did your visit with King go? Find out anything you'd like to share with us, Cooper?"

Emmanuel felt a kick of fear in the pit of his stomach. Did he really have the steel to withhold evidence from the Security Branch? If they found out, they'd make him pay in blood.

"I did a search of Captain Pretorius's hut," he said, "but didn't find anything. It was clean, like someone had tidied the place up."

"Hut?" Dickie's brain was just firing up. "What hut?"

"The captain built one on King's farm. He used it for R&R." Emmanuel spoke directly to Dickie. "That's rest and recreation, for those of you who don't speak army bachelor talk."

Dickie stubbed his cigarette out with a grinding action that made the ashtray creak. "One day you going to get that clever head of yours kicked in, my *vriend*. You wait and see."

Emmanuel smiled. "Headkicker is one up from shitkicker, isn't it? Your ma must be proud."

The veins on Dickie's neck swelled and he stepped forwards. He clenched his fists.

"Sit down, Dickie," pockmarked Piet ordered calmly. "Cooper here is just playing with you. Aren't you, Cooper?"

Emmanuel shrugged.

"About the hut . . ." Piet continued where Dickie had lost the thread. "You'll take us there tomorrow morning and show us everything of importance."

"That's not possible," Emmanuel said. "It's Sunday. I'll be in church for the morning service."

"You religious?" Piet asked with a trace of disbelief. There was no mention of it in the thin intelligence file.

"Aren't you?" Emmanuel asked.

The lieutenant took a long drag of his cigarette. "That's twice you've turned the questioning around onto us, Cooper. Once with Dickie and now with me. Must be force of habit, hey?"

"Must be," Emmanuel said and upped the likelihood of being found out for withholding evidence. Piet Lapping was coolheaded and clever.

"So, you finally turned up." It was Paul Pretorius, looming in the doorway to the police cells.

"I was out working the case," Emmanuel said. The spit and polish soldier swaggered into the room and set himself up behind Hansie's desk.

"Tell me," Paul said and leaned back in Hansie's chair, square jaw jutting out. "Why are all the suspects on your list whites?"

Emmanuel looked at Lieutenant Lapping. Who was in charge of this investigation, him or the tin soldier?

"Answer the question." The words barely made it out from between Piet's clenched teeth. Having Paul Pretorius along for the ride wasn't Lapping's idea. Some bigwig must have pulled strings.

"You think Jews are proper whites?" Emmanuel threw the question out and waited to see if the bait was taken.

"No," Paul replied without hesitation. "They're different from us, but we need their brains and their money to build a new South Africa. We don't have to worry about them mixing blood with us or the kaffirs because it's against their religion. Blood purity is part of their thinking."

"Are they the chosen people?" Emmanuel wondered out loud and made a close study of the captain's second-born son. His barrel-like chest was puffed up like a bellows.

"They may have been the chosen people in the olden days, but it's our turn now. We've been given a covenant by God to rule over this land and keep it pure." Paul Pretorius leaned across the desk as if it were his own personal pulpit and continued his sermon. "In years to come, the world will look at us for guidance. You mark my words. We will be a beacon."

"Guidance in all areas or just . . ."

"Detective Sergeant Cooper!" Piet Lapping couldn't contain his frustration. "I said answer the question. How did you compile your list of suspects?"

Dickie and Paul were easy to distract but Piet kept his pebble eyes on the prize: relevant information. If Emmanuel were caught out, it would be by Lieutenant Piet Lapping.

"Preliminary inquiry found that Zweigman and Rooke both had motive. The captain suspected Zweigman of crimes under the Immorality Act and was known to have reprimanded him. Rooke blamed the captain for his arrest and imprisonment. Mrs Pretorius supplied me with the names. Both suspects provided alibis."

"What about this man King?" Piet asked. "Was there bad blood between him and Captain Pretorius?"

"Not that I could find. They seemed to have liked each other. The captain even built his own bush hut on King's farm."

"Rubbish." Paul Pretorius leaned farther across the desk. "My father had nothing in common with that Englishman. They hardly knew each other."

"That doesn't change the fact that your father had a deal with King to retain some of the old family farm."

"Rubbish again." Paul waved the information away with a flick of his hand. "Anything King says about my pa is an out and out lie."

"Okay." Lieutenant Lapping ground his cigarette out. "Let's leave that for a moment. Anyone else on your list, Cooper?"

Emmanuel stopped himself from rubbing the lump at the side of his head. At the top of his personal list was the bastard who'd smashed his skull, pissed on him, and then stolen the evidence.

"I'm looking at another lead. A Peeping Tom who molested some coloured women a year or so back."

"Who was it?"

"Don't know yet," Emmanuel replied. "It's possible this man killed the captain to keep his secret hidden."

Paul snorted out loud. "No man, no white man in Jacob's Rest, would interfere with coloured women. That sort of thing might happen in Durban and Jo'burg, but not here. Have you questioned any native or coloured men?"

"None of them presented as suspects," Emmanuel replied evenly.

"They're not going to hand themselves over." Paul spoke with blunt force. "You have to go in there and show them who's boss and then they'll start talking."

"Okay . . ." Lieutenant Lapping tried to keep the discussion on the rails.

"No, man, it's not okay." The seams of his blue army uniform stretched under the strain of Paul Pretorius's muscled bulk. "With your help my brothers and I could shake the investigation up. Get information flowing instead of following up some stupid rumour put around by the coloureds to shift blame onto an innocent white man."

146

Piet pulled another cigarette from the pack and took his time lighting it before he answered. "You and your brothers are the injured party, but you are not the law. I am the law. Understand?"

"*Ja.*" Paul looked almost sulky. For a soldier, he didn't take orders very well.

"Good," said Piet and took a drag of his cigarette. "When the time comes to get your brothers involved in the investigation, I'll let you know."

The lump on Emmanuel's head throbbed back to life. Giving the Pretorius boys a slice of the investigation would create the potential for disaster. Did the lieutenant support the idea of a family vendetta or was he just trying to keep Paul and his powerful backers on side?

"You think there's something in the pervert story?" Piet asked.

Enough to make two angry coloured men threaten violence in an attempt to protect their women. The stalker was no storybook phantom.

"The new laws make men with particular appetites nervous," Emmanuel said. "Public humiliation and jail time are good enough motives for murder. Even here in Jacob's Rest."

"Any political leads?"

"Haven't looked into that yet. The bus boycotts and pass burnings haven't made much of an impact out here."

"Not yet." Piet was grim. "This resistance campaign is like a fucking disease. The whole country is set to go up in flames. There is nothing the comrades won't do to crush the government. They want a revolution. They want to destroy our way of . . .”

The door to the police station crashed open and the Pretorius men washed into the small room on a wave of crumpled black suits and beer fumes. Shabalala remained out on the porch, sober and impassive.

“Howzit? Howzit?” Henrick slumped against the edge of Hansie’s desk and addressed no-one in particular. His suntanned face was mottled with patches of red brought on by alternating bouts of crying and beer drinking.

“Detective Sergeant . . .” It was Hansie, lobotomised by a few drinks too many. “You find anything? You find anything good at King’s?”

“Nothing,” Piet Lapping said and looked over at Emmanuel while he said it. All information was going out through the Security Branch, and the Security Branch alone.

Emmanuel kept quiet. He needed time to work out the calendar while Piet and Dickie crash-tackled their way through the political side of the investigation.

“You didn’t find anything, Detective?” It was Louis; the only Pretorius male not glassy-eyed and slack-jawed.

“Nothing,” Piet said.

Emmanuel shifted uncomfortably under Louis’s continued scrutiny. Despite Piet’s definitive answer, the boy was waiting for him to reply. He shook his head no and made sure to keep direct eye contact.

Out of the corner of his eye Emmanuel glimpsed Shabalala moving quickly off the veranda and onto Piet

Retief Street. There was the sound of a shuffle and a loud cry.

"Captain . . ." a drunken voice called out. "Captain! Please!"

"What the fuck is that?" Paul was on his feet, ready to play the commando.

"Captain. Captain. Please!"

The Pretorius men pressed out of the building in a rush. Emmanuel followed close behind and saw Harry, the old soldier, in the middle of Piet Retief Street. Shabalala was trying to guide him away, but the grey-coated man refused to move.

"Captain," he continued to bay. "Captain! Please . . . My letters . . ."

Paul and Henrick made it first down the stairs. One push on the chest and the skeletal old man fell back onto the hard surface of the road with his arms and legs askew.

"We buried my pa this morning." Henrick bent low over the crumpled figure. "Hold your tongue. Hear me?"

"My letters . . ." The warning passed Harry by. He struggled to his feet and continued towards the police station. "Captain. Please. Come out."

Erich grabbed the addled soldier's face. "My father's dead. Now shut up."

Emmanuel pushed past Piet and Dickie, who watched the action with bemused smiles. Drinking and fighting were natural Saturday night activities and getting between white men and a feeble-minded coloured one wasn't worth the effort.

"Shut up." Paul grabbed the old soldier by the lapels and shook him like a dry cornstalk. Johannes and Erich joined their brother and the medals on Harry's coat rattled a discordant tune as they pushed him from one to the other. Louis hung back.

Emmanuel approached the phalanx and felt Shabalala move with him. They shouldered their way into the circle and stood either side of the old man.

"What you doing?" Erich's blood was high and ready to boil over.

"He's crazy," Emmanuel said quietly. "Constable Shabalala and I are going to take him home. His wife will do a much better job of beating the shit out of him than you ever will."

"Home." Harry grabbed Emmanuel's jacket sleeve. "Not home. No. Not home."

"See?" Emmanuel said. "He'd rather stay here with you than go home to his wife."

"Not home." Harry's thin voice went up an octave. "Not home."

Paul laughed first, followed by his brothers.

"He sounds like an old woman, hey?" Erich imitated the shell-shocked old man. "Not home. Not home."

The laughter stepped up a notch and Emmanuel and Shabalala moved slowly out of the circle with Harry between them. They went down Piet Retief Street. They kept their pace measured and deliberate. Walking. Just walking home.

"Go back to your wife," Henrick called after them, his mood lightened by the violence and the old man's comic turn. "You lucky this time, Harry."

150

"Captain . . ." Harry whimpered softly. "Captain. Please."

"Here." Shabalala pointed to a small path that ran along one side of the police station. "Go here."

They slipped onto the path and moved briskly until they were out on the veldt. Harry turned back towards the station; his palsied hands held out like a beggar's.

"Captain," he said. "My letters."

Shabalala picked the old soldier up and raced along the narrow kaffir path. Emmanuel struggled to keep up with the black policeman who worked fast to put distance between them and the volatile Pretorius brothers. Guard dogs snarled and barked at a perimeter fence as they slipped past houses lit by the gentle flame of gas lanterns. Night began to fall.

Shabalala stopped at a rickety wooden gate and put the old man back on his feet. A sheen of sweat on the black constable's brow was the only indication he'd done more than stroll from the police station.

"This is his house," Shabalala said. "You must go in and give him to his wife."

"You're coming with me."

"Captain or Lieutenant Uys go in with the coloured people. Not me."

"The captain's dead," Emmanuel said. "Tonight, there's only you and me."

Shabalala nodded and followed him in through the gate and past a narrow vegetable patch that ran the length of the yard and pressed up against the back *stoep* of the house. Emmanuel pounded on the door.

"The letters." Harry started towards the gate. "The letters."

"Get him," Emmanuel said as the sound of footsteps approached the back door. "Police. We have Harry."

The door opened and Angie, the old soldier's wife, stepped out. She wore a brown cotton housecoat double stitched along the collar and sleeves to reinforce the fraying material. Her dark crinkly hair was pulled up and stretched taut across the curve of huge plastic rollers.

"Where did you find him?" she asked curtly. Harry went walking almost every day. Most of the time he found his way home without trouble.

"Outside the police station," Emmanuel said.

"The letters," Harry wailed. "The letters."

Angie crossed the *stoep* in five quick steps. "You talk about the letters? You say about the letters, you stupid man?"

Emmanuel rested a warning hand on her shoulder, then withdrew it. "He's had a hit or two already. He doesn't need any more."

She saw the bruised flesh around her husband's left eye. "Who hit you, Harry?"

"I want the letters," Harry said. "I want the letters."

She addressed Shabalala. "Who hit my Harry?"

"Madubele. He and his brothers."

Angie took her husband's arm and led him into the small cinder-block house. She looked back towards the gate, fearful of what lay beyond it in the gathering darkness.

152

"Inside. Quick," she said to Harry, who shuffled in ahead of her.

Emmanuel followed without an invitation.

He signalled to Shabalala, who reluctantly stepped into the house and stayed with his back pressed against the closed door.

The house consisted of two plain rooms joined together by a cracked seam of mud and plaster. The kitchen, a collection of mismatched pots and plates on a chipped sideboard, sat directly opposite a curtained alcove that contained a double bed and a small chest of drawers with a bevelled mirror.

They were in the sitting area: four wooden chairs and a moth-eaten loveseat that must have been transported by sea and bullock train from the mother country to the outer edges of southern Africa decades before. A round table with the diameter of a tin bucket displayed two photos in tarnished frames: one of Harry as a young soldier bound for the glory of the battlefield, the other a family portrait of Harry and Angie with a trio of white-skinned girls. The picture was identical in setup to the one he'd seen in the captain's house, a family group formally arranged against a plain backdrop. The travelling photographer had done a good trade in Jacob's Rest.

Harry sat on the edge of the double bed, his palsied hands resting unsteadily on his knees. Angie pulled the curtain closed around them. The clink of campaign medals was followed by the metal sigh of the springs as the old soldier lay down to rest.

Emmanuel picked up the family photo and motioned Shabalala over. "Where are the daughters?" he asked. There was no sign of them in the cinder-block house, not a ribbon or a hairpin.

"Gone," Shabalala answered. "To Jo'burg or Durban. For work."

The girls in the photo had taken after their father. Skinny and pale-skinned with fair hair and freckles, they were a race classification nightmare. Pose them against the cliffs of Dover and they'd blend right in. They were white girls, pure and simple. Only someone who knew the family could say any different.

"What's on their papers?" he asked Shabalala. "Mixed race or European?"

Shabalala looked at the floor. "I have not seen their papers."

"Those are my girls." Angie re-entered the sitting area and took the photo from Emmanuel. She wiped the frame down with her sleeve, as if to clear it of germs.

"Where are they?"

Angie tilted the photo so the light hit it fully. "That here is Bertha, she lives in Swaziland. Then Alice and Prudence, they live in Durban now."

"How long have they been gone?"

"Six months or so."

"The letters Harry was asking for. Were they from Alice and Prudence?"

"No." Angie put the photo down and angled it away from the room. "Harry doesn't know what he's talking about. The mustard gas, it's made him imagine things."

154

"He seems certain about the letters," Emmanuel said.

"That one is certain about a lot of things. But that doesn't make it so."

Angie moved across his line of sight and blocked the photo from view. She was the lioness at the gate whose job it was to stand guard over the family secrets.

"Make sure Harry stays in until morning," Emmanuel said. "Tonight's not a good night for him to be wandering around."

"I'll make sure he stays right where he is." The furrowed lines on Angie's bulldog face softened and she showed them out of the back door. "Thank you for helping my Harry home, Detective."

Emmanuel and Shabalala exited via the back gate. The moon was on the wane but its light still shone strongly enough to see by. Out on the kaffir path, Emmanuel turned to the black policeman.

"Tell me about the letters," he said.

"I have not seen any letters," Shabalala replied simply.

Emmanuel studied the closed face of his partner.

"Did the captain see the letters?"

"Uhhh . . ." Shabalala cleared his throat nervously. "He saw them. Yes."

"Who did the captain say they were from?"

"Those inside. The two youngest children of the old man."

"Why was the captain collecting letters for Harry?"

"Uhhh . . ." This time, the black constable's lips closed firm and sealed the words in.

155

Emmanuel watched him, saw the gates slam shut.

"Nobody else will know what you tell me tonight, Constable," he said. "That is a promise."

Shabalala took off his hat and turned it like a spinning wheel in his broad hands. The hat stopped spinning, and he breathed out.

"The old man's daughters, they are living among the white people. They cannot write to their own people in case someone finds out."

"How did they get white ID papers?"

"They are white, just like the Dutchmen. Captain said they must register in the city and if there was a problem he would say they were from a European family."

"Captain tell you this?"

"Yes."

"Why did he do it?" From all he'd seen, the Pretorius family were firmly in the racial segregation corner. In their world, race mixing wasn't in bad taste; it was a crime.

"I do not know why he did it." Shabalala put his hat back on and pulled it low on his forehead.

"If you knew, would you tell me?" Emmanuel asked.

The constable spread his hands out in a conciliatory gesture. "I have told you all I can," he said politely.

The black policeman would tell him all he could, not all he knew. Was it possible that the strong bond between black and white playmates, so common in childhood, had actually survived the transition to adulthood for Captain Pretorius and Constable Shabalala?

156

"Those men at the station," Emmanuel said. "They won't wait for you to tell them what they need to know. They will get information the fastest way. You understand that?"

"I understand fully."

"They can do as they please."

"I have seen this," Shabalala replied.

Emmanuel turned to leave, then stopped. "You said Madubele and his brothers hit Harry. Who's 'Madubele'?"

"The third son of the captain and his wife."

"Erich?"

"Yes. The third son has a temper. He is always exploding like a rifle shot, that is why he was given that name."

"Tell me the others," Emmanuel said. The names given to people by the natives always had a core of truth to them that was instantly recognisable.

Shabalala held his hand up like a schoolteacher and worked his way from thumb to little finger. "The first one is Maluthane. He deceives himself in thinking he is the boss. The second is Mandla because he is strong like an ox. Three is Madubele and fourth is Thula because he is quiet. Five is Mathandunina, meaning he is loved by his mother and he loves her."

Each name was a thumbnail sketch of the Pretorius boys, each one broadly accurate in its content. Even Louis, the runt of the litter, was described not in his own right but in connection with his mother.

"What's your name?" Emmanuel asked.

"It is long. You speak Zulu, but even you will not be able to pronounce it."

Emmanuel smiled. It was the first time the black constable had made a joke in his presence. In five or ten years' time Shabalala might come around to telling him the truth about the captain.

"Tell me what it is," Emmanuel said.

"Mfowemlungu."

Emmanuel did a quick translation. "Brother to the white man."

"*Yebo.*"

"The captain was the white brother?"

"That is correct."

Emmanuel thought of the people on the Pretorius family farm, their hearts soaring as the young Shabalala and Pretorius ran the length and breadth of the property like warriors in the Zulu *impi* of old.

"Mrs Pretorius, what does she think of this name?"

"She believes we are all brothers in God's sight."

"You and the captain were like twins?"

"No," Shabalala said. "I am always the little brother."

Emmanuel sensed Shabalala's resignation. Never the man, always the garden boy. Never the woman, always the cleaning girl.

"Did the captain think of you that way?"

"No."

"You felt for him as one who is a true brother?"

"*Yebo,*" the constable said.

The leaders of the Afrikaner tribe made a great deal out of blood bonding. Their most secret organisation, the Broederbond, meant blood brothers. What happened when the bond went across the colour line, and tied black to white?

158

"I will find out everything," Emmanuel said. "Even if it hurts you and the captain's family, I will find it out."

"I know this to be true."

"Goodnight, Shabalala."

"*Hambe gashle*. Go well, Detective Sergeant."

Emmanuel followed the narrow kaffir path that led to the coloured houses and the shabby strip of businesses serving the non-white population. He needed a drink and the Standard Hotel was the last place he was going to look for one. Time to pay Tiny and his son an after-hours visit.

The path skirted the grounds of the sports club. Farm families, overnighting in town after the funeral, were camped out in trucks, which were drawn into a circular formation like the wagon *laagers* of frontier times. Emmanuel ducked low to avoid being seen. He came up to his full height when the dark outline of the Grace of God Hospital became visible.

Past a stretch of vacant land decorated with scraps of windblown garbage, he entered the small grid of coloured people's homes. The first house, set on a wide span of land, was well hidden behind a high timber wall and a row of mature gum trees. Emmanuel ran his hand along the fence. His fingertips brushed against the wood and the small gate that led into the garden. It was good to walk in the dark: silent and undetected.

This is how Captain Pretorius must have felt: free and godlike as he moved across every boundary in his small town. It was here, on this stretch of the kaffir path, that he beat Donny Rooke to a pulp. Out on the main streets, in the houses and the stores, the captain was a good man: moral and upright. But off the grid, in the shadows of the kaffir path, who was he?

Emmanuel passed the burned-out shell of Anton's garage, two more houses, and a small church. The path swung hard to the left to run along the edge of the vacant lot adjoining Poppies General Store. The next shop along was the Fine Liquor Merchants. Emmanuel slowed at the gate, but didn't go in. A woman's voice, shrill and liquored up, drifted out over the back fence.

"You bad, Tiny. You a bad, bad man."

"How can I be bad, when I make you feel so good, hey? How's that?"

Emmanuel found a gap in the fence large enough to see through. He pressed his eye to the slit. Tiny and his son, both shirtless and drunk, were working the clothes off two well-used coloured girls. Emmanuel recognised the woman sliding herself over Tiny's hardened stomach like a grease cloth. She was the one he'd seen in front of Poppies, walking a toddler along the street.

"Mmm . . . *Ja* . . ." The coarse-haired woman gave a practised groan and sucked on a hand-rolled *dagga* cigarette. "You bad, Tiny."

"I'm about to get badder," Tiny promised in a sodden voice. "Let me see some."

The woman threw her unbuttoned shirt to the floor and lifted a drooping breast up for inspection. "This what you want?"

Tiny was on her nipple in a second. The wet sound didn't bother Theo, who hammered away at a fat brown girl with two missing front teeth. The girl, built to absorb maximum thrust, managed to take deep sips

160

from a whisky bottle even as Theo worked his magic on her.

Emmanuel stepped back. No chance of a drink just at the moment, but Captain Pretorius was on to something. A night on the kaffir paths was worth twenty door to doors.

The split where he'd lost his late-night visitor was up ahead. The rustle of footsteps broke the peace. Someone else was out, skirting the town in the dark. Emmanuel retreated into the shadows.

Louis trotted past. Emmanuel waited until he got well ahead, then followed. The boy wasn't lost; he walked as if he owned the kaffir path. The light from Tiny's courtyard cut into the darkness. Louis moved in on it like a moth.

The boy stopped and knocked on the gate. The noises from inside drowned him out. He tried again.

Emmanuel slipped into the space between the liquor store and Khan's Emporium. A shirtless Tiny opened the gate to Louis.

"What you want?" the coloured man asked. He was in a foul mood.

"Give me something small," Louis said.

"No dice. I promised your father. Never again."

"The captain's gone," Louis said.

"What about your brothers? What happens when they find out?"

"They won't."

"*Ja*, well . . . they better not," Tiny said and retreated into his courtyard before reappearing with a small bottle of whisky.

161

"How about a smoke?" Louis asked and slipped the bottle into his pocket.

"What? And get my business burned down when Madubele finds out?" Tiny waved the boy away. "Make tracks."

"He won't find out."

"If he does? You going to make him pay compensation like the captain did for Anton? You lucky I gave you anything. Now get moving before someone sees you."

"The captain's gone to the other side," Louis repeated. "There's no-one to see us."

Tiny ended the conversation by closing the gate in Louis's face. The boy unscrewed the whisky bottle, took a long swallow, then raised his free hand to the sky with his palm held open. Another swig from the bottle and Louis's clear voice graced the empty lot and the night sky.

He sang "*Werk in My Gees Van God*" — "Breathe in Me Breath of God" — a well-known Afrikaans hymn. The tune was the source of uncomfortable memories and even now Emmanuel could recall the words: *Blend all my soul in Thine, until this earthly part of me glows with thy fire divine.*

Was Louis able to distinguish between the whisky fire in his belly and the divine fire of the Holy Spirit? The back gate to the liquor store swung open and Tiny pushed his face out.

"Keep it for church, Pretorius. You're spoiling the mood."

Louis raised the bottle in a salute, then sidled off in the direction of the coloured houses and the sports club where the overnighting white families were camped. What was he going to do there? Give a sermon? Or find a dark corner to do a little of the devil's work?

The kaffir path was a gold mine of information and Emmanuel sensed that at least part of the answer to the captain's murder lurked out here in the shadows of the town.

The main street was in darkness, as was the dirt road running to the Protea Guesthouse. He passed the police sedan, its locked boot home to the filthy suit and the captain's marked calendar. Tomorrow he'd find a proper home for the sensitive items. The Security Branch could jimmy a boot lock with no effort.

The door to his room was ajar and the light was on. He stepped inside. Piet and Dickie lounged on either side of the bed. Clothes and papers were dumped onto the floor.

Piet yawned and lit a fresh cigarette.

"You always pack this lightly, Cooper?"

"A hangover from the army," Emmanuel said. "You need to borrow a clean tie, or was it starched underwear you were after?"

"Your fondness for old soldiers?" Dickie asked. "Is that a hangover also?"

Emmanuel pulled up a chair and sat down. "I confess. I got to the rank of major by bending over for all the allied generals. What else do you want to know?"

"We didn't come to ask questions," Piet said. "We came to tell you something."

"I'm listening."

"In the next day or two . . ." Piet spoke through a curtain of smoke, "we're going to know everything about you, Cooper. What you drink. Who you're fucking. Where you buy those sissy ties. We'll know it all."

"I drink tea white, no sugar. Whisky neat. Water when I'm thirsty. I haven't fucked anyone since my wife ran back to England seven months ago, and I get my sissy ties from Belmont Menswear on Market Street. Ask for Susie. She'll help you find the extra-large sizes."

"It's good you have a sense of humour," Piet said. "You'll need it."

"When you take the credit for any arrests? Or when you dump a bad result on me?"

Piet's smile was a slash cut into his acne-scarred face. "Either way, you and your boyfriend van Niekerk are going to regret trying to grab a piece of our investigation."

"I thought the two of you came to my room because you wanted to be friends. You won't be bunking with me tonight, then?"

Dickie flushed red. "No wonder your wife left you."

"You're the one who came to my room uninvited," Emmanuel said. "Have a good time looking through my underclothes, Dick?"

Dickie leapt to his feet.

"Sit down," Piet instructed him. "I have to tell Cooper a few things."

"Threaten away," Emmanuel said. It was getting late and he'd had enough of the Security Branch.

164

"Seven am tomorrow morning we will go to King's farm. You will show us over the hut. You will then investigate the Peeping Tom story. All other leads are our territory."

"There's only two of you," Emmanuel noted.

"No," Piet corrected him. "The local guys, Hepple, Shabalala and Uys will make up the rest of our team."

Emmanuel had no trouble interpreting the information. The Security Branch was officially shutting him out of the case.

"Nice to see some people still make house calls," he said when Piet and Dickie squeezed their giant frames through the doorway.

Piet stopped and flicked his lit cigarette butt into the garden. "Let me tell you how this will end, Cooper. If you work against us, I will find you out and then Dickie here will beat the English snot out of you. That's a promise."

Emmanuel closed the door on the Security Branch. His breath was tight in his chest. He resisted the urge to gather his scattered clothes, throw them into his bag, and head back to his flat in Jo'burg. He was in Jacob's Rest on Major van Niekerk's orders. The choice to leave wasn't his to make.

Fuck them up. It was the sergeant major with some gentle late-night advice. *"Go in hard. Take no prisoners."*

Emmanuel looked up at the ceiling. He'd hoped he'd heard the last of the Scotsman and his deranged pronouncements out on the road.

"Take the tyre iron. Give them a taste of steel."

Emmanuel touched the lump on his skull. His head ached, but not enough to bring on a delusional episode. He emptied five white pills into the palm of his hand and chased them down with water. He lay back down. The voice would go away as soon as the medication took effect.

"Use the element of surprise." The Scotsman continued his barrage. *"Get them before they get you, soldier."*

"It's peacetime." He didn't bother answering out loud. He knew the sergeant major would hear him fine. *"Killing people isn't legal anymore."*

"What are you going to do, then?" The sergeant major was at a loss now that brute force wasn't an option.

"Figure it out," Emmanuel said. *"Find the killer."*

"Hmm . . ." The prospect of a peaceful solution threw the Scotsman off balance. *"How are you going to do that?"*

"Don't know yet."

"Do you have a plan?"

"Not yet."

"I see . . ." The sergeant major's voice drained away into the darkness.

The pattern on the ceiling changed when the wind moved the tree outside the window. Figure it out? That was easy to say, but what did he have? A couple of coloured girls passing as white, a father and son who played with cheap whores, and a wily white boy with a taste for whisky and *dagga*. Big news in a little town,

166

but no match for the solid evidence he'd let slip away from him at the hut. And who'd left the note with King's name on it in the dead of night? The killer or someone trying to help the investigation?

"*You have the calendar.*" The sergeant major fought his way past the flow of medication.

True, he had the calendar. But how was he going to get across the border without drawing the attention of Piet and his gorilla?

"*Sleep,*" the sergeant major instructed in a slurred voice. "*I'll keep the dogs at bay for you.*"

Darkness closed in and Emmanuel floated down to a blackened barn smouldering in twilight. The sergeant major sat in front of the ruin surrounded by a dozen soldiers in torn and bloodied uniforms. One of the soldiers turned to Emmanuel. His face was reduced to lacerated flesh and smashed bone.

"*All eyes to me,*" the sergeant major ordered. "*Gather round, lads, and let's talk about drinking and fucking. And women and children and home. Our man Cooper needs a kip.*"

The soldier with the smashed face laughed. The troops pressed close around the sergeant major. Emmanuel closed his eyes and fell asleep.

CHAPTER
NINE

Emmanuel eased the Packard into the space next to the Security Branch Chevrolet at 6:55 the next morning. The police station appeared small and abandoned in the morning light. Piet wound his car window down and leaned out.

"Change of plan, Cooper. Follow us." He gave the command and Dickie flicked the engine on. "We'll make a stop at the black location first, then go to Pretorius's hut."

"Whatever you say, Lieutenant."

Dickie and Piet swung a right at the Standard Hotel and headed west on the main road. Emmanuel turned in behind them and pressed the accelerator.

He couldn't get a handle on why the Security Branch was heading to a black settlement outside a small country town. Not a single clue led in that direction.

They peeled off onto a pitted dirt road and minutes later entered the black location, a haphazard planting of cinder-block houses and mud huts on a dusty span surrounded by veldt. Children in Sunday clothes played hopscotch in front of a dilapidated church with a rusted tin roof.

The Chevrolet pulled to a stop near the children and Piet waved a boy over. It was Butana, the little witness from the crime scene.

"Shabalala —" Piet raised his voice to a near shout so the kaffir boy understood "— go get Constable Shabalala. Understand?"

"Yes, *baas*," Butana raised the volume of *his* voice so the Dutchman understood, then slipped off his too big shoes and took off down the dirt road that bisected the location. The other children followed behind, happy for an excuse to put some distance between themselves and the white men in the big black automobiles.

Emmanuel got out of the Packard and scoped the scene. It was a clear spring day. Fallow cornfields ran from the edge of a grassed area to a stream swollen with night rain. Beyond that, a lush carpet of new grass and wildflowers spread out beneath a blue sky and a roll of white clouds.

Breathtaking, Emmanuel thought. But you can't eat scenery.

He turned his attention to the irregular grid of dwellings. They were ramshackle constructions put together with whatever was at hand. A corrugated iron roof patched with flour sacks to keep out the rain. A 55-gallon drum rolled into a doorway to keep out the draft. It was spring, but the memory of a hard winter lingered over the native houses.

The young and fit could move to E'goli, the City of Gold — Johannesburg — where even a black man had the chance to become rich. Or they could stay in the location with their families and remain poor. Most chose the city.

The church door opened and a wizened pastor with watery eyes peered out. Emmanuel lifted his hat in greeting and received a wary nod in return. From down the dirt lane came the sound of children's voices.

Constable Shabalala hurried towards the cars, followed by a long train of children. The black policeman was in his Sunday clothes: a greying white shirt, black trousers, and a corduroy jacket with leather patches at the elbows. The bottom seam of his trousers had been let out to their full length, one inch too short to cover his socks and boots. Perhaps the captain's hand-me-downs.

He approached the Security Branch car with his hat in his hand. He knew that Afrikaners and most whites set great store by a show of respect. Piet pulled a piece of paper out of his pocket.

"N'kosi Duma," Piet said. "Where is he?"

Shabalala spread his palms out in an apologetic gesture. "That man, he is not here. He is at the native reserve. He will be home maybe tomorrow."

"Christ above." Piet lit a cigarette and blew smoke into the clean spring air. "How far is it, this reserve?"

"Before *baas* King's farm. One hour and a half on my bicycle."

Piet had a quick discussion with Dickie, who was hunkered down behind the wheel.

"Get in," Piet told Shabalala. "We'll go and get him."

Emmanuel made his way over, determined to wedge himself into the situation somehow. He felt the beat of his heart. Piet knew whom to ask for. How the hell did they know a man named N'kosi Duma lived on a location outside of Jacob's Rest?

"Constable Shabalala can ride with me," Emmanuel said. "I've got enough fuel."

"He's with us," Piet said coolly. "Your job is to show us the hut."

"The reserve is between here and the hut." Emmanuel knew he was pushing his luck but kept going. "Should we call in there first?"

"The hut," Piet said.

"It's a hunting camp," Dickie said after they'd examined the captain's clean little space. "Only an English detective from the city would think it was anything else."

"A waste of time, just like I thought," Piet muttered. "Let's move on."

Emmanuel didn't show them the hidden safe.

They left through the hole in the tall stick fence and rejoined Shabalala, who waited patiently between the cars.

Piet motioned Dickie into the black Chevrolet and turned to Emmanuel. "You will go back to town," Piet said with a glimmer of pleasure in his pebble eyes. "The Peeping Tom story is your area of investigation. Remember?"

"It's Sunday. I don't think there's much chance to make inroads there."

"You're a religious man, aren't you? Here's your chance to get to the church service in time. That's what you wanted, isn't it?"

171

"Amen," Emmanuel said and approached Shabalala, who'd stepped back to allow the Dutchmen some room. The Peeping Tom story was all he had to keep him in Jacob's Rest and close to the main game. He had to follow that trail and do it with a smile.

"The coloured church," he asked Shabalala. "Where is it?"

"You must go past the old Jew's store. The *ma'coloutini* church is at the end of that road."

"Let's roll." It was Dickie, chomping at the bit like a racing hippo out for the derby day sweepstakes.

Shabalala hesitated. "You will be at the station this afternoon, Detective Sergeant."

It was a request, not a question.

"I'll be there," Emmanuel said and Dickie gunned the engine. The chassis on the Security Branch Chevrolet dipped a half-foot closer to the ground when Shabalala got into the car. There was enough collective muscle in the vehicle to pound a steel girder into shape.

Piet leaned his head out the window. "Go first," he instructed. "We'll follow you out."

Emmanuel did as he was told. The Security Branch needed to see him run off with his tail between his legs. It gave them pleasure. It wasn't hard to hand them what they wanted. He got in the Packard and drove back to town.

Emmanuel made a sweep of the police files and hit the letter Z with nothing. No files under P for pervert, or Peeping Tom. No files at all for any of the women in the

172

old Jew's shop or for Zweigman himself. There was no written evidence the molestation case ever existed.

He pulled out files at random. Cow theft. A stabbing. Damage to property. The usual small town complaints. He searched for Donny Rooke and found him — charged with the manufacture and importation of banned items. The photos of the girls were signed into evidence, but not the camera.

Was it possible the coloured women's complaints weren't taken seriously enough to write up? Or had the files been lifted? Donny Rooke's stolen camera proved the captain wasn't above confiscating evidence when it suited him.

The Security Branch and the National Party machine wanted a respected white policeman struck down in the line of duty. They *didn't* want complications to that story. Under the new race laws, everything was black or white. Grey had ceased to exist.

Physical intimidation, theft, and the possible importation of pornographic items — Captain Pretorius may have appeared to be a straightforward Afrikaner but something more complicated lurked beneath the surface.

The small stone church overflowed with worshippers. Families, starched and pinned in their Sunday best, spilled out onto the front stairs that led to the open wooden doors. The captain's premature death was good for business.

An organ wheezed "Nearer My God to Thee", and the coloured families stood to sing the final hymn. Twin

173

girls in matching polka-dot dresses broke free of their plump mother's embrace and ran into the churchyard. They threw themselves down beside a flowerbed and peered into the foliage where Harry, the old soldier, was curled around the stem of a daisy bush, fast asleep.

Emmanuel leaned against the wall between the church and the street and watched the Sunday service let out.

Every colour from fresh milk to burnt sugar was on show. There was enough direct evidence in the churchyard to refute the idea that blood mixing was unnatural. Plenty of people managed to do it just fine.

A clutch of wide-hipped matrons in flowered dresses and Sunday hats brought pots of food to a table set up in the shade of a large gum tree. Men in dark suits and polished shoes milled around waiting for the signal to pounce on the food.

At the bottom of the stairs Tiny and Theo kept company with two respectable coloured women. Emmanuel needed someone to get him into the community and introduce him around. A white man hanging off the edge of a mixed-race gathering had an unsavoury feel. He also had to show the Security Branch something to convince them he was hard at work on the pervert lead now that the station files had yielded nothing.

"Tiny." He put his hand out in greeting, aware of the murmur of the congregation around them.

"Detective." The coloured man was all scrubbed up. Any trace of last night's debauchery had disappeared. "This is a surprise. What can I do for you?"

174

The liquor merchant was ill at ease, his handshake a quick brush of the fingers. The crowd thinned as people moved back to ascertain the situation.

"Sorry to disturb you on a Sunday, Tiny. I need to reinterview all the women who filed complaints about the Peeping Tom." He took off his hat in a friendly gesture. "I was hoping you could give me a hand."

"Um . . ." Tiny hesitated. It didn't seem right, talking about a degenerate on a potluck Sunday when all the good families were gathered around.

"I won't talk to them now," Emmanuel reassured him. "I need a list of names, that's all."

"Well . . ."

"There were four of them." The tightly girdled woman next to Tiny spoke up. She was fair-skinned, with two blobs of rouge painted high on her cheekbones. "Tottie and Davida, who work for the old Jew. Della, the pastor's daughter, and Mary, Anton's little sister."

"Detective, this here is my wife, Bettina." Tiny fell into line. "And this here is my daughter, Vera."

While Tiny and Theo were up late with the whores, the women in the family stayed safe at home working the hot comb. Both mother and daughter were starched and neat with hair that hung in a lifeless curtain to the shoulder. Burn marks, now a faint red, marked the skin along their hairlines — battle scars earned in the war against the kink.

"Are all the women still in town?" Emmanuel asked.

"Tottie is there by the steps . . ."

175

Honeypot Tottie was surrounded by a swarm of suitors. She wore a tailored green and white dress with a neckline cut just low enough to produce un-Christian thoughts. The girl was ice-cream on a hot day.

"Della is there next to her father." Tiny's daughter, Vera, pointed to a long, skinny girl with breasts a giant would have trouble getting his hand around. The pastor's daughter was plain in the face, but all souped up under the hood.

"Davida lives with Granny Mariah but she's with her mother at Mr King's lodge today and Mary is over there, helping serve the food." Mrs Hanson indicated a pixie-sized teenager working the tight space between two hefty matrons. Mary was halfway across the bridge between childhood and adulthood.

The women were different from each other, and distinct from the crowd in their own ways. There was Tottie, the allround beauty and bringer of wet dreams; Della, the generously endowed pastor's daughter; and Mary, the pocket-sized woman-child. That left Davida, whose only distinction, as far as Emmanuel could tell, was the fact that she didn't stand out in any way. You had to get close to her to see anything of interest.

Now he had the women's names it was time to chase up the garage fire story. Anton the mechanic was absent from the gathering.

"Anton not a churchgoer?" Emmanuel said.

"We're all churchgoers, Detective," Tiny's wife said primly. "This is a righteous town, not like Durban and Jo'burg."

The round-heeled women from the liquor store were missing in action.

"Drinking, *dagga* smoking, loose women, and loose morals." He looked at Theo meaningfully for a moment. "I'm glad Jacob's Rest doesn't have that kind of thing, Mrs Hanson."

"You want to see Anton, Detective?" Theo asked, anxious for the conversation to move on. "He's in the church. Come, I'll show you."

"Thanks for your help." Emmanuel tipped his hat to the straitlaced pair and followed Theo through the crowd and into the church. Anton was inside, stacking hymnbooks. The stained-glass windows cast a jigsaw of colours onto the stone floor.

The mechanic looked up. "Got you working Sundays, Detective?"

"Every day until the case is closed."

"How's it going?"

"Slowly," Emmanuel said, then waited while Theo left the church. "I need information about the captain and his family."

Anton emptied the last pew of books. "Can't say I can help. The Dutchmen keep to themselves, the black men keep to themselves, and we do too."

"What about the fire? How did you and the captain arrange compensation?"

There was a pause while the lanky coloured man placed the pile of books next to the pulpit. "How'd you know about that?" he asked.

"I've got big ears," Emmanuel said. "Tell me about the fire."

Anton shook his head. "I don't want to get the Pretorius boys off side. Without the captain to control them, anything could happen."

"Does King know about the fire?"

"He's one of my investors," Anton said. "He knows everything."

"Good. If I have to I'll tell the Pretorius boys that King let the story out. King is too big for them to mess with, isn't he?"

"He is," the mechanic agreed, then got a cloth from a cupboard and began wiping down the wooden lectern with a vigorous hand. He worked for a minute in silence. Emmanuel let him get to the story in his own time.

"I used to work at the Pretorius garage," Anton said. "Five years. Not bad work, but Erich is a hothead, always on about something or other. One day, Dlamini, a native who owns three buses, got me to do some work out at the black location and it got me thinking maybe I could go it alone, you know?"

Emmanuel nodded. He could see where the story was headed.

"I talked to a few people. King, the old Jew and Granny Mariah put up the seed money and I was on my way. Things went good for a while. The Pretorius garage kept the white trade and the holidaymakers moving through town." Anton worked the dust rag over the wooden pews. "I kept the black and coloured trade. It was a fair split, seeing the Dutchmen own most of the cars."

"What happened?"

"King's nephew was visiting and his roadster needed new spark plugs. He brought the car in to me and that started it off."

"A red sports car with white leather interior?" Emmanuel asked.

"The very one," Anton replied. "Well, you can imagine the fuss in a town this size. An actual Jaguar XK120. White, black, coloured, they all piled into my shop for a look. I was excited myself. A car like that doesn't come around every day."

"You forgot," Emmanuel said.

"That's right." The coloured mechanic managed a smile. "I forgot it was a white man's car and off limits. Didn't think about it until the old Jew came pounding on my door that night."

"How does he fit in?"

"He saw the whole thing," Anton said. "He saw Erich pour the petrol, light the match and walk away. It was Zweigman who went to the police station the next morning to file a witness statement. Wouldn't be talked out of it by anyone, not even his wife."

For someone trying to hide out in a small town, Zweigman managed to attract a lot of attention.

"Did you try to talk him out of filing the statement?"

"I was scared my house would be firebombed next," the mechanic said. "I wanted King to handle it."

"Did he?"

"He didn't have to. Captain Pretorius himself came to see me in the morning and told me Erich would pay for the rebuilding of the garage and for the replacement of my lost stock."

"In exchange for what? Getting Zweigman to withdraw his statement?"

The mechanic flushed. "It's not possible to live here and be on the wrong side of the Pretorius boys, Detective. I asked the old Jew to withdraw the statement like the captain asked. He wasn't happy, but he did it."

"How long ago was this?"

"Four months."

"Did Erich pay you the whole amount in cash?" Where would anyone, with the exception of King, get that kind of money?

"Half upfront, the rest due next week."

"How much?" Emmanuel asked.

"One hundred and fifty pounds still owing." Anton balled the cleaning rag and threw it into the corner with a hard click of his tongue. "Not that I'll see a penny of it now the captain has passed. There's no papers, no nothing, to prove Erich owes me a thing."

"No criminal record to connect him with the fire and no more debt," said Emmanuel. Hot-headed Erich was now a person of interest to the investigation. "How did Erich feel about paying the money?"

"He was furious." Anton sat down in a cleaned pew. "Marcus, the old mechanic who works at the garage, said the captain and Erich had a real head to head about it. Erich thought his pa was siding with the natives instead of supporting the family."

That piece of information didn't surprise Emmanuel. The Pretorius brothers were princes of Jacob's Rest, who took their father's protection for granted. It must

180

have stunned Erich to find he'd overstepped the line from privileged Afrikaner to criminal.

"Why do you think the captain made Erich pay?"

"The old Jew," Anton said. "He was one hundred per cent certain he saw Erich start the fire and he was ready to swear to it in a law court. Said he'd even swear on the New Testament Bible. It took me an hour of begging to make him go to the police station and withdraw the statement."

The captain was level-headed enough to see that paying the money was the best option. It wouldn't do for Frikkie van Brandenburg's grandson to be held in a place of confinement with the detritus of European civilisation. Even though it was likely that a hand-picked jury of whites would decide in favour of Erich, the pure-bred Afrikaner, over a Jew. Captain Pretorius, it seems, was an expert at keeping things off the record and out of public view.

"The next payment is due?" Emmanuel asked.

"This Tuesday."

"You going to ask for it?"

Anton got to his feet. "You believe a coloured man can walk into a Dutchman's place and demand his money? You really believe that, Detective?"

Emmanuel looked at the floor, embarrassed by the raw emotion in Anton's voice. Both he and Anton knew the simple truth. The mechanic didn't have a hope of getting the money unless a white man, one more powerful than Erich Pretorius, made the approach.

The church door opened a fraction and Mary the woman-child peeked in.

"Anton?" Her lips clamped shut and she stood like a gazelle caught in a hunter's spotlight.

"What is it?" Anton asked.

"Granny Mariah's curry . . ." she said, then withdrew her head and disappeared from sight.

Anton forced a smile. "That's my sister Mary. I think she wanted to say Granny Mariah's curry is going fast. It's a popular dish at potluck Sunday."

"She was one of the victims in the molestation case?"

"*Ja.*" The mechanic rubbed a finger along the edge of a pew. "That's why she's like you see her now. Frightened of men she don't know."

"Who interviewed her?"

"Lieutenant Uys, then Captain Pretorius."

Emmanuel stepped into the aisle and moved towards the front door. "Was Mary interviewed at the police station or at home?" he asked.

"Both." Anton followed behind. "Why? Is the case being looked into again?"

"I'm looking into it," he said.

"Good." This time the mechanic's smile was real. "It never sat right with us that nothing came of the complaints."

"Something about the case doesn't sit right with me, either," Emmanuel said, thinking of the absent police files and Paul Pretorius's dismissive attitude towards the idea that any member of his chosen race would cross the colour line in search of thrills.

Anton pushed the door open and allowed Emmanuel to exit first. Outside, the potluck lunch was in full swing. The smell of mealie bread and curry flavoured

182

the air. Most of the families sat on the grass with plates of food spread out in front of them or stood in the skirt of shade cast by the gum trees. The matrons had begun to serve themselves from the depleted bowls on the long table.

"Think there's any of Granny Mariah's curry left?" Emmanuel asked. The look of powerlessness on Anton's face when he talked about the money was still with him.

"Hope so." Anton waved a hand towards the serving table. "Would you like a plate of food, Detective? You don't have to. I'm sure the Dutch church has its own potluck, it's just . . . I thought maybe . . ."

"I'll take a plate," Emmanuel said. Lunch with Hansie and the Pretorius brothers would be as much fun as the time the field medic dug a bullet out of his shoulder with a penknife. Besides, the Security Branch's insistence that he follow up the molestation case meant he'd be spending a lot of time going in and out of coloured homes. This was a good chance for them to see him and get used to his presence.

The crowd stilled while Anton and Emmanuel approached the food table. A mother smacked her daughter on the hand to stop her talking and the congregation kept a wary eye on his progress.

Emmanuel kept his posture relaxed. A white detective from the city was never going to be the most popular person at a non-white potluck Sunday lunch. Anton handed him an enamel plate edged in blue. Emmanuel walked along the table and, army mess style, received heaped spoonfuls of potato salad, roast chicken, lentils and spinach from the matrons, all of whom kept their attention on the serving plate.

The last of the matrons looked directly at him. He nodded a greeting at the woman, whose light green eyes shone like beacons in her dark face. Her wavy grey hair, pulled back into an untidy bun, was untouched by the hot comb.

"You investigating one of our people for the captain's murder, Detective?" There was nothing in the matron's manner to indicate any deference to the fact that she was a coloured woman talking to a white man in authority. The churchyard went quiet.

Emmanuel kept eye contact and smiled. "I'm here for some of Granny Mariah's curry," he said. "Any left?"

"Hmm . . ." She reached under the serving table and produced a silver pot. "Lucky for you, we saved some for Anton."

The formidable old lady split the curry between the two plates and the crowd started talking again.

"Thanks," Emmanuel said and turned to face the picnicing congregation.

"Best we eat over there," Anton said and they made their way to a red gate and set their plates on a stone wall. They were as far away from the congregation as they could get without actually leaving the churchyard.

Emmanuel pointed to the dark-skinned matron who was busy tidying the serving table. "Who's the woman with the cat's eyes?"

"Granny Mariah." Anton laughed. "You almost got her to smile with that curry comment. That would have been one for the books."

"Why's that?"

"Well . . ." The coloured man heaped his fork with yellow rice. "Granny doesn't have much time for men. Doesn't matter what colour. We all a bunch of fools so far as she's concerned."

"I got that feeling," Emmanuel said and got stuck into the food. They ate in silence until the plates were half empty.

Anton wiped his mouth. "You want to know what's really going on, Granny Mariah's the one to talk to. She knows everything. That's another reason men hold their tongues around her."

Emmanuel recalled Tiny and Theo's late-night antics. "Does she have anything on you?" he asked.

"Just the usual stuff." The gold filling in Anton's front tooth flashed bright when he smiled. "Nothing that would shock an ex-soldier or a detective investigating a murder."

"I don't know," Emmanuel said. "What passes for the usual stuff in Jacob's Rest?"

"I'm not about to confess my sins to the police. No offence, Detective Sergeant."

"That's wise," Emmanuel said. Harry, the war veteran, crawled out from under the daisy bush and grabbed at the plate of food set out for him. He shovelled handfuls of rice into his mouth, barely chewing the food.

"Harry eats every two or three days," Anton said. "He won't touch anything in between. Nobody knows why."

He's in the trenches, Emmanuel thought, starving until the next ration trickles down from the supply line. Harry's body was back in South Africa, but a part of his mind was still knee-deep in European mud. Emmanuel knew that feeling.

"Anyone here work at the post office?" he asked Anton as Harry cleaned the plate in four quick licks.

"Miss Byrd." The mechanic indicated the church steps. "She's the one in the hat."

Several women on the stairs wore hats but Emmanuel spotted Miss Byrd easily. "The hat" Anton referred to was designed to draw all eyes to its glorious layers of purple felt and puffed feathers. Miss Byrd's Sunday crown transformed her from a sparrow into a strutting peacock.

"What does she do at the post office?"

"Sorts the mail," Anton said. "She also serves behind the non-whites counter now the whites have their own separate window."

Emmanuel finished his lunch and wiped his mouth and hands clean with his handkerchief. Miss Byrd was perfect for what he needed.

"I'd like an introduction," he said to Anton.

CHAPTER
TEN

The town was deep in a Sunday afternoon slump. All the shops were closed, the streets empty of human traffic. A stray dog limped across Piet Retief Street and onto a kaffir path running beside Pretorius Farm Supplies. Emmanuel's footsteps were loud on the pavement. He peered into Kloppers Shoe Store. Hard-wearing farmer's boots and snub-nosed school shoes clustered around a pair of red stilettos with diamantes glued to the heel. The strappy red shoes sat at the centre of the display like a glowing heart. The order for the red shoes must have been made while fantasy images of dancing and champagne blocked out the dusty reality of life in Jacob's Rest.

The Security Branch Chevrolet was parked out the front of the police station with its doors locked and windows wound up. A sharp-faced man with clipped sideburns sat on the *stoep* and stared across the empty main street. His tie was loosened, his shirtsleeves rolled up past the elbow to reveal pink strips of sunburned flesh. Lieutenant Uys was back in town after his holiday in Mozambique.

"Lieutenant Uys?" Emmanuel held his hand out. "Detective Sergeant Emmanuel Cooper, Marshal Square CID."

"Lieutenant Sarel Uys." The lieutenant got to his feet for the formal introductions and Emmanuel felt the brief crush of sinewy fingers around his hand. Sarel Uys barely scraped the minimum height required to join the force, which explained the "show of force" handshake.

"You've heard?" Emmanuel asked.

"About a half-hour ago." The lieutenant slumped back down in his chair. "Your friends broke the news."

Emmanuel ignored the reference to the Security Branch. Deep furrows of discontent ran from the corner of Sarel's mouth to his jaw line.

"Did you know the captain well, Lieutenant?" he asked.

Sarel grunted. "The only one who knew the captain was that native."

"Constable Shabalala?"

"That's him." Sarel looked like he'd sucked a crateful of lemons for breakfast. "He and the captain were tight."

Sandwiched between the giant forms of Captain Pretorius and Constable Shabalala, the wiry little lieutenant was number three at the Jacob's Rest police station. It seemed that fact cut deeper than the captain's murder.

"Have you been stationed here long?" Emmanuel continued with the informal fact gathering.

"Two years. I was at Scarborough before."

"That's quite a change," Emmanuel said. Scarborough was a prime post. Policemen fought hard to get into the wealthy white enclave and then, if they were smart

188

enough, they made some influential friends to ensure they only left Scarborough to retire some place sunny. A transfer to Jacob's Rest smelled of involuntary exile. He'd get someone at district headquarters to dig up the dirt on Lieutenant Uys's transfer to the cattle yard.

"That's why I spend my holidays in Mozambique or Durban," he said. "I prefer the ocean to the countryside." Sarel Uys smiled and showed a row of teeth the size of dried baby corn kernels. Everything about the man was small and hard.

"Most people in town go to Mozambique a couple of times a year, don't they?"

"Everyone but the natives," Sarel said. "They don't like the water."

The blacks' dislike of water was a tired belief that ceased to apply the moment whites needed their clothes washed or their gardens watered.

"Did Captain Pretorius go often?" Emmanuel asked.

"A couple of times a year."

"With the family or by himself?"

The lieutenant was suddenly curious. "You think maybe someone from over there did it?"

"Maybe. Do you know if Captain Pretorius ever went to LM for business?"

"Ask the native," the lieutenant threw back. "He'll tell you if he has a mind to."

"You've been here two years," Emmanuel continued. It was getting harder to maintain a friendly tone with this man. "Surely you got to know Captain Pretorius a little?"

"This murder is typical of the captain." Sarel shook his head in disbelief. "I tell you, it's typical of the way he treated me."

Emmanuel had trouble following the logic. "How so?"

"He got himself killed while I was away on holiday so I didn't get to find the body or call in the detectives. My one chance to get back to Scarborough and he makes sure I'm not here to take it."

"Captain Pretorius didn't plan on getting murdered," Emmanuel said.

"He knew everything that went on in this town. He must have known he was in danger. I could have helped him if he'd just told me what was going on." The lieutenant's slender fingers rubbed a bald spot into the material of his trousers.

Perhaps Sarel Uys needed a permanent holiday from the force instead of six days in Mozambique.

"He never asked for my help." Uys stared across the quiet street. "I could have been his right-hand man if he'd given me the chance."

The bitter tone had changed to longing. Uys had never left the playground or outgrown the desire to be close to the most popular and athletic student. The captain had denied him the small pleasure of living in his reflected glory.

"I've heard you helped the captain with a lot of cases. You both worked the molester case, didn't you?"

"Oh, that." The little man was dismissive. "Catching a man who interferes with coloured women doesn't get you noticed with the higher ups, believe me."

190

Emmanuel leaned a shoulder against the wall and thought of Tiny and Theo out on the veldt with a loaded gun and itchy fingers. They'd taken the law into their own hands because the law didn't give a damn what happened to their women.

"Captain Pretorius didn't care about promotion," Sarel went on. "He was happy here with 'his people' as he called them. He didn't have any plans to move up. Not like me."

Emmanuel doubted Lieutenant Uys was moving anywhere but sideways and eventually out of the force. He'd end his days warming a bar stool and complaining about his missed chances.

"Did the investigation run for a long time?" Emmanuel asked.

"Maybe two months or so. There were times I couldn't get through a week without hearing some coloured woman complaining about being followed or being touched up."

Emmanuel recalled Mary, the woman-child, darting away from the church door like a startled springbok. Who had put the fear of men into her? The Peeping Tom or Lieutenant Uys?

"You filed all the interviews?"

"In one big fat folder. Under U for 'unsolved'," Sarel said with satisfaction.

The file wasn't under U or any other letter. The files were no longer "absent", they'd been taken. Sarel had no idea the file was missing, but even if he'd noticed he'd have let it ride: there was no glory in hunting up a file concerning a non-white problem. The new laws were set to make old attitudes worse. Non-white cases were already at the bottom of the pile. That's why the Security Branch was so pleased to offload the molester case onto him. Only grunt cops with too much time and too few brains dirtied their hands exclusively with non-white cases.

Emmanuel pushed himself off the wall. Why would someone take the files unless there was something in them worth hiding?

He left Uys to his bitter musings. The filing cabinet needed to be searched again and then he'd move on to Constable Shabalala and see what shards of information he could extract from the black man.

Emmanuel entered the front office. A dog-eared paper folder lay on Hansie's desk. The folder was dark blue and not like any of those in the police station's filing cabinet. It was not like anything he'd seen at Marshal CID, either. A pale yellow snakelike S was hand-drawn on the front — a Security Branch file. Emmanuel checked the front door and the side door leading to the cells. He couldn't lock either without drawing attention to himself, so he moved quickly.

He unbuttoned the fastener: inside the folder was a stack of mimeographed papers stamped along the top with the bright red warning "Highly Confidential". The word "Communist" was repeated on every page above lists of names neatly drawn into two columns underneath.

A pamphlet with the optimistic title "A New Dawn for South Africa" was clipped to the front of a hazy black-and-white graduation photo. The face of a young

192

black man wearing thick-rimmed glasses was circled in red. At the bottom of the photo was the school's name, Fort Bennington College.

Emmanuel knew the school by reputation. It was an Anglican mission school famous for turning out the black academic elite. The first black lawyer to open his own law firm, the first black doctor to run an all-black practice, the first black dentist, had all come out of the school. Fort Bennington College educated blacks to rule the country, not just carry a bucket for the white man. Afrikaners and conservative Englishmen hated the place with a passion.

A cough from the direction of the cells forced Emmanuel to close the file and rebutton the fastener. The folder was proof that Piet and Dickie were the attack dogs of a powerful political force with vast intelligence-gathering capabilities. His hands shook as he repositioned the blue folder and moved to the filing cabinet, where he checked under the letter U and found nothing.

The door to the cells opened. It was Piet with his shirtsleeves rolled up and a cigarette hanging from the side of his puffy lips. The Security Branch officer undid the fastener on the blue folder and slid a piece of paper into the middle.

"Have fun at the coloured church?" Piet asked and took a deep draw on his cigarette.

"Not much," Emmanuel said.

"Shame." Piet grinned. "Van Niekerk won't like to hear his number one boy has come home empty-handed."

Piet blew a series of smoke rings into the air and Emmanuel's heartbeat spiked. The Security Branch had found something. N'kosi Duma had given them something good. Piet could hardly contain his glee.

"Is Constable Shabalala around?" Emmanuel asked. There was nothing to gain from going up against the Security Branch in a cocksure mood. He had to sidestep them and find out as much as he could from other sources.

"Out the back," Piet said. "You can come through, but be quick about it."

Emmanuel walked through to the police station yard and saw Dickie standing by an open cell door. A gaunt black man, who he assumed was Duma, cowered against the hard metal bars.

"Don't worry . . ." Dickie spoke to the terrified miner in a grotesque parody of motherly concern. "I'm sure your comrades will understand why you did it."

"Dickie." Piet encouraged his partner to move his tanksized body farther into the cell. The black man flinched and held his arms over his head in a protective gesture. Dark bruises marked Duma's skinny arms and a low animal whimper came from deep in the terrified man's throat. The Security Branch always got what they wanted: one way or another.

"Keep moving," Piet ordered. "Your business is outside."

Two steaming cups of tea rested on the small table by the back door. Emmanuel exited and found Shabalala seated by the edge of a small fire that burned

194

in the outdoor hearth. Piet slammed the back door shut.

"Detective Sergeant." Shabalala stood up to greet him.

Emmanuel shook the black man's hand and they sat down side by side.

"What happened in there?" he asked in Zulu.

"I have been outside," Shabalala answered.

"What do you *think* happened?" Emmanuel pushed a little harder. Unlike Sarel Uys and Hansie Hepple, the black policeman showed a real aptitude for the finer details of police work. Constable Shabalala needed to know that nothing he said could be used against him by the Security Branch later.

The black policeman checked the back door to make sure it was still shut. "The two men, they want to know if Duma has seen a piece of paper with . . ." he paused to retrieve the unfamiliar word ". . . communist writing on it when he worked in the mines."

"Did they get an answer from him?"

"Those two did not get an answer from Duma," Shabalala said with a trace of contempt. "It was the *shambok* that got the answer."

Emmanuel took a breath and looked deep into the fire. The liberal use of the rawhide whip, the *shambok*, readily explained the bruises on the miner's arms. Hard questioning was one of the things that made the Security Branch "special".

"What did Duma say?"

"I did not hear," Shabalala said. "I could not listen anymore."

This time Emmanuel didn't push. The sound of a man being broken during interrogation was enough to turn the strongest stomach. Shabalala had walked away and Emmanuel couldn't blame him.

"Did they find out anything about the captain's murder?"

"No," Shabalala said. "They wanted only to know about the writing."

If a link, however tenuous, was proved between a communist and the murder of an Afrikaner police captain, Piet and Dickie were set for a smooth ride to Pretoria and a personal meeting with the prime minister of the Union. After the ministerial handshake they'd get fast-tracked promotions and an even bigger *shambok* to wield.

It seemed the Security Branch was in the middle of an investigation that somehow tied in with Captain Pretorius's murder. Piet Lapping was no fool. He was in Jacob's Rest because something in his confidential folder drew him to the town with the promise of netting a genuine communist revolutionary.

"Are all the police files for this station kept inside?" Emmanuel steered away from the dark swamp of torture and political conspiracy that Piet and Dickie waded through for a living. The Security Branch could continue chasing communist agitators. He'd play his hunch that the murder was tied to one of the many secrets Captain Pretorius kept.

"Sometimes," Shabalala said, "Captain took the files home to read. He did this many times."

"He has an office at home?" Emmanuel asked. Why hadn't he thought of that when he was at the house?

"No office," the black constable said. "But there is a room in the house where Captain Pretorius spent much time."

"How would a person get into such a room?" Emmanuel wondered aloud.

"A person must first ask the missus. If she says yes, then he can go into the room and see things for himself."

"If the missus says no?"

The black man hesitated, then said very clearly, "The man must tell me and I will get the key to the room from the old one who works there at the house. She will open this room for the person."

Emmanuel let his breath out slowly.

"I will ask the missus," he said and left it there.

They sat side by side and watched the flames without speaking. The bond, still fragile, held firm. The Security Branch had a file crammed with enemies of the state but he had the inside track on the captain's shadow life.

The back door opened and Piet stepped out into the backyard with his cup of tea. His pebble eyes had an unnatural sheen to them, as if he'd swallowed a witch's brew and found that what killed other men made him strong.

"We're through." Piet spoke directly to Shabalala. "You can take him back to the location but make sure he doesn't go anywhere until our investigation has finished. Understand?"

"Yes, Lieutenant." Shabalala moved quickly towards the back door. When he drew level with Piet, the

Security Branch agent put his hand out and patted his arm.

"Good tea," he said with a grin. "Your mother trained you well, hey."

"*Dankie*," Shabalala replied in Afrikaans, then stepped into the station without looking at him.

Emmanuel marvelled at Piet's ability to mix an afternoon of torture with harmless banter. It didn't matter that Shabalala and Duma knew each other and might even be related. When pockmarked Piet looked at Constable Samuel Shabalala he didn't see an individual; he saw a black face ready to do his bidding without question.

The Security Branch lieutenant sipped his tea and took in the dusty yard with a sigh.

"I like the country," he announced. "It's peaceful."

"You thinking of moving out here?" Emmanuel said and made for the back door. He didn't have the stomach to listen to Piet waxing lyrical about the beauty of the land.

"Not yet." Piet wasn't letting anything penetrate his bucolic reverie. "When all the bad guys are behind bars and South Africa is safe I'll move to a small farm with a view of the mountains."

"Home sweet home." Emmanuel pulled the back door open and walked into the police station. Captain Pretorius had lived the dream. He was a powerful white man on a small farm with a view of the mountains. He'd ended up with a bullet to the head.

"*Woza.* Get up, Duma, and I will take you home." It was Shabalala trying to coax the traumatised black man out of the cell. The injured miner was still pressed up against the bars with his arms over his head.

Shabalala put both his hands out like a parent encouraging a toddler to walk for the first time.

"*Woza*," Shabalala repeated quietly. "Come. I will take you to your mother."

Duma struggled to his feet and steadied himself against the bars of the cell, then limped painfully towards the door. The miner's left leg was half an inch shorter than the right and twisted at an odd angle. Even before the Security Branch abuse, Duma must have been a pitiful sight.

Emmanuel felt a flash of heat across his chest. Not the familiar surge of adrenaline that accompanied a break in the case but a hot, white bolt of rage. The captain was shot by an able-bodied man with keen eyesight, a steady hand, and two feet planted firmly on the ground. Duma didn't come close to presenting a match with the killer.

Shabalala held the crippled miner's hand and led him out of the cell towards the back door. The front door and the front offices were for whites only. Emmanuel's rage turned to discomfort as he stepped back to allow the black men passage. Shabalala and his charge would spend the next hour dragging themselves across the veldt until they reached the location five miles north of town.

"Stay by the front door to the hospital," Emmanuel said quickly before sanity returned and he changed his mind. "I will come and pick you up."

"We will be there," Shabalala replied.

Emmanuel walked through the front office and out onto the veranda, where Dickie and Sarel were watching a line of three cars driving down the main street. The sour-faced lieutenant looked like a ventriloquist's dummy next to his hefty companion.

"Weekenders coming back into SA from Mozambique." Sarel Uys indicated the country-style traffic jam. "They'll make a dash for home before the sun sets."

Dickie drank his tea with noisy enjoyment. Like pock-marked Piet, he had the look of a man with the wind at his back and the road rising up to meet him. What had Duma said? The Security Branch had released him, so they weren't looking to hang the captain's murder on him. What then? He could try to find out but Duma wasn't in a fit state to talk to anyone. The connection between a communist plot and Captain Pretorius's murder remained a mystery for the moment.

"Any luck with the pervert?" Dickie called out with great cheer.

"Not yet," Emmanuel said and turned in the direction of the Protea Guesthouse, where the Packard sedan was parked. Justice be damned. He'd find the killer first, not to serve justice, but to see the look on Dickie's face when he shoved the result down his throat.

Duma was slumped in the back seat of the Packard with his eyes rolled back in his head. A low whimpering was the only sound he made. Emmanuel pulled the car to a stop in front of the church and glanced at Shabalala, who was nursing the half-crazed man.

"How was he before this afternoon?" he asked Shabalala.

The black constable shrugged. "Since the rock crushed his leg, he has been bad. Now he is worse."

A group of older black women approached the car. They were cautious and fearful in their movement, not knowing what to expect once the car doors opened. The women stopped short when Shabalala got out and approached them. There was the quiet murmur of Zulu before a pencil-thin woman in a yellow dress gave a shout and ran for the Packard. Emmanuel stilled as the woman hauled the miner into a sitting position in the back seat and wailed out loud. The sound was an ocean of sorrows.

Shabalala pulled the woman away and lifted Duma from the car. The women followed the black policeman who carried the cripple down the narrow dirt road towards home.

The skinny woman's cries carried back to him and Emmanuel switched on the engine to drown out the sound. Five years of soldiering and four years picking over the remains of the dead and still the sound of a woman's grief made his heart ache.

CHAPTER
ELEVEN

He came up to the big white house early the next morning and found Mrs Pretorius planting seedlings in the garden. A wide straw hat covered her head and her delicate hands were protected from the dirt by sturdy cotton gloves.

"Detective Cooper." Her blue eyes were hopeful as she greeted him.

"No news yet," Emmanuel said in response to the look. "I've come to ask you if I could see the spare room where Captain Pretorius slept."

"On Wednesdays," she told him with the diamond-hard look he'd seen at their first encounter. "Willem only slept there on fishing nights."

"Forgive me. I know you and the captain were dedicated to each other. Everyone in town commented on it. Even the non-whites."

"We tried to set an example. We hoped others would see us and follow the path to a true Christian union."

"A good marriage is a rare thing," Emmanuel said. Mrs Pretorius might believe herself to be half of a Christian partnership, but the sin of pride was heavy on her.

"You're married, Detective Cooper?"

Emmanuel touched a finger to the spot where his wedding ring had been. Any mention of a divorce was sure to set her against him and get the door to the spare room slammed in his face. Mrs Pretorius wouldn't countenance a morally flawed outsider touching her saintly husband's belongings.

"I lost my wife almost seven months ago." He told the truth to the degree he could and hoped she'd fill in the blanks.

"God has his reasons," she said.

She touched his shoulder. Even when cast down into the valley of grief, Mrs Pretorius had to be the one to shine her light onto the world.

"I'm trying to understand," Emmanuel said. He was thinking of the captain and the homemade safe cunningly hidden from view. He was starting to see into the dark places in Willem Pretorius that his wife's goodness failed to illuminate.

"You may go into the room," she said with a nod. His confusion, which she took for spiritual struggle, branded him worthy of her help. "Come with me."

Emmanuel followed Mrs Pretorius across the garden and noticed the imprint of her boots in the freshly turned soil. A work boot with deep straight grooves almost identical to the prints left at the crime scene. He remembered what Shabalala told him: that the Pretorius men and Mrs Pretorius had won many medals for target shooting.

"You'll have to get Aggie to open up for you. Willem used the room for work and kept it locked when he wasn't at home."

The words nudged something in her and she began to cry with a soft mewling sound. Her face collapsed with grief. If the fragile blonde woman had killed her husband she regretted it now.

She pulled off her gardening gloves and wiped away the tears. "Why anyone would hurt my Willem. He was a good man . . . a good man . . ."

Emmanuel waited until the sobs lessened in intensity.

"I'm going to find out who did this to your husband and I am going to find out why."

"Good." The widow took a deep breath and got herself under control. "I want to see justice done. I want to see whoever did this hang."

The diamond-hard look was back and Emmanuel knew Mrs Pretorius meant every word. She planned to be at the prison when the hatch opened and the killer took the long drop to the other side.

"Aggie —" Mrs Pretorius called out into the large house. "Aggie. Come."

They waited in silence while the ancient black woman shuffled across the entrance hall to the front door. Her ample body was bent in on itself after a lifetime of domestic work, her hands were gnarled from years of washing laundry and scrubbing floors for the ideal Afrikaner family. Emmanuel doubted she did much of anything anymore.

"Aggie." The volume of Mrs Pretorius' voice dropped only a fraction. The maid was deaf into the bargain. "You must take Detective Cooper to the spare room the captain used. Open up for him and lock it when he's finished."

The ancient maid motioned Emmanuel in without speaking. What was her position in the household? Hansie said the old woman was no good anymore but that the captain wouldn't let her go. Most Afrikaners and Englishmen had a black servant who was almost part of the family. Almost.

"You must have tea with me after, Detective Cooper," Mrs Pretorius said. "Get Aggie to show you to the back veranda."

"Thank you."

After tea with Mrs Pretorius he was going to see Erich. The doors to the Pretorius family home were going to shut in his face after he questioned the volatile third son about the fire at Anton's garage and the fight he'd had with his father over compensation. He had to get information while he could.

Aggie stopped in front of a closed door and rummaged in her apron pocket. It took her an age to fit the key into the lock and turn it with her arthritic hands. She pushed the door open and motioned him in without a word. Emmanuel wondered if the black maid was mute as well as deaf.

He viewed the room before he disturbed the contents. It was a large, pleasant space with a neatly made bed, bedside table, dark wooden wardrobe, and writing desk positioned by a window that looked out over the front garden. It was another example of the clean, ordered spaces Captain Pretorius specialised in.

Emmanuel moved to the bedside table and pulled the drawer open. It contained a black calfskin-covered Bible and nothing else. He picked up the Bible and examined the well-thumbed pages. The good book wasn't just for show. Captain Pretorius read the words of the Lord on a regular basis. There was no Bible at the stone hut, however — just a camera stolen from a snivelling pervert and an envelope with something worth pissing on a man for.

Emmanuel turned the Bible upside down and gave it a shake to see if anything fell out.

"Ayy . . ." It was the maid Aggie, scandalised by his rough treatment of the Word. Seems she wasn't mute or blind, just reluctant to use her dwindling energy stores on talking. Emmanuel gently closed the Bible and turned it the right way up. With the old maid looking on, he flipped through the pages as if he were a preacher seeking pearls of wisdom for an upcoming sermon.

Emmanuel put the Bible back into the drawer. There was nothing in the book but the word of the Almighty. The bed was made with a plaid blanket over clean yellow sheets. He lifted the pillow. A pair of blue cotton pyjamas nestled underneath. The maid gave another soft gasp and Emmanuel replaced the pillow exactly as he'd found it. The room already had the feel of a shrine with everything in it destined to remain untouched until the captain returned on judgement day.

The wardrobe was a handsome piece of furniture with double doors and mother-of-pearl handles. Two ironed police uniforms on wooden hangers hung side by side. Two pairs of shiny brown boots glowed with polish and waited for the captain's size 13 feet to fill them.

Patience, Emmanuel told himself. The room was locked for a reason. He opened the writing desk's top drawer and his heart began to pound. Inside, a fat police file lay next to a slim hardcover book. He undid the tie and flicked the file open. The first page was an incident report filed in August '51 in which the luscious Tottie James was subjected to a gasping noise coming from outside her bedroom window. No surprises there. Emmanuel guessed that most men made gasping noises when she was in the immediate vicinity.

He flipped to the end of the reports and failed to find a humorous angle in the description of Della, the pastor's daughter, who had been grabbed from behind in her own room and held face down on the floor while the perpetrator ground his hips against her backside. Peeping Tom implied distance, a furtive individual coveting the desired object from afar. Physical assault resulting in bruising and a cracked rib was another matter entirely.

Tonight, he'd read the file in detail and try to get some idea of the man who committed the offences and why the captain and his lieutenant failed to find and apprehend him.

Emmanuel put the police file down and examined the hardcover book in the drawer. Small enough to fit into a jacket pocket, the slim volume was a high-end item. He felt the smooth leather cover. The title intrigued him: *Celestial Pleasures*.

He opened the hand-cut pages at random and skimmed a couple of lines: "*Plum Blossom stretched out on the plush sedan, her only covering a red and gold tassel that hung from her exquisite neck. Wisps of opium smoke escaped her parted lips and rose up into the air."*

Curiosity got the better of him and he skipped to the middle. There was a line drawing of a naked oriental girl with downcast eyes kneeling on a cushion. Classy, Emmanuel thought, and edging on literary, but a stroke book nonetheless. He slipped it into his pocket.

"Hmm . . ." Aggie was alerting him to the fact she'd seen him take the book.

Emmanuel kept his back turned. He was leaving the Pretorius house with the police file and the book no matter how outraged the deaf servant might be.

The rest of the drawers revealed the captain's love of starched undershirts, plaid pyjamas and olive drab socks. He moved back to the bed, checked underneath it and found not a speck of dust.

Emmanuel approached the generously padded black maid, who was resting her weight against the doorjamb. It was nine-thirty in the morning and she looked ready for a nap.

"What do you do in the house?" he shouted in Zulu. Holding a conversation in English was likely to send the maid into a coma.

"Clean," she replied in her native language. "And keep the key."

"What key?"

She rummaged in her apron pocket and pulled out the key to the spare room. She displayed it in the palm of her hand but didn't say anything.

"You keep the key to this room?"

The maid nodded.

208

"How did the captain get in?"

"He asked for the key."

Aggie the trusted servant was the gatekeeper, but how did Willem Pretorius gain access when he came home late from fishing?

"Did he wake you and get the key when he came home after dark?"

"No. He said where I must leave the key."

"You left the key on a table," Emmanuel said. "Somewhere like that?"

"He said where I must leave the key," she repeated and waved him out of the room impatiently. She was ready to move on.

Emmanuel stepped into the corridor.

"Where did you leave the key?" he asked.

"In the flowerpot, behind the sugar sack, in the teapot. Wherever he said I must put it."

"Really?" Emmanuel marvelled at the captain's relentless need for secrecy. He acted like an undercover policeman whose real identity was his greatest liability.

"Why do you think he changed the place for the key?" he asked while Aggie pushed the key into the lock with her gnarled hands.

The worn-out old woman gave a shrug that implied she'd long since given up trying to understand the mysterious ways of the white man.

"The *baas* says 'Put it in the teapot'. I put it in the teapot."

That was the end of the matter as far as the maid was concerned. A servant didn't question the master or try to make sense of why the missus needed the shirts hung on the line a certain way.

"Aggie!" Mrs Pretorius called from the back veranda. "Aggie?"

The black maid didn't hear the missus. She was busy turning the key in the lock with as much speed as her brittle fingers allowed.

"I will go outside and have tea with the *nkosikati*," Emmanuel said and walked through to the back of the house. If he waited for Aggie it would be lunchtime when they finally made it outside.

He stopped by the display cabinet running along the side of the large sitting room and picked up the picture of Frikkie van Brandenburg and his family. He was used to seeing the dour clergyman, the Afrikaner oracle, as an older man with a furrowed brow and fire in his eyes but even in his youth the unsmiling Frikkie looked ready to set the world to rights.

What would van Brandenburg make of his daughter's family? *Dagga* smoking Louis, Erich the arsonist and Willem the deceiver were all tied to him by blood and marriage. Would Frikkie be proud or would he doubt, for just a moment, that the Afrikaner nation was set on a higher plane than the rest of humanity?

Emmanuel replaced the photograph and continued towards the kitchen, where a younger black maid set up the tea service on a silver tray.

"*Sawubona* . . ." he said good morning to the girl and stepped onto the vine-covered veranda. Mrs Pretorius waved him over to a table overlooking a small vegetable garden. A garden boy, a squat man in his thirties, weeded the rows and turned the earth with a hand fork.

Emmanuel sat down opposite Mrs Pretorius and placed the police file on the ground. He kept the book in his pocket. The young black maid came out with the tea service and set it down on the table before she disappeared back into the house.

"How do you take your tea, Detective Cooper?" Mrs Pretorius asked.

"White, no sugar," he replied and studied the late Willem Pretorius's wife. She was beautiful in a refined way. There were no rough edges to her despite the steel he sensed within.

"You have a lovely garden," Emmanuel said and accepted his tea. This would be his first and only chance to get a bead on the captain's home life.

"My father was a gardener. He believed that with God's help and hard work, it was possible to create Eden here on earth."

"I thought your father was a minister. An exceptionally well-known one."

She made a weak attempt to wave off the reference to her famous father. "Pa didn't pay any attention to the stories written about him. He liked better to work in his orchard than to speak to a hall full of people."

Like many powerful men, it appeared that Frikkie van Brandenburg had greatness thrust upon him.

"He was a homebody?" Emmanuel asked with a smile. The newly written history books made a point of mentioning van Brandenburg's zeal in spreading the message of white superiority and redemption. No meeting was too small or insignificant. No town too isolated to escape the gospel according to Frikkie. The great prophet travelled to them all.

"He was home when he could be. We knew how important his work was for our country. Four of my brothers followed in his steps and became ministers of the Dutch Reformed Church. My two sisters are married to ministers."

"You're the odd one out."

"Not at all," Mrs Pretorius answered. "Willem could easily have become a minister of the church. He had the strength for it, but he wasn't called."

"I see," Emmanuel said. Perhaps the captain realised early in life that the path of moral rectitude wasn't for him. Beating a small-time pornographer with your bare fists was not on the list of pastoral duties. And of course, *Celestial Pleasures* wasn't required reading at the seminary.

"Louis is going to be a minister," Mrs Pretorius said with satisfaction. "This was his first year at theological college."

Emmanuel didn't show his surprise. After witnessing Louis hassling Tiny for booze and smokes it was hard to imagine him leading a congregation or dispensing Christian wisdom.

"What's he doing home?" It wasn't holiday time. All the schools and colleges were still in full swing. The summer break would begin in late December.

Mrs Pretorius sipped her tea and considered her answer. It took her a few moments to find the correct words. "Louis wants to be part of our people's new

212

covenant with God, but he's too young to be away from home. The separation didn't suit him."

Emmanuel waited. He'd seen a flash of doubt escape through a chink in the widow's holy armour. Louis was her weak spot and there was something more to his early return from theological college.

"My father took a break from his studies, you know. When he returned to the church he was stronger than before, more able to lead the people on the Way. Louis will spend time on Johannes's farm, get to know the land and the concerns of the *volk* . . . He'll go back to theological college and when he comes out he'll be a lion of God."

There was absolute belief in her eyes.

"Maybe Louis will be a farmer or a businessman like his brothers?"

"No. Not Louis." Her smile formed icicles on the rim of her teacup. "He's not like the others. Even as a child he had a gift for gentleness and compassion. He is destined for greater things than what can be found in this town."

Mrs Pretorius dreamed big, he'd give her that. Her sons ruled Jacob's Rest but her ambitions were grander. She wanted a leader of the people who could make the nation into a holy land. The boy's complete unsuitability for the job was a fact that escaped her completely.

"Did the captain share your dreams for Louis?"

"They're not my dreams, Detective Cooper. They're Louis's." This time Emmanuel felt the chill from her smile in his bones. She was certainly van Brandenburg's

213

daughter. To go against her wishes was to go against the wishes of God.

It was no wonder Willem Pretorius and his son travelled the kaffir paths in the dark. A woman with fire in her eyes and ice in her heart ruled their home.

Emmanuel drank his tea. Mrs Pretorius's home was a showcase for her vision of how Afrikaner life should be. If he proved a link between the captain and the importation of banned materials, she'd burn the house down to purify it.

"Willem loved this place and these people." The widow's blue eyes glistened with tears as she looked over the back fence to the veldt. "He was like a native that way. The land was all. I know you English laugh at our belief that we are the white tribe of Africa, but in Willem's case it was true. He was an African man."

The captain certainly had an affinity with the Africans. His closeness with Shabalala was the source of Sarel Uys's bitterness and maybe the lieutenant wasn't the only one uncomfortable with Willem Pretorius's relationship with the black constable.

"Do you think some whites resented the captain's good relationship with the natives?" he asked. He was thinking of Uys and the fact he'd just returned from Mozambique. Did the hard-faced little man park his car across the border, swim the width of the river, then back again after committing the crime? He would have had two days to lie low and get a suntan before showing up at Jacob's Rest again.

"Willem didn't mix with them socially," Mrs Pretorius said firmly. "He knew all of them because he grew up here. As police captain he had to talk with them and spend time among them. People understood that."

"Of course." Emmanuel set his teacup down. Willem Pretorius did more than police the native community. He'd chosen Shabalala and Aggie the arthritic old maid to keep his secrets safe. That implied trust.

The new segregation laws formalised the longstanding idea that the black tribe and the white tribe were created by God to be separate and to develop along separate lines. Each tribe had its own natural sphere. Only degenerates crossed over into unnatural territory. In the eyes of some whites, Captain Pretorius might have done just that: crossed the line into the black world.

He's not like other Dutchmen. That's what Shabalala said on the first day of the investigation. Maybe that difference got the captain killed.

"Thank you for the tea, Mrs Pretorius." Emmanuel retrieved the molester files from the floor. He had to see Erich and then he'd dig deeper into the "white man gone to black" lead. "I'll be in contact if there are any developments." He held his hand out, aware that this was the last time he'd have physical contact with her. After he interviewed her son, Mrs Pretorius would freeze him out.

She shook his hand and stared at the police file. "What's that?" she asked.

"A file on the molestation case involving some of the coloured women in town." He told her the truth. She didn't like dirt in her house and he wanted to gauge her reaction to the news that Willem Pretorius had brought darkness into her world.

"Oh . . ." She took a half step back. "Was it in the spare room?"

"Yes," Emmanuel said. "The case was unsolved and probably due for a review to see if any fresh leads came up."

Her brow wrinkled with distaste. "It was most likely one of them. One of their own who did it."

"Did Captain Pretorius say that?"

"He didn't have to." She regained her composure and moved on to a topic she knew a lot about, the weakness of others. "The man who committed these acts still has strong primitive traits. We Europeans are further away from the animal state than the blacks or the coloureds."

Emmanuel wanted to tell her that every night he dreamed of the terrible things that civilised Europeans did to each other with guns, knives and firebombs.

He slipped the file under his arm. Every hour of every day someone somewhere in South Africa commented on the strange behaviour of those outside their own racial group. The Indians, the blacks, the coloureds and the whites pointed the finger at each other with equal enthusiasm.

"Strange . . ." Mrs Pretorius's voice was soft. "Willem didn't say anything about working on the case. He said it was closed."

The widow looked at the bulging file with a hungry curiosity. It was as if she wanted a taste of the shadow world her husband had worked to contain.

216

"Did he discuss his cases with you?"

"Not all of them," she said. "But this one was special. It upset him to work on it. There were nights he couldn't sleep for worrying about the town's morality."

"Unsolved cases can do that to a policeman."

"That's why . . ." Her focus on the file was complete. "I don't understand why he didn't say he was looking it over again. He . . . Willem told me everything."

The presence of the file in her house without her knowledge cracked the foundation of Mrs Pretorius's fantasy world. The certainty of her true Christian union with the captain had been called into question.

"I'm sure he didn't want to trouble you." Emmanuel gave her an easy way out. She'd face a real test of her beliefs if he found the captain's business in Mozambique was criminal.

"Of course." She smiled at her own doubts. "Willem was a natural protector. He lived to keep our family and the town safe."

The tears returned as the word "lived" left her mouth. It was the past tense. Every conversation she held about her husband was now a conversation about the past. Mrs Pretorius's sorrow was genuine but he had a feeling that if she'd caught her beloved Willem in an immoral act she'd have pulled the trigger herself.

"I'm sorry . . ." she said. "I'm keeping you from your investigation. You could be using this time to hunt down the killer and bring him to justice."

"I do have some people to talk to. I'll let you know if there's a breakthrough."

Grief and vengeance would be Mrs Pretorius's constant companions for the next few months. Emmanuel left through the trimmed garden. He needed to see Erich Pretorius soon, but first he was going to ask Miss Byrd, the coloured postal clerk, for his second favour in as many days.

"Where is the *nkosana?*" Emmanuel asked the black teenager manning the pumps at the Pretorius garage.

"Office." The stick-legged boy pointed to a room adjoining the mechanical repair shop.

Emmanuel knocked twice on the door labelled "Pretorius Pty. Ltd." and waited for an answer.

"Whozit?"

"Detective Sergeant Emmanuel Cooper."

"What is it?"

Emmanuel pushed the door open. If he got through this encounter without a fist to the chin he'd consider himself lucky. The third Pretorius son was in a filthy mood and the interview hadn't even begun.

"What do you want?" Erich looked up from a stack of paperwork on his desk.

"The polite thing to say is 'How can I help you?'" Emmanuel said. Spare parts and piles of old invoices littered the office. Unlike his mother, Erich Pretorius was comfortable with disarray.

"You want something?" Erich pushed the unfinished paperwork away.

"This must be a good business," Emmanuel said and studied a farm supply calendar highlighting the latest in

218

tractor technology. "A corner position on the main street. You've done well."

"I do okay. What's it to you?"

"I'm just saying that business must be good, especially now you're the only garage in town."

Erich leaned across the desk with a smile that promised a world of pain. "Who's been whispering in your ear? That coloured?"

"King was the one who explained to me that your next payment is due here." Emmanuel returned to the calendar and tapped a finger to Tuesday.

"What payment?" Erich sneered.

"Fire insurance," Emmanuel said. "Or don't you need to pay it now your father is dead?"

Erich was on his feet in half a second. "What the fuck has the payment got to do with my pa dying?"

"He was the only one keeping the deal on the level." Emmanuel felt the heat coming off Erich. He was about to combust with rage. "With your pa out of the way, there's no proof you owe Anton a thing."

"You think I'd kill my own father for a hundred and fifty pounds?"

Emmanuel stood his ground as the Afrikaner brick rounded the desk and moved towards him.

"People have been killed for less, Erich." He kept his tone amiable and calculated how fast he could make a dash for the door if need be.

"Get out." Erich was close enough to spray spit. "Get out of my place, you piece of English shit."

Emmanuel didn't move. Erich was loud, but he was used to being second in command. He was the muscle of the Pretorius household, not the brains, and he'd fold as soon as it was clear who was boss.

"Where were you the night your father was murdered?" Emmanuel asked calmly.

"I don't have to answer that," Erich said.

"Yes, you do." Emmanuel stared the furious man down and showed no fear in the face of hopeless odds. The Afrikaner was big enough to break his jaw with one swat.

"I was with my family." Erich broke off eye contact. "My wife and our maid can vouch for me. We were all up at 11 p.m. with little Willem. Croup."

Emmanuel pulled out his notebook. "I'll have to talk to your wife and verify your alibi."

"Fine by me," Erich said without hesitation. "She's just around the corner. Moira's Hairstyles is her store."

Moira's Hairstyles, set on the main street, was another slice of Jacob's Rest belonging to the Pretorius clan. The captain's family didn't need the pro-white segregation laws to give them status; they were doing fine without the government leg-up given to whites under the new government.

Emmanuel sized up the man-mountain standing in front of him. He might not have killed his father, but was he angry enough about the debt to arrange a severe form of punishment for him?

"How do you feel about paying all that money to a coloured?"

"I got no choice." Erich swung back to his desk with a grim expression. "Pa said if I don't pay, that prick

220

Englishman Elliott King will have the town crawling with Indian lawyers."

Emmanuel made a sound of understanding. Indian lawyers were universally acknowledged as being on a par with the Jews when it came to brains and ambition.

Erich opened a drawer and retrieved a bulging paper bag.

"One hundred and fifty pounds." He let the bag fall onto the desktop. A bundle of twenty-pound notes slid out. "I'd shove it up your arse but I have to deliver it to the old Jew this evening."

"What was your father thinking?" Emmanuel mused out loud. "Making you give money to a Jew to pay to a coloured?"

Erich kept his temper in check. "You're clever," he stated. "But not clever enough to make me confess to a murder I didn't commit. I never in my life raised a hand to my father."

"You were angry with him, weren't you?"

"Of course," Erich said. "Ask the boys out there. They'll tell you we fought about the payments. If the old Jew stuck to his story, I'd have to hire a lawyer to defend me. Then I'd have to close up shop for the trial, which could last weeks and weeks. In the end it was a hell of a lot cheaper to pay the money and be done."

Interesting that the captain hadn't argued the right and wrong of his son's actions with him. He'd gotten to Erich through the hip pocket. It was about the money. Mrs Pretorius lived in a world governed by a moral code, but her departed husband had been a pragmatist.

221

"Does your ma know about the fire?" Emmanuel asked. He was curious to see the degree to which Willem Pretorius kept his wife's fantasy world intact.

"No." Erich blushed, an odd sight in a man so big. "Pa thought it was best if we didn't bother her with . . . um, details."

"I see."

Willem Pretorius had succeeded at concealing many of the . . . um, details, but somewhere along the line he failed to safeguard all his secrets. Someone knew about the stone hut. Someone knew about the stash of goods in the safe. The theft of the evidence was not random. The wooden club proved that the perpetrator was prepared to commit violence to keep one step ahead of the law.

While Captain Pretorius had kept watch on the people of Jacob's Rest, someone had watched him as well.

"Is that all?" Erich crammed the money back into the bag, an activity that clearly incensed him.

Emmanuel decided to take a run at his "white man gone to black" lead. He had to follow every avenue in the hope that one of them led him back to the stolen evidence.

"Your father was tight with the non-whites, wasn't he?"

"Pa grew up with the kaffirs but he wasn't a *kaffirboetie* if that's what you're getting at."

Kaffirboetie, brother to the kaffir, was one of the most potent insults to sling at a white man who wasn't a native welfare worker.

222

"Do you think any of the whites believed he was too close to the natives?"

"Maybe some of the English. You people have a hard time understanding that we don't hate the blacks: we love them. They're in and out of our homes, with our children and our old people. Blacks are family to us."

"Like Aggie?"

"Exactly. She's useless, but Pa kept her on because she's been with us since I was in nappies. Aggie was a second mother to me and my brothers."

Emmanuel didn't dispute Erich's sentiments. His feeling for the old black woman with the gnarled hands was genuine. The wheels fell off the Afrikaner love cart, though, the moment non-whites wanted to be more than honorary members of the blessed white tribe.

"So." Emmanuel slipped his notepad into his pocket. "No problems among the whites that you can think of?"

"None," Erich said.

That brought him back to Sarel Uys. He was the one white person to exhibit real animosity towards the captain's ties to Shabalala. How much bitterness did the jealous policeman have stored in his gut?

"Thanks for your time," Emmanuel finished with the standard sign-off to an interview. "I'll call in at Moira's Hairstyles on my way back to the station."

"Do that," Erich said and dumped the money back into the drawer.

Emmanuel closed the office door behind him. The sound of the telephone handset being lifted filtered through. Erich was calling his commando brother at the police station to report on the questioning. The Security Branch would have an ear to the phone as well.

The police station was a no-go area for the rest of the day. He had to find another place to conduct his business, somewhere across the colour line.

CHAPTER
TWELVE

Emmanuel stepped out of Moira's Hairstyles and headed straight onto the kaffir path. Everything had checked out. Little Willem was up with croup at 11 p.m. and again at 2 am. The black maid, Dora, was willing to swear on the life of her own sons to that effect. Erich Pretorius might be a human flamethrower, but he was safe at home on the night of the murder.

The captain's third son was a long shot, so it was no surprise to learn that he'd had no direct physical involvement in the homicide. Evidence at the crime scene pointed to the killer's lack of physical strength. Erich was capable of pulling a loaded freight train to Durban in an afternoon. The killer had a cool head. Erich was seventy per cent muscle and thirty per cent combustible fuel.

Emmanuel crossed a vacant lot thick with weeds and untidy clumps of grass. It was close on lunchtime and the street was quiet when he turned a sharp right in the direction of Poppies General Store. The old Jew sat behind the long wooden counter, reading a book. The hum of sewing machines filtered out from the back room. Zweigman glanced up when he entered.

"Detective."

Emmanuel had come to ask for use of the shop telephone but he'd remembered something else.

"How did Captain Pretorius know you were a qualified doctor?" he asked. Zweigman the surgeon and Zweigman the storekeeper still seemed at odds to him. If Sister Angelina and Sister Bernadette had kept their promise, Zweigman would have remained just another Jew trading his wares in the marketplace, practically invisible.

"Knowing things was the captain's speciality," Zweigman replied dryly.

There was more. Emmanuel could see it in the German's face, in the peculiar way he held his head tilted slightly to the side when he spoke. When Shabalala withheld information, Emmanuel suspected it was to protect the memory and reputation of his childhood friend. Who was Dr Zweigman protecting?

Emmanuel wrote "time of doctor recommendation from Shabalala" onto a clean page in his notebook. When did the captain tell his black right-hand man to see Zweigman instead of Dr Kruger if he needed help? Was it before or after the little boy was run over in front of the store? If it was before, then the captain had advance knowledge of Zweigman's true status.

"I've come to ask you for the use of your phone," Emmanuel said.

"There is a telephone at the police station for just such business." Zweigman's brown eyes burned with enough curiosity to kill six cats.

"The homicide case and the police station have been taken over by the Security Branch." Emmanuel told the

226

truth. "I need another place to carry out my investigation."

"You are reopening the case involving the molester?"

"That and a few other things," Emmanuel said, thinking of the files lying in their safe hiding place, waiting to be read. He'd report to van Niekerk and send out feelers for new information first, though.

"If that is so . . ." Zweigman reached below the countertop and retrieved a weighty black telephone connected to miles of fraying cord. "I am happy to do you this favour, Detective Cooper. You may call from the back room."

The women sitting at the sewing machines looked up when they entered, this time with less trepidation. He nodded at each of the seamstresses and made sure to give Hot Tottie an extra long pass as he followed Zweigman through to the sitting room. Focusing on the show pony was a sure way to cover up his connection with the shy brown mouse at the captain's hut.

Tottie's emerald green eyes sparkled with amusement. She was a queen and he was yet another supplicant come to lay his desire at her door.

Davida was laying out a paper pattern onto a cutting table under Lilliana Zweigman's guidance. Her head, covered by a green scarf, remained bowed. She gave no indication he'd talked to her and touched her and asked her to keep his secrets safe.

"Here." Zweigman placed the black Bakelite phone onto the tea table and indicated a chair. "My wife and the ladies will come through this room to go out to the backyard in twenty minutes. Lunch break."

"I won't be that long." Emmanuel sat down and pulled the phone towards him. Zweigman left the room and Emmanuel waited until the busy hum of the sewing machines started up again. The fragile Lilliana had stopped all activity until her husband emerged unharmed from the back room. Something in the past still cast a shadow over the Jewish couple. How many people in towns and villages and cities lived with the firsthand knowledge that nothing is safe? History, written with the help of bullets and firebombs, swept away everything in its path.

He rang through to the operator and waited to be connected to district headquarters. The line was clear.

"Cooper?" Van Niekerk's voice was clipped hard. Something was going on at the office.

"Yes, sir."

"Call me back on this number in ten minutes. Local area code." The major gave the number, then cut the line without explanation. The familiar *beep, beep, beep* came down the line followed by the operator's voice.

"You've been disconnected, sir. Shall I try again?"

"No. Thank you." Emmanuel hung up and checked his watch. Ten minutes gave van Niekerk just long enough to walk the two city blocks from headquarters to a public telephone box. The Security Branch had flushed the major out of his private office and onto the streets.

The white noise of the sewing machines contrasted with the jagged beat of his heart. He read over the notes he'd made at the crime scene. Was Captain Pretorius's murder the corner piece of a bigger puzzle the Security Branch was working on?

Emmanuel looked around him. He was in a small tearoom annexed to the back of a sweatshop operating on the dark side of the colour line. The Security Branch and their heavyweight political backers occupied the power seat while he trawled through the grubby entrails of the victim's private life. A feeling of doubt came over him and he closed his eyes to think. A needle of pain pricked his eye socket.

"Jesus . . ." the sergeant major's voice whispered. "*What if those fuckers are right and the murder was a political assassination?*"

Emmanuel pushed the voice away and revisited the basic laws of homicide investigation. Most murders are the result of banal and human impulses: a robber kills for money, a husband kills for revenge, and a misfit kills for sexual release. Ordinary, sad, and confused human needs lifted the hands of killers.

"*The Security Branch doesn't operate in your ordinary world, laddy,*" the abrasive Scotsman said. "*While you're sifting through underwear drawers and skiving on kaffir paths they're shaping the map of South Africa and every country around it. You are a foot soldier and they are the general's personal aides.*"

Emmanuel tried to ignore the sergeant major's comments, but couldn't. There was too much truth in what he said. Why would the Security Branch go after this murder so fast and so hard if they didn't already have evidence to back up their political revolution theory?

The words "neat" and "sniper-like" in his notes caught his attention as never before. Professional assassins targeted the head and the spine. Professional assassins left no traces behind. Had he misread the crime scene by looking for personal elements where none existed?

He dialled the number van Niekerk had given him.

"Cooper?" The major was out of breath and out of sorts when he answered on the second ring.

"It's me. Why the change in telephones?"

"The Security Branch has big ears and I'm not about to give them information for free," van Niekerk replied. "Are you calling from the police station?"

"I'm using a private telephone."

"Good. What's your news?"

"The Security Branch is going hard after the communist link. They have a confidential file with lists of Party members and their affiliates. It seems Captain Pretorius's murder is tied into an existing investigation."

"Operation Spearhead," van Niekerk said with the casual superiority that set half the detectives who worked homicide or robbery against him. "The National Party plans to break the back of the communist movement by arresting agents crossing into South Africa with banned writings and pamphlets. They conduct raids at illegal border crossings and hope they net a Red fish to fry up on treason charges."

"Captain Pretorius was shot along a stretch of river used by smugglers," Emmanuel said. "The Security Branch may have been watching."

230

"This coming Thursday they were due to hit the Watchman's Ford crossing where Captain Pretorius was found, acting on a tip-off. The Security Branch wants to salvage that operation by finding a link between the murder and a specific communist agent they've had under surveillance."

The depth of van Niekerk's political and social connections impressed Emmanuel and gave him pause. Was there any piece of information beyond the grasp of the ambitious Dutchman?

"Is the suspected agent a black graduate of Fort Bennington College?"

"Now it's my turn to be impressed," van Niekerk replied with a trace of humour. "That fact is known to less than a hundred people in the whole of South Africa. Are you sure you don't want to join the Security Branch? They're looking for bright young men."

"I'm not interested in redrawing the map of the world with a thumbscrew and a steel pipe."

"Have they gone that far?"

"Yes." The crippled miner's bruised arms and wild eyes came to mind.

"Has any of it come your way?"

"Not yet," Emmanuel said. "But it's just a matter of time."

"What have you got on Captain Pretorius?" Van Niekerk's voice took on a new urgency.

"Nothing conclusive. I'm chasing something now that could knock the captain off his pedestal, though."

He didn't mention the stolen evidence. That wound was too fresh to open in front of van Niekerk.

"Find it," the major said. "Information on Frikkie van Brandenburg's son-in-law is the only ammunition that will stop the Security Branch in their tracks if they come after you."

"You think I'll need to fight my way out of a corner here?"

"I'm talking to you from a filthy call box on a side street. You're calling from God knows where. We're already in a corner, Cooper."

"What do I do with the dirt when I find it?" The security arrangements he'd rigged up in Jacob's Rest weren't enough to stop a Security Branch raid. He needed a second net to catch him if he fell.

"Go to the local post office. I'll telegraph through what you need in half an hour."

The hum of the sewing machines begin to wind down. It was almost lunch break for Lilliana Zweigman and the seamstresses.

"I have to go," he told the major as the sound of chairs pushing back filtered into the tearoom.

"Emmanuel . . ."

The use of his first name held him on the line.

"Sir?"

"There's an information satchel being sent by courier to the Security Branch tomorrow morning. One of the things in it is a personal dossier on you. I can't stop it. I'm sorry."

"What does it have?" He couldn't stop himself asking the question. He needed to know.

"Everything. That's all the more reason to collect whatever dirt you can on the Pretorius family. You're going to need it regardless of who catches the killer first."

"Thank you, sir."

He hung up the phone and reached into his pocket for a handful of magic white pills. Fear joined his feeling of doubt and he wondered how his life was going to keep from flying off the narrow rails he'd painstakingly built since returning to South Africa. He swallowed the pills with a glass of water from the tearoom tap. It was too late to stop the folder and too late to withdraw from the investigation.

"*Stop feeling sorry for yourself, for Christ's sake,*" the sergeant major said. "*Get off your arse and get to work. You still have a murder to solve.*"

The women filed out into the back courtyard and Emmanuel made his way onto the kaffir path running towards the post office. A squadron of yellow-winged grasshoppers flew into the air at his approach and settled on curved stalks of field grass. He didn't want to think about the personal dossier, but it was on his mind.

"*Dark, isn't she?*" the sergeant major mused aloud. "*What does it say about you, Emmanuel . . . the fact that Davida stirs you?*"

"It means nothing," he said quietly.

"*Really?*" The sergeant major was amused. "*Because it makes me wonder if what the jury said about your mother was true after all. What do you think about that, laddie?*"

Emmanuel didn't answer. The pills he had swallowed at Zweigman's would kick in soon. He shut the sergeant major out and locked the gate. Under no circumstances was he going to think about what the mad Scotsman had said.

Harry the shell-shocked soldier was sitting on the post office steps when Emmanuel emerged from the one-room building with van Niekerk's telegram safe in his pocket. It was early afternoon and the main street was bathed in shimmering springtime light. Down the road, a barrel-chested white farmer whistled a tune while his farmboys loaded his pickup truck with hessian sacks of fertiliser and seed.

"Little Captain —" Harry's voice was a rough whisper "— Little Captain . . ."

The jangle of medals and an insistent tugging at his sleeve let Emmanuel know that the veteran was talking to him and not a mustard gas phantom.

"I'm Detective Sergeant Emmanuel Cooper from Jo'burg," he reminded the old soldier. "You met me at Tiny's shop. Remember?"

"Little Captain." Harry paid no attention to what he said. "Little Captain."

Emmanuel didn't correct Harry a second time. He had to get off the main street before the Security Branch got wind of his whereabouts and decided to convey their displeasure at his questioning of Erich Pretorius.

"How can I help you, Harry?" he asked.

"Tonight?" Harry's bony hand curled around his wrist and held on. "Tonight, Little Captain?"

234

Emmanuel looked around to gauge how much attention was coming his way. None of the people walking along the street paid any mind to the unusual sight of an addled coloured man holding onto a white man's wrist. Harry was the village madman: no-one expected him to behave like a normal resident of Jacob's Rest.

"Maybe tonight," Emmanuel answered Harry's question once he'd made sense of it. "Maybe tonight. I don't know yet."

"Good, good." Harry's smile lit up his face and revealed who he was before the war: a charming light-skinned man with his thoughts in the right order. "Good, Little Captain. Good."

"Go along. I'll come tonight."

"Good, good." The old soldier dropped his hand and turned in the direction of the police station. Emmanuel touched his shoulder and spoke close to his ear.

"Don't go to the station, Harry. Captain Pretorius doesn't live there anymore."

"Home," Harry said. "Home."

Harry shuffled his way along the street like a daylight spectre. Where would he be without Angie the bulldog to watch over him and without his play-white daughters? The world was an unkind place for old soldiers.

"Are you friends with Harry?"

It was Louis. He had materialised like an apparition in the spring sunshine.

"I've met him a few times," Emmanuel said.

"He's a soldier, just like you. But that doesn't make him the same as you."

"That so?"

Louis must have picked up information about his stint in the army from the brothers.

"We have to be on guard against our feelings for them," the Pretorius boy said. "They can never be our spiritual equals, which is why we must remain separate and pure."

The glow in Louis's eyes made Emmanuel uncomfortable. This kerbside sermon came out of nowhere and it reminded him of the hymn Louis sang behind Tiny's liquor store.

"Was your father in the army?" A "brothers in arms" bond might explain Captain Pretorius's decision to deliver the letters to Harry and to help the old man's daughters gain white identification.

"My father didn't fight in the English war." Louis seemed a lot like his mother: soft on the outside but with a diamondhard core. "Two of my grandfathers were commando generals in the Boer War. Our family are true *volk*."

The blacks had it right. Louis and his mother shared an overwhelming pride in the family's Afrikaner bloodline and a taste for spiritual superiority. If pride comes before the fall, Emmanuel thought, then Louis and his mother were due for a nosebleed dive into hell.

"You coming to collect the part for your motorbike?" Emmanuel asked. He remembered the mechanical rattle he'd heard at the stone hut before passing out. Could it have been a motorbike engine?

"It hasn't come yet," Louis said.

Dickie lumbered out onto the front porch of the police station and lit a cigarette.

"Maybe today's your lucky day," Emmanuel said. It was time to make for the kaffir path. The afternoon was slipping away and he still had to retrieve the files and read them over.

"Detective . . ." Louis called to him. "I almost forgot. My brothers are looking for you."

"They'll find me soon enough," Emmanuel said and hurried by the stretch of white-owned businesses on Piet Retief Street. He had to get onto the kaffir path before drawing level with Pretorius Farm Supplies, Moira's Hairstyles, and the garage. The captain's family was everywhere.

Emmanuel paused at the entrance to the path. Louis stood on the post office stairs and watched him with the intensity that his mother had used when she fixed her gaze on the police files. The teenager waved goodbye and disappeared into the building where the coffee-coloured Miss Byrd and the pink-skinned Miss Donald boxed the mail by race grouping and sold stamps.

Out on the kaffir path Emmanuel thought about Louis. There must have been tension in the Pretorius household over the boy and his future. Mrs Pretorius saw in Louis a holy prophet. A pragmatic realist like Willem Pretorius would have seen something different.

CHAPTER
THIRTEEN

Sunlight filtered through the branches of the lemon tree in the backyard of Poppies General Store and threw a patchwork of shade over the police incident reports of the attacks on the coloured girls. Six months of violence and perversity with no result.

Emmanuel checked the dates again. There were two distinct stretches of time during which the molester was active. The first was a ten-day blitz in late August when he spied through windows at women. Then, in December '51, he went on a two-week spree of increasingly bold physical assaults. Each report read darker than the last.

The perpetrator began the December stretch peeping through windows, and in fourteen days had progressed to an attack involving broken ribs and deprivation of liberty. A white man found guilty of such crimes was, in the view of the courts and the public, a deviant and a traitor to his race. Paul Pretorius laughed off the idea that his father's murder was connected to an unsavoury case involving non-white women but a European man, especially, might be inclined to use drastic measures to keep his shameful secret hidden.

Emmanuel picked up the last report, written in Afrikaans by Captain Willem Pretorius himself.

Molestation Case Summary
28 December 1951

After re-interviewing the women concerned I believe the likelihood of an arrest remains unlikely for the following reasons.

1. None of the women is able to identify the offender, as the attacks occur at night and the victims are grabbed from behind.
2. The racial group of the offender remains unknown.
3. The offender's accent suggests he is a foreigner who may come into South Africa undetected for the purposes of attacking women outside his home territory. Our border location makes Swaziland and Mozambique the offender's most likely place of origin.
4. Due to the high likelihood that a foreign national or a vagrant camping along the border is committing the attacks, apprehension of the offender remains difficult.
5. The case files will be reopened if and when new attacks occur.

Signed,
Captain Willem Pretorius

Fast work. Two days after the last attack and Pretorius had the case summed up and the files tucked away in his private room. *"If and when new attacks occur . . ."* The captain had anticipated a cessation to the attacks despite every sign the molester was sliding into serious and compulsive criminal behaviour. A week after the captain's intervention the activity stopped. No fresh sightings. Nothing but a sweet country silence where there'd been the sound of breaking ribs the week before.

Emmanuel drummed his fingers on the incident report. A foreign national or a vagrant camping on the veldt: who could have guessed Pretorius had such a lively imagination? Putting on an accent was presumably beyond the capability of a South African — born male. The flimsy summary didn't feel right. Had the captain found the attacker and tightened the reins without laying charges?

At the back of the file was a list of suspects interviewed by the captain during his investigation. Anton Samuels the mechanic and Theo Hanson were both questioned twice with no result. At the end of the list was a Mr Frederick de Sousa, a travelling salesman from Mozambique passing through Jacob's Rest with a suitcase of cheap undergarments. He was in town during two of the attacks but couldn't be tied to any others.

De Sousa was all the excuse Emmanuel needed to cross the border into Mozambique and visit the photo studio that had advertised on Captain Pretorius's calendar. He'd face off with the Security Branch in the

240

morning and then pretend to limp off to Lourenço Marques to continue his vice work.

Emmanuel pushed the police report away. There was no excuse for the total disregard for the job evidenced in the shoddy files. He believed in the law and the difference it made to people's lives. He got up and walked to the back of Poppies General Store.

"Mrs Zweigman?" He stuck his head into the workroom and attracted her attention as gently as possible. "Can I talk to Davida and Tottie? It's police business."

"Please . . . to . . ." The fragile woman stumbled over the words. "Wait . . ."

Lilliana Zweigman disappeared into the front of the store and returned with her husband, whose hand rested on her arm.

"I need to talk to Davida and Tottie," Emmanuel said. The hum of the machines died down and an expectant silence took its place.

"I will accompany you. Davida and Tottie, come with me, please. Angie, could you take care of the counter?"

"Yes, Mr Zweigman." Angie pushed her chair back and went to take her place at the front of the shop. The sewing machines whirred to life and the two remaining women went to work attaching sleeves to half-made cotton dresses.

Emmanuel motioned the women over to a table positioned beneath the shade of the lemon tree. He avoided eye contact with the shy brown mouse. He couldn't afford to expose her and the information she had about the calendar to anyone. Zweigman stood at the back window of the store with his nose pressed against the glass. He showed an almost paternal concern for the women in his wife's care. Or was it more than that? Captain Pretorius certainly thought so.

"Sit down," Emmanuel instructed Tottie and Davida and slid two pieces of blank paper and two pencils across the table. "I want you to draw me a map of your houses. Label the rooms. Draw the windows and doors. Mark the room where the Peeping Tom made his appearance."

"Yes, Detective." Tottie gave him a smile guaranteed to pop the buttons off a grown man's fly. The coloured beauty didn't care how many moths got burned against her flame.

Davida was bent over her paper with intense concentration. She drew the outline of a house with a small servant's room out the back.

"Detective?" Hot Tottie was thrown into confusion by an uncharacteristic lack of male attention. "Is this what you want?"

Emmanuel made sure to maintain eye contact before looking down at the map, which was hastily drawn but adequate for the task at hand.

"It's exactly what I want," he said and smiled.

The shy brown mouse slid her finished map across the table without a word. She didn't look up once. Emmanuel placed the drawings side by side and studied them, paying particular attention to the location of the rooms where the Peeping Tom struck.

He tapped a finger to Tottie's map. "Your room is here at the back of the house?"

242

"It used to be." The beauty flicked a strand of dark hair over her shoulder to give a clearer view of her exposed neckline. "My daddy moved me to the front room after it happened the second time."

"Your room is here, separate from the house?" he asked Davida.

"Yes. My room is the old servant's quarters."

"Do you live with Granny Mariah?"

Her grey eyes flicked up in surprise. "Yes."

Emmanuel wanted to ask why she didn't live in the house with her grandmother but concentrated on the maps again. Both Davida's and Tottie's bedrooms were at the very back of the house, with windows facing the kaffir path. Was that a common element in all the crime scenes?

"Do either of you know the layout of Anton's house?" he asked.

"You know where the bedrooms are in Anton's house, don't you, Davida?" Tottie said and almost purred with satisfaction when Davida blushed two shades darker.

Davida didn't rise to the bait, just pulled a piece of paper across the table and drew a quick sketch.

"Mary's bedroom is in the back." She slid Anton's house plans back over to him. "Della's bedroom is also in the back of the house."

"Does the kaffir path run close to the rear boundary of all the houses?"

"I don't know anything about the kaffir path," Tottie said. "My daddy only lets me use the main streets. You have to get Davida to answer that question for you, Detective."

Emmanuel took stock of Tottie. The curvy beauty was a spoiled little miss who liked to take a cheap shot. She'd as good as called her workmate a kaffir by implying that respectable girls, girls with a daddy to look out for them, didn't go near the native byway. Why was the shy brown mouse a target for Tottie?

"The path runs by them all," Davida said without moving her attention from the tips of her fingernails.

The connection between the rooms and their proximity to the kaffir path was too obvious to miss. How had the attacker managed to evade the captain, who policed the path and the streets most days of the week? Then a radical thought occurred to him.

"The attacker? Was he a big man like Captain Pretorius?"

"I don't know," Tottie announced with a triumphant smile. "That man didn't lay a finger on me. My daddy and my brothers made sure I was safe."

A teaspoonful of Hot Tottie went a long way. Emmanuel had enough of a taste to last a full week.

"You can go back to work," he told her. "I have a few more questions for Davida."

"You sure, Detective?"

"I don't want to embarrass you with the sordid details of the attacks. You shouldn't have to hear such unpleasantness."

"Of course," Tottie said. She looked disappointed at missing the good stuff.

244

He waited until she sashayed into the shop before he turned to Davida.

"Was the attacker big like Captain Pretorius?" he asked again.

"He was bigger than me but not as big as the captain."

"How can you be sure?" The connection between the captain and the molester was too strong to dismiss. Willem Pretorius travelled the kaffir paths with impunity day and night and he had the power to pull the plug on the investigation when things got too hot. Was he protecting himself all along? "Did you know the captain well enough to be certain that he wasn't the man who grabbed you?"

"Captain Pretorius was very tall with wide shoulders. Everyone in town knew that." She moved her hands from the table to her lap so he couldn't see them. "The man who grabbed me wasn't so tall."

"You think it was a white man?"

"It was dark. I didn't see him. He had a strange accent. Like a white man from outside South Africa."

"Could he have been a Portuguese?"

"Maybe, but I don't think so."

Emmanuel noticed the old Jew still had his nose pressed hard against the back window of the store. So, Hot Tottie wasn't Zweigman's fancy. It was the shy brown mouse he had an eye for.

"You sure you're not used to being touched by one of my kind?" Emmanuel asked straight out. Maybe the grey-eyed girl was keeping his secrets and a few more besides.

She shifted in her chair but didn't look up. "Just because I don't have a daddy, doesn't mean I run around."

"What about Anton? Did you run around with him?" He wanted to know if he'd been mistaken in his judgment that she was a silent and watchful woman who kept to herself.

"I saw Anton a few times but it didn't work out."

"Have you told me the truth about everything, Davida?"

"Why would I lie?"

"I don't know."

He had a perverse desire to pull her head covering off and unbutton her shapeless cotton shift so he could search for the hidden places he sensed below the surface. She glanced upwards suddenly and he had to look away.

"You can go back to work." He pretended to shuffle the reports into place and then watched her disappear into the back room of the store. Was Davida hiding something or was he simply revisiting the shameful sense of power he'd felt over her outside the stone hut?

Emmanuel deviated off the path and swung past the post office before making his way to the police station's back entrance. He rested against a tree and waited for Shabalala to appear on his bicycle. It was sunset and the kaffir path was busy with blacks funnelling back to the location for the night.

"They have been looking for you," the constable told him after they'd exchanged greetings.

246

"Are they still looking?"

"There were many phone calls from Graystown and now they are not looking for you anymore."

"Phone calls about what?"

"A man. A communist," Shabalala said. "That is all I heard."

"And how did you hear that?" Emmanuel asked. How did a six-foot-plus black man move in and out of a Security Branch investigation without drawing attention to himself?

"Tea." Shabalala gave a straight-faced answer. "My mother. She taught me how to make good tea."

"Ahh . . ." The invisible black servant was etched into the white way of life. Shabalala had used that to its full advantage.

They moved along the rear property line of the houses on van Riebeeck Street and soon drew level with the captain's house. The shed door was open and the sound of contented humming drifted out onto the kaffir path.

Inside, Louis was at work on the Indian motorcycle, which was close to fully assembled. The boy's overalls were covered in grease, his leather work boots splashed with oil and dirt. Did the contents of a hymnbook get Louis humming out loud with happiness?

"That one." Emmanuel pointed back in Louis's direction once they'd passed the captain's house. "He is going to be a pastor?"

"The madam has told everyone that it is so."

"You don't see it?"

"I see only that he is different."

"I see this also," Emmanuel said and they continued along the narrow path. The icy Mrs Pretorius was aware that Louis was not like her other sons, but she chose to interpret this as a sign of his greatness.

"I've been thinking . . ." Emmanuel stayed with the Afrikaner family for a moment. "When did Captain Pretorius tell you the old Jew was a doctor?"

"Before the middle of the year," Shabalala said. "I think in April."

"Before the accident in front of the shop," Emmanuel said. "How did he know Zweigman was a doctor?"

"The captain did not tell me how he knew this. He said only that the old Jew would fix me better than Dr Kruger."

Better. That was a value judgment. Willem Pretorius knew that Zweigman was more than your run of the mill general practitioner. Clever Captain Pretorius had tabs on everyone in Jacob's Rest except the killer.

"The old Jew, where is his house?" Emmanuel asked.

"It is on the same street as the Dutchmen's church. A small brick house with a red roof and a gum tree near the gate."

They walked on in silence until they came to the Grace of God Hospital. Sister Angelina and Sister Bernadette were kicking a patched-up soccer ball across a vacant lot with a group of orphans. Dust rose in the twilight as the diminutive Irish nun dribbled the ball through the opposition defence and made a run for goal. A shout erupted from the barefoot soccer team when Sister Angelina lunged to the side and caught the

248

ball as it sailed towards the mouth of the net. To thrive in Africa, nuns had to take and block a few shots on goal.

Emmanuel waved a greeting and he and Shabalala moved onto the grid of coloured houses where a pick-up truck painted with the words KHAN'S EMPORIUM was backed up to a wooden gate. Two Indian men loaded crates of sealed jars into the vehicle while Granny Mariah watched.

"Detective. Constable Shabalala." The steely-eyed matriarch greeted them with a brisk nod. "How's the investigation coming?"

"Still checking into things," Emmanuel said. A huge vegetable plot crowded with rows of furrowed earth ran the entire length of the backyard. To the far right of the market garden stood the one-room building that once served as the servant's quarters.

"That's Davida's room?" He pointed to the whitewashed structure hemmed in by flowering herbs and empty wood crates stacked to the windowsill.

"Yes. What's that to do with anything?" Granny asked.

There was a clear view from the kaffir path to the curtained window. He checked the locking mechanism: a piece of timber that slotted into two brackets at either side of the entry held the gate shut.

"Was this always here?"

"I had it put on after that man grabbed Davida. We had no problems once the lock was there."

Did the assailant give up indulging his compulsion when access to the women became difficult? Tottie was moved to the front of the house where her brothers and father surrounded her and the gate to Davida's yard was locked tight.

"Did the other women who were attacked have extra security put in?"

"Oh, yes." Granny Mariah paused to direct one of the Indian men to the last crate of bottled pickles. "When it first happened back in August last the men started patrolling the kaffir path at night but after three weeks, not a whisper. It was like the man just disappeared so everyone went back to their business. Then came the December troubles and we all got locks put in."

"What did the captain have to say about the patrols?"

After dark, the kaffir path was Willem Pretorius's domain. He might not have welcomed a rival patrol.

"He said fine so long as the men kept to the coloured area. They weren't allowed past the hospital or Klopper's shoe store on the other side of town."

Despite what Davida said about the size of her attacker he couldn't let go of the niggling feeling that Willem Pretorius might be the right fit for the perpetrator. The Afrikaner man knew the kaffir paths like the back of his hand and he was used to travelling on them without arousing suspicion. He knew the women and where they lived. The patrol was no barrier to his activity. No group of mixed-race men would dare stop a white police captain for questioning.

If Willem Pretorius was involved in the attacks, that fact opened up a whole new set of possibilities regarding his death. What lawful avenue was open to a coloured man when he found a white police captain was molesting his sisters? Tiny and Theo had come after Emmanuel himself with a loaded gun.

He leaned his shoulder against the open gatepost. Candlelight flickered out from behind the curtain in Davida's room. A shadow moved past the window. Signs of a small and secret life. Just what did the shy brown mouse do when night fell?

"You checking the other girls' rooms or just Davida's?" Granny Mariah's question was hard-edged.

"I was just wondering how the attacker avoided Captain Pretorius. The captain was out here all the time, wasn't he?"

"Here? Who says he was here at my place?"

"I meant the kaffir path. Captain ran past here a couple of times a week, didn't he?"

"Sometimes he went past and sometimes he didn't. He didn't hand out a timetable."

"No, he didn't."

Emmanuel raised his hat goodnight and set off with Shabalala. Once the last of the house servants headed home the path became the domain of Willem Pretorius and a handful of coloured men breaking up from a once-a-week poker game. Did the captain abuse his power and molest women he knew were unlikely to be taken seriously by the law? What option did a mixed-race man have but to pick up a gun and go after the offender in order for justice to be served?

"*Hamba gashle.* Go well, Shabalala," Emmanuel said and the tall policeman swung his leg over his bicycle and steadied himself against the handlebars. He couldn't bring up his suspicions about the captain just yet.

251

"*Salana gashle*. Stay well, Detective Sergeant." The black man rode off into the failing light. Soon he was gone, leaving behind a red sunset.

Emmanuel walked on past the coloured church and shops. He moved past backyard fences locked and barred against the night, past the path that ran to the Protea Guesthouse and his room, then around the outside curve of the town that showed him civilised backyards pushing against the untamed veldt.

He kept his pace up until he reached a rickety back gate. He took out a letter he had retrieved earlier that afternoon from Miss Byrd at the post office. It was addressed to the captain, but it was actually for Harry from one of his daughters. Now living as white, she had no other way to communicate with her father without putting her new social status in jeopardy.

The ghost of Willem Pretorius breathed in Emmanuel. He walked to Harry's back door, rapped twice, and slipped the Durban-postmarked letter into the old soldier's shabby room. He moved away quickly, as he knew the good captain had, and made his way back onto the path.

Darkness surrounded him. He stopped now and then to listen to the voices drifting out of back rooms. An evening prayer over dinner, an argument, a child's unsettled cry ... The people of Jacob's Rest were preparing to say goodbye to another day.

At Granny Mariah's again he leaned back against the barred gate and pictured Davida's little room surrounded by herbs and flowers. Gum leaves rustled and the wind sighed.

252

Off to his right a catlike footfall disturbed the undergrowth, then fell silent. Emmanuel stilled. Another footstep advanced in the dark. Something or someone was moving slowly in his direction. He eased his weight forwards and the gate fell back into place with a loud *click*.

There was a sharp release of breath and the slither of a body in the dark. Emmanuel wheeled off the kaffir path and turned full circle as he tried to pinpoint the source of the furtive movements. The whisper of grass and leaves was the only sound. He released his breath and the night enveloped him. Under the cloak of darkness, he felt a human presence close by. Someone was out on the veldt, watching.

Next day, Emmanuel walked into the police station at 9:20 a.m., ready for anything after he had questioned Erich Pretorius. Instead of an ambush, he found the Security Branch policemen and commando Paul Pretorius clustered around the captain's desk. The phone rang and Piet jumped on it.

"*Ja?*" he said, tapping a fresh cigarette from his pack and inserted it into the corner of his mouth. Paul and Dickie leaned close to the phone. There was an electric current in the air that signalled the beginning of a big push. The Security Branch was ready to make a move.

"Don't do anything." Piet sucked the nicotine from his cigarette. "We'll be there in three hours. You will wait for us. Understood?"

The phone was slammed down and Piet swung to Dickie.

"Go to the hotel and get our bags ready. We move tonight." He turned to Paul. "You coming?"

"Wouldn't miss it for the world." The hulking soldier was primed for action, his neck and shoulder muscles knotted tight in expectation.

"Just enough for one night," Piet cautioned him. "We'll bring the package back here sometime tomorrow. Do the work under the radar."

Emmanuel pushed himself off the wall and approached them. He wanted to report in and be dismissed in quick order. The border crossing into Mozambique was only minutes away.

"Anything I can do to help?" he asked the Security Branch team.

Piet blew a plume of smoke into the air. "Where have you been?"

"Looking into the molester case. I'm following up a suspect who lives in Lourenço Marques. An underwear salesman."

Piet's eyes narrowed and Emmanuel wondered if he'd gone too far by including the underwear comment. The Security Branch officer scrutinised him for a moment and tried to work out the angles on the Mozambique lead.

The phone rang and Piet picked it up before Dickie or Paul got a chance. Pockmarked Piet loved being in command.

"Don't do anything," Piet hissed down the line. "Follow and observe. That's all. We will direct the operation when we arrive."

He slammed the phone down and turned his attention back to Emmanuel. His smile was an unpleasant trench dug into his irregular face.

"This Mozambique trip better be in connection with the molester case. I don't want a repeat of yesterday."

"That was a mistake." Emmanuel told Piet what he wanted to hear. "I overstepped the bounds and it won't happen again."

"Better not." Paul Pretorius moved towards him with his index finger stuck out like a sword. "You're lucky we didn't find you yesterday, my *vriend*."

There was a pinprick of pressure on his chest as Paul gave him a hard jab. The fact that Emmanuel would escape punishment made Paul angry.

"Go pack your things," Piet instructed calmly. "If Cooper crosses the line again, we'll deal with him in a more thorough manner. Understood?"

"Good," Paul said. The lure of a future beating was enough to placate him and get him moving towards the door.

Piet collected the files on the desktop and handed them to Dickie. "Pack these and put petrol in the car. I'll meet you back at the hotel."

Emmanuel gave the Security Branch plenty of room to make their exit. He'd allow them an hour to clear town, then head to the border with the name of the photo studio tucked in his jacket pocket.

Piet paused at the front door and glanced over his shoulder with cold eyes. He was still bothered by the Mozambique lead and didn't like the idea of the

English detective roaming over international boundaries unsupervised.

"Remember my promise?"

"The English snot beaten out of me?" Emmanuel said. "Yes, I remember."

The Security Branch team disappeared onto the street. A big Red fish was on the hook and that far outweighed the need to punish a flatfoot assigned to chase a deviant.

Emmanuel walked through to the back of the station and found Hansie and Shabalala sitting in the yard.

"Where's Lieutenant Uys?" he asked, taking a seat between the boy policeman and the Zulu constable.

"Gone," Hansie said. "He gets to ride with the others."

Exclusion from the carload of hard-knuckled men obviously upset him. Even Hansie understood that being sent outside with the kaffir while the other white men talked business marked a low point in his law enforcement career.

"Go inside," Emmanuel told Hansie. "You can sit behind the captain's desk and answer the phone."

Hansie was up and running before the sentence was finished. Evidently, he'd never been allowed to sit in the captain's chair before.

"What have they said you must do?" Emmanuel asked Shabalala in Zulu.

"Stay here. Go home when it is dark and come again tomorrow."

"I have to go to Lourenço Marques for only one day. Can you keep that boy inside, out of trouble, and doing his job?"

"I will do what I can," Shabalala said.

"Detective Sergeant —" Hansie called out in a shrill voice. "Detective Sergeant Cooper?" Hansie was jumping from foot to foot in the back doorway. "A messenger. He has a special envelope."

Emmanuel's stomach tightened with excitement. Could he really be this lucky? He rushed to the front office, where a dust-covered messenger waited by the captain's desk. Hansie followed a half-step behind.

"Can I help?" Emmanuel asked.

"Envelope for Lieutenant Piet Lapping." The young man in the brown travelling overalls spoke through a tight mouth.

"Are you a courier?" Emmanuel asked, knowing full well that the Security Branch trusted no-one outside the organisation to relay information.

"No." The messenger's mouth became a hard line of discontent. "I'm the Security Branch."

Emmanuel understood the reason for the taciturn speech pattern. The young messenger, the cream of the police academy and hand-selected for the Security Branch, was not pleased at being chosen for the lowly task of delivering an envelope to a backwater. The value of information had not become apparent to him yet.

"Detective Sergeant Emmanuel Cooper," Emmanuel introduced himself. "You've missed Lieutenant Lapping, I'm afraid. He's out on a mission and doesn't know when he'll be back."

"They've all gone." Hansie spun a circle in the captain's chair. "They even took Lieutenant Uys with them."

"I'm happy to sign for the envelope." Emmanuel moved in on the disgruntled messenger and his package. "I'll make sure Lieutenant Lapping gets it when he gets back."

"It has to be signed over to Lieutenant Lapping. Those are my orders."

"Lieutenant Lapping has to be the one to sign for the package?"

"That's right."

"You could place it into the police mailbox at the post office," Emmanuel suggested. Miss Byrd had explained the workings of the postal service to him in great detail at their first meeting. "Only Lieutenant Lapping will be able to sign it out and he'll have to produce identification before they let him have the package."

"I don't know . . ." The messenger rubbed at the dust that had collected on his smooth-shaven chin when he'd turned onto a farm lane by accident, then had to double back to the main road. The motorbike tyres still had fresh cow dung stuck in the treads.

"Maybe Lieutenant Lapping will be here tomorrow when they send you back with the package," Emmanuel went on. "Or maybe he'll be here the next day. I can't make any promises."

The messenger looked around the small town police station like a doctor inspecting a plague house. He didn't want to set out before dawn and travel across the country only to be turned back again and again.

"Only Lieutenant Lapping can sign it out?"

"With identification," Emmanuel emphasised.

258

"Okay." The messenger pretended to give the idea serious thought even as he pulled his motorcycle gloves on in preparation for the trip back to the city. "Is the post office close by?"

"Down the street," Emmanuel said. "I'll take you over and get Miss Byrd to sign the envelope into the police box."

CHAPTER
FOURTEEN

It was 12:15 in the afternoon when Emmanuel parked the Packard on the beachside strip in Lourenço Marques. The calm waters of Delagoa Bay lapped the sand and seagulls wheeled overhead. Tourists of every skin colour strolled along the promenade, the women dressed in bright cotton dresses, the men in casual drill shorts and open-necked shirts.

Emmanuel took a deep breath of the fresh salt air. It felt good to stand in the sun and know that the Security Branch and the Pretorius brothers were in another country. He crossed the wide avenue to the ocean. The tide was in. Fishermen cast nets into the water and low-slung Arab-style *dhows* skimmed the horizon line. To the south stood a long wooden jetty with boats moored alongside.

A group of red-faced anglers loaded a wide trawler with supplies for an offshore fishing safari. The jetty was the obvious place to find a paid guide to take him to the photo studio.

"Hot samosas, ice-cream . . ." Vendors called out their wares as he strolled along the beachside. A sallow-faced street performer amused a group of tourists by throwing peanuts into the air for a monkey tethered to a fraying rope. At the entrance to the jetty, homemade placards advertising island visits and fishing charters crowded together. One sign stood out. It advertised Saint Lucia Island. A sleek wooden sailboat, a hymn to expensive old-fashioned craftsmanship, was tied up behind the sign. *Saint Lucia Lady* was written along the sailboat's stern.

"*Baas . . . senhor . . .* mister . . ."

A group of streetwise boys waited for the opportunity to shake the change loose from the pockets of visiting tourists. A spindly-legged youth ran over to him.

"Prawns, beer, peri-peri chicken? Whatever the *baas* wants I will get it," the youth said. The last part of the sentence was accompanied by a vaudeville wink and a smile that revealed two missing front teeth. The boy was about seven years old and already familiar with white men in search of illicit pleasure.

Emmanuel fished the name of the photo studio from his pocket and read it out loud. Chances were the worldly little guide with the stick legs couldn't read or write. The street was his classroom.

"Carlos Fernandez Photography Studio. You know this place?"

The boy said, "I know all the places in Lourenço Marques. I will take you for only fifty pence, *baas*."

Emmanuel handed twenty-five pence to the boy. "Half now, the other half when we reach the studio. Okay?"

"Come." The boy waved him along the seaside strip and past an array of ice-cream vendors, grilled corn sellers and trinket pedlars. The streets pulsed with life and Emmanuel relaxed for the first time since finding Captain Pretorius floating in the river.

They moved across a wide avenue bordered by flame trees and straggly jacarandas and then navigated the edges of an open-air market selling fresh fruit and fish. Further on, the little guide took a left, then a quick right before stopping in front of a nondescript building without a street number or business name to identify it. The front window display, an old-fashioned light box camera, positioned against a dusty, blue velvet drop curtain, gave the only indication of the building's purpose.

Emmanuel handed his guide the balance of his payment and pushed the door to the photo studio open. A corpulent Portuguese man sporting an oily black toupee and a half-dozen gold necklaces around his tyre-wide neck sat behind the low wooden counter. He smiled and showed a mouth full of gold and silver fillings.

"How can I help?" The greasy fat man sounded as if his windpipe was lined with loose gravel.

"I'm here to collect for Willem Pretorius," Emmanuel said. "He's been detained and can't make this month's pick-up."

The man stroked the quivering folds of his neck and pretended to think. "Pretorius? I don't recall that name."

"This is Fernandez Photo Studio, isn't it?" Emmanuel kept cool and kept pushing.

"Of course. But I still do not recall the man you are collecting for."

"He's big, with a broken nose and short blond hair."

The man who Emmanuel assumed was Fernandez moved to stroke the gold chains hanging around his neck. The green silk shirt he wore was unbuttoned low enough to display his ample cleavage. "No." He shook his head. "I have no memory of this man."

"Perhaps someone else who works here does remember. It's not worth my life to return to South Africa without his order and this is the address he gave me."

"Ahmed!" the Portuguese bullfrog called with a loud croak. "Ahmed!"

A wiry, dark-haired man with nervous seal pup eyes darted out of a back room and hovered close to Mr Fernandez. He looked to be a mix of Arab and black African and wore a white lab coat; he smelled of chemicals and sweat. A crocheted skullcap was attached to his head with four oversized hair clips.

"Ahmed. This gentleman is looking for an order for a . . ." Fernandez paused dramatically and looked to Emmanuel for help.

"Willem Pretorius. Big man with a broken nose." Emmanuel repeated the description for Ahmed, whose attention bounced from one object in the room to another without settling on anything in particular.

"Mr Fernandez?" Ahmed tapped his boss on the shoulder with yellow-stained fingers and waited patiently for recognition.

Fernandez manouevred his bulk anti-clockwise and stared at his assistant. "Answer this gentleman's query so that he can be assured that he is in the wrong place."

"The samosas. Rose has delivered the samosas and coffee. They are still hot."

The fat man, animated by the promise of fried food and caffeine, heaved his weight out of the chair and struggled to his feet. "I'm sorry we have not been able to help you locate your friend's order but now we are closing the studio in honour of my saint's day. Ahmed, show the gentleman to the door and lock up behind him."

"Of course, Mr Fernandez." The lab assistant scuttled to the front door and swung it open with a flourish. "This way, please."

Emmanuel reviewed his options and found the only one open to him was to leave and return when the abundant Mr Fernandez was fed and rested. As he stepped through the doorway, Ahmed leaned closer.

"You must go for a swim and then have an ice-cream." The assistant spoke in a loud stage whisper. "At five o'clock you must go to the Lisbon Café. I will be there at that time also."

"Five o'clock, the Lisbon Café?"

"Yes. If I am late you may wish to order the fish curry. It is very good."

The door shut behind him and Emmanuel saw his little guide waiting farther up the street. The boy ran to his side.

"I need to buy a pair of bathers," Emmanuel said. "You know a place?"

"Of course," the boy replied. "But first I will take you to a place to exchange your money. I will get the best rate for you, *baas*. Then I will take you to get the bathers. At this shop, I will get the best price for you."

"Okay," Emmanuel said. "Can you get me to the Lisbon Café at five o'clock sharp?"

"Yes. I can do this for the *baas*," the guide said. "When you are there, you must have the fish curry. It is the best in Lourenço Marques."

The assistant from the photo studio slipped into the café and performed a quick check of the patrons. He clutched a slim leather satchel in his arms. Emmanuel lifted his hand in greeting and Ahmed made his way over to the table.

"Mr Curious White Man." The assistant sat down next to him and angled his chair to face the door. "I, Ahmed Said, have decided that I must talk to you."

"About?"

"The photos, of course." The assistant removed a handkerchief from his jacket pocket and wiped his forehead. He was sweating a river. "But first, I think you must buy me a drink. Double whisky, if you please."

Emmanuel nodded at the knitted skullcap covering Ahmed's glossy head. "I thought drinking was against your religion."

"It is," Ahmed replied without rancour. "But I am a very bad Muslim. Which is why I have come to talk to you about this policeman's photos. I will tell you all I know as soon as my throat is not so dry."

"Double whisky and a strong coffee." Emmanuel gave the order to a passing waiter, then turned back to his informant. "How do you know the man I was asking about was a policeman?"

"Please. What else could he have been? Even his khaki shorts had a pleat down the front, just like a uniform."

"You always so observant of the clients who come into the studio?"

"Only the ones who ask for me by name. They are the ones willing to pay Mr Fernandez for my extra special service."

Emmanuel paid the waiter and paused until he'd moved to another table.

"Developing pornographic photos?"

"*Art* photographs," Ahmed corrected him with a smile. "The client must specifically ask for Ahmed to develop art photos or we do not touch the film."

"The policeman knew what to ask for?"

"Certainly." Ahmed worked the whisky tumbler with spinster-like sips. "At first I thought he might be spying on us, trying to get evidence to shut us down, so I said I wasn't taking in any more art photos."

"Then?"

"He was cool, that one. Most men are sweating like I am now, afraid they'll be caught red-handed, but not him. He looked me straight in the eye and said, 'Don't worry, these are for my own personal use.'"

Emmanuel swallowed a mouthful of tar-black coffee. "And were they 'personal use' photos?"

266

"Oh, yes." The assistant's dark eyes lit up. "And very good ones, too. None of the usual images of women licking penises like lollipops or being done from behind like a cow. These were very . . . unusual."

"Two girls?" Emmanuel ventured a guess.

"No." Ahmed checked his watch, then drained his glass in one gulp. "I see that kind of thing every day. These photos are not like the others, but I promised myself that I would not tell you too much. You must see them for yourself."

"You have copies?" Emmanuel sat up. This was more than he could have hoped for. The bastard who'd knocked him cold wouldn't be the only one with access to the evidence.

"That is why I'm here." Ahmed sighed. "I am a bad Muslim who is about to marry a good Muslim woman. Much as it pains me, I must cleanse myself of the filth I have gathered over the years."

"You have the photos with you?"

Ahmed stood up abruptly. "No. They are in the safe at the photo studio. You must break in and steal them in ten minutes."

"What?"

"Mr Fernandez is cheap," Ahmed explained. "The night watchman comes on duty one hour after the studio has closed. That gives you one hour to go in, get the photos, and leave Lourenço Marques before the police are alerted."

Emmanuel couldn't believe his ears. "I have to steal the photos? I thought they belonged to you."

"They do." Ahmed checked his watch again. "We must get moving. I will explain on the way."

The buzz in the café increased when a large group of sunburned tourists came in for an early dinner of cheap wine and prawns. Breaking and entering was as much a crime here as it was back in South Africa and Ahmed was not the ideal accomplice; his shirt and jacket were soaked through with sweat and they hadn't even set the wheels in motion yet.

"What makes you think I'm willing to break the law to get the photos?"

"You've come all the way to Mozambique. Something tells me you would not like to go home empty-handed. Now, please. We must hurry. I promise I will explain on the way."

"You have between here and the photo studio to convince me," Emmanuel said and followed Ahmed into the sunset.

Outside, the air smelled of charcoal fires and the ocean. The pink- and brown-skinned beach crowd surged along the sidewalk in search of spicy food and holiday trinkets. In the crush, Ahmed caught hold of Emmanuel's sleeve and led him into the middle of the moving traffic.

"It's faster this way," Ahmed shouted over the blast of horns that accompanied their reckless scramble past car bumpers and smoking exhausts. He appeared not to notice the screeching tyres or the irate drivers yelling at them in Portuguese. For the second time Emmanuel questioned the wisdom of going anywhere with a backsliding Muslim pornographer.

"Tell me more about the photos," Emmanuel said once they'd cleared the sweating asphalt and stepped onto the opposite side of the boulevard. "Did the policeman come once a month to pick them up?"

They turned into a laneway flanked by African women selling carved animals and shell jewellery. A skinny black girl held out a fat wooden hippo for their inspection. Ahmed waved her away and they continued to move at a clip towards the photo studio.

"He came twice only, in January and again in March. Each time with one roll of film."

"You sure?"

Ahmed stopped to catch his breath and mop the deluge of sweat from his face and neck. "I told you. I always remember my special clients. He came twice only."

"Is it the same woman on both rolls?" If the du Toit girls weren't starring, then who was?

"Who said it was a woman?" Ahmed gave an evil giggle and squeezed himself into a tight alley running between two *turista* hotels with painted wooden shutters and breezy "ship to shore" curtains at the windows. Emmanuel didn't make it into the narrow corridor. Shock held him prisoner.

"The photos are of a man?" he asked bluntly. Maybe Louis, with his blond hair and girlish mouth, really *was* his father's son. How could you keep a secret like that in Jacob's Rest? Almost impossible, but the captain had already proved his ability to keep parts of himself hidden from public view.

269

Ahmed waved him in with a grin. "Who said it was a man?"

"What does that mean? It has to be one of the two."

"Does it?" the assistant laughed, clearly enjoying the game. "You cannot imagine the things I see in my work. It is for this very reason that I myself can never own a pet."

Emmanuel smiled at the lab assistant. Against his better judgment, he'd taken a liking to Mad Ahmed.

"Not even a chicken?" Emmanuel asked when they set off again. "Surely some things are sacred, even in your line of work."

"Hmm . . ." Ahmed gave the subject serious thought. "You are right. I have seen eggs in unnatural places, but never the chicken itself. My new wife and I will have chickens, thanks to you. Chickens, and maybe some grasshoppers. Yes, that's what we'll do."

Emmanuel was laughing out loud now. There weren't enough doctors in the army psych unit to cure whatever Ahmed had.

"Who is this woman you're marrying?" he asked.

"A poor one," came the quick answer. "My mother found her in the countryside."

"She has no idea what you do."

"No," Ahmed said as they crossed a dirt laneway and came to a stop behind the back entrance to the photo lab. "That is why I must make every attempt to rid myself of my little problem."

Emmanuel checked the high walls crowned by coils of barbed wire and broken glass. The back gate was padlocked. Ahmed's madness wasn't so funny anymore.

270

"Why are the photos in the safe if they belong to you?" Emmanuel asked. This was the moment to walk away and leave the nervous assistant to do his own dirty work.

Ahmed pulled a key from his pocket and slipped it into the padlock. "They are in the safe for my own protection. After a year or two of working here, I began to spend too much time with my friends."

"Who?"

"The ones in the photos. I cannot tell you the hours I spent in solitary pleasure with them. Once I did not come out of my room for the whole weekend. Every Monday, I was exhausted after milking my body of its life fluids. Buckets . . ."

"Okay . . ." Emmanuel interrupted the nostalgic memoir. "You grew hair on your palms. What then?"

"No." The assistant pulled the padlock open and held his sweaty palms out for inspection. "My palms remained normal but my mother began to worry. She talked to Mr Fernandez, who came to my house and took my friends from me. He put them in the safe. I am allowed to see them twice a week for one hour at a time."

The back gate creaked open a fraction. Walk away, Emmanuel told himself, that's the smart thing to do. New evidence was sure to turn up in Jacob's Rest.

He stayed put. "Go on," he said. "Where's the problem?"

Ahmed was shamefaced. "I have begun breaking into the safe when Mr Fernandez is out. I fear there will be no life fluid left for my wife if my friends and I continue meeting."

"What happens when you get the photos? You going to lock yourself in a room with your friends until you're tapped dry?"

"No. I will destroy the photos. You and I together will burn them in a fire."

"*We'll* burn them?" Emmanuel stepped back. "What makes you think I'll do any of this?"

Ahmed turned from crazy to cunning in a flicker. "You came to Mozambique alone and you have not asked the help of our local police even though you are also a law man. Like my special clients, what you crave is not available to you legally."

"I'm looking for evidence. That's different from being one of your special clients."

"Even so, I am the only one who can help you procure what you need."

The word "procure" made him sound like a pervert haunting the streets after dark. It wasn't too far from the truth. "How do I know the photos have anything to do with the policeman?"

Ahmed put his hand on his heart. "I offer no proof. I give only my word."

"Your word may be gold in the tugger's world, Ahmed, but I need more than that."

The pornographer shook his head. "To speak of the photos cheapens the experience of seeing them, virgin, for the first time. I will not do that to myself or to you. I am sorry."

Emmanuel patted the sweaty man's shoulder. "Good luck with the break-in. I'm going to get myself a drink and head back to the border."

He turned to leave. The assistant scuttled around him and held the empty satchel up like a stop sign.

"No images. No favourites. No order. Location. Yes. Location. I will give you a place."

"Go ahead."

"A police station with two cells, side by side. A desk with a chair, near the back door. Above the desk, a row of keys, a *shambok* and a *knobkerrie*. That is all I will say of the photos. Push me no more!"

It was a clear description of the Jacob's Rest police station. "What's the combination to the safe?" Emmanuel said.

Ahmed pulled a piece of paper from his pocket and held it up between his thumb and forefinger. "I give you this only because our cause is pure."

"You've been in the business too long, Ahmed. We're breaking and entering to steal a stash of hardcore. A judge will find another word to describe our cause."

"There will be no judge. You will please go straight to the back door. Here is the key. The office is the first door on the left. The safe is hidden at the bottom of a long cupboard behind the desk. You may use this bag to put the envelopes in and leave the safe open in order to simulate a robbery. When you are done, come out to me."

"Easy as that?" Emmanuel slipped the key and the safe combination into his pocket. It was too clean and too simple, but the description of the police station pushed him on. Twenty paces away was the envelope that dealt the dirt on the captain: fat with admissible evidence. He was no better than Ahmed's special clients. He was ready to risk jail for a taste of the forbidden.

"Godspeed," Ahmed whispered and Emmanuel slipped into the backyard. Two garbage cans stood flush against the back wall of the studio.

Twelve steps to the back door. He inserted the key and entered the building. On the left was the door Ahmed had described. A dim light fell in through a window. Night was falling.

He moved quickly into the office. His breath was hard in his chest as he knelt down next to the safe and dialled the numbers Ahmed had given him. He felt a click beneath his fingers, the door eased open, and he reached in. The thick wad of files neatly bound in brown cardboard felt like gold in his hand.

He stuck the files into the satchel and sped towards the yard. It was time to skip and run. A short sprint and the file was his. It was as easy and clean as Ahmed promised. He stepped outside.

A white shaft of light hit him full in the face.

He caught a fist flat against the head, fell hard and looked up, dazed. The security guard, a lean black man, came at him like a pickaxe. Pain shot through his ribcage, then along his jawbone as the guard took the cruel to be kind approach with his heavy boots.

Emmanuel rolled and a second kick went wide. He felt the weight of the envelopes as he struggled to his

274

feet and judged the odds. Not good. The guard took up the whole doorway and he wasn't going anywhere.

Emmanuel waited for the guard to move. The black man stared him down, nostrils flared with the scent of wounded prey. Emmanuel faked a move to the left and the guard came at him fast. He crouched low, tipped the guard's legs from under him and heard a wet smack when the guard's body landed on the hard concrete.

The guard pulled himself up to a kneeling position. Emmanuel legged it to the fence. He wasn't too proud to run from a foe seconds away from beating the crap out of him.

He reached the gate. It was closed. He hammered his fist against the steel.

"Open up!"

"You must go over the fence," Ahmed instructed him calmly from the other side. "I cannot let you out this way."

"Open the fucking door!"

"You must go over the fence. Over the fence."

The top of the fence was too high to jump over, the surface too smooth to get a toehold. The guard came towards him with his nightstick raised. The weight of the files tugged at his shoulder and his plan fell into place. First beat the living hell out of the guard, second get a garbage can and climb out, third beat the living hell out of Ahmed. Not up to the scale of the D-Day invasion, but it would do.

Emmanuel let the guard get close enough to taste victory, then dodged to the right. The nightstick swung down and grazed his shoulder, but he kept moving. He was at the garbage can in two seconds flat. He picked up the half-filled container and turned to get a close view of the nightstick making a comeback. This time it landed square against his arm and sent the garbage can crashing down.

Emmanuel scooped up the lid and held it over him like a shield. The nightstick worked double time, each hit making a dull metal clank in the night air. An alley cat howled as Emmanuel rolled the can towards the fence. He steadied it against the wall and turned his attention to the guard, who was hammering away at the lid with grim precision.

He crouched low, reached out from behind the safety of the lid, grabbed the guard by the ankles, and pulled. The guard fell hard a second time. The nightstick rolled free and Emmanuel threw it over the fence. That was one less thing to worry about. He jammed the lid in place on top of the can, then stripped off his jacket and threw it over the coil of barbed wire along the top of the fence. He placed a foot on the lid and the nightwatchman hit him square between the shoulder blades.

Emmanuel turned, ducked a blow, then landed a solid punch against the guard's jaw. The man wobbled unsteadily. Emmanuel hit him with his right fist, then again with his left, and the guard went down for good. Emmanuel quickly climbed onto the garbage can and scrambled over the wall. A shard of broken glass sliced into his calf as he hauled himself over. He landed in the alley, bruised and bleeding, and saw Ahmed waiting. He picked up the nightstick.

Ahmed ran.

$\star$ $\star$ $\star$

Emmanuel caught the sweaty lab assistant and swung him hard against the wall of an empty shop.

"You are angry. I understand this."

Emmanuel slammed Ahmed back again.

"I am mildly annoyed," Emmanuel said. "Angry is when I break both your kneecaps with this nightstick."

"The guard, of course. I had every confidence you would deal with him efficiently."

"Did you?" Emmanuel made sure Ahmed felt the press of his thumbs as he dug them deep into the tender muscle flesh of his shoulders.

"Please." Ahmed winced in pain. "You must listen to me. We must hurry to complete our plan."

"It's your plan, Ahmed. My plan was to get the photos and walk out the back door."

"The photos. They are yours now." The assistant was unbalanced enough to sound enthusiastic. "You can take them across the border if you allow me to guide you."

Emmanuel eased the pressure of his thumbs on Ahmed's shoulders.

"Another stunt like the one you just pulled and you will get a taste of this nightstick. That's a promise."

"Follow me and we will complete our mission," Ahmed said and slid into the dark with the certainty of an alley rat. They followed a dusty back lane and turned into a wide tree-lined boulevard fronted by white stucco colonial buildings in the Portuguese style.

Ahmed picked up his pace and they walked past a group of older men playing cards outside a brightly lit café. They cut across the centre of a night market

277

offering monkeys in cages, racks of cotton suits, and fiery bowls of chilli prawns for sale. After ten minutes trudging steadily upwards they stopped at a wooden gate hanging off its hinges. Ahmed squeezed through the entrance and motioned Emmanuel into an overgrown garden with a zigzag pathway leading to a small tumbledown shack.

"My house," Ahmed announced with pride and led the way to a cleared corner of the garden where there was a circle of stones filled with dry leaves and kindling. A can of petrol lay next to the hearth.

"You were expecting me?" Emmanuel said.

"Every week I say to myself, 'Ahmed, burn the filth and be done', but I have not had the strength to do so. Now, with your help, I will say goodbye to all my friends."

The smell of petrol was strong in the air as Ahmed doused the dry leaves and dropped a lit match onto the incendiary mix. There was a *whoosh* when the fire ignited the leaves.

Emmanuel placed the satchel on the ground. Ahmed was welcome to do what he wanted with his "friends" but he needed the captain's photos and he needed to get the hell out of Mozambique. He knelt down to unpack the stash of pornography and his leg and shoulder spasmed with pain. The cut from the broken glass was raw, the hit from the nightstick throbbed.

"Give me my photos," he said. "I need to get back to SA before the border closes."

Ahmed removed the envelopes from the leather bag and laid them out on the ground at evenly spaced intervals. His index finger stroked every envelope before stopping two from the end of the row.

"This is yours." He picked up two identical envelopes but made no move to relinquish them. "You must promise me to look at the photos in order. This is very important. It cannot be done any other way. It *must* not be done any other way."

"What for?" Emmanuel asked with as much patience as he could muster.

"You must promise," Ahmed insisted. "You must look at them one at a time and lay them out on a table in order."

"How do I know the correct order?" Emmanuel said, humouring Ahmed, who was now hugging the envelopes to his chest like a cherished loved one.

Ahmed reached into the first package and carefully withdrew two photos. "I have numbered them," he said and laid the prints down next to the fire. "You must arrange them just so."

Photo number one was a picture of the cells at the Jacob's Rest police station. Photo number two was of the desks in the front office. Light from the fire flickered over the banal images. Despite the pain and the difficulty of obtaining the photos, he was intrigued. He'd been beaten and pissed on at the captain's hut for whatever was in the envelopes Ahmed was holding.

"I promise to look at them in order," Emmanuel said. He'd promise his first-born if that made Ahmed hand over the goods sooner.

"You will not regret it." Ahmed replaced the photos and reluctantly surrendered the package. "You are a very lucky man. I am filled with envy at your joyous introduction to this special friend."

The worn skin of the envelope rested softly in Emmanuel's palm. He was one step closer to the truth about Willem Pretorius and hopefully one step closer to catching the killer. He turned to leave.

"Mr Policeman," Ahmed said. "Please stay a moment. I need you to make sure I complete my task."

"Go ahead," Emmanuel said and Ahmed pulled the photos from their envelopes and threw them onto the fire. Heat blistered and distorted grainy images of naked blondes, brunettes, black women, white women, twins and couples arranged in every imaginable configuration. Ahmed's collection ranged far and wide. Within minutes, all that remained of the mad pornographer's "friends" was a pile of grey ash on the glowing twigs.

Ahmed sobbed. He took a handkerchief from his pocket and blew his nose with gusto. "Thank you, Mr Policeman. You have been my redemption. I will be faithful to my wife as the creator intended. Please take this leather case as a token of my esteem."

Emmanuel accepted the gift and slipped his envelopes inside. For Ahmed he was the redeemer: for the Pretorius family he might be the destroyer.

CHAPTER
FIFTEEN

The dark blanket of night had spread over Jacob's Rest by the time Emmanuel arrived back from Lourenço Marques. He parked in front of his room at the Protea Guesthouse and eased his aching body out of the driver's seat. The Security Branch was conducting a raid in another part of the country and that left him free for the first time to use his own accommodation without fear of intrusion.

He limped to his room with the leather satchel in his hands and unlocked the door. Inside, he flicked the light on and pulled the drawers of the bedside table open. He checked the empty cavity; fingers sweeping into every corner in the hope that one magic pill had come loose from the pack.

The drawer was empty and Emmanuel calculated a window of perhaps half an hour before the pain burning along his calf worked its way to his shoulder, then up to his head — a half-hour tops before he was limping along the kaffir path towards Dr Zweigman's modest brick bungalow.

Drops of sweat broke out on his top lip when he reached down and pulled the photos from the first envelope. His injured shoulder protested at the movement and he narrowed the window of rational function to fifteen minutes.

He opened the envelope and laid out numbers one to four. The photographs showed the cells, the desks, the table with tea and cups and the back window. Harmless images that could have been taken by a keen twelve year old on a Voortrekker Scouts excursion. Numbers five to ten showed the station's backyard. A tree. A chair. The circle of stones used for the *braai* fire.

A rising sense of panic swelled up. Was Ahmed so desensitised by years of developing hardcore that only images of ordinary things turned him on? The urge to split the pack of photos and check the middle was strong, but Emmanuel resisted. Maybe there was method to Ahmed's madness.

He laid out numbers eleven and twelve and his luck took a turn. Photo number eleven was a sunlit boulder out on the veldt. Number twelve was the same rock, but with a young woman leaned back against it, her tanned arms crossed over her torso. She was fully clothed. An unremarkable image except for the fact that it was a photo of a mixed-race woman taken by a white man and the woman's face was not shown.

Emmanuel laid the rest of the photos from the first package out in order and examined them one at a time. Each image was a fumbling, almost adolescent revelation of the woman's body; the photographer a novice asking for just a little more in each frame. The woman's dress, a plain cotton frock tailor-made for church hall revivals and family picnics, was undone two buttons at a time and the sleek curves of breasts, thighs and hips gradually revealed themselves. Then the modest covering was gone. The images contained brown skin, sunlight, dark, hard nipples and pubic hair.

The last photograph in the pack, number twenty-five, was the woman, face still unseen, leaning naked against the rock with her legs spread wide. She was a beautiful, sunlit invitation to bliss.

Emmanuel examined the slow-motion striptease. He could see why Ahmed loved the photos: they documented a shedding of innocence more profound than the removal of clothing. There was the sense in every shot that the woman and the photographer were moving slowly and inexorably to a place they had both never been before.

As evidence, there was a lot less to like about the images. There wasn't one single element in the photographs to connect Willem Pretorius to the mystery woman. Anyone with access to the police station could have taken the first few shots and there was only Ahmed's word that the Afrikaner captain was the one to hand over the undeveloped rolls for processing. A dark-skinned half-Arab Muslim pornographer was not a reliable witness in a South African court of law.

"*Open the second envelope.*" The sergeant major slid into the room on a wave of pain and took his position at the head of the parade. "*You'll not get the pills until you know exactly what you have, laddie.*"

Emmanuel opened the envelope and pulled out a fresh stack of photographs. His shoulder ached with an intense throbbing that spread across his back and forced him to breathe through an open mouth.

He laid out the first five photos with shaking hands. Same woman in a different location: a bedroom with a wide wrought-iron bed and lace-edged curtains at the window. It wasn't the stone hut with its narrow single cot. The room in the photos was a feminine space, possibly the woman's own bedroom.

"*The naked female is a wondrous thing, is it not, soldier?*" The Scotsman was in awe. "*Look at that arse. I could bounce a shilling off it it's so tight.*"

Emmanuel kept flipping, quicker now as the pain worked its way up towards his neck. In five minutes his head was going to be alive with the sound of jackhammers. The photos flashed in front of him in a blur of hardcore images. The woman naked on all fours, then naked from behind, thighs open to display every fold and detail of her shaved sex.

"*Oh, yes, lad.*" The sergeant major was delighted. "*After food and water and whisky, this is the stuff of life. Exactly what the doctor ordered, hey?*"

"Unless I can tie these photos to Willem Pretorius," Emmanuel said aloud, "the Security Branch will throw them out the window as unrelated to the case. Smut and communist infiltrators don't mix."

"*Not so fast . . . You're missing all the good bits, lad. Can't you take a moment to enjoy your work? Take a look at the last one.*"

Emmanuel picked the photo up. The woman was lying naked on the unmade bed with her hips tilted upward and her hand buried deep between her legs. He

284

backtracked and examined the preceding photo, which showed the woman lying on her side with her face masked by the fall of her long dark hair. A new element was added and he'd all but missed it. Around the woman's neck was a necklace, an opened flower with a small diamond at the centre.

"*Pretty,*" the sergeant major cooed. "*I like the look of that.*"

"The necklace or what it's resting against?"

"*Both. Jewellery on a naked woman is a sacred thing, my lad.*"

"You'd say that if she had a tyre iron around her neck," Emmanuel said. The pack of photos thinned to nothing and he flicked the last two photos onto the bed. The woman's identity was going to remain a mystery. The slim waist ruled Tottie out and the long hair and bold physical presence of the woman's body made Davida Ellis an unlikely suspect. Was the captain's model someone from an outlying farm or hamlet? Emmanuel placed the last photo down and felt its mesmerising power grab hold of him.

"Well, well," he said. The pain in his body drained away and was replaced by an unassailable sense of wellbeing. Maybe he was going to win the war after all.

"*What in hell makes a man do something so . . . unsavoury?*" the sergeant major blurted out.

Emmanuel wiped the sweat from his forehead, and examined the last photograph. A naked man lay on the unmade bed with his forearm thrown over his eyes in a playful parody of the woman's efforts to hide her identity. A crumpled sheet was pulled low over his hips to expose an edge of wiry blond pubic hair. The hard shape of the man's erect penis strained against the cotton sheet, proof of his readiness to go again, despite the fact that the smile on his mouth suggested he'd already spent a good deal of time thrusting his way to heaven.

"*Jesus!*" The image made the cast-iron sergeant major ill at ease. "*It's wrong for a man to parade himself like that.*"

"She asked him to pose. And he said yes."

"*He did it to please her?.*"

"Yes."

"*Well . . .*" The Scotsman considered that fact for a moment. "*There's not much a man won't do for pussy.*"

"There's more to it than that," Emmanuel said and traced a finger over the broken nose and the unique gold-faced watch that clearly identified this slab of Afrikaner manhood as one Captain Willem Pretorius, moral defender of the town of Jacob's Rest and enthusiastic amateur photographer. Pussy, as the sergeant major suggested, was only part of the reason for such a flagrant act of self-revelation. Willem Pretorius had taken a life-threatening risk by posing for the camera.

"He loves the fact she's looking at him: seeing him for who he really is. Check the expression on his face. He's not Captain Willem Pretorius, upholder of the sacred covenant with the Lord. He's a bad man who's spent the afternoon doing bad things to a woman his tribe says is unclean and he couldn't be fucking happier."

286

"*Maybe it was love made him do it?*"

"I doubt it," Emmanuel said. The morphine-like sense of wellbeing ebbed away and the pain surged up to his jawline. "Forty-something pictures of her doing every imaginable thing for his pleasure and one photo of him looking like the king of cock hall. Being the white *induna* is what he loved."

"*The necklace cost a few pounds.*"

"A trinket." Emmanuel began packing the photos. His thoughts had taken a turn to a dark place. "A piece of insurance to gain her loyalty. You really think he'd stand by her if it affected his perfect Afrikaner family? He'd have her on a bus to Swaziland with ten pounds in her pocket or six feet underground with nothing."

"*What the hell are you so angry about? I only meant that he gave her presents and made sure no-one knew who she was. He protected her, didn't he?*"

"He protected himself," Emmanuel said and returned the pictures to the leather satchel as quickly as he could without damaging them. He needed the pills. He needed something to stop him from limping over to the captain's house and shoving the feast of hardcore down Mrs Pretorius's lily-white throat.

"*You're not going to do that,*" the sergeant major cautioned. "*The old Jew will fix you up and first thing tomorrow you'll send this lot off to van Niekerk, fast post. This shit is going to save your life, soldier.*"

The sergeant major was right but that didn't diminish the anger Emmanuel was feeling. It was the last photo: the satisfied look on Willem Pretorius's face needled him into an incomprehensible rage. He could almost hear the woman's teasing voice coaxing the naked Dutchman to smile for the camera after she had arranged the sheet just so.

Emmanuel clipped the satchel shut. He had to dream of a woman in a burned-out cellar while Pretorius got the real thing. The rage was sharpened by another emotion. He stopped short. He was blindingly, furiously jealous of the captain and the woman who'd spent the afternoon fucking and then shared a dangerous joke.

The pain pushed Emmanuel onto the kaffir path towards the old Jew and his scarred leather doctor's kit.

Emmanuel knocked on the door a third time and waited. It was 10:35 p.m. and Jacob's Rest was a small town: the residents had locked up for the night and it would take Zweigman a while to answer.

"Yes?" the German asked through the door.

"Detective Sergeant Cooper. I'm here on a personal errand."

The double lock clicked open and Zweigman peered out. His white hair stuck out at odd sleep-tossed angles but his brown eyes were sharp and focused. He was wearing plain cotton pyjamas under a tatty dressing gown that sported a moth-eaten velvet collar.

"You are injured," Zweigman said. "Come this way." He indicated a doorway immediately to his right and Emmanuel shuffled his aching body into a room barely large enough to house the leather sofa and armchair that stood at its centre. There was a gramophone on an occasional table with a stack of records in paper sleeves resting next to it, but what dominated the space were the books. They lined the walls and jostled for room in the corners and at the ends of the sofa. There were more books than could be read in a lifetime.

Zweigman picked up an old newspaper from the leather armchair and threw it aside, not caring where it landed.

"Let us see what damage you have done," he said.

Emmanuel sank into the cracked leather chair and pushed his injured leg out with some effort.

"Some aches and pains. Nothing that a few painkillers won't fix."

"That is for me to decide," Zweigman said and gently lifted the torn trouser leg out of the way to examine the wound. He emitted a satisfied grunt.

"Painkillers will help but the wound is deep and needs both cleaning and stitching. May I see your shoulder, please?"

Emmanuel didn't ask the German how he knew about the other souvenir collected from the guard in Lourenço Marques. Despite his current circumstance, Zweigman couldn't shrug off the mantle of intellectual superiority that hung from his stooped shoulders. He had commanded respect in another life and Emmanuel imagined the good doctor's expertise was once dispensed to gold-plated families in rooms with polished furniture.

Emmanuel's shirt was half unbuttoned when there was a knock at the door that started out as a soft tap and rapidly turned into a manic pounding when the call wasn't immediately answered.

"Liebchen?" The woman's voice was husky with tears. *"Liebchen?"*

"Please stay seated," Zweigman said and walked to the door and opened it gently. Lilliana Zweigman stumbled into the room in a pale silk dressing gown embroidered with dozens of purple butterflies in flight. Her hands reached out and patted her husband's face and shoulders like a field medic searching for hidden injuries.

"We have a visitor." Zweigman gave no indication that his wife's behaviour was in any way unusual. "Would you be kind enough to make us a pot of tea to be served with your excellent butter biscuits?"

"Is he?" Lilliana mumbled. "He is?"

"No, he is not. The detective is a book lover and we were discussing our favourite writers. Is that not so, Detective?"

"Yes." Emmanuel picked up the book closest to him and held it up. His shoulder screamed in protest but he didn't let it show. "I was hoping to borrow this copy for a few days."

"Ahh . . ." Lilliana became bright as a welder's spark now that the danger had passed. "Yes, of course. I will make the tea."

She floated out of the room and Emmanuel wondered at the capacity of the human mind to mould reality to its will. He was seated in Zweigman's house with bloodied trousers, an unbuttoned shirt, and a copy of *A Field Guide to Spores and Fungi* in his hand, and Lilliana had willed herself into believing it was a social call.

290

"The shoulder." Zweigman continued as if they had not been interrupted. "Let me see it, please."

Emmanuel removed his shirt slowly and hot pain coursed through his muscles. The guard would be able to tell Mr Fernandez, the Portuguese land whale, that he'd given the thief a taste of suffering.

"An old bullet wound overlaid with a new bruise. I will not ask how you acquired such aggressive injuries." Zweigman pressed his fingers around the edge of the bruise. "Arnica to take down the swelling and painkillers to take away the pain. Nature will do the rest in its own time."

The doctor found his medical kit among the chaos, snapped it open, and rifled through the contents. He pulled out a container of pills and shook four into the palm of his hand.

"Swallow these with your tea," Zweigman instructed before digging into his bag to extract a tub of cream. "Please rub this into your shoulder while I arrange for the washing bowl and sterilise a needle from my wife's sewing kit."

Emmanuel scooped ointment out of the jar and spread it over his shoulder as the doctor left the room. Zweigman was right. The nightstick had brought the pain of his old injury back to life.

Zweigman re-entered the room and set up the bowl next to the gramophone. He moved with such certainty that Emmanuel wondered again what had landed the old Jew and his wife in Jacob's Rest.

"How did the captain know you were a doctor?" he asked.

The German dipped a cloth into the washbowl and started cleaning the cut. "You asked me once before and I have told you that I do not know."

"Something happened back in April that tipped him off. What was it?"

"I recall no such incident, Detective." Zweigman reached up for a pair of tweezers and began digging into the cut. "Hold still, please. I have found the source of your discomfort. There." He lifted the tweezers to show a jagged piece of clear glass. "Once again, I will not ask how you came by this."

"Very kind of you. But I can't return the favour."

The doctor didn't respond to the statement and set about preparing the sewing kit. At some point during his fall from grace the German had learned to keep his mouth shut. He would not volunteer any information.

"Which one of the coloured women was the captain close to?" Emmanuel asked the question straight out.

"Close?" Zweigman gave a topnotch impression of a penniless migrant hearing the English language for the first time. "What does this mean, Detective?"

"It means close enough to stick his tongue in her ear and a few other places besides," Emmanuel said and the doctor flushed.

Zweigman said nothing for a moment. "If you repeat that accusation outside this room, even in jest," he warned, "it will take a team of surgeons to sew you together and I am not sure they will succeed."

"Was it one of the women in your shop?" Emmanuel asked as the German threaded a needle and tied a knot in the surgical thread. His hands were steady, but there was an odd tilt to his head, as if he was trying to get as far from the conversation as possible.

"Tottie or maybe Davida?"

"I'm afraid that I cannot help you," Zweigman said and closed the cut. He stitched the flesh together with the quick skill of a surgeon used to mending much deeper wounds. Emmanuel was sure that the old Jew knew more than he was telling but, unlike the Security Branch, he preferred confessions to be voluntary.

"You know what's strange?" he said to Zweigman after the thread was tied off and the sting in his flesh had subsided. "You didn't tell me I was mistaken about the captain. The suggestion that a morally upright white policeman might be fooling around with a coloured girl didn't get a response from you. No surprise. Nothing at all."

Zweigman carefully packed everything back into his wife's sewing kit. He looked old and worn out, his shoulders pushed down by a heavy weight.

"We are men of the world, Detective. We have been through a war and seen cities burn. Does an affair really have the power to shock either of us?"

"Maybe not. But the rest of the town and the country will see it differently. The Immorality Act is the law and the fact that it was broken by a policeman will shock plenty of people."

"The Immorality Act." Zweigman snorted. "The forces of nature are more powerful than any law made by men."

The door to the lounge-cum-library opened and Lilliana Zweigman backed into the room carrying a tray containing a teapot, cups and a plate of butter biscuits cut into the shape of snowflakes.

"Here." Zweigman took the tray from his wife and balanced it on the wide arm of the sofa. "You are a marvel, *liebchen*, a true wonder. You have earned a rest. Why don't you go to bed now while we talk?"

Lilliana didn't move. She sensed something not quite right about the detective's presence in her house.

"Please help yourself to tea and one of my wife's biscuits."

Emmanuel bit into a pale yellow disc of pastry sprinkled with sugar. It was delicious and he hadn't eaten for hours. He finished the biscuit in two bites and reached for another one.

"You see?" Zweigman patted his wife's arm. "You have not lost your touch. I'm sure our visitor would appreciate a small tin of your pastry to take home."

"Yes." Lilliana backed out slowly. "I will pack him some in the container with the red roses on the outside."

"The ideal choice," the doctor said and gently closed the door behind her.

"Please excuse my wife, Detective. She's not comfortable with members of the police."

"No offence taken," Emmanuel said and swallowed the painkillers with a mouthful of tea.

Zweigman sat down and rested his teacup on his knee. A wealth of past sorrows seemed to surround the doctor and the melancholy reached out and embraced

294

Emmanuel like an old friend. Men of the world, Zweigman had called them. Men formed by war and cruelty — and unexpected kindnesses.

Emmanuel picked up a book to break the morbid spell and ran his fingertips over the smooth calfskin cover. *City of Sin* was embossed on the spine. It was the same size and style as *Celestial Pleasures*, the slim volume he'd found in the captain's locked sanctuary. In a town the size of Jacob's Rest, the book of erotica could only have come from this room.

"Did Pretorius borrow any of these books?"

"He never honoured me with such a request," Zweigman said. "I believe the Bible was his mainstay."

"Do you lend books from here?"

"Everyone is welcome, Detective."

Emmanuel breathed out in frustration. "No specific names to give me, I suppose. No clue as to who borrowed a book entitled *Celestial Pleasures*."

"I have no memory of that particular book and no idea who may see fit to read it."

Emmanuel finished his tea and pushed himself out of the deep folds of the leather armchair. The painkillers surged through his blood and he felt just fine.

"When Constable Shabalala avoids telling me something, I know it's to protect Captain Pretorius. Who are you protecting, Doctor?"

"Myself," Zweigman answered without hesitation. "Everything is done to protect my soul from further onslaughts of guilt and blame."

"I was hoping for something as simple as a name," Emmanuel said and turned to leave. He needed sleep.

Tomorrow he had to try and identify the woman in the photos and hope that she would lead him to the man who'd stolen the evidence from the stone hut.

"Detective." Zweigman held the jar of ointment out. "Apply this to your shoulder once every two to four hours. It will help reduce the swelling."

"Thanks. I also need more painkillers. I'm out."

Zweigman's brown eyes made a close study of the wounded detective before he answered.

"You received a three-week ration less than one week ago. What has happened to the rest?"

"Gone," Emmanuel said, conscious of how that must sound to a medical professional. "I don't normally run through them so quickly."

"What made you lift your dosage?"

The sergeant major's voice and the memory of running through the smoke of wood fires were not things he was prepared to share with anyone, even a highly qualified surgeon. The town of Jacob's Rest opened all the cages he normally kept locked and he couldn't find a reason for that.

Zweigman went to his medical kit and returned with a half-filled container of white pills.

"These are for physical pain. They will not cure the pain you are feeling in your heart or your mind. That pain can only be cured by feeling it."

"What if the pain is too much to bear?" Emmanuel asked. The army psych unit was big on drugging the pain away: on the patient not feeling anything that ruled out a return to active duty. Fit enough to pull the trigger meant fit enough to return to the killing fields.

296

"You will go mad." Zweigman smiled. "Or you will transform yourself into a new being, one that even you will not recognise."

"Is that what you've done? Transformed yourself?"

"No." The old Jew looked as ancient as Jerusalem stone. "I am merely hiding from who I used to be. A sad and cowardly end in keeping with the rest of my life."

"You stood up for Anton. You protect your wife and the women in your care. How is that sad and cowardly?"

"Rearguard actions to keep the past at bay." Zweigman opened the front door and let fresh air into the room. "Come to the store tomorrow, I will check on your injuries and give you my wife's tin of biscuits. It appears she has been delayed."

Quiet sobbing came from the back of the house and Emmanuel stepped out into the sleepy embrace of Jacob's Rest.

"Thank you," he said and limped to the front gate. It seemed to him that the German refugee and his wife had run from the past only to find they had brought it with them to a distant corner of Southern Africa.

Zweigman watched the injured detective slip away into the night, then rushed to the kitchen tucked at the back of the small brick house. His wife stood at the table with the tin of butter biscuits held tightly to her chest.

"That man . . . he will take what we love from us."

"No, *liebchen*." Zweigman tried to remove the rose-covered tin from his wife's hands but found her grip impossible to loosen. He touched her cheek. "I promise that will not happen to us again."

Emmanuel was halfway back to the Protea Guesthouse when the singing began. It was a popular tune rendered almost unrecognisable by a high-pitched voice that broke on every fifth word and then started up again like a scratched record. He located the drunken songbird behind the coloured church.

"Hansie," Emmanuel greeted the tottering figure. "What are you doing out here?"

"Sarge, howzit?" The teenaged policeman held up two bottles of whisky triumphantly. "See? Louis said he wouldn't give it, but he did when he saw the uniform. *My* uniform."

"Tiny gave you those bottles?" One of them was already half empty. Hansie was having the time of it.

"Won't give any to Louis. But he gives to me because of the uniform."

"Where are you going with the bottles, Hansie?"

"Louis bet me I couldn't but I did." Hansie thumped his chest. "Because I am the law and people respect the law."

"You going back to Louis's house?"

"The shed." The boy squinted out across the dark veldt, then turned in an unsteady circle. "Louis said take the kaffir path but I don't know . . . where . . . where's the way back?"

Emmanuel put his arm around Hansie's shoulder. He was interested in how the lion of God managed to

298

talk his friend into shaking down a coloured merchant for liquor.

"I'll show you," he said and turned Hansie in the direction of the non-white houses in order to get more time to "interrogate" him. "Why didn't Louis get the bottles? He knows the kaffir path better than you, doesn't he?"

"See." Hansie held the bottles up. "I got them. Me."

"Good job." Emmanuel tried another tack. "Does Louis normally get the bottles?"

"*Ja*. But he sent me this time."

"Why?" It was hard to stop himself from smacking some sense into the idiot constable.

"He went but Tiny said no, no, no dice."

"Why?"

"Captain found out about the drinking. He sent Louis away to a farm in the Drakensbergs . . . long way away up in the mountains." Hansie gave a full-bodied burp that echoed across the empty veldt. Up ahead, the light from the captain's work shed punctuated the darkness.

"That's the shed. Go in but don't tell anyone you saw me. Understand?"

"*Ja*." The drunken Afrikaner lurched forwards, eager to show his spoils.

Emmanuel spun Hansie around to face him and levelled the police boy a severe glance, the kind used by headmasters about to hand out a six-of-the-best caning.

"Forget you saw me. That's an order, Hepple."

"Yes, sir, Detective Sergeant, sir."

Emmanuel launched Hansie towards the light with a gentle push. The inebriated boy stumbled towards the open door with the bottles held aloft like the conquering hero. A chorus of cheers greeted his entrance. Louis wasn't the only one waiting for the whisky river to start flowing.

At the open shed door, Emmanuel risked a quick look in. Hansie, Louis and two freckle-nosed teenagers sat on an oilstained blanket and passed the half-empty whisky bottle among them. The second bottle of amber was placed in the middle of the circle with its top off in readiness.

"Hey, Hansie." A boy with a train-tunnel-sized gap between his front teeth took a swig. "Louis here says that Botha's daughter isn't the prettiest girl in the district. Says he's seen better."

"Who?" Hansie was flabbergasted. "Who could be better than her? No-one."

"I've got different tastes from you." Louis pushed his messy blond hair from his forehead. "Just remember that no matter how modest women are in their appearance, no matter how shy and clean, they are the reason Adam fell into sin."

"That's exactly what I'm hoping for, man!" Hansie replied.

The policeman's answer set off a round of laughter that continued even as Emmanuel slipped away into the veldt. He didn't have to stay longer to know how the evening would unravel. There'd be talk of girls, imagined and real, then someone, most likely Hansie, would lie about having lost his virginity. There'd be more talk of girls and cars and the next big social dance. And during all this, Louis, the sleeping lion of God, and Louis, the juvenile delinquent, would jostle for supremacy.

CHAPTER
SIXTEEN

Emmanuel called in at the Grace of God Hospital early the next morning and found Sister Bernadette and Sister Angelina supervising a breakfast of cold porridge without milk for the twenty or so orphans collected on the open veranda. He waited until they'd dished up the last bowl, then approached them. He had no idea how to ask for what he wanted.

"Sisters . . ." He cleared his throat and started again. "Sisters, I'd like you to witness a likeness of Captain Pretorius for me."

"Of course," Sister Bernadette said. The tiny white nun wiped her pale hands on her apron. "Do you have a pen, Detective?"

"Yes, I do . . . it's just that . . . I . . ." He trailed off.

"Yes?" Sister Angelina prompted.

"I should warn you that it's a . . . a provocative image. One that might upset or shock you."

"Oh . . ." Sister Bernadette's smile was strained. "In that case we should get it over and done with as quickly as possible."

God bless the pragmatic Catholic sisters, Emmanuel thought and pulled the second of the two envelopes from the leather satchel. In fifteen minutes the photographs were due on an express bus to Jo'burg with Miss Byrd's cousin, Delores Bunton.

Sister Angelina motioned him over to the far end of the veranda to an old gurney covered by a sheet. They were out of sight and earshot of the children. Emmanuel hesitated then pulled the image free.

"Look at the photo," he said, "then turn it over and write 'I swear that this is a true image of Captain Willem Pretorius.' Sign your names underneath and date it, please."

He put the image face-up on the trolley and felt the heat of a blush in his cheeks.

"Oh, my," Sister Bernadette gasped.

"Gracious." Sister Angelina crossed herself and blinked hard.

"This is a surprise . . ." the little Irish nun muttered. "I had no idea."

"*Yebo*." The black nun pursed her lips. "Who knew the captain had such a big smile."

"Yes." Sister Bernadette pushed an imaginary strand of hair into her head covering. "I don't recall seeing him this happy before."

The sisters stood motionless and stared at the photograph. Emmanuel turned the image over and heard a sigh from the nuns. He handed over the pen and watched them sign and date the photo. He placed it back in the envelope.

"Thank you, sisters," he said. "If anyone from the Special Branch or the Pretorius family asks about this photograph, deny ever having seen it. It's the safest way."

★ ★ ★

Poppies General Store was quiet. The normal hum of sewing machines was replaced by the soft scrape of Zweigman's shoes as he unpacked cans of sardines from a box and stacked them on a shelf.

"Detective." The shopkeeper greeted him with a nod. His hair, normally chaotic, was now positively Medusa-like with warring white strands fighting each other in an epic battle for control.

Emmanuel motioned in the direction of the silent back room. "Nobody home?"

"My wife is unwell," Zweigman said. "She has given the ladies a day off."

"Anything to do with my visit?"

"The damage was done long before you appeared." The German stacked the last can of sardines on the shelf. "You have come for your check-up, yes?"

"That and use of the phone, if I may." He had to let van Niekerk know that the satchel of photographs was already on its way to the address he'd telegraphed through two days ago.

"Of course." Zweigman picked up the phone from the counter and shuffled into the back room, where the rows of sewing machines stood with their night covers still on. Poppies felt deserted without the ladies bent over patterns and pins under the watchful eye of Lilliana.

"I will be in the front unpacking." Zweigman put the phone on the tea table. "Call me when you are ready for your examination."

Emmanuel sat down and dialled the operator. He wanted to be at the Jacob's Rest police station within

304

the half-hour to see if the Security Branch raid had netted a big Red fish during the night.

He got through to headquarters without any trouble and was given a new number to call. Van Niekerk knew how to fly under the Security Branch radar.

"I've sent you something," Emmanuel said once the major picked up.

"Is it useful?" Van Niekerk was in high spirits for a powerful man forced to dirty his hands in a public callbox. Like a prized bloodhound he sniffed something on the wind.

"Extremely useful," Emmanuel said.

"Smut? Dirty money? Political?"

"Smut."

"Can it be tied to our departed friend or a member of his family?"

"Let's just say the captain was as good behind the camera as he was in front of it."

"My God! Are you absolutely sure it's him?"

"One hundred per cent," Emmanuel said. "I had the image signed and verified by two people who knew him."

He felt guilty using Sister Bernadette and Sister Angelina, but nuns were hard witnesses to push around on the stand. It was uncharitable to attack a bride of Christ.

"Good man," the major said. "I knew you'd come up with the goods. You always do."

Giving the information to van Nierkerk didn't feel as rewarding as Emmanuel thought it would. Willem Pretorius's homicide was still unsolved and that was the only reason he'd come to Jacob's Rest. The pornographic pictures were of value only if they helped catch the killer.

"The packet will be hand-delivered this evening to the address on the telegraph." He was suddenly impatient with van Niekerk. Catching the killer was secondary to the power that possession of the photos gave the major over the Security Branch and factions of the National Party. "I have to go and check out what the Security Branch dragged in," Emmanuel added. He wasn't leaving Jacob's Rest until he found out who'd killed Willem Pretorius and why.

"They got him," van Niekerk stated bluntly. "Your man from Bennington College."

"How do you know?"

Van Niekerk laughed, as if the question itself was too stupid to answer.

"I just do, Cooper."

"Anything else you can tell me?" Emmanuel asked. There was no way Piet or Dickie would let him in on the questioning.

"He was at the crossing on the night the captain was killed," the major said. "That's a solid fact. The miner Duma from the location was his contact. You may want to start entertaining the possibility that the Security Branch is on the right track."

"I'll do that, sir," Emmanuel said, before signing off. He knew in his bones that the communist agent wasn't a fit for the murder. Why was the body dragged to the water when it could have been left on the sand? And Shabalala was sure the killer had swum back to

306

Mozambique. Maybe the Security Branch had some answers.

He went to the front of the store where Zweigman was busy cleaning the shelves with an ostrich feather duster.

"I'll come back for my examination this afternoon," he told the shopkeeper and set the phone back on the counter. "I have to check in at the police station."

"Of course. I will be here until approximately five-thirty."

Emmanuel stepped onto the pitted dirt sidewalk fronting Poppies and the liquor store.

It was time to hammer on Shabalala's door until the black man told him everything he knew about Willem Pretorius's secret life.

Four Chevrolet sedans were parked in front of the police station, the shiny chrome trim of each car flecked with dust and the dried bodies of crushed insects collected on the night drive. A handful of plain-clothes officers in creased suits mingled on the porch, smoking and talking to a plump man with a camera slung around his neck. Press, Emmanuel guessed. The reporter would be in the employ of one of the toady Afrikaner newspapers that ran with the official National Party line no matter what the real story was.

Emmanuel climbed the stairs ready for the brush-off. The Security Branch machine had a stranglehold now on the police station and he wasn't on their list of invited guests. One of the new Security Branch officers stepped forwards.

"This is a restricted area," said the moon-faced man in the badly cut suit. "No entry without Lieutenant Lapping's say-so."

Emmanuel stepped back. He was unlikely to get pockmarked Piet's nod of approval in this lifetime.

"I was looking for the regular police — Constable Shabalala, Lieutenant Uys and Constable Hepple. I'm working a local investigation."

"Check out the back." Moonface smiled then said, "Hey, you caught the pervert yet, Detective Sergeant?"

Emmanuel walked away without answering. Lieutenant Lapping had isolated him from the murder investigation and made him a figure of fun into the bargain. He'd eat humble pie for as long as it took to find Shabalala and until he'd finished sifting through Willem Pretorius's dirty laundry.

He opened the side gate to the police station's backyard. Paul Pretorius and the diminutive Lieutenant Uys were sitting in the shade of the avocado tree with three men he didn't recognise. Was there anyone left at the Security Branch offices?

Paul Pretorius stood up and closed the gap between them with his slow swagger. "So." The hulking soldier smiled at him for the first time in their acquaintance. It was an unpleasant sight. "How does it feel to be at the arse end of the investigation, Detective Sergeant?"

"You've got a confession from the suspect?" Emmanuel said.

"Another hour or two and it'll be done," Paul said, stroking the bristles on his chin to emphasise how long a night it had been for those at the centre of power. "I tell you what, those boys inside know what they're doing."

"They're sure he's the one?"

"Absolutely. And you thought Pa's killer was some degenerate white man. Looks like you'll have to run back to Jo'burg with empty pockets. Shame, hey?"

Emmanuel knew just the thing to wipe the smile off Paul Pretorius's face: a single image of the respected white police captain nursing a giant hard-on in a coloured woman's bed. That would do the trick. It was just as well the packet of pornographic photographs was on its way to van Niekerk and well out of his reach.

"The constables aren't here?" He continued with the conversation as if the arrogant Pretorius son hadn't taken the whip to him. Paul was destined to find out the truth about his father one day and Emmanuel hoped he'd be there to witness the moment.

"Hansie's out with his girl and Shabalala I haven't seen." Paul Pretorius strolled back towards the group of men seated in the shade with a shrug that implied he had more important things to do now he was finished baiting a detective with no power and no credibility.

Emmanuel moved onto the kaffir path. He had to find Shabalala and explain to him that protecting Willem Pretorius's memory was a waste of time. With enough pressure he might even be able to find out the identity of the mystery woman in the photos.

At the juncture of the kaffir path and the main street he spotted Constable Hepple nestling close to a hugely betitted brunette with milkmaid's arms. It was the girl from the churchyard; the one Hansie had targeted after the captain's funeral. The lovebirds didn't notice him until he was almost on them.

"Detective Sergeant." Hansie sprang back and straightened his jacket over his slim boy hips. "I . . . I didn't see you."

"You were busy," Emmanuel replied and the girl made a hasty attempt to straighten the neckline of her dress. "Do you know where Constable Shabalala is?"

"The location." Hansie's breath was short and his colour high. "Lieutenant Lapping said for him to come back tomorrow."

"Lieutenant said Hansie could have the day off as well." The girl's work-worn hands fluttered up over her enormous breasts to stroke the diamond centre of her necklace. "We were going for a walk."

Emmanuel pointed to the necklace nestled in the girl's cleavage. "That's an unusual design. Can I take a closer look?"

"Of course." The milkmaid flushed with self-importance and lifted her chin to allow a better view. "It's real gold and diamonds."

"A flower," Emmanuel said and examined the gold petals set with a sparkling diamond stamen. It was the necklace worn by the brown-skinned woman in the captain's flesh extravaganza. Hansie shuffled closer, intent on protecting his girl from the big-city detective's attentions. Emmanuel ignored him. The farm girl's

310

mammaries were important only because their eye-popping size ruled her out as the model in the photos.

Emmanuel's brain leapt from one bizarre scenario to the next in an attempt to explain the appearance of the gold flower around the neck of an Afrikaner brunette. Did Captain Pretorius have a multicoloured harem of women he rewarded with identical gold flower necklaces?

"Where did you get the necklace?" he asked.

"Hansie." The girl beamed at her idiot boyfriend. "He gave it to me just now."

That explained the sweaty clinch. It wasn't every day a farm girl was given an expensive piece of jewellery to flash around.

"You've got good taste, Constable." Emmanuel placed his hand on Hansie's shoulder and moved him farther onto the kaffir path. "Where did you get the necklace?"

The boy tensed at the serious tone and scraped the toe of his boot into the sandy path.

"I don't remember."

"Tell me."

"I . . . I found it."

"Where?"

The constable's cornflower-blue eyes filled with tears just as they had when the Pretorius brothers made a move to beat the daylights out of him at the crime scene.

"By the river. On the path leading to the veldt."

Emmanuel regretted not letting the Pretorius boys give Hansie a solid pounding. It was more than the imbecile policeman deserved.

"You're talking about the riverbank where the captain was found?"

"*Ja.*" Tears rolled down the constable's face and dripped onto his starched uniform. His mother was going to have to spot clean the fabric this evening.

"The necklace was on the path the boys used to get back to the location?" Emmanuel clarified the facts and struggled to stop his fingers digging into the flesh of Hansie's shoulder. Surely the National Party government realised that giving a uniform to a boy like this was the same as giving it to a monkey?

"*Ja,* on that path."

"Why didn't you call me to look at this unusual thing?"

Hansie chewed on his thumbnail and gave the question his best efforts. It was an excruciating exercise to watch. "Well . . . A woman's necklace has nothing to do with the captain dying. I mean . . . it would be like a woman was there with him . . . and . . . there wasn't a woman with him, so . . . because . . . Captain wasn't like that."

"Hepple." Emmanuel dropped his hand from the young man's shoulder and rifled in his jacket pocket for the car keys. "That necklace is evidence. You have until this afternoon to get it back from your girlfriend and give it to me. You understand?"

"But . . . She . . . she really likes it."

312

"This afternoon," Emmanuel said and made for the Packard. He had an idea now of what Shabalala was hiding and why the Zulu policeman was covering up for his boyhood friend, Willem Pretorius.

He ran through the unplanned maze of dilapidated dwellings on the lookout for the pink door that he was told marked the Zulu constable's house. He found it and pounded twice. The door swung open and Shabalala stepped back in surprise.

"A woman was with him," Emmanuel said. "There was a woman with Captain Pretorius at the riverbank on the night he was shot."

"It rained and many of the marks . . ."

"Don't give me that rubbish, I'm not buying it today. You're a tracker. You knew Pretorius wasn't alone that night."

The Zulu-Shangaan made an effort to speak and when that failed, he reached into the pocket of his overalls and pulled out a blank-faced envelope, which he handed over without saying a word.

"What's this?"

"Read it, please, *nkosana*."

Emmanuel tore the envelope open and extracted a folded piece of paper with two lines of text written on the lined face. He read the words out loud. "*The captain had a little wife. This wife was with him at the river when he died.*"

"You were the one who sent me to King's farm," Emmanuel said. He recognised the hand. It made sense now. The person who'd left the note ran like no-one

313

he'd ever seen; ran with a relentless stride that had left him gasping for breath out on the veldt. Captain Pretorius and Shabalala stirred the hearts of the old people as they crossed the length and breadth of the Pretorius farm without stopping, without drinking. Like so many white men, Emmanuel thought, I was beaten by a warrior of the Zulu *impi*.

"What happened that night on the riverbank? I'm not going to tell the Pretorius family or the other policemen. So go ahead and just say it."

Shabalala paused as if he couldn't bear to put into words the things he'd kept bottled up for so long.

"The captain and the little wife were together on the blanket. Captain was shot and fell forwards. The little wife, she struggled from under him and ran on the sand to the path and then the man pulled the captain to the water. This is all I know."

"Christ above, man. Why didn't you tell me straightaway?"

"The captain's sons. They would not like to hear these things. None of the Afrikaners would like to hear this story."

The Pretorius boys were the unofficial lawmakers in Jacob's Rest. Anton and his burned garage were an example of the rough justice they meted out to offenders. What chance did a black policeman stand against the mighty hand of the Pretorius family?

"I understand," Emmanuel said.

Shabalala had to live in Jacob's Rest. Writing unsigned notes was the simplest way for him to help the investigation and stay out of harm's way. It was better and safer for everyone involved if a white out-of-town detective was the one to uncover the truth about the captain.

"Detective Sergeant." The Zulu constable motioned to the back of the house. "Please."

Emmanuel followed Shabalala through the neat sitting room into the kitchen. A black woman stood near a table. She looked up with a concerned expression but did not make a sound.

Shabalala led Emmanuel through the back door. They took seats at either side of a small card table. In the yard behind Shabalala's house there was a chicken coop and a traditional *kraal* for keeping animals overnight. Behind the *kraal* the property fell away to the banks of a meandering stream.

Both men looked towards the distant hills as they talked. The serious business of undressing Captain Pretorius could not be done face to face.

"Do you know who the woman is?"

"No," Shabalala said. "Captain told me of the little wife but not who she was."

Emmanuel sank back in his chair. He'd had about enough of Willem Pretorius's firewalls. Why didn't he boast about his conquests like a normal man?

"What did he tell you about the girlfriend?"

"He said he had taken a little wife from among the coloured people and that the little wife had given him . . . um . . ." The pause lengthened as Shabalala sought the most polite way to translate the captain's words.

"Pleasure? Power?" Emmanuel prompted.

"Strength. The little wife gave him new strength."

"Why do you call her little wife?" He'd seen the photographs and there wasn't one thing in them that his own ex-wife Angela would have agreed to do.

"She was a proper little wife," Shabalala stated. "The captain paid *lobola* for her, as is the custom."

"Whom did he pay the bride price to?"

"Her father."

"You're telling me a man, a coloured man, agreed to exchange his daughter for cattle?" He leaned towards Shabalala. Did the Zulu policeman really believe such a far-fetched story?

"Captain told me this is what he did. He had respect for the old ways. He would not take a second wife without first paying *lobola*. This I believe."

"Yes, well. I'm sure the white Mrs Pretorius will be delighted to hear her husband was such a stickler for the rules."

"No. The missus would not like to hear this." Shabalala was deadly serious.

The sound of a woman's voice singing in a far-off field carried back on the breeze. Spread out before them, a great span of grassland ran towards distant hills. This was one Africa, inhabited by black men and women who still understood and accepted the old ways. Five miles south in Jacob's Rest another Africa existed on parallel lines. What made Willem Pretorius think he could live in both places at the same time?

"We have to find this woman." Emmanuel pulled the Mozambican calendar from his pocket and laid it out on the small table between them. The time for secrets was over. "She was the last person to see Pretorius alive and maybe she can tell us what he was doing on these particular days."

Shabalala studied the calendar. "The captain was in Mooihoek on the Monday and Tuesday before he died but he did not leave the town on the other days."

"What do you think those red markings mean? Did he go somewhere for a few days each month?"

"No. He went to Mooihoek to buy station supplies and sometimes to Mozambique and Natal with his family, but not every month."

"These markings mean something." Emmanuel sensed another dead end coming up. "If Pretorius was doing something illegal . . . smuggling goods or meeting up with an associate . . . would you have known?"

"I think so, yes."

"And was he doing anything like that?"

Shabalala shook his head. "Captain did not do anything against the law."

"You don't think the Immorality Act counts?" Emmanuel was amazed by the tenacious respect Shabalala still held for his dead friend. Of all the people in Jacob's Rest Shabalala had earned the right to be cynical about Willem Pretorius, the lying, adulterous white man.

"He paid *lobola*. A man may take many wives if he pays the bride price. That is the law of the Zulu."

"Pretorius wasn't a Zulu. He was an Afrikaner."

Shabalala pointed to his chest just above the heart. "Here. Inside. He was as a Zulu."

"Then I'm surprised he wasn't killed sooner."

There was a shuffle at the back door and the round-faced, round-bottomed woman from the kitchen carried a tea tray onto the *stoep* and set it down on the table.

"Detective Sergeant Cooper, this is my wife, Lizzie."

"*Unjani*, mama."

Emmanuel shook hands with the woman in the traditional Zulu way, by holding his right wrist with his left hand as a sign of his respect. The woman's smile lit up the *stoep* and half the location with its warmth. She was a fraction of her husband's height but in every way his equal.

"You have good manners." Her greying hair gave her the authority to speak where a younger woman would have stayed silent. She gave the calendar a thorough look-over.

"My wife is a schoolteacher." Shabalala tried to find an excuse for his wife's inquisitive behaviour. "She teaches all the subjects."

Lizzie touched her husband's broad shoulder. "*Nkosana*, may I see you in the other room for just a moment, please?"

There was an awkward silence before the Zulu policeman stood up and followed his wife into the house. It didn't do well for a woman to interrupt men's business. The murmur of their voices spilled out from the kitchen. How Captain Pretorius arranged the purchase of a second wife was not as important as finding the woman herself. She was the key to everything.

Shabalala came back out onto the *stoep*, but remained standing. He tugged on an earlobe.

"What is it?"

"My wife she says this calendar is a woman's calendar."

"It was the captain's. I found it at the stone hut on King's farm."

"No." Shabalala fidgeted like an awkward schoolboy. "It is a calendar used by women to . . . um . . ."

Shabalala's wife stepped out from the kitchen and picked up the calendar.

"How silly can a grown man be?" she asked Shabalala with a click of her tongue. She pointed to the red-ringed days. "For one week a month a woman flows like a river. You understand? This is what this calendar is saying."

"Are you sure?"

"I am a woman and I know such things."

Emmanuel was stunned by the simplicity of the explanation. It would never have occurred to him in a hundred years of looking. The calendar was about the woman and her cycle, not an elaborate puzzle of illegal pick-up dates and activities. The camera, the calendar and the photos were all linked to the shadowy little wife, whoever she was.

"Thank you," he said, then turned to Shabalala. "We have to find the woman before the Security Branch beats a confession from the man in the cells and then throws all the other evidence out the window."

"The old Jew," Shabalala suggested. "He and his wife also know many of the coloured people."

"He won't speak," Emmanuel said. "But I know someone who might."

Emmanuel crossed the street to the burnt-out shell of Anton's garage and Shabalala set up watch in the vacant lot next to Poppies General Store. If Zweigman took flight during Emmanuel's talk with Anton, the black policeman had orders to follow and observe from a distance.

Emmanuel entered the work site and the coloured mechanic looked up from the wheelbarrow of blackened bricks he was cleaning with a wire brush. Slowly, a sense of order was being imposed on the charred ruins of the once-flourishing business.

"Detective." Anton wiped his sooty fingers clean with a rag before shaking hands. "What brings you to these parts?"

"You know most of the coloured women around here?" Emmanuel didn't waste time with preliminaries. If he didn't get anything from the mechanic, then he'd move on to the old Jew.

"Most. This got to do with the molester case?"

"Yes," Emmanuel lied. "I want to find out what set the victims apart from the other coloured women in town."

"Well . . ." Anton continued moving bricks to the wheelbarrow. "They were all young and single and respectable. There are one or two women, I won't mention names, who are free and easy with their favours. Molester didn't go after them."

320

"What about Tottie? You know anything about her private life?"

"She hasn't got one. Her father and brothers have her locked down so tight a man's lucky to get even a minute alone with her."

"No rumours about her taking up with a man from outside the coloured community?"

The mechanic stopped his work and wiped drops of sweat from his top lip. His green eyes narrowed.

"What you really asking me, Detective?"

Emmanuel went with the flow. There was nothing to gain now from being shy or subtle.

"You know any coloured man who practises the old ways? A man who might take a bride price for his daughter?"

Anton laughed with relief. "No dice. Even Harry with the mustard gas would never swap his daughters for a couple of cows."

It was highly likely the deal, any deal with native overtones, was done in secret to avoid the scorn of a mixed-race community that worked tirelessly to bury all connection to the black part of the family tree.

"Has any coloured man come into money that can't be explained?"

"Just me." Anton grinned and the gold filling in his front tooth glinted. "Got my last payment a couple of days ago but I don't have a piece of paper to prove where it came from."

The secretive Afrikaner captain and the coloured man who'd bargained for sexual access to his daughter were not likely to advertise their venture in any way.

Only a traditional black man, steeped in the old ways, would talk openly about the bride price paid for his daughter.

"Okay." Emmanuel abandoned the line of questioning and backtracked. "Have there been rumours about any of the women in town or out on the farms taking up with a man from outside the community?"

Anton carefully selected a charred brick and began scrubbing in earnest. "We love rumours and whispers," he said. "Sometimes it feels like the only thing that keeps us together."

"Tell me."

"If Granny Mariah hears I repeated this, she will hang my testicles out to dry on her back fence. I'm not exaggerating. That woman is fierce."

"I promise she won't get that information from me."

"Couple of months back . . ." Anton chose to talk to the brick in his hand, "Tottie let slip to some other women that she thought the old Jew and Davida were close. Too close."

"Any truth in it?"

"Well, Davida was over at the Zweigmans' house all hours of the day and night. She walked in and out whenever she pleased and it didn't seem right, one of us being so comfortable with whites."

"Did anyone ask her what she was doing there?" He couldn't connect the heated exchange of bodily fluids with the shy brown mouse and the protective old Jew. His relationship with her seemed paternal, not sexual.

"Reading books, sewing, baking, you name it, she always had an explanation for being there." Anton worked a lump of ash out of the brick's surface with his fingernail. "I was sweet on Davida at the time. We went walking and I even got some kisses in but she changed, Davida did. It was like she went into a shell once the talking started. She wasn't like you see her today, all covered up and quiet. The girl had some spark back then."

"Really?"

"Oh, yes. Beautiful wavy hair down to the middle of her back; all natural, not straightened. At socials she was the first one up to dance and the last one to sit down. Granny had her hands full with her, I'll tell you."

The description didn't remotely match the cloistered woman hiding under a headscarf. But the fact that the shy brown mouse once had long black hair did make her a possible match for the model in the captain's photographs. What was her body like under the shapeless clothes that hung from her like sackcloth?

"What happened?" Emmanuel asked.

"I still can't figure it," Anton said. "She got through the molester thing okay and then one day the hair is all gone and she won't walk with me anymore."

"When did this change take place?"

"April sometime." Anton threw the damaged brick into a wheelbarrow. "Zweigman and his wife nursed Davida through a sickness and when she came out, well, nothing was the same as it was before."

April. The same month Captain Pretorius discovered the German shopkeeper was actually a qualified surgeon. Did Zweigman reveal the extent of his medical skills during treatment of Davida's mysterious illness?

323

And if that were the case, how had Willem Pretorius found that out? The shy brown mouse was the only common link between the two men.

"Thanks for your help, Anton," Emmanuel said and held his hand out to end the informal interview. "Good luck with the clean-up."

He wanted to run through the connections between Willem Pretorius and Davida Ellis with Shabalala so he could clarify the links in his own mind. First, Donny Rooke sighted the captain behind the grid of coloured houses on the night he was murdered. Then Davida appeared at the stone hut. Somehow *Celestial Pleasures* had travelled from Zweigman's study to Pretorius's locked room as well. The elements were beginning to connect.

"Detective." Anton stayed half a step behind him. "I wasn't joking about Granny Mariah. She'll never forgive me if I cause trouble for her granddaughter."

Emmanuel didn't know how to tell the mechanic that Davida's troubles were likely to run far deeper and wider than a rumour spread by an ex-boyfriend. If the shy brown mouse proved to be the principal witness in the murder of a white police captain, everyone in South Africa was going to know her name and her face.

CHAPTER
SEVENTEEN

Granny Mariah and Davida were at work in the garden, planting seeds into a long row of freshly turned earth. The older woman's green eyes widened at the sight of the white policeman and his black offsider walking across her garden on a spring day.

"What do you want?" She straightened up and put her hands on her hips.

"I need to speak to Davida." Emmanuel remained calm and pleasant in the face of Granny Mariah's hostility. There wasn't much a non-white woman could do once the force of the law turned against her.

"What do you want with her?"

"That's between Davida and myself."

"Well, I won't have it. I won't have you coming in here and making trouble for my granddaughter."

"It's too late for that," Emmanuel said. He felt sorry for the fiery woman and admired the strength she showed in the face of overwhelming odds. This was a battle they both knew he was going to win.

"Granny ..." The shy brown mouse stepped forward. "It's all right. I'll talk to the detective."

"No. I won't have it."

"He's right," Davida said quietly. "It's too late."

The brown-skinned matriarch held onto her granddaughter's hand and squeezed tight. "Use the sitting room, baby girl," Granny Mariah said. "It's more comfortable."

"We'll talk in her room." Emmanuel walked to the small white building at the edge of the garden and opened the door. Inside the old servant's quarters he pulled up a chair from which to survey the interior of the room. The wrought-iron bed and bedside table were instantly familiar from the photographs. On the floor closest to the pillows was a neat stack of leather-covered books taken from Zweigman's library. All that was missing was a giant slab of white meat lying resplendent on the bed.

Davida entered the room and the images Emmanuel had seen after getting back from Lourenço Marques flashed through his mind. The fall of long dark hair across her face, the jewel hardness of her erect nipples against the white sheets, the sleek lines of her legs ending in a thatch of dark pubic hair . . . and Willem Pretorius ready to taste it all.

"Did you know Captain Pretorius?" he asked.

"Everyone knew him."

"I mean did you know him well enough to, say, have a talk with? That sort of thing?"

She turned to face the window, her fingers toying with the lace edge of the curtains. "Why are you asking me these questions?"

"Why aren't you answering?"

326

"Because you already know the answer. That's why you're here." Her breath made an angry sound as it escaped her mouth. "Why must I say it?"

"I need to hear it from you, in your own words."

"Okay." The shy brown mouse turned to him and he glimpsed the fighting spirit of Granny Mariah alive and well in her. "I was sleeping with Captain Pretorius in that bed right there. You happy now?"

"'Sleeping with' as in napping or 'sleeping with' as in fucking?"

"Most nights we did both." She was defiant, ready to burn all the remnants of herself as a good woman.

He liked the angry Davida a lot better than the milk-and-water version she peddled to the world.

"I'm wondering why a mixed-race woman would get involved with a married white man whose family lives just a few streets away. Do you like taking risks, Davida?"

"No. It wasn't like that."

"How was it?"

"I didn't want to." She scraped curls of flaking paint off the windowsill and rubbed the residue between her fingers. "He didn't want to."

"He forced himself, did he?" Emmanuel didn't try to hide his scepticism. How long did it take Willem Pretorius to raise the white flag and surrender to the pleasure of the wrought-iron bed? A day, a week, or possibly a whole month?

"He tried," Davida insisted. "First with abstinence and then with the photos, but those things didn't work."

"Tell me about the photographs," he said.

She'd volunteered the information without knowing he was in possession of printed copies. Maybe it made her feel better to admit to the things in her life that had been locked in the internal vault. Being a model in pornographic photographs was an illegal activity sure to have her barred from membership in the League for the Advancement of Coloured Women.

"Captain said if he had some photos to look at, then he wouldn't have to touch me. He said looking at pictures was a lesser sin than committing adultery."

"I see."

The differences between the two envelopes of photographs was stark. The first pictures were naive and gentle, the second explicit and untamed. Some time between shooting roll number one and roll number two, sin had won the battle for Captain Pretorius's soul.

"But the photographs didn't work and the two of you ended up committing adultery? Is that right?"

"Yes." Her voice dropped to a whisper. "That's what happened."

"What was your relationship like?"

"I already told you."

"So, Captain Pretorius would have sexual relations with you and leave immediately afterward? There was nothing more to it?"

"No. Captain liked to stay and talk for a while afterward."

"How would you describe your relationship with him? Good?"

"As good as it could be." She shrugged her shoulders. "There was never going to be wedding bells."

"Then why did you do it? Anton or any of the other coloured men in town would have been more suitable choices, wouldn't they?"

She made a sound of disbelief low in her throat. "Only a white man would ask a question like that and expect an answer."

Emmanuel felt he was seeing her for the first time. The meek coloured girl he could deal with, even ignore, but this furious sharp-eyed woman was something else altogether.

"What's the question got to do with my being white?"

"Only white people talk about choice like it's a box of chocolates that everyone gets to pick from. A Dutch police captain walks into this room and I say what to him? 'No, thank you, Captain sir, but I do not wish to spoil my chances for a good marriage with a good man from my community, so please *ma baas* take yourself back to your wife and family. I promise not to blackmail you if you promise not to punish my family for turning you away. Thank you for asking me, Mr Policeman. I am honoured.' Tell me, is that how it works for non-white women in Jo'burg, detective?"

Emmanuel felt the truth of her words. It was as if she'd slapped him hard with an open hand. He sat forward and considered the implications of what she'd said. A secret and illegal affair with an Afrikaner certainly delayed any chance of getting married or of beginning a serious relationship with someone in her own race group. Jacob's Rest was too small to cover that level of illicit activity. Davida Ellis was stuck in limbo: an unmarried mixed-race woman tied to a married white man.

"When was the last time you saw Captain Pretorius?"

The rush of colour brought on by her tirade against the white man ebbed away, leaving her curiously ashen.

"The night he died," she said.

"Where?"

"He came here to the room. He said for me to get my things because we were going out to the river. I didn't want to go but he was angry and said we were going."

"What was he angry about?"

"He caught Donny Rooke spying on him and had to give him a hiding as a warning. I cleaned the captain's hands with a cloth before we left because he'd split the skin on his knuckles."

That was one up for Donny and confirmation that Pretorius leaned hard when he had to. It was unlikely that Donny, the outcast, could have organised an assassination and a foray into Mozambique to cover his trail after the beating he'd taken. Donny wasn't nearly smart enough or strong enough for that.

"You didn't want to go out that night?"

"No." She fell back into her old ways and concentrated on her hands while she spoke. "I never liked going outside with the captain. I was scared that someone would see us."

330

"Pretorius had no such worries?"

"He said it was okay now that he knew who was spying on him and the river was his favourite place to . . . you know . . . to go."

Emmanuel remembered his impression of the crime scene and the distinct feeling that the victim might have been smiling when the bullet struck. Not so far off the mark, then.

"Captain Pretorius thought someone was spying on him before he caught Donny that night?"

"He said he knew there was someone out on the veldt and that he was going to catch him."

"When did he first tell you that someone was spying on him?"

"Three, four weeks or so before he died."

"He thought that man was Donny?"

"Yes. That's what the captain told me."

What on earth would lead Willem Pretorius to believe that Donny Rooke, of all people, was capable of cunning undercover surveillance? The watchful presence was still out there in the dark, and it sure as hell wasn't Donny.

"What happened then?" He believed everything Davida had said so far and wondered when she'd slip and try to cover up a hole in her story. Everyone had something to hide.

"We went to the police van and I got under the blanket in the back. We drove to Old Voster's farm. Captain got out and checked to see if everything was okay. He didn't come back for a long time and . . ." She took a deep breath. "I got scared, but then he came and said it was all clear, so we went down to the river."

She was breathing harder now, her chest rising and falling in an unsteady rhythm. She was like this in the stone hut. Scared to death.

"Go on."

"Captain spread the blanket out and then . . . well . . . that's when it happened. Two popping sounds and he fell forwards just like that."

"Captain Pretorius was standing by the blanket and you were sitting down?" Emmanuel asked. Something was missing from her description of the events.

"We were both on the blanket." She stared out the window like a prisoner watching a flock of birds soar above the barbed wire. "We were . . . he was . . . you know . . ."

"Davida, turn around and look at me," he said. "Tell me exactly what happened on the blanket. Don't leave anything out. I won't be angry or shocked."

She turned back to him but didn't lift her gaze from the middle button of his jacket. After what she'd done in the photographs, it was amazing to see a blush work its way up her neck and darken her skin.

"Captain was doing it to me from behind." Her voice was a reedy whisper of sound. "He finished and was doing up his buttons when I heard the two popping sounds. I didn't know what it was and then the captain fell forwards and I couldn't move. He was on me, lying on top of me. I tried to move but he was on top of me."

"What did you do then?"

"My heart was beating so loud that my ears were ringing. I was crying, too. Trying to get out from under the captain. That's how come I didn't hear him until he was behind me."

"Who?"

"The man."

"What man?"

"The man with the gun. He kicked my leg and said, 'Run. Look back and I'll shoot you.' I pushed myself out from under the captain and I ran. I fell over on the kaffir path and my necklace snapped but I didn't stop to look for it. I got up again and I ran until I got back home."

"This man. What language did he use?"

"English. With an accent."

"Tell me about the man. Did you see any part of him?"

"I was facing away and the captain was behind me. I didn't see him. I only heard him telling me to run."

"From his voice," Emmanuel said, "what would you guess? White, coloured, black, or Indian?"

"A Dutchman," she answered straight off. "A proper Afrikaner."

"Why do you say that?"

"His voice. A Boer used to giving orders."

That description matched ninety per cent of the men who'd attended Willem Pretorius's funeral. It was the same as finding a match for a man wearing khaki work pants or overalls.

He was sceptical about the appearance of "the man". Wasn't it a little too improbable, and convenient, to have a phantom Afrikaner descend from the sky to absolve her of involvement in the captain's murder?

"Did you know the man, Davida?"

"No, I didn't."

"Was it a coloured man? Someone from town?"

She looked up now, alert to the change in atmosphere. Her eyes were the colour of rain clouds.

"It was a white man," she repeated. "He spoke to me like I was a dog; like he enjoyed giving orders."

"Did you know the man, Davida?" He hit the question again and waited to see where she went with it.

"I told you. No." Her voice was pitched high with frustration. "I don't know who it was."

Emmanuel studied her face; strikingly pretty now that she'd ditched the novice nun pose and he could see her clearly. "He did you a favour, didn't he? The man. No more posing for illegal photos. No more lifting your skirt every time Pretorius came calling."

"That's not right. I didn't want to hurt the captain."

"Why not?" Emmanuel countered. "Sleeping with you is against the law. Making pornographic photographs is also against the law and yet he forced you to do both those things. That's right, isn't it? You couldn't say no to an Afrikaner police captain."

"That's true." The rain clouds burst and she wiped the tears from her face with a quick hand. Crying for a dead Dutchman in front of an Englishman. Could there be a more ridiculous thing for a mixed-race woman to do?

334

"You had feelings for him," Emmanuel said. He'd seen the photograph she'd taken of Pretorius. Davida and the captain shared more than just a mutual physical pleasure.

"I didn't love him." She was angry about the tears and the cool way he watched her struggling for control. "But I didn't hate him, either. He never did anything to hurt me. That's the truth."

"There's plenty of ways to hurt someone without raising a hand to them." His own anger came in a flash and he let ten per cent of it out to breathe. "What will happen when you testify in court and everyone in South Africa hears about the photos and the fact that you were a white policeman's *skelmpie*? Will that feel good or will that hurt? No matter. You can always remember how considerate Willem Pretorius was when he led you down the road to nowhere."

"You're cruel," she said.

Emmanuel stayed quiet for a moment. He'd gone too far.

"I'm sorry," he said. "Let's get back to the riverside. Is there anything else you can tell me about the man who shot Captain Pretorius? Anything at all will help."

It took her a while to recover from the terrifying spectre of the courtroom and the public fallout from the murder trial.

"He was quiet," Davida said. "Like a cat. I didn't know he was there until he was right behind me."

"You were frightened and crying," Emmanuel reminded her. "Hearing anyone would have been hard."

"I know but . . . it was like the time the Peeping Tom grabbed me. I didn't know he was there until right before he jumped. It was like that."

"Was the killer's accent the same as the man who grabbed you?" Emmanuel asked. No matter which way the case turned, the molester was always there, like a shadow.

"They both sounded strange." She looked directly at him, the connection clicking into place. "Like someone putting on a voice."

Well, if she was lying about the man at the river, he couldn't fault her performance. She appeared amazed not to have made the link before now between the killer on the riverbank and the molester.

Emmanuel digested the new information. It supported his sense that the captain's murder was tied to small-town secrets and lies and not part of an elaborate communist plot to derail the National Party government.

He stood up and brushed the creases from the front of his trousers. Two days ago he'd believed Davida was a shy virgin who shrank from the touch of men not of her own "kind". That perception was now a confirmed pile of horseshit and he was forced to give serious credence to her version of events regarding the captain's murder. He no longer trusted his instincts when it came to the captain's little wife.

Was that because, as the sergeant major suggested, there was something in her that stirred him? Emmanuel avoided looking at the wrought-iron bed and resisted the flood of uncensored images that came to him in a rush. Of all the times for his libido to rise from the dead, this would have to be the worst. Davida Ellis was a mixed-race woman and a key witness in the murder of an Afrikaner policeman: the devil's very brew.

Emmanuel turned his back on the bed and faced the window where she stood. "When did you take up with Pretorius? Before or after the molester stopped?"

"After. The first time the captain came into this room was to interview me about the attacker. That was the end of December."

"Do you remember being asked anything unusual by the captain?"

"Well . . ." She considered her answer. "Everything about the interview was strange. Not like with Lieutenant Uys, who asked three questions and then chased me out of the police station."

"Strange in what way? Tell me about it."

"Captain came here to this room by himself." She let that breach of protocol sink in. "He asked me to sit down on that chair and close my eyes. I did and then he asked me to think about the man who'd grabbed me. He asked a lot of questions. Was the Peeping Tom bigger or smaller than me? I said bigger but not by that much. What was his skin like? Rough or smooth? I said smooth with only a little roughness, like a man who works with his hands now and then. Did his skin smell of anything in particular? Coffee, cigarettes, grease, or soap — any of those things? I said no but his hands did smell familiar. Captain told me to keep my eyes shut and try to remember. Where had I come across the smell before?"

"Did you remember?"

"I said that Anton's hands smelled the same way. Like crushed gum leaves."

"You think Anton's the Peeping Tom?"

"No," Davida said. "Anton's hands are rough, like sandpaper, and his arms are hard with muscles. The man who grabbed me had soft hands and a smaller body than Anton's."

He didn't ask her how she knew those intimate details about Anton. Presumably she did a lot more than take the air when she went out walking with the lanky mechanic.

"How did Captain Pretorius react when you told him about the smell on the molester's hands?" There was no mention of the gum leaf smell in the record of interview typed up and filed after the captain's informal visit to the old servant's quarters. There had to be a reason for the omission.

Davida shifted uncomfortably, and then seemed to realise that both her reputation and the captain's were lost beyond any hope. Head up, she spoke to Emmanuel directly, in much the same way as Granny Mariah had outside the church.

"My eyes were closed. I didn't see his face but I know he was pleased. He stroked my hair and said, 'You're a clever girl to remember that, Davida.' I opened my eyes and he was halfway out of the door."

What was it about the town of Jacob's Rest? The heat, the isolation, or maybe just the proximity of the race groups appeared to make the exercise of power over others irresistible. Emmanuel himself had almost touched Davida's wet hair outside the captain's stone hut because he'd tasted the thrill of knowing that she was under his command and would keep his secrets safe. Wasn't that feeling of power just an extension of the white *induna* fantasy that the National Party was now enacting into law?

"Did you ever tell Anton about the connection with the Peeping Tom? Ever ask him what the crushed gum leaf smell was?"

"Captain Pretorius came back here three or four days later and it was hard to talk to Anton after that. I don't know what the smell was and the captain never mentioned it again."

"Did you always call him 'Captain'?"

The bold act evaporated and Davida went back to looking at the magic spot in front of her right toe. "He liked to be called Captain before and during and then Willem afterward."

Yes, well. A relationship with a morally upstanding Dutchman with a taste for pornography and adultery was bound to come with a dizzying level of complications and arcane rules. Emmanuel glanced around the room and took note of the hastily made bed and the dust motes dancing over the painted concrete floor. Seemed that Willem got all the neatness he needed at home and then came to this room to wallow in the mess and untidiness.

"Did you visit Pretorius at the stone hut?" he asked. The stone hut that was kept as fastidiously clean as the locked study in the immaculate Cape Dutch house but without the help of a maid.

"Yes, I did."

"When you'd finished calling him Captain Pretorius and then Willem, did you clean for him?"

She looked up now, grey eyes sparking with indignation. "I'm not a maid," she said.

No, she wasn't a maid and not overly fussy about housekeeping on the whole. Somebody had cleaned the stone hut to a hospital ward level of cleanliness. The only thing missing was the astringent smell of pine antiseptic. "Was the captain fussy about the interior of the hut? You know, did he have a place for everything and everything in its place?"

"No. He didn't care so much about keeping neat."

"Not in this room and not at the hut," Emmanuel said. In every other respect Willem Pretorius had kept himself very neat indeed. The immaculate white house with his immaculate white wife, the starched police uniform and spotless undershirts were all outside indications of his clean and spotless soul. Flip a coin and you got the shadow Willem, slumming naked in an unmade bed with a smile on his face. Why was the stone hut so clean? The captain hadn't been expecting any visitors.

"What were you doing at the hut?" Emmanuel asked.

"Getting the photos." She was nervous now, her shoulders straightening as she pulled herself out of her slouch. "I didn't want anyone to find them."

"Did your mother clean up the hut, Davida?"

"No."

"What did your father think about your relationship with Captain Pretorius? Did he approve?"

340

That threw her and she cupped a hand to her flushed cheek. "What are you talking about? My father died when I was a child. In a farm accident."

"I thought Willem Pretorius arranged for a bride price to be paid to your father in exchange for you?"

"Wh — what? Where did you get that from? That's a lie."

"Which lie are we talking about? The one about the bride price or the one about your father being dead?"

Davida quickly hid her fear and confusion in her shy brown mouse persona. "I told you the truth about Captain Pretorius and myself. I even told you what we were doing when he got shot. Why would I lie to you now, Detective Sergeant Cooper?"

"I don't know." He noted the correct use of his title. "But I'm sure you have your reasons."

He walked to the door, conscious of Shabalala waiting outside and of the gathering speed of the investigation. He had to make the connection between the molester and the captain's killer real enough to stand up in court. He needed evidence.

"Are you going to take me to the station?" she said.

"No."

The Security Branch and the Pretorius brothers were the last people he'd expose her to. She was safe so long as she remained an anonymous coloured woman working for an old Jew in a shabby local store. Once she'd been revealed as Captain Willem Pretorius's doxy the knives were going to come out and the punishment for her transgressions would be fierce.

"What do I do now?" She sounded lost now that everything about her secret life had been exposed.

"Stay here. You can help your granny in the garden but don't leave the property until I get back and tell you it's okay to move around."

"When will that be?"

"I don't know." He pulled the door halfway open, then stopped. "What happened back in April?"

"How do you know about that?"

"I don't. That's why I'm asking."

She hesitated, then said, "I had a miscarriage. Dr Zweigman made sure everything was cleaned up and healed but the captain thought he killed the baby. They had a fight about it. I never talked about Dr Zweigman with the captain after that and I never talked about the captain with Dr Zweigman, but we all knew."

"I'm sorry," Emmanuel said and stepped out of the room and into the garden. He was sorry to have ever heard of Jacob's Rest. He was also sorry to discover that the disconnect switch, the one that allowed him to endure the grisliest murder investigations without getting emotionally involved, no longer worked.

CHAPTER
EIGHTEEN

"Crushed gum leaves . . ." Emmanuel said to the mechanic after he and Shabalala had made their way back to the garage. "What do you use on your hands that has that particular smell?"

Anton rummaged in a wooden bucket and pulled out a tin can stamped with an impression of a slender leaf with jagged thunderbolts spiking out from it. "Degreaser. Us mechanics use it to clean up. It gets the dirt up from around the nails and between the fingers."

"Who would use this particular cleaner?" Emmanuel prised opened the top and sniffed the thick white slurry. The gum leaf smell was intense. "Just mechanics, or anyone fixing machinery?"

"Well, it's not cheap, so it wouldn't be used by someone fiddling around with their bicycle or bore pump. The only other place I've seen this stuff in town is at the Pretorius garage."

"Is that where you get your supply?"

Anton laughed. "Good heavens! Can you imagine Erich Pretorius letting me buy anything from his place? No, I get my little sister to bring back two or three cans when she comes home from Mooihoek for the holidays.

She's at boarding school there. She was only down this weekend because of the funeral."

"You'd notice if a can was missing?"

"Definitely. I string my supply out over the year. Like I said, it's expensive. December's supply has got to last to Easter, then I have to stretch the next one to August."

"December and August?" Emmanuel gave the can of precious cleaner back to Anton and pulled out his notebook. Something was nudging his memory. "Why those months in particular?"

"School holidays," Shabalala said. "My youngest son comes home also at these times."

The molester was active during two distinct periods: August and December. Emmanuel gave his notes a quick check. That was right. He checked specific dates with Anton. The attacks occurred during the holidays and at no other time of year. The attacker might be partial to schoolgirls. Or on school holidays himself.

"Gentlemen." Zweigman appeared holding a container of his wife's butter biscuits as an entrée into the conversation. "My wife will be upset if I do not deliver these as promised."

"The molester? What made you think it was a white man?" Emmanuel said.

"I have no proof. Just a feeling that the colour of his skin is the reason why he was not caught and brought to trial."

"Okay." Emmanuel included all three men in the conversation. "Let's assume the molester was a

Dutchman. Are there any white men that you know of who are only here in town for the big school holidays?"

Zweigman, Anton and Shabalala all shook their heads in the negative. Emmanuel moved on. "Which white boys were at boarding school last year? I'm talking about boys over the age of fourteen."

"The Loubert boys, Jan and Eugene," said Anton. "Then there was Louis Pretorius and I believe the Melmons' son Jacob. I don't know about the Dutch boys out on the farms."

"What about Hansie?" It was a ludicrous thought but Emmanuel had to cover all the bases. Whittling down the suspect list by scraping together pieces of information on white schoolboys was a primitive science at best.

"Training," Shabalala answered. "The constable was at the police college during the last half of the year."

"The boys who were away at school last year? Did any of them ever get caught on the kaffir paths after dark?"

"Louis and the Loubert boys," Anton replied. "They were using the path to obtain . . . um, things that the captain thought were unhealthy."

"Liquor and *dagga* from Tiny? Is that right?"

"*Ja.*" Anton lifted his eyebrows in amazement. "I thought only Captain Pretorius and the coloured people knew about that. It was kept pretty quiet."

"Small town," Emmanuel said. "Which of those three boys would have access to the cleaner?"

"Louis for sure," Anton answered again. "The boy is always messing around with engines and fixing things up. He's good with his hands and Erich lets him have whatever he wants from the garage."

"Was Louis home for the August and December holidays?" Emmanuel asked Shabalala.

"Yes," Shabalala said. "He came back for all the holidays. The missus does not like him staying too long away."

That was three out of three for Louis. He knew the kaffir path almost as well as a native; he was home for the holidays; and he had easy access to the eucalyptus-scented cleaner. Those facts alone warranted an interview even though the idea of the boy as the molester still seemed ludicrous.

Emmanuel went back to the bit about Louis being good with his hands. On the first day of the investigation Louis had given the distinct impression that his father was the mechanical whiz. He'd said as much.

"I thought the captain was letting Louis help him fix up an old motorbike," Emmanuel said.

"Other way around. The captain was helping Louis. There's not much that boy doesn't know about engines but the captain was always asking for help after he'd stuffed something up."

"You think Louis is capable of finishing that Indian motorbike without help?"

"Completely." Anton placed his precious supply of antigrease cleaner into the wooden bucket. "Beats me why he went to bible college when he should have been working at his brother's place. Being a mechanic suits him a hell of a lot better than being a pastor."

346

"Yes, but it doesn't suit his mother." Mrs Pretorius had a pretty clear idea about her youngest son's future: a future free of oil stains and overalls.

"The school holiday inquiry is an interesting one," Zweigman broke in politely. "But that does not explain why the attacks stopped in the middle of the Christmas holidays and have not recurred."

"You're right, December twenty-sixth was the last reported attack. That still leaves how much of the holiday?"

"The first week of January," Shabalala replied so softly that Emmanuel turned to him. The Zulu constable looked just as he had on the banks of the river the moment before they pulled Captain Pretorius from the water. His face carried sadness too deep to be expressed with words.

"The Drakensberg." Emmanuel remembered Hansie's drunken ramblings out on the veldt. When had the captain sent Louis "a long way away" after discovering the drinking and *dagga* smoking? "Is that where he was, Shabalala?"

"*Yebo*," the Zulu man said. "The young one, Mathandunina, was taken by the captain on the first day of January to a place in the Drakensberg mountains in Natal. I do not know why."

Emmanuel scribbled van Niekerk's name and phone number and a query onto a page in his notebook, tore it out, and handed it to Zweigman.

"Call this number and ask this man, Major van Niekerk, if he has an answer to this question. Constable

347

Shabalala and I will be back within the hour. If not, look for us in the police cells."

It was five past twelve and Miss Byrd was sitting on the back steps of the post office, chewing on a canned meat sandwich made with thick slices of soft white bread. She was startled to see both the detective sergeant and the Zulu policeman walking towards her.

"The engine part that Louis Pretorius is waiting for? Has it come in yet?" Emmanuel said.

"It came the day before his father passed. Tragic, hey? Captain not getting to ride the motorbike after all the hard work he and Louis put into it. To be so close and not . . ."

"I thought Louis was coming to the post office every day to check for the part?"

"No." Miss Byrd smiled. "He calls in to collect the mail for his mother. He's very considerate that way, a very sweet young boy."

"Yes, and Lucifer was the most beautiful of all God's angels," Emmanuel said. He and Shabalala walked back onto the kaffir path. They started as one towards the captain's shed. He'd told the Zulu constable about the attack in the stone hut and the mechanical rattle he'd heard just before passing out.

"Looks like he dismantled the bike after he finished it, so no-one knew he had transport." Emmanuel took a guess at the sequence of events. "I'm willing to bet that Pretorius didn't know anything about the engine part arriving from Jo'burg."

"He said nothing of it to me."

They picked up the pace and jogged in unison across the stretch of veldt that swung around the back of the police station and curved past the rear fence line of the houses facing onto van Riebeeck street. The noon sun had burned away the clouds to reveal a canopy of blue.

"You don't have to come in," Emmanuel said when they'd stopped outside the shed door. "Right or wrong, this is going to cause big trouble."

"That one inside." Shabalala hadn't even broken a sweat on the run. "He is the only one who knew which kaffir paths the captain was running on. I wish to hear what he has to say to this."

Emmanuel gave the door a shove with his shoulder, expecting resistance, but found none. The door swung open to reveal the darkened interior of the work shed. He stepped inside. Both Louis and the motorcycle were gone. Emmanuel walked over to the spot where the Indian had been resting on blocks and found a large oil stain but nothing else.

"The little bastard's taken off on his motorbike. You have any idea where he could have gone, Shabalala?"

"Detective Sergeant —"

Dickie and two new Security Branch men wrestled the Zulu constable from the open doorway then shoved him back onto the veldt. Lieutenant Piet Lapping entered wearing a sweat — and ash-stained shirt and rumpled pants. Lack of sleep had made his craggy face look like a bag of marbles stuffed into a white nylon stocking.

"Lieutenant Lapping." Emmanuel smelled the anger and frustration coming directly off Piet's sweat-beaded skin and concentrated on remaining calm. The Security Branch couldn't nail him for anything. Not yet.

"Sit down." Piet indicated the chair in front of the hunting desk. Dickie and his two bulldozer pals followed and took up positions at either side of the door. Emmanuel did as he was told and sat down.

"Dickie." Piet held out his hand and took a thin folder from his second in command, which he held up for closer inspection. "You know what this is, Cooper?"

"A file," Emmanuel said. It was the information folder delivered by special messenger on the day he'd gone to Mozambique.

"A file . . ." Piet paused and rummaged in his pants pocket for a cigarette. "Sent especially to us by district headquarters. Have you seen this particular file before, Cooper?"

"No, I have not."

Piet lit his cigarette and allowed the flame from his silver lighter to burn longer than necessary before snapping it shut with a hard click. He placed the file gently onto Emmanuel's lap.

"Take a good look at it. Open it up and tell me if you see anything unusual about the contents."

Emmanuel cracked the yellow cover and made a show of checking the inside before closing the file and resting his hands on the folder.

"It's empty."

"Hear that, Dickie? It's empty." Ash from the lieutenant's cigarette fell onto the file but Emmanuel did nothing to remove it. "It's obvious to me now that Cooper was promoted quick smart because he's sharp.

350

He's got it up here, in the *kop*, where it counts. Isn't that so, Detective Sergeant?"

Emmanuel shrugged. They weren't having a conversation; Lieutenant Lapping was running through the standard textbook interrogation warm-up that demanded the interrogator make at least some attempt to extract information via voluntary confession. Beating suspects was hell on the hands and the neck muscles and from the look of him Piet was coming off a heavy night in the police cells.

"I'm not angry." The lieutenant went down on his haunches like a hunter checking a spoor trail. "I just want to know how the fuck you managed to extract the contents of a confidential file while it was under lock and key."

Up close, Emmanuel saw the blue smudges of exhaustion under pockmarked Piet's eyes and smelled the gut-churning mix of blood and sweat coming off his person. It was a rank abattoir fug overlaid with the mild lavender perfume of a common brand of soap.

Emmanuel did his best not to pull back from the Security Branch officer. "Maybe district headquarters forgot to include them," he said.

Piet smiled, then took a deep drag of his cigarette. "See, with any other team of police I'd buy that explanation. But this is my team and my team doesn't make mistakes."

"I'd go back to district headquarters and see who typed the report and posted the file," Emmanuel suggested.

"Done all that," Piet replied almost pleasantly. "And what I found was this: you, Detective Sergeant Cooper, were the person who helped the messenger sign the folder into the police box when it arrived in town."

"I was being polite. One department of the police is supposed to help another department, isn't it?"

"My first thought is that your close friend van Niekerk tipped you off about what was in the folder. You knew the file was coming and somehow you managed to lift the contents. Did one of those spinsters at the post office let you into the police box? We've been too busy to ask them in person but I think an hour alone with me will get them to open up, so to speak."

The Security Branch operatives laughed at Piet's provocative turn of phrase and Emmanuel sensed the group's anticipation at the possibility of questioning two country maids. Affable and trusting Miss Byrd with her fondness for feather hats. Five minutes in Lieutenant Lapping's company and she'd be broken for good.

"Why are you chasing postal clerks? I thought you had a communist in the bag, ready to confess. Did something go wrong at the station?"

Piet's dark eyes were dead at the very centre. "The first thing you will have to accept, Detective, is that I am smarter than you. I know you took those pages and I will find out how. I will also find out why."

"No confession, then? What a shame. Paul Pretorius was certain it would only take and hour or two for the suspect to open up, so to speak."

352

Piet smiled and the dark centre of his pupils came alive with a bright flash of intent. "I promised Dickie that he could work on you if the time ever came, but I've changed my mind. I'm going to enjoy seeing you crack myself."

"Like you cracked the suspect at the station?" Emmanuel said. A Security Branch officer he might be, but Lieutenant Lapping had superiors to report to, generals and colonels hungry for a victory against enemies of the state.

Lieutenant Lapping blinked hard, twice, then got to his feet and strode to the doorway. He put his hand out and Dickie placed a brown paper envelope in it with a look that sent a chill down Emmanuel's back.

What the hell did they have? It was good. It had to be. Keep calm, he told himself. You've been through a war. You've seen things that killed other men and you survived. What was there to be scared of?

"You know what's in here?" Piet held the envelope at eye level.

"I don't have a clue." Emmanuel found that he sounded calm despite the sick rolling of his stomach. What the hell was in the envelope? Had they somehow got a new background report on him in the last fourteen hours?

Piet opened the envelope and extracted two photos, which he held up with schoolmarmish precision. "Tell me, Cooper, have you seen these images before?"

There wasn't time to slip the mask of indifference back into place. He tried to make sense of it, to see all the angles at the same time, but he couldn't get past the stark black-and-white images of Davida Ellis first with her legs spreadeagled and then stretched out on the bed like a cat waiting to be stroked. His copies were halfway to Jo'burg, safely packed under a layer of pink plastic rollers in Delores Bunton's luggage. Unless . . . unless the Security Branch had somehow intercepted his courier.

"So . . ." Piet ground his cigarette out with the heel of his shoe. "You have seen them before."

"Where did you get them?"

"We found them exactly where you left them. Under your pillow."

Was Piet telling the truth or just trying to catch him out in a lie? He had no idea and that was just the way the Security Branch boys liked it. Until he knew exactly where the photographs came from he was going to play for time and information.

"What were you doing in my room?" he asked. "You looked through it the other day and didn't find anything."

"Some fresh information came to light." Piet signalled to Dickie, who took the photos, but remained standing by his partner's side. "Information concerning your personal tastes."

Dickie made a tutting sound and leered at the images of the woman. "That's two laws broken right there, Cooper. If it was a white woman or a light-skinned one we might have turned a blind eye but this . . . this is serious business."

"Where did you get the information from?" Emmanuel asked. It seemed that both Dickie and Piet

354

were playing the personal angle. They were tying the photographs to his alleged perversions and not to the homicide investigation. Good. That meant the bundle of photos he'd sent off on the "Intundo Express" bus this morning were safe. The feeling of triumph passed quickly. He was still in hot water, caught in possession of banned materials.

"Who told us about the photos, Dickie?"

"A little bird," Dickie replied as if the expression was something he'd just made up off the top of his head.

Emmanuel glanced at the photos. If his copies were safely on their way to van Niekerk in Jo'burg, then these images must have come from the safe in the captain's stone hut. It was the only logical explanation, and all the connections he'd made this morning pointed to the thief being the captain's youngest son.

"Was it pretty boy Louis who told you where to find the photos?" Emmanuel kept his eye on Dickie to see if the name and the description triggered a reaction. What he got wasn't a subtle clenching of the jawline but a teeth-baring snarl.

"How you can even mention his name after what you —"

"Dickie!" Piet interrupted. "I know this kind of activity upsets you but you must remove your personal feelings from the work. We are miners and it is our job to find the seam of gold in the dirt. You cannot let the dirt bother you."

Activity? The word stuck with Emmanuel. What activity would upset Dickie enough to warrant professional counselling from his superior officer in the

355

middle of questioning? The answer made Emmanuel sit up straight. How deep was the hole the angelic-looking boy had dug for him?

"Louis says I molested him?"

"What exactly are you doing here in the shed, Cooper?"

"Gathering evidence." Emmanuel stemmed the rising panic. The blond boy had set a stunning trap baited with banned images and topped it off with an accusation guaranteed to outrage every red-blooded male in Jacob's Rest.

Dickie snorted. "A pervert looking for a pervert. That's a good one."

"Go back and stand with the others," Piet instructed his partner with a flex of his knotted shoulder muscles. "I'm too tired to question Sergeant Cooper and instruct you in the finer points of the work."

"But —"

Piet gave Dickie a look that sent him lumbering back to his corner, from where he glared at Emmanuel as if it was his fault that he'd been dismissed from the action.

"Well, which one is it?" Emmanuel asked. "Do I enjoy looking at dark girls or chasing white boys?"

"They're not mutually exclusive. You could have used the photographs to stimulate the interest of a boy who would otherwise find you unattractive. You get my drift?"

"Why the hell would I choose to show an Afrikaner boy photographs of a coloured woman in order to arouse him? What kind of sense does that make?"

"Maybe those are the only photographs you could get hold of."

"We're policemen. Either one of us could get pictures of a white girl doing everything except fucking a gorilla. The cops and the criminals always have the best stuff, you know that."

"You're right." Piet patted his shirt pocket and extracted a squashed cigarette pack. "But that doesn't take Louis Pretorius's complaint away. A jury won't think about the finer points, like the race of the woman in the photos. The fact that it's a coloured woman will only get you more prison time."

Why had Louis exposed himself so openly? He must have known that planting the photos would finger him as the person who'd stolen the evidence from the stone hut and yet he'd done it anyway.

"Did Louis swear out a formal complaint against me in writing?" Emmanuel asked. How serious was Louis about keeping him hemmed down and out of action?

"Yes."

"Show it to me," Emmanuel said.

The Security Branch men were in the middle of breaking the biggest case of their careers. Where did they find the time to pen a formal report on the matter of an English pervert attempting to corrupt an Afrikaner country boy? Small potatoes compared to getting a confession from a Communist Party member tied to the premeditated murder of a police captain married to Frikkie van Brandenburg's daughter.

"You don't get to ask us for anything," Piet said.

"Arrest me and charge me," Emmanuel said clearly, to make sure there was no confusion. He didn't believe they had more than Louis's verbal complaint and that wasn't enough to hold a fellow white policeman behind bars. Right at this moment he had better things to do than provide a break for the exhausted Security Branch officers.

"You know what I think?" Piet said. "I think the file you stole had the dirt on you and your pal van Niekerk, on your mutual affection and your shared interest in boys. Penny to a pound, that's the reason he tipped you off about it."

"Why don't you call district headquarters and get them to tell you exactly what was in the file, or is it a bad time to admit you lost the pages? No confession and no file. Your superiors will be pleased to hear that."

There was movement at the door and Dickie shuffled aside to let the moon-faced policeman in the badly cut suit into the shed.

"*Ja?*" Piet gave the newcomer permission to speak.

"It's been an hour, Lieutenant. You said to find you and alert you of the time."

Piet checked his watch with a weary shake of his head. Where did the minutes go? "You are free to leave, Cooper, but before you go I should warn you about something."

Emmanuel waited for the threat. He wasn't about to play second fiddle in Piet's grand orchestration of events by asking him to specify the nature of the warning.

358

"Louis came to the station and complained to his brother about your . . . attentions. You're lucky we were there to stop Paul Pretorius and the rest from coming after you straight away. I can't make any promises regarding your safety because we have more important things to attend to at the moment."

The Security Branch officers had regained some of their spark. They were letting him go because he was a minor impediment to the smooth running of their investigation. An hour to shake the tree for the information about the missing file contents and Louis's allegations was all they'd allowed while Moon Face kept watch on the real prize back at the police cells. God knows what position they'd left the young man from Fort Bennington College in while they took a quick break: strung up by his thumbs or suffocating in a wet post office canvas bag?

"Has it ever occurred to you," Emmanuel said, "that the man at the station hasn't confessed to the murder because he isn't the killer?"

Piet turned on him. "The kaffir was at the river at the same time and the same place as Captain Pretorius. We have the right man and by nightfall we'll have a signed confession. What have you got, Cooper? Some sad pictures of a coloured whore and a whole family of Afrikaner men ready to skin you alive. You were only on the case because Major van Niekerk was desperate for a piece of the action and now it is time for you to fuck off and let us get on with our jobs. You are way out of your depth. Understand?"

"Perfectly," Emmanuel said. How would he end the day: beaten and kicked to shit by the Pretorius brothers or with the killer behind bars? A betting man would lay two to one on a beating. The only unknown factor was the time and the severity of the punishment.

The shed emptied. The wide stretch of the veldt spread all the way to the horizon. How was he going to find one boy in all that space?

The call, a series of short whistles followed by a soft coo, was nothing Emmanuel had ever heard before. He stepped onto the kaffir path and the birdcall repeated with a loud insistence that caught and held his attention for a second time. A thick tangle of green scrub stirred and Shabalala materialised from the underbrush like a phantom. The Zulu constable stood to his full height and waved towards the bush with an insistence that seemed to say "run like hell", so Emmanuel did. He ran across grass and dirt, followed now by the sound of male voices in the captain's garden. He was level with the wild hedge when Shabalala grabbed him and threw him down to the ground.

Emmanuel tasted dust and felt his shoulder spasm with pain as he was held down on the ground by the Zulu's powerful hands.

"Shhh . . ." Shabalala put his finger to his lips and pointed in the direction of the captain's shed.

Emmanuel peered through the slender gap Shabalala had made in the bush cover. The Pretorius brothers were in the empty shed, searching for the English detective who'd tried to corrupt their baby brother. Henrick and Paul were the first ones out onto the kaffir path, rifles slung across their backs in a show of armed strength.

"Fuck." Paul spoke the word with venom, his frustration evident in the hard set of his shoulders.

"He can't have gone far." Henrick was calmer. "Take Johannes and go round the hospital and the coloured houses. Erich and I will go this direction past the shops. We'll meet up behind Kloppers."

"What if he's not on the kaffir path? What if he's gone bush?"

"Englishmen from the city don't go bush." Henrick was dismissive. "He'll be in town, hiding somewhere like a rat."

Johannes, the quiet foot soldier of the Pretorius corps, stepped out of the shed with his hands sunk deep into his pockets. "The motorbike. It's gone but I don't see how. Louis is still waiting for the part to come from Jo'burg."

"We're not looking for the fucking motorbike." Paul turned his frustrations onto his brother. "We're trying to find that detective."

"Well, he's not in the shed." Erich joined the musclebound trio. "He must have heard us coming and taken off into the veldt."

"If he's out there, he won't last long," Henrick said. "First we'll check the kaffir path and then the Protea Guesthouse. If we don't find him, we'll have a sit-down and decide which houses to search."

The brothers split up and moved along the grass path in opposite directions. Only Johannes appeared uncertain as to the purpose of their mission. He gave the empty shed one last puzzled glance before following Paul in a quick march towards the Grace of God Hospital.

The hunting party begin their first sweep of the town. The Pretorius boys had taken the law into their own hands and no-one was going to stop them.

"How am I going to find Louis and dodge his brothers at the same time?" Emmanuel wondered aloud. The smallness of the town made it impossible to escape the Pretorius family and the unbroken stretch of veldt made it unlikely that the boy could be found without an army of searchers.

"We will find him," Shabalala said.

Emmanuel turned to the Zulu policeman; Shabalala needed to know exactly how deep the water was before he stepped into it. "Louis has told his brothers that I interfered with him. It is not true, but the brothers believe him and if you are caught with me they will punish you also."

"Look." The black man shrugged off the warning and pointed to a shallow dip carved into the ground and camouflaged by the thick brush. Inside the hollow was a can wrapped in oilskin cloth. He pulled out the package and handed it over for inspection. Emmanuel unwrapped the can and sniffed at the still damp oilskin wrapping.

"Petrol," he said. "Louis's?"

362

"I think the young one kept it here to fill his motorbike. The can is empty."

"Mathandunina is planning to travel," Emmanuel said. "The border was just a few miles away. If Louis slipped across to Mozambique it would take months to track him, and that's if the Mozambican police decided to cooperate. Can you point the direction Louis is headed in?"

"I can find where the young one has gone," Shabalala said without arrogance. "I will go to the shed and follow the tracks. You must follow me out here on the veldt. It is not good for you to be on the path."

"Agreed," Emmanuel said and the Zulu constable walked to the deserted shed and stood for a while, examining the prints in the sand. He turned in the direction of the Grace of God Hospital and set off at a measured pace. Louis hadn't taken off across the veldt in a haze of petrol fumes and churned grass like an impulsive teenager blowing off steam. He had stuck close to the outer edge of the town for some reason. And, Emmanuel figured, there had to be one: everything Louis had done so far was planned and thought out. The boy was slippery enough to fool his own father about the motorbike — an impressive task when you considered just how secretive and two-faced the captain had been. Like father, like son.

Emmanuel picked up his pace to catch up with Shabalala, who followed the trail to the edge of the sports club playing fields. They crossed from the white side of Jacob's Rest to the rows of coloured houses and then the paths that led north to the black location. Where the hell was Louis headed?

The buildings of the hospital came into view. Emmanuel and Shabalala sidled past the morgue and the non-whites' wing. It was the same stretch of the kaffir path where the captain had parked when he came to pick up Davida Ellis for their last outdoor frolic — and where Donny Rooke had had the bad luck to be at the same time.

The distinctive line of gum trees that marked Granny Mariah's property was visible up ahead and to the left. A memory stirred and Emmanuel moved faster. He had good reason to know this place as well. It was here, within sight of that back fence, that he'd encountered the watchful human presence breathing in the darkness.

Shabalala stepped off the kaffir path and headed into the veldt at a right angle so that he was almost directly in front of him.

"What is it?" Emmanuel asked when he reached the spot where the Zulu constable was crouched down to inspect an area of disturbed earth.

"He has come off the path and parked his motorbike here." Shabalala pointed to markings in the dirt that wouldn't make sense to anyone but a tracker. "The young one has parked and then walked back in that direction."

They looked towards the line of gum trees. The back gate to Granny Mariah's garden swung back and forth on its hinges in the breeze. Thoughts of the Pretorius brothers' vigilante rule vanished and he and Shabalala ran to the kaffir path and the open gate.

364

One step into the yard and Emmanuel spotted Granny Mariah lying in a furrow of turned earth, the blood from the gash in her forehead feeding the newly planted seeds in a steady red stream. He ran to her side and felt for a pulse. Faint but there. He turned to Shabalala, who was wisely locking the gate behind him.

"Go out the front door and get the old Jew. Tell him to bring his bag and his wife's sewing kit with him."

Shabalala hesitated.

"Go out the front," Emmanuel insisted. The coloureds of Jacob's Rest would just have to deal with the shocking sight of a black man leaving and entering Granny Mariah's house in plain sight. "The Pretorius boys are still on the kaffir paths, so you have to use the main streets. Get back as quickly as you can without causing a commotion."

"*Yebo.*" The Zulu constable disappeared into the house and Emmanuel took off his jacket and rolled it under Granny Mariah's battered head. He felt her pulse again. No change, so he went to search the old servant's quarters, already certain he would find it empty. He put his head in and looked for signs of Davida before checking under the bed to make sure she wasn't hiding there.

"Davida? It's Detective Sergeant Cooper. Are you here?" He opened the wardrobe. A few cotton dresses and one winter coat with fake tortoiseshell buttons. He walked out to the garden, where he soaked his handkerchief in the watering bucket and gently wiped Granny Mariah's bloodied face. This mess was exactly what the information in the molester files pointed to:

an escalation of violence leading to deprivation of liberty and God knows what else. The captain had only delayed the inevitable by sending Louis off to a farm in the mountains and then on to theological college, where, it would seem, the Holy Spirit had failed to dampen the fires of sin burning within him.

Granny Mariah groaned in pain but remained unconscious. Just as well. The disappearance of her granddaughter would be a heavy burden for the normally resilient old woman to shoulder in her weakened state. She'd be lucky to get her head off the pillow in the next few days.

Zweigman hurried into the garden with Shabalala trailing close behind. The white-haired German got to work quickly, his expert hands checking vital signs and determining the range and extent of injuries.

"Bad. But, thank God, not fatal."

"How bad?"

"A laceration to the scalp which will require stitching. Severe concussion but the skull is not fractured." Zweigman the surgeon took control. "We will need to move her inside so I can clean her up and begin closing this wound. Please, go into the house and locate towels and sheets while Constable Shabalala and I move her to a bedroom."

Emmanuel followed orders and soon Zweigman was setting up. He snapped open his medical bag and placed bandages, needles, thread and antiseptic on a dresser closest to the double bed where Shabalala had laid the unconscious Granny Mariah.

Emmanuel signalled to Shabalala to move out to the garden. They stood at the back door and in view of the bloodied row of turned earth.

"Davida is gone. The captain's youngest son has taken her. There can be no other explanation," Emmanuel said.

"I will see." Shabalala examined the markings on the ground. He worked his way slowly to the back gate, unlocked it and continued out onto the veldt. Why, Emmanuel wondered, did he find it necessary to have the Zulu constable confirm the obvious? Was it because he still didn't trust his instinct where Davida was concerned and therefore couldn't rid himself of the niggling feeling that maybe, just maybe, Davida and Louis were somehow in this together? Two star-crossed lovers bound together by the cold-blooded murder of Willem Pretorius. But that conclusion was no more far-fetched than the teenaged boy turning out, in all probability, to be the molester.

Shabalala re-entered the garden and locked the gate behind him. His expression was grave. "It is so," he said. "The young one has taken the girl with him and they have gone on the motorbike."

"Did he take her or did she go with him?"

Shabalala pointed to scuffled lines in the dirt. "She ran but he caught her and pulled her back to where the old one was lying in the dirt. After that, the girl went with him quietly."

"Why would Louis show his hand before we'd even questioned him?"

"We must find Mathandunina," Shabalala said with simple eloquence. "Then we will know."

Finding Louis would be a massive task requiring manpower and time — two things he didn't have and was unlikely to get any time soon.

"What direction did he go in?" Emmanuel asked, visualising the enormous stretch of veldt that surrounded Jacob's Rest on all sides and spread out across the border into Mozambique. He brought himself back to the blood-soaked garden. He had to work with what he had: a Zulu-Shangaan tracker and an enigmatic German Jew. Things could be worse; he could have been left with Constable Hansie Hepple.

"Towards the location. It is also the way to *Nkosana* King's land and the farm of Johannes, the fourth son."

"Where would a white boy on a motorbike go with a brown-skinned girl he's holding against her will?" The whole thing carried the stamp of disaster. Surely Louis saw that?

"Not to the location."

"Or to his brother's farm. Wherever he goes, Louis is going to attract a lot of attention. My guess is he's going to have to keep well hidden until he's —"

"Done with her." Zweigman finished the sentence from where he stood in the dim hallway, his shopkeeper's shirt and trousers stained with blood from the operation. "That is what you were thinking, is it not, Detective?"

"I don't know what to think. As far as I can see, the whole abduction makes no sense."

368

"Maybe it makes perfect sense to Louis Pretorius."
Zweigman reached into his pocket and pulled out a
piece of paper, which he handed over. "Your major said
to pass this on to you as soon as possible."

Emmanuel unfolded the lined sheet and read the
information. Deep in the Drakensberg Mountains of
Natal was a farm, a retreat, known as Suiwer Sprong,
or Pure Springs, where high-bred and wealthy
Afrikaners with close ties to the new ruling party sent
their offspring to be "realigned" with the Lord. Shock
therapy, drug therapy and water therapy were some of
the ways that "realignment" was delivered from the
hands of the Almighty to the suffering few. A Dr Hans
de Klerk, who'd trained under the pioneering German
eugenicist Klaus Gunther prior to the outbreak of the
Second World War, was head of the set-up.

"A nut farm with a religious bent. Is van Niekerk
sure of this?"

"Your major sounds like a man who is sure of many
things. He is certain that this place in the Drakensbergs
is the only institution that a family such as the
Pretoriuses would use to seek treatment for a
psychological illness."

The family should get their money back. Whatever
therapy Louis underwent hadn't stuck. A few weeks
back in Jacob's Rest and Louis had fallen into his old
habits in a more dangerous way than before.

Emmanuel considered the steps that had led to the
abduction and assault. Louis wasn't unbalanced
enough to overlook the fact that Davida Ellis was the
only one who could tie him to the molester case and to

the murder of his father. With Davida out of the way, all that stood between him and freedom was the word of the English detective he'd accused of trying to seduce him. It was a clever plan, well executed. So far.

"This abduction may not be as irrational as it looks." Emmanuel recalled the information from the molester files. Reading them had given him the feeling that the perpetrator was headed for a violent culmination to his fantasy life. "Louis gets to finish what he started in December and he gets to eliminate the only person who can connect him, however vaguely, to the murder of his father."

"If that is the case," Zweigman observed quietly, "he will keep her alive until he has enacted his fantasies."

"I think so." Emmanuel didn't want to delve into the German's statement. He turned to Shabalala. "Where could Louis go and hide out without being found? It has to be a place large enough to hold two people. I don't think he'll go to the captain's hut. It's not secret enough. Is there a cave or maybe an old hunting shack?"

The Zulu constable glanced up at the sky for a moment to think. Then he quickly picked up a long stick and drew a crude map in the dirt. He made three crosses at almost opposite ends of each boundary.

"There are three places on *Nkosana* King's farm that are known to me. The captain and I hid here many times when we were boys. The young one, Louis, has also been to these places with his father when the land was still with the family."

"Can we get to all three in an afternoon?"

"They are far from each other and this one, here, we must go to on foot. It is a cave high on the side of a mountain and the bush is thick around."

"The other two?"

"This one is an old house where an Afrikaner lived by himself. It is falling in but some of the rooms have a roof over them."

"What's it like? The area around the house?"

"Flat. The house is sad, like the white man who used to live in it."

"That's not the place." Emmanuel pictured the crime scene at the river, the sweep of land and sky shimmering with a quintessentially African light. It was a beautiful place to die. Louis and his father both shared a taste for forbidden flesh and they might have been sufficiently alike to prefer courting women in an outdoor setting. There was nothing like the raw beauty of nature to arouse an Adam and Eve fantasy in which the apple was eaten to the core and the racial segregation laws were nonexistent.

"To which one of these places would you take a girl to show her the view?"

Shabalala pointed to the location of the mountain cavern. "From the ledge in front of the cave you can see the whole country and a watering hole where the animals come to drink. It is a place to stir the heart."

Just the sort of isolated and romantic spot a deranged Dutch boy might take a woman on her final outing. The Afrikaner love of the land was as tenacious as the influenza virus.

371

The cave was a long shot. But it made sense. The boy hadn't torn out onto the veldt with a captive girl without a specific place to hide already in mind. And Louis wasn't going to hide on a working farm trampled over by labourers and herds of cattle. King's personal fiefdom, once the Pretorius family home, had plenty of open space and very few people to spoil the illusion that South Africa was, in fact, empty when the white man arrived. Louis could hide there for a long while without drawing attention.

"How far on foot to this place?" Emmanuel asked.

"We must park and walk for maybe half an hour to the bottom of the hill and then fifteen minutes to the top."

Emmanuel rounded it up to one hour. The Zulu-Shangaan tracker covered more ground in a shorter period of time than anyone he'd ever met, and that included soldiers running like hell from the fall of mortar shells.

"We should check the cave. An isolated and sheltered place on a deserted piece of land seems right for what Louis most likely has planned. I've got nothing to back up my case. It's just a feeling. That's all."

"Your instinct and Constable Shabalala's knowledge of the land are all you have, Detective, so you must move and move quickly," Zweigman said. "The men at the police station will not drop even one pen to set out in search of a dark-skinned girl."

"Not unless she's a communist," Emmanuel said and turned to the towering black man standing at his side.

Without Shabalala's help, the wheels were going to fall off the already shaky wagon.

"We'll need to get my car and head out to King's farm. Are you still with me?"

"Until the end," Shabalala said.

CHAPTER
NINETEEN

They chanced the main streets in the hope that the Pretorius boys were still prowling the kaffir path. All was clear when they eased onto Piet Retief Street and moved past the white-owned businesses. The garage was open, but under the temporary management of an old coloured mechanic who shouted orders at the black petrol pump attendants from his spot in the shade. No sign of Erich the flamethrower or his big brother Henrick at Pretorius Farm Supplies, either.

A Chevy farm truck carting the wide, rusty disks of a plough provided enough cover to get them past the police station and onto the dirt road to the Protea Guesthouse. Emmanuel and Shabalala crossed the raked tidy yard. Sun sparked off the silver hubcaps of the black Packard. A twig snapped and the Zulu constable tensed, catlike. Another twig snapped and the black policeman released a pent-up breath.

"There is someone behind the big jacaranda tree," he said. "We must leave this place quickly."

The car was parked beyond the jacaranda and there was no way to get to it without one of them being caught in the ambush. He couldn't risk losing Shabalala.

374

Emmanuel checked their line of retreat. It was clear. He nodded at Shabalala and they ran fast and low towards the whitewashed fence and the dirt street freshly sprinkled with water to keep the dust down.

"Go, go!" Paul Pretorius was in full commando mode, calling out orders to his second in command.

Johannes stepped out from behind the fence and took up position in the middle of the driveway. Emmanuel heard the sound of Paul's boots crunching on the loose gravel behind him. Shabalala split off to the right of Johannes. Emmanuel split off to the left and together they ran a full press towards the startled fourth son. The Pretorius boys expected him to be alone and their haphazard ambush reflected the bone-deep belief that an English detective in a clean suit was easy prey.

"Stand your ground," Paul Pretorius called out.

Brutal rounds of boarding school rugby training and bruising matches on forlorn country fields surged from the dark pit of Emmanuel's memory as Johannes moved to block his path. Left hand out, he pushed hard against Johannes's chest and heard the satisfying crunch of the fourth son's body hitting the dirt road. It was the first time that the tutelage he had received at the heavy hands of Masters Strijdom and Voss had amounted to anything.

"This way." Shabalala sprinted towards Piet Retief Street and across the sweating asphalt to the kaffir path opposite. A shout from the direction of Pretorius Farm Supplies was enough to push them onto the grass path in record time. Now they had the whole Pretorius clan after them.

"Here." Shabalala pulled back two loose palings in a splinter-faced row of pickets and they crawled into a squat yard with a smokehouse at its centre. The garden boy, milky-eyed with a bony face and ash-white hair, looked up with a start.

Shabalala put his finger to his lips and the old man went back to weeding the flowerbed as if nothing unusual was happening.

"Peter?"

"Yes, missus?" the garden boy answered and Emmanuel and Shabalala moved behind the smokehouse for cover. They leaned against the corrugated iron wall and waited for the appearance of the Pretorius boys or the nosy white missus.

"What's that, Peter? I thought I heard something."

"Just the wind, missus."

"Okay." The voice grew fainter as the missus moved back into the sitting room. "You make sure those weeds are gone, hey?"

"Yes. All gone, missus." Peter's milky eyes darted up to check the position of the white detective and his third cousin by marriage, the police constable, Samuel Shabalala.

"Keep going. Down that way." The sound of Henrick Pretorius's voice kept Emmanuel pinned against the smokehouse wall. One call from the gardener or the missus and that would be the end of the rescue mission. Shabalala rested easily against the smokehouse wall. Emmanuel took his cue from the black constable and relaxed his clenched jaw. The pounding of footsteps

376

diminished, then disappeared as the Pretorius boys continued the chase.

"My car's no good," Emmanuel said. "If they have any brains they've slashed the tyres or left someone sitting on the bumper to guard it."

"We must find another car. There is one close by."

"Where?"

"The police station."

"The police station? How are we going to manage that, Constable?"

Shabalala moved to the front of the smokehouse and indicated a brick dwelling with coloured glass panels set into the front door and a wagon wheel fence along its wide *stoep*.

"The young policeman. He lives with his mother and his sisters. That is his house."

"You want Hansie to get the car?"

"I can think of no other person who can get the police van from the front of the station."

"God help us."

Emmanuel crossed the street with Shabalala and knocked on the front door with two clear raps. Through the coloured glass panels he saw the young policeman make his way down the corridor.

The door swung open and Hansie peered out with a sullen expression on his face. His blue eyes were rimmed with red and his nose glowed a dull pink from constant blowing.

"I got the necklace." He sniffled. "I got it back just like you said, Detective Sergeant."

"Good work." Emmanuel stepped into the corridor and forced Hansie back a few feet. Shabalala closed the door behind them. "I need you to get me one more thing, Constable."

"What?"

"The police van," Emmanuel said. "I need you to go to the station and collect the police van."

"But Lieutenant Lapping gave me the day off. He said I didn't have to come in till tomorrow."

"I'm putting you back on duty." Emmanuel made it sound like an instant promotion. "You're the best driver on the force. Better than most of the detectives I work with in Jo'burg."

"Honest?" The compliment perked the boy up enough to forget about the necklace and the day off.

"Honest," Emmanuel looked directly at Hansie in order to gauge just how deeply his words were sinking in. "I want you to go to the police station, get the van, and drive it back here. Can you do that?"

"*Ja.*"

"If anyone asks you where you're going with the van, tell them you are looking for a stolen . . ." His city knowledge hit against the reality of country life. What was there to steal in Jacob's Rest?

"Goat," Shabalala supplied. "You are looking for a stolen goat."

"Have you got that?"

"I'm looking for a stolen goat."

"Go straight to the police station and come straight back here with the van." Emmanuel repeated the instructions, hoping some of the information stuck in Hansie's muddled brain.

"Yes, Detective Sergeant."

The boy straightened his uniform and quick-marched towards the front door with wind-up-toy precision. Everything — Louis's apprehension, Davida Ellis's safe return, and the service of justice — all rested in the hands of eighteen-year-old Constable Hansie Hepple. A feeling of dread assailed Emmanuel.

A skin-and-bone blonde girl, her hands and apron covered in sticky bread dough, appeared. Blue eyes, darker and denser than her brother's, glimmered with a faint internal light.

"That was a pretty necklace," she said in Afrikaans. "Hansie cried when he had to take it back and his sweetheart was angry with him. Ma's gone to the store to get bicarb of soda to settle Hansie's stomach."

"We have got to find an alternative way out of here. This is no place for men like us to end," Emmanuel said to Shabalala.

They pushed through the rough country, drawn on by the looming mass of towering rock and clouds. In an ancient time, long before the white man, the mountain must have had a spiritual significance. Emmanuel felt the pull of it as he struggled to keep tabs on Shabalala's agile navigation through the monotonous blur of branches, thorns and termite mounds.

Fifty-five minutes and one brief break later, they reached the foot of the mountain and encountered a solid rock wall softened here and there by tufts of grass and stunted trees growing from crevices carved by centuries of wind and rain. As natural formations went, it had a handsome but unfriendly face.

"How do we get up?" Emmanuel leaned back against a sun-warmed boulder that nestled beside the mountainside like a schoolboy's marble. It was good to have a break; to feel the air coming in and out of his lungs without the fiery afterburn caused by lack of oxygen.

"We go around and then up," Shabalala said, and Emmanuel noted with satisfaction that the Zulu constable had broken a sweat on the cross-country trek.

"Is the goat on the mountain?" Hansie asked, after drinking deeply from his water canteen. The boy policeman's face had progressed from white to pink and then finally to a coal-fire red that rivalled a split watermelon for sheer depth of colour.

"I hope so," Emmanuel said and followed Shabalala around the base of the massive rock outcrop. They walked for five minutes until they came to a deep crease in the mountainside. Shabalala pointed to a path that wound upward and disappeared behind a windblown tree with branches bleached like bones.

"Up here." Shabalala led them onto the skinny dirt lane, slowing now and then to check a clump of grass or a snapped twig.

"Any sign of them?" Emmanuel asked as he scrambled over loose rocks and exposed roots. Louis and Davida could be a hundred miles in the opposite direction.

"There are three paths to the cave. I can say only that they have not come along this way."

"Maybe they haven't come here at all." The fear that had tugged at him since speeding out of town and heading to the mountain was now lodged like a splinter in his gut. He'd made a meal of the scraps thrown to him throughout the investigation and now he was about to find out if all the hunches and conjecture amounted to anything.

Shabalala stopped at the intersection of three paths that joined up into one and examined the ground and the surrounding loose stones.

"They are here," he said.

A moment of relief washed over Emmanuel and then he moved quickly up the path, his exhausted muscles fed by adrenaline. Louis had a good three-hour lead on them and God knows what had happened to Davida Ellis in that time.

The grass trail ended at a wide, flat rock ledge that jutted out over the steep fall of the mountainside and offered a breathtaking view of untamed country running to all points of the compass. A martial eagle, white chest feathers flashing starkly against the pale sky, circled on a warm air current in front of them. Far below on the plain, a watering hole sparkled in the late afternoon sunlight. It was as Shabalala said, a place to stir the heart.

"There." The Zulu constable pointed across the ledge to the dark mouth of the cave hollowed into the rock face.

"Detective Sergeant . . ."

"Shh . . ." Emmanuel silenced Hansie. "Wait behind this bush and guard the path. If anyone comes, call out to me. Understand?"

"*Ja.* Call out."

"Good." Emmanuel unclipped the holster at his hip, the first time he'd done so since arriving in Jacob's Rest, and pulled out his .38 standard Webley revolver. With Shabalala at his side, he ran low and fast across the rock ledge with his ears straining for the sound of voices or the click of a rifle bolt sliding back. An eerie silence followed them into the cave.

Emmanuel did a visual sweep of the interior and holstered his weapon. The cave was a scooped out oval, large enough for a Voortrekker Scout troop to hold an all-night sing-along inside. Diffused afternoon light illuminated an unsettling domestic scene. A thin bedroll made up of a sheet and grey blanket was laid out in the middle of the space and next to it, a lantern and a bucket of water. A container of rusks, strips of dried beef, and two enamel plates and cups lay on a flat stone. An open Bible, a box of candles and a coil of rope were placed on an empty rucksack, that served as an altar. Emmanuel holstered his weapon.

"Where are they?" he said. The cave was set up to imitate a living place, a place to sleep and eat and do who knows what with the Bible and the rope. The teenager had every intention of spending the night and possibly longer holed up in his private chapel.

"I will see." Shabalala checked the tracks on the floor and stepped out of the cave to investigate further. He returned quickly.

"They have gone along the narrow way to a place with a waterfall. It is spring. The water will be flowing."

"Can we follow?"

"It is narrow. There is space for only one person to walk at a time. I can take you."

"Let's go," Emmanuel said. "I don't want to take the chance of finding a second corpse in the water."

Emmanuel swung in behind his colleague and they approached the mouth of the pathway, which disappeared like the tail of a snake into the mountainside. A low, sweet voice singing an Afrikaans hymn stopped them at the entrance. A few swift steps and he and Shabalala were crouched behind a spiked bush with the teenaged constable, who was hot-cheeked and flustered.

"What is it?" Hansie asked.

"Whoever steps out from that pathway, you are not to make a sound," Emmanuel said. "Understand? Not even a whisper."

Davida Ellis stumbled onto the flat rock ledge in her bare feet with her arms wrapped protectively around her midriff. She was soaking wet and her pale green dress clung to her brown skin. Drops of water splashed onto the rock surface and formed a small puddle at her feet. She shivered despite the mild spring heat.

Louis Pretorius appeared, stripped naked to the waist with a rifle slung across his shoulder like a native scout. He continued singing and dried his face and hair with a handkerchief, which he returned to the pocket of his damp jeans. The words of the Afrikaans hymn circled high into the clouds, as if on a fast track to the Almighty. Louis had the face and the voice of an angel.

He finished his song and laid his hand lightly on Davida's shoulder. She flinched but he didn't seem to notice her reaction to his touch. He spoke close to her ear. "I will sprinkle clean water on you and you will be clean. Ezekiel 36:25. It feels good to be cleansed and made new, doesn't it?"

His hand moved to her neck, his fingers brushing the delicate bones of her oesophagus. "God hears better if we speak out loud and raise our voices to Him."

Emmanuel made ready to sprint across the rock ledge if the boy's fingers encircled Davida's throat.

"Agghhh . . ." Hansie released a scandalised breath that travelled across the open space and bounced off the hard rock surfaces. He might as well have thrown a stone. Louis tensed and swung his rifle across his chest so it nestled firmly in his hands. His finger rested on the trigger and aimed the gun's barrel towards the bush.

"Come out," he called in a voice that was close to friendly. "If you don't I'll unload this chamber into the bushes. True as I stand here."

"Don't —" Hansie jumped to his feet, his hands raised in surrender. "Don't shoot. It's me. It's Hansie."

"Who's with you?" Louis asked. "You're not clever enough to have made it here on your own."

"Not clever? What —"

Emmanuel and Shabalala stood up. Emmanuel didn't want Louis to panic and send Davida on a shortcut to the Lord God via the sheer drop just two feet to his left. And he sure as hell wasn't going to let Hansie Hepple conduct the negotiations for release of the hostage.

"Detective Sergeant Cooper." Louis greeted him with a nod of his head as he would someone he'd met on the street corner or the church steps. "I see you got out of the jam I fixed for you. And you brought along Constable Shabalala for company. What brings the three of you out to the mountain?"

"We could ask you the same thing." Emmanuel kept his tone friendly and noted the supremely self-confident way the bare-chested boy handled his rifle. He looked born to the ways of the bandit. Davida shivered next to him.

"This is a long way to come for a shower, isn't it, Louis?" he said and tried to appraise Davida's condition. She stared at him with the mute shock he'd seen many times on the faces of civilians caught in the crush of two warring armies. Her eyes pleaded for rescue and restoration.

"I am acting on God's command. I don't expect you to understand what it is I do here today, Detective."

"Explain it to me. I want to understand."

"And He shall wash away the sins of the world." Louis circled a hand around Davida's arm and jerked her against his hip. "I have purged the dirt from her physical being with pure water and stones and now I will cleanse her soul of the sin that has made her an impure vessel."

"Last time I checked you weren't the Lord God. You were Louis Pretorius, son of Willem and Ingrid

Pretorius of Jacob's Rest. What qualifies you to clean anyone's soul but your own?"

"And He hath put a new song in my mouth, even praise unto our God: many shall see it, and fear, and shall trust in the Lord."

In a trade-off of scripture verses, Emmanuel was sure he would lose out to Louis. The young Pretorius boy was so tightly wrapped in his holy vision that he didn't even recognise that what he'd done to Davida and her grandmother was sin itself. For Louis, it was all holy bells and whistles backed up by a chorus of angels.

"But . . ." Hansie was having trouble keeping up with the conversation. "That girl is a darkie. What are you doing up here with one of them?"

The fire in Louis's eyes was bright enough to rival his grandfather Frikkie van Brandenburg's incendiary glare. "When I was a child, I spoke as a child and when I was grown I put away all childish things. You, Hansie, are one of those childish things."

"What are you talking about?" Hansie asked. "You're not supposed to be washing or doing whatnot with one of them. It's against the law and I know that your ma won't be happy to see you standing so close, either."

"My mission does not concern my earthly family or you. God called me and you are standing in the way of His works."

"Let me get this straight." Emmanuel tried to gauge the depth of Louis's delusion. "God, the redeemer of souls, has called you to the theft of pornographic images, lies, assault, and the kidnapping of unclean women? When did you get this calling, Louis? At

Suiwer Sprong or afterwards at the theological college?"

Louis's pretty face seemed to distort. "Everything I do is in the service of the Lord."

"Did the Lord call you to molest those women last year?"

"That was the work of the devil. I broke free of his chains and have been cleansed of all my sins."

"Is this how they drove the sin out of you on the farm? With outdoor showers and fear?" Van Niekerk had listed "water therapy" as one of the cures being offered at the quasi-religious nut farm. What methods had the German-trained Dr Hans de Klerk used to clean the sin from the Pretorius boy?

Louis blinked hard. "Everything that was done to me was in the service of the Lord. I was lost and now I am found."

Emmanuel felt an unexpected stab of pity. Louis was brought up by his mother to believe he was the light of the world, but he'd inherited his father's taste for life outside the strict moral code of the *volk*. He was torn in two, lost, and made more dangerous by a spell of "realignment" deep in the Drakensberg Mountains.

"Was your father an impure vessel, Louis?" Emmanuel asked. He was interested in Louis's attitude to the captain's hypocrisy.

"Pa was led astray by the work of the devil, same as me." The boy looked over at the Zulu constable. "My pa was a good man, hey, Shabalala? A godly man."

"I believe it."

"I'm not disputing your pa's goodness," Emmanuel said, "I'm just wondering how hard he struggled with the devil. You went away to the farm and conquered the devil, but your father stayed on, and well . . . he let the devil win a few nights a week. For almost a year."

"Captain Pretorius wasn't in league with the devil!" Hansie's voice rose three octaves higher. "You didn't know him. He was clean inside and out."

"No man is clean inside and out." Emmanuel returned his attention to Louis and kept his tone even and nonconfrontational. "You know what it is to struggle with the devil, don't you, Louis? You want to be holy and yet here you are on top of a mountain with a terrified woman, a gun, and a piece of rope coiled on your Bible."

"This woman is the root of all the problems." Louis curled his hand tightly around Davida's forearm until she gasped in pain. "She is the one who needs to be cleansed of her carnal nature."

"Like you cleansed your father at the river?" Emmanuel tested the connection between the molester and the murderer. An unbalanced boy with a sighted rifle and delusions of godhead was a dangerous animal. "That's what you did, isn't it? You arranged a face-to-face meeting with the Almighty and then you dragged his body to the water to cleanse him of sin. Is that how it happened?"

"I don't know what you're talking about."

"You killed your father to cleanse him, didn't you, Louis?"

"Of course not."

"You knew he wasn't going to stop sinning, so you helped him break free of Satan's trap. I understand that. I understand how it happened."

Louis loosened his grip on Davida's arm and levelled a damning stare at the English detective. "I loved my father. When the devil had me in his claws, my father prayed with me and together we found a way out. I would never raise a hand to him. He saved me."

"You didn't shoot him at the river?"

"No. Honour your mother and your father so your days may be long on the earth. That's God's promise."

"But you spied on your father when he was alive. That wasn't an honourable thing to do, was it?"

"Witnessing." Louis let go of Davida's arm and pushed the messy blond hair from his forehead. "I had to witness the depth of his wrongdoing to understand just how far he'd strayed from the path of righteousness."

"You didn't enjoy it?" Emmanuel saw Davida slump back against the rock face and draw great mouthfuls of air into her lungs. She was still shivering and probably in shock. "You got no pleasure from watching your father having sex with one of the women you'd messed with the previous December? How many times did you witness your father straying from the path, Louis?"

"I can't remember," the boy muttered.

"Surely once was enough? You see your father with a brown-skinned woman and you know, don't you? You know that a sin is being committed without having to come back a second and a third time."

"I was witnessing. I didn't enjoy what I saw."

"Truly?" Emmanuel had the tiger by the tail and he had every intention of shaking it until it coughed up a lung. "I think you were doing something that began with W, but it wasn't witnessing. You got as much pleasure as your father did, only from a distance."

"Shabalala." The bare-chested boy appealed to the black policeman. "You know my family. We are from pure Afrikaner blood. You are from pure African blood. This business has come about because of those with impure blood among us. Is that not so?"

"Your father was pure. The woman is pure. When they were together, there was no wrong in them."

"You can't believe that." The boy was thrown by Shabalala's calm and forgiving statement. "She's the reason my father went astray and was killed. The fault is in her."

"That one there. She was your father's little wife and I tell you again, there was no wrong in them. The captain made the arrangement for her in the old way and did not intend any disrespect to come to her during his lifetime and even now after he has gone."

Louis blushed at the Zulu constable's criticism but didn't lower his weapon. "Your native ways are not for the *volk* to live by. Our God does not permit the tainting of our bodies or our blood with those from a lesser sphere. It is written so."

Davida, still shaking, had inched her way along the rock wall and was now out of arm's reach of the teenage prophet.

Emmanuel stepped forward and drew Louis's attention to him. "Did you ever offer your father the chance to come here and cleanse his sins in the waterfall?" he asked.

"No."

"Why not?"

"There was never a good time to bring it up. I didn't know how to tell him that I knew what he was doing."

"Well . . ." Emmanuel said. "How about after he'd finished and both of you were satisfied and feeling good about the world? You could have met him out on the kaffir path and exchanged notes before praying together."

"You are a foul-minded Englishman. It's a pity my brothers didn't catch you and teach you a lesson."

Emmanuel shrugged and stared over the rock ledge to the vast sweep of country. Davida was inches from the cave mouth and safety. "By their deeds shall ye know them." He dragged out a biblical quote from the deep vaults of memory. "What's a jury going to make of an Afrikaner boy out here with a kidnapped coloured girl? Do you really believe your brethren will understand that you washed her body to cleanse her and spied on your father having sex with her in order to bear witness to the Lord?"

"God is my guide and my staff. It is not for man to pass judgement on what I have done."

"Things are different now, Louis. When you got rid of your father you got rid of the one person who was willing to break the law to protect you."

Louis's finger was tight on the trigger. "I had no hand in what happened to my father. He was struck down before his time and I pray to the Almighty that he sees into Pa's heart and forgives his transgressions."

"Louis . . ." Hansie's vacant blue eyes brimmed with tears of frustration. "Tell the detective sergeant this is all a mistake. You didn't touch those coloured women and Captain didn't do like what he says . . . with the sex and the devil and the little wife."

Louis smiled, truly the most beautiful of God's angels. "You know what my pa told me once, Hansie?"

"No."

"That you cannot know God until you have wrestled with the devil and the devil has won." He turned to Davida to illustrate his point and found her gone. The rifle swung easily in the boy's hands and he raised it to his eye and took aim at the cave mouth where the woman appeared as a dark fleeting shape. His legs were spread in the classic marksman pose that gave stability to the torso and increased the likelihood of hitting the mark.

"Drop the weapon, Louis!" Emmanuel shouted across the rock ledge, handgun squarely on target. "Drop it or I will shoot you."

The shadow disappeared from the cave mouth and Louis slowly lowered his rifle to his hip. His fingers twitched around the barrel but the gun stayed put.

"Do not move." Emmanuel's voice was clear and authoritative as he closed the distance between them. "Drop the gun to the ground and kick it towards me. Now."

Louis loosened his grip and the rifle clattered across the ledge where Constable Shabalala picked it up and

392

swung it across his back. The captain's youngest son sank down into a crouch and stared out across the miles of brown- and green-speckled veldt. It was midafternoon and the light had a soft and yielding quality that made the scrub appear hand-painted on the canvas of the Earth.

"Now," Louis said, "she will never be saved."

Emmanuel signalled to Shabalala to stand guard while he checked the cave.

"Davida." He called out her name and stepped into the interior of Louis's bizarre mountain home. She sat near the cave entrance with her knees drawn up tightly underneath her. Emmanuel crouched next to her but didn't touch her despite the fact that her body shook with a bone-rattling intensity. She'd had enough of white men trying to help her for a lifetime.

"It's okay. You're safe now," he said. Her skin was scratched with fine red lines from the wash-down Louis had given her with rocks and pure spring water. "Did he hurt you anyplace that I can't see, Davida?"

"Not like you think. Not that way."

"Can you tell me what happened?"

"No, not now. Did you find my granny?"

"Zweigman is with her. He says she's injured, but she's going to be all right. You know he'll take good care of her."

"Good. Good." She started to cry and Emmanuel retrieved the grey blanket from the made-up bedroll. He held it out for her to see.

"Can I put this on you? You need to get dry and warm before we make a move."

"Outside. I'll put it on outside. I don't want to stay in here."

They left the cave and she huddled near the entrance; her instincts telling her to stick close to shelter. Emmanuel wrapped the blanket around her shoulders and noticed that she didn't look across to where Louis was under guard.

"It smells of him," she said. "Like flowers on a grave."

"You'll need to keep it on until you're warm, then we'll head back to Jacob's Rest."

"I'll go when you go," she said and rested her chin on her knees to watch long wisps of white cloud stretch across the sky. Emmanuel walked over to Shabalala and stood by his side. The Zulu constable looked weary, as if this end to things was more terrible than he had imagined.

"What now?" Louis asked over the sound of Hansie's snivelling. "Are you going to arrest me?"

"I've got no choice," Emmanuel said. "You are charged with assault and kidnapping. Both are criminal offences and you will have to stand trial."

"My mother . . ." There was a glimmer of fear in Louis's eyes. "She'll know all the ways the devil has led me astray."

"Most likely, yes." Emmanuel checked the position of the sun. It was time to get moving if they wanted to make it back to Jacob's Rest before nightfall. The police station was still out of bounds. They'd have to use Zweigman's store as a holding cell for Louis at least until Davida Ellis was safely returned home. After that he'd have to make a dash for Mooihoek with the captain's youngest son in custody. The Pretorius boys would skin him alive and boil his bones for soup if they caught him in the company of their sweet little brother.

"You're going to put him in prison?" Hansie was shocked.

"That's generally where people accused of assault and kidnapping end up, Hepple. That is the law."

"But it's not right putting a white man in jail over one of them. It's not decent."

"What's decent or not is for a judge to decide. Collect the evidence, complete the docket, and present the case in court. That's my job. And yours, too." Emmanuel checked Davida to see if she'd stopped shivering. The long march back to the car was going to be difficult with Hansie, Louis, and a traumatised woman in tow.

"I'll get her," he said to Shabalala. "You get Mathandunina."

They split off to their separate duties but didn't get far. The distinct sound of a safety catch releasing caught them midstep. Emmanuel turned to see Hansie standing, tear-stained and snotfaced, with his Webley revolver aimed right at his midsection. A bullet in the gut administered by a dull-minded Afrikaner boy was a lousy way to die.

"Constable Hepple." He used the title to remind the teenager that he was an officer of the law. "Put the gun down, please."

"No. I won't let you take Louis to jail."

"What should we do with your friend, Constable Hepple?"

"Let him go."

"Okay," Emmanuel said and left Hansie to fill the sudden power void.

"Go," the boy policeman urged his friend. "Go. Run."

The bare-chested prophet was crouched down, staring out across country, as if mesmerised by the colours of the veldt spread out below him.

"Louis." Hansie's voice was loud and raw in the arena of rock and cloud. "What are you doing? Go."

The teenaged boy stood up and walked to the very edge of the rock platform, where he spread his arms out wide to feel the wind blowing in from the bush lands. He turned back to face the cave, his hair bright as a halo.

"This is a holy place. Can you feel it, Detective? The power of God so close."

"I can," Emmanuel said.

"You're right, Detective. I should have brought my father here and tried to save his soul. If I'd done that he'd be alive today."

"It wasn't your job to save him." Emmanuel could feel the pull of gravity dragging on Louis's heels, threatening to suck him over the edge and into the void. "A man is responsible for the health of his own soul. You did nothing wrong."

Louis smiled. "The sin is that I didn't try. I left him adrift in a sea of iniquity."

396

"It's hard for sons and fathers to talk. You said yourself that it was difficult to bring up the topic of what your father was doing."

"I didn't want him to stop. You know there were evenings when, right after Pa had finished, I'd lie out on the grass and look up at the stars. What happiness I felt inside, knowing that he and I were alike. I was my father's son, not Mathandunina."

Hansie lowered his revolver so it was now aimed somewhere between Emmanuel's pelvis and his kneecaps. There was still no room to make a sudden move towards Louis, who remained perilously close to the cliff. Constable Hepple was too dull of mind to understand that the threat to his boyhood friend came entirely from within.

"Remember, Shabalala?" Louis switched to Zulu. "When I was a child the people would say, 'Look at this one. Whom does he belong to? Can he really belong to that man there?'"

"Your father knew well that you were his son," Shabalala said. "He had you close in his heart."

"That's why it pains me that I did nothing to save him."

"You were not at the river." Shabalala threw out a lifeline in the hope that it reached the boy's hands. "The man who shot your father is the one who is at fault in this matter."

"The wages of sin is death. I knew that and yet I did nothing because what Pa did gave me pleasure also. My mother will hear of this but she will not understand. She will never forgive."

"Your mother loves you also."

"She will be in disgrace because of me. Her family will cast her out if I go to jail."

"You are loved by her." Shabalala walked slowly towards the boy. "She will take you back into her arms. It is so."

The wind rising up from the veldt was cold on Emmanuel's face. Even Shabalala with his breathtaking physical speed would not be able reach the melancholy boy in time to stop him from testing his angel's wings.

"You'll tell her I'm sorry, hey, Shabalala? You'll say to her that I know we will meet one day on the beautiful shore."

"*Nkosana . . .*" Shabalala sprinted towards the boy he'd seen stumble and fall as a child. His hands were outstretched with the mute promise: "Hold on to me and I will keep you safe from harm."

"Stay well," Louis said and stepped backwards off the cliff and into the Lord's embrace. There was the dry snap of branches, then the breath of the wind as it stirred the silence.

CHAPTER
TWENTY

Emmanuel stood at the edge of the sheer drop. There was no sign of Louis Pretorius. He wasn't in a crevice with minor injuries or balancing precariously on a tree limb awaiting rescue. The boy had fallen all the way to the veldt floor.

"I must get him," Shabalala said and headed for the path that led down the mountain. He was breathing hard, his giant chest rising and falling under the starched material of his uniform. "I must find him and return him to his home."

"You are not at fault." Emmanuel felt the black man's pain. It was deep in his flesh like a thorn. "You did all that could be done for Mathandunina in his last moments."

Shabalala nodded, but kept his own counsel. It might take years for the thorn to work its way to the surface and fall away.

"We will meet you by the boulder." Emmanuel let the black constable get on with the job of recovering the dead. Nothing he could say would take away the pain that Shabalala felt for failing to save the son of his friend. "We will wait there until you are ready."

The Zulu constable started on his journey without looking back at the cave where he had played for long hours as a boy. He would not return to this place again without a powerful medicine woman, a *sangoma*, by his side. Ghosts and spirits were so thick in the air a person could not draw breath without choking. Mathandunina's body and spirit must be picked up and together taken back to his home in order to avoid more bloodshed and misfortune.

Shabalala disappeared into the bush and Emmanuel pulled the bottle of white pills from his pocket. A place to stir the heart or crush it, he thought as he chewed the painkillers and looked out over the African plains. The light here was completely different from the cool, white sunshine that lit the sky during the European winter, but with Louis's death he felt the same: old and tired.

"Dear Jesus." Hansie was on his knees, his hands clasped together in prayer. His words came out between broken sobs of grief. "Help him. Give him strength to overcome the fall. Raise him up, Lord."

"He's dead, Hansie."

"*Ja* . . ." The boy made a mournful sound and rocked back onto his heels. "I should have helped take him off the mountain when you said."

Emmanuel didn't have the strength to reprimand Hansie. He waited until the boy's sobs lessened.

"You weren't to know," he said.

Hansie shook his head as if to clear it. "I'm sorry, Sarge. I still don't understand what happened."

"In time. Maybe."

Emmanuel walked to where Davida sat with the blanket draped over her shoulders. She'd stopped shaking and gazed at the breathtaking vista.

"We have to go." Where to exactly, Emmanuel didn't know. Returning Davida to Jacob's Rest was out of the question. As soon as the news of Louis's death spread, she would become kindling for the fire that would engulf the small town. She was safer with her mother out here on King's farm.

Davida stood up and let the blanket drop to the dirt. She walked to the ledge and stared into the void.

"I hope the lions eat him," she said.

The lights of Elliott King's homestead clustered on the horizon and glowed bright against the night sky. Emmanuel breathed deeply. He felt sick. In the back of the van, Shabalala cradled Louis Pretorius's body: an empty cocoon of flesh and bone now broken beyond repair. The Zulu constable was convinced that Louis's spirit was conjuring a violent revenge against them. The only way to avoid trouble, Shabalala said, was to take the boy's body back to his mother, but Emmanuel couldn't let that happen.

"Park close to the stairs," he said, once they'd crossed the cattle grid at the entrance to the drive. They had to deliver Davida to her mother, then drive Louis to the nearest morgue. A police inquiry into the death was certain and a public inquest couldn't be ruled out. The spotlight would illuminate all the secrets of Jacob's Rest.

Hansie pulled in behind the red Jaguar in the driveway and cut the engine.

Elliott King and his picture-perfect nephew Winston stood at the top stair to the porch. The world was going to hell while they sipped sundowners and admired their own little piece of paradise.

A black ranger in a Bayete Lodge uniform appeared from nowhere and stood guard at the front of the police van with a nightstick in his hands. Like all chiefs, the rich Englishman had his own private army.

King dismissed the ranger with a wave of his gin and tonic and Emmanuel reached for the door handle. Davida grabbed hold of his arm. She trembled.

"I don't want to go out there," she said.

"Hepple," he instructed the constable, "go into the house and fetch the housekeeper, Mrs Ellis. Tell her to come straight away."

Hansie slid out of the driver's side door and took the stairs two at a time. He crossed paths with the King men on their way down to the van.

"Your mother's coming," Emmanuel told Davida and she pressed closer to his side. "I have to talk to King."

"Don't let them near me," she said.

"I won't," Emmanuel promised and swung the door open and stepped out. King and Winston peered through the front window at Davida's huddled shape.

"Has she been hurt?" King demanded.

"Where's my Davida?" Mrs Ellis stumbled down the stairs towards the triangle of white men standing between her and her daughter.

402

Emmanuel waved King and Winston aside so the housekeeper could coax Davida out of the vehicle and into the house.

"Take her inside. I'll take her statement in a little while. Stay with her until I get there."

"Statement?" The housekeeper was dazed and afraid. "Why does my baby need to give a statement?"

"Take her inside," Emmanuel repeated, "and get her a blanket and a cup of tea. Keep her warm."

"Davida? Baby girl?" Mrs Ellis leaned into the van and put her arms around the balled-up shape hiding there. "It's mummy. Come on, darling . . ."

Davida reached up and the two women clung tightly to each other. Emmanuel stepped further away and tried to block out the sobbing.

"Come on, baby . . ." Mrs Ellis said and led Davida towards the stairs.

Emmanuel watched the women disappear into the house. Soon he would talk to Davida about the man at the river.

"Did you do that?" Winston said. "Did you put those bruises and scratches on her, Detective Sergeant?"

"No."

"That was Louis," Hansie cut in. "He's the one who did it."

"Louis Pretorius?" Winston asked.

"*Ja*. He took her up to the mountain and washed her with stones under the water. He was trying to save her. That's what he said."

"He raped her?" King asked.

"I don't believe so." Emmanuel was sure that something else, possibly just as unpleasant and intrusive, had happened under the waterfall.

Winston seemed stunned and angry.

"I'll know more once I've spoken to her." Emmanuel kept King and Winston back from the van. He didn't like the look in Winston's eye.

"Well," Winston said. "Where is Louis? Is he in custody?"

"He's in the van with Shabalala," Hansie said. "Shabalala wants to take him back home to his ma, but we can't. Not yet."

"What?" Winston moved fast towards the back of the van and grappled with the door handle. Emmanuel grabbed him, spun him around by the shoulders, and pushed him hard towards the house. Winston turned to face him and stepped towards him again. Emmanuel stopped him cold with two hands on his chest.

"Move away from the van."

"He has to pay for what he did," Winston said.

"He will," Emmanuel said. "Now move away from the van."

Winston stared him down for a moment and Emmanuel recognised something in his look. Where had he seen that look before? Winston broke eye contact and strode in the direction of the house. King reached out a sympathetic hand, but Winston pushed him away and climbed the stairs.

Something is going on, Emmanuel thought. Why is Winston this angry about the assault of a housekeeper's daughter?

404

"You need to move away," Emmanuel told King. "I don't want to see you or Winston within ten feet of this police van. Understood?"

King nodded. "What happens now?"

"I'll take Davida's statement and then we'll transport Louis to Mooihoek."

"You won't take him home?"

"No," Emmanuel said. "Go inside and finish your drink. Constable Hepple will escort you."

Hansie followed the Englishmen up the stairs and took up position between the *stoep* and the vehicle. Emmanuel unlocked the back doors of the police van and motioned Shabalala out.

The tension in the Zulu constable's face and body was obvious. "Are you all right?" Emmanuel asked.

"This one —" Shabalala pressed a hand against the doors. "He will cause trouble wherever he goes. He will try to take one of us with him to the other side. I feel it is so."

"If we bring him to his house, that will cause trouble also. He won't be easy to handle wherever we go."

"I know this." The Zulu policeman made eye contact with Emmanuel. "You must be careful, *nkosana*. Mathandunina knows it was you who found out about the mountain and it was you who took the little wife from him. You have touched her and he does not like this."

"I did no such thing."

"You put his blanket around her, that is what I mean, *nkosana*."

"So —" Emmanuel said after the surge of embarrassment at his denial ebbed. How could a corpse know about the conversation in Davida's room or the quickening of his senses at the sight of her so close to the wrought-iron bed? "What must we do, Shabalala? I can't see any way to avoid trouble over Louis."

"We must tell his mother where he is. Maybe if we do this, things will not go so badly for us."

"When we get to the place where his body will be examined," Emmanuel said, "I'll call Mrs Pretorius and let her know where her son is."

"That is good." Shabalala still looked worried. "I will tell him and if he hears it correctly, he will not want more blood to be spilled."

"I'd like that," Emmanuel said. Less blood to be spilled. He'd spent three years hoping for that very thing and yet he'd come home and stepped right back into the company of the dead.

Emmanuel read the handwritten statement a second time and looked across the table at Davida. She was flushed and uncomfortable as if the heat from the kitchen stove had suddenly gotten to her. Mrs Ellis hovered close to her daughter's shoulder like a guardian angel afraid of failing a major assignment.

"The man at the river. You sure you didn't see who it was?"

"Yes."

"Did you know the man who shot Captain Pretorius, Davida?"

406

"No." She was adamant. "I didn't see who it was. I don't know who it was."

"He sounded like the molester, is that right? Like someone putting on a voice?"

"Yes."

"Louis admitted to being the molester," Emmanuel said. "But he denied killing his father."

"You believe that mad Dutchman but you don't believe me?" Her grey eyes sparked with anger. "White men always tell the truth, that's what you policemen believe. It makes catching criminals easy. Just look for the dark skin, don't bother with evidence."

Her accent caught his attention. It was not quite to the manor born, but desperate to get there by any road possible.

"Where did you go to school, Davida?"

"What?"

"Tell me where you went to school."

"Stonebrook Academy." She paused. "Why?"

"Your accent . . ." he said, "it's . . . elegant."

"So?"

"What are you doing in Jacob's Rest, working for the old Jew and his wife in their little rag factory?"

"My granny and my mother live here," she said. "I came to be with them."

"Surely you were meant for more? An accent like that doesn't come cheap."

"I like cutting patterns."

"Did you fail your matric, Davida?"

She flashed an angry stare at him, then thought better of defending herself against the insult to her intelligence. The dangers hidden in the answers she gave were suddenly clear to her. She shut her mouth tight.

"Tell him, Davida." Mrs Ellis took up the fight on her daughter's behalf. "She passed with flying colours and got accepted at the University of the Western Cape. Top of her class in four subjects."

"What happened?"

"She came to visit Granny and me for the Christmas holidays and decided to stay on for a year. She'll be going to university next year, hey, Davida?"

Emmanuel sat forward pulled towards Davida by a thread of understanding. All those days spent in the company of the old Jew and his wife, reading, dreaming of the world out there. He'd done the same thing at boarding school — gazed out over the dusty fields to the world beyond.

"Look at me, Davida," he said and waited until she did. "You weren't going anywhere, were you?"

"No," she whispered.

"That's why the captain built the hut. A little place out of town for the two of you. A home."

"That's right."

"No . . ." Mrs Ellis muttered. "This doesn't make sense."

Emmanuel maintained eye contact and the thread with Davida strengthened. Her breath became shorter.

"Pretorius made the arrangement for you to be his little wife . . . that's right, isn't it, Davida?"

"What?!" Mrs Ellis broke from the perfect servant mould and hit her palm on the tabletop. "You can't

408

come into my house and talk to my daughter like this. My baby's got nothing to do with Captain Pretorius. She delivered some papers to him for Mr King a couple of times, but that was it."

Davida looked older and wiser than her mother by a hundred years when she leaned back against the tiles depicting pretty rural scenes and wrapped her arms around her waist.

"Ma . . ."

Silence filled the room for a moment.

"No. No." Mrs Ellis stepped close to her daughter. "That life isn't for you, my baby. You're going to go to university so that you don't have to be that kind of woman. You're going to stand on your own two feet and have a profession."

"What country do you think we live in, Ma?" The question was full of sadness. "A coloured woman doesn't get to choose the life she wants. Not even after she's been to university. This, here, is how things are."

Emmanuel wanted to look away from Mrs Ellis's face, the death of her dream for her daughter written clear upon it. He watched the tragedy unfold across the kitchen table.

The housekeeper cupped her daughter's cheek with her palm and brushed away a tear that lay there.

"It's okay, my baby," she said, spinning a new vision for the future. "We'll forget this business and go on like before. You're young enough to start again without anyone knowing . . . That's right, hey?"

"Detective Sergeant!" Hansie called from outside. "Sergeant! Hurry."

Footsteps and the sound of glass smashing came from the front of the house. Emmanuel rushed out of the stifling kitchen and through the hushed luxury of the primitive-themed sitting room to the *stoep*. Elliott King stumbled against the drinks cabinet, his nose dribbling blood onto the front of his linen suit. Winston stood over him with his fist clenched.

"Fuck." The Englishman found an embroidered serviette and held it to his nostrils to stem the blood. "Christ, that stings."

Emmanuel looked past King and saw the rear lights of the police van fading into the night. He jumped off the steps onto the gravel drive and started to run.

"Shabalala's gone . . ." Hansie called out.

Emmanuel sprinted across the cattle grid and onto the dark ribbon of dirt road that split the King property in two. He ran for five minutes. The sound of the engine faded and then disappeared ahead of him. He stopped and gasped for breath. He rested his hands on his knees and tried to figure out what had happened.

After a minute he straightened up and glanced at the stars puncturing the night sky. The one person he trusted to stay by him had driven off with Louis's body because of a native superstition. Black policemen weren't even allowed to drive official vehicles. Emmanuel turned and walked slowly back towards King's house. Is this how it ends? he wondered. Abandoned and empty-handed on a deserted country road?

The silent landscape absorbed the crunch of his footsteps and the hiss of his ragged breath. He'd had worse days struggling across winter-hardened fields but today was the peacetime equivalent. The moment Shabalala delivered Louis's body to his mother, the Pretorius family would explode. King's farm and Davida were going to be the targets of extreme vengeance.

He broke into a steady run, then heard a faint sound behind him. He checked over his shoulder. Red taillights blinked in the darkness as the police van reversed down the dirt road towards him. He met the van halfway and pulled the driver's door open once the vehicle had stopped.

"What happened?"

"The young man." Shabalala's top lip was swollen from a recent hit. "He fought with *Nkosi* King and then he came to the van and he fought with me. He said he wanted Louis but I would not let him in, so he said he was going to get a gun and 'bang' shoot me and shoot the van also. He ran to the house and *Nkosi* King said to drive because the young man, he was serious."

"Did Winston give you that fat lip?"

"*Yebo*," the constable said. "I let him hit me many times, but I do not wish to be hit with a bullet many times."

"You did well." Emmanuel checked the lights of the homestead. Something had come loose in Winston. "Stay here. I'll send Hansie for you when things have settled."

"I will return when you say so."

"Thank you," Emmanuel said. Shabalala had gone against his instincts and given up the opportunity to take Louis back to his mother. Winston's violent threats were reason enough not to return to the homestead, but the Zulu constable held the course.

Emmanuel raced back to the house and found Hansie waiting for him at the cattle grid. The teenager's uniform was streaked with dust and embedded with pieces of loose gravel.

"That Winston pushed me down the stairs," Hansie said. "Then he went after Shabalala."

Emmanuel tried to make sense of Winston's actions. What fool goes after the police? For what reason? He leapt up the stairs, thinking of Shabalala's swollen lip and Hansie's dishevelled appearance.

"Stay out here and make sure no-one comes in or out of the house, Hepple."

"Yes, sir."

The *stoep* was empty and Emmanuel went inside. The sound of voices drew him across the sitting room to the kitchen, where he paused at the open door. Mrs Ellis leaned over King and wiped his bloody nose with a wet face towel, while Winston stood in a corner looking at the floor. Davida sat at the table and twisted a spoon in her hands.

"Careful," King groaned. "You have to be more careful with me, Lolly."

"Shhh . . ." The housekeeper whispered close to King's ear, "It's not so bad, you silly man."

Emmanuel entered the room.

"You're a family," he said, stunned by the revelation. "Mother, father, sister and brother."

412

"Don't be ridiculous." King gave each member of his illegitimate family a warning glance. "You have no proof of your allegations and if you repeat that slander again my lawyers will deal with you, Detective Sergeant."

"Shabalala was right." Emmanuel ignored King and spoke directly to Davida. The undervalued sale of the Pretorius farm suddenly made sense. "The captain did pay a bride price, but it wasn't in cattle or money, it was in land. The land we're standing on."

Davida glanced at her father, waiting for a cue.

"King was the one who cleaned the hut up after the captain died," Emmanuel went on. "He sent you to get any evidence he'd missed when he wiped the place down. That's right, isn't it?"

"Davida." King used her name like a blunt instrument. "The detective sergeant is wearing a suit but he's a police officer and his job is to enforce the law. Do you understand what I'm telling you?"

"Yes, Mr King."

"You don't have to protect him anymore, Davida. Tell me what happened."

She shut herself up behind her shy brown mouse mask and Emmanuel wondered how he would break through.

"Bride price?" Mrs Ellis placed the wet face towel down on the table. "What does that mean?"

"The detective is playing games, Lolly," King said.

Winston snorted in disbelief and the housekeeper took a half-step back. She glared at the injured Englishman.

"You knew what was going on," she said.

"No." King sounded calm but his thumb drummed against his thigh. "Pretorius was someone I did business with, that's all."

"You say you don't like the Afrikaner, yet you talked with that one for hours about how you both loved Africa. Why did you spend so much time with him?"

"Business," King said. "It pays to have interests in common with whoever you're dealing with. If something happened between Davida and that Dutchman it was her choice, nothing to do with me."

The slap came from nowhere. An arc of crimson blood sprayed from King's wounded nose and landed on Mrs Ellis's starched uniform and the handpainted tiles. Emmanuel caught the housekeeper's hand before she went in for a second hit.

"Liar!" Mrs Ellis was in a cold rage. "You said this one belonged to me but you broke your promise. You stole her and you sold her."

"Lolly —" Red bubbles flew from King's nostrils while he tried to stem the bleeding and talk at the same time. "Don't. Not in front of the police, for God's sake."

Years of hard work had made her strong and Emmanuel struggled to keep her away from King. If he let her go, she'd scratch King's eyes out.

"How could you do this to her? She was going to study to become a teacher, or even a doctor —"

"Christ above, Lolly. How long do you think it would take a dark-skinned girl like her to earn even close to what we made on the land deal? Fifteen, twenty years if she was lucky? Pretorius was willing to give me far more than she was worth —"

Emmanuel loosened his grip and let Mrs Ellis fly. Elliott King didn't know when to shut up.

"Lolly —" King tried to fend off the blows but the housekeeper slapped him down and tore into the suntanned skin of his neck and chin with her nails. His chair tipped over and King went with it, landing on the floor with a thud.

Mrs Ellis followed him down and her hands began to rip his hair. Emmanuel gave her another moment and when she showed no signs of slowing he pulled her away; he already had one dead body to deal with.

"Okay —" He lifted the vengeful woman up and held her arms loosely by her side until her muscles relaxed and she fell against him fighting for breath. "It's okay now," he said.

Winston stepped towards his mother and she surged violently towards him. Emmanuel held her back.

"You knew," she cried. "The two of you knew about it."

"No," Winston said. "I was supervising the lodge on Saint Lucia for the last six months. I didn't know anything about the land deal until it was done. I would never have let that Dutchman touch her."

"You're lying —"

"I will not take the blame for setting up that deal," Winston said.

"Stop." Davida pushed her chair back and sprang to her feet. "Stop it!"

King struggled to stand, holding onto the back of a chair for support. His hair resembled an abandoned bird's nest. Mrs Ellis began to weep quietly and Emmanuel released her into Davida's arms.

The name Saint Lucia rang a bell. Emmanuel dug around in his memory and came up with the sign at the jetty in Lourenço Marques and the beautiful wooden sailboat moored in the berth behind it.

"What's Saint Lucia?" he asked.

"An island." King was happy to shift the focus away from the land deal. "We opened a lodge there at the beginning of this year."

"What do you do on the island, Winston?"

"I run it," Winston said.

Emmanuel took that information on board. The captain's killer had slipped into Mozambique. What if the killer had simply gone home?

"What did you think of Captain Pretorius?" he asked Winston.

"*Die Afrikaner Polisie Kaptein —*" Winston mimicked the rough-edged Afrikaans tongue perfectly "— meant nothing to me."

Davida gasped and Emmanuel turned to her. The blood had drained from her face.

"If I closed my eyes," Emmanuel said, "I'd think you were a proper Afrikaner. An Afrikaner used to giving orders."

Winston went very still. "Plenty of people can put on that accent."

"Did Davida ever tell you about the man who molested the coloured women last year?"

416

Winston shrugged. "We all heard about it."

"He put on an accent," Emmanuel said, "to cover up his own voice."

"And?"

"Did Davida ever tell you that man had an accent?"

"I don't remember," Winston said.

"Did you tell him, Davida?"

"No ..." Her fingers twisted together. "I don't remember."

Emmanuel held his gaze steady on her. "Was it Winston's voice you heard at the river?"

"It wasn't him." She spoke in a rush. "It was someone else. I swear it."

"Where were you last Wednesday night, Winston?"

Mrs Ellis stopped crying and the room went quiet again. Davida's face was pinched tight with shock. A horrified realisation had just begun to register on King's bloodied face.

"Were you on the South African side of Watchman's Ford last Wednesday night, Winston?" Emmanuel asked and a phone began to ring in another part of the house.

"He was in Lourenço Marques collecting supplies for the island." King wedged himself into the conversation. "I can have a dozen signed witness statements attesting to that fact on your desk by tomorrow afternoon."

"I'm sure you can," Emmanuel said. The telephone continued its insistent ring. He walked to the door and called out, "Constable Hepple! Come in, please."

Hansie poked his head around the doorjamb.

"Could you please answer the phone and tell the caller that Mr King and Winston are busy."

"Yes, sir."

"Now, where were you last Wednesday night, Winston?" He asked the question again as the ringing fell silent. "Take your time and try to remember."

"I told you. He was buying supplies —"

"Everyone out of the room," Emmanuel said. "Winston. You stay."

"Sergeant —" Hansie stood fidgeting in the doorway. "It's for you. The telephone."

"Who is it?"

"It's the old Jew. He says it's urgent and I must get you *now* now. Straightaway."

Davida hurried to him and whispered "Granny Mariah" so that her mother didn't hear it.

"I'll check," Emmanuel said, then spoke to Hansie. "Stand guard and don't let anyone leave until I get back. You understand? No-one."

"No-one." Hansie repeated and took up position in the middle of the doorway, hands on his hips in a direct imitation of a police recruitment poster printed in the English and Afrikaans newspapers. "Why stay on the farm or serve in a shop?" the advertisment seemed to say. Why indeed when a few months training translated into instant authority over ninety per cent of the population?

Emmanuel walked into the office where King had shown him the native spells kept by Pretorius senior and picked up the telephone on the desk.

"Detective Cooper?" Zweigman sounded like he'd run a mile in wooden shoes.

"Is it Granny Mariah?"

"No, she is recovering. Davida?"

"Recovering also."

"And the boy?"

"In custody," Emmanuel said. "We'll be transporting him to Mooihoek in a few hours."

"Good." Zweigman dropped his voice to a whisper. "Do not come near the town and be careful on the roads also."

"What's happened?"

"The brothers searched my house and Anton's. Nothing serious. Torn books, overturned furniture. Amateur theatrics . . ." The old Jew was unfazed by the thuggish actions of the Pretorius boys. No doubt he'd seen several libraries' worth of books burned on Nazi bonfires and watched a continent bombed to rubble. He didn't scare easily.

"They are still searching for you," Zweigman added.

Emmanuel listened carefully. There was no possibility of returning to town, not after what had happened to Louis on the mountain.

"What did you mean about the roads?" he asked. If he couldn't get to Mooihoek this evening he needed to make alternate plans. On the King farm he was a sitting duck for the Pretorius brothers and the Security Branch.

"The Security Branch has sent four teams of men out to set up roadblocks leading to and from the town."

"Why?"

"This I do not know. Tiny was ordered to take his finest liquor to the police station and it was he who passed this news to me."

"Any idea where the roadblocks are? Or what they're looking for?"

"No idea."

Emmanuel paused to consider his position. If the roadblocks were set up between King's farm and Mooihoek, then he was trapped until daybreak.

"Doc," he said after a pause. "What's the best way to store a dead body overnight?"

Emmanuel sat down opposite Winston at the kitchen table and studied him for a moment. The rest of the family were in the sitting room under Hansie's guard. Winston appeared composed. Zweigman's phone call had given him time to collect his thoughts.

"Let's talk about Captain Pretorius," Emmanuel began. He kept his tone friendly and relaxed.

"I only met him a few times," Winston said.

"Funny, the way history repeats itself. Your mother must have been about Davida's age when she took up with your father. Maybe a little younger."

"I've never done the maths," Winston said.

"I think you have. You know better than most people the kind of life Davida was headed for."

"My mother's been very comfortable."

"One child taken away and dressed up to pass as white, the other traded for a piece of land. That's comfortable?"

420

Winston got up abrubtly and walked to the stove, where he warmed his hands despite the heat in the kitchen. "I made a mistake," he said. "I realise that now."

"Explain that to me, Winston."

"I should have gone after my father instead."

Emmanuel asked slowly and deliberately: "Did you kill Captain Pretorius at Watchman's Ford last Wednesday night?"

Winston looked him in the eye. "He took Davida's chances away when she had so few to begin with. That was unforgivable."

"Did you kill him, Winston?"

"I was in Lourenço Marques on Wednesday night. I bought supplies for the Saint Lucia Lodge. I have five witnesses who will testify to that in court."

"Only five? Surely your father can afford more."

"He can. But five will do."

"I'm curious. Captain Pretorius was pulled into the water," Emmanuel said. "Why?"

"Maybe the killer didn't want to leave him on the sand with his fly open and reeking of sex. Maybe the killer felt sorry for him in the end."

"You have some regrets, then, about shooting Captain Pretorius last Wednesday night?"

A hardness showed itself beneath the surface of Winston's face. Surviving as a fake in the white man's world had taught him how to protect himself and his family at all costs. He smiled but said nothing.

Emmanuel wondered what kind of world Winston King lived in. His whole life was a lie. Even his fair skin and blue eyes were a lie. It didn't help that he lived in a time when the term "immorality" was applied to interracial sex and not to the raft of laws that took away the freedom of so many people.

"What about Davida?" Emmanuel asked. "Do you have any idea what will happen to her?"

"She didn't kill Pretorius. She has no case to answer."

Emmanuel wanted to slap Winston across the face. He showed no remorse for Captain Pretorius's murder and no understanding of how his actions would affect his darker-skinned sister.

"Davida gets to walk into the sunset? Is that what you think?" Emmanuel said. "All thanks to you?"

"She'll go to Western Cape University and she'll get to live her own life. Surely that's worth something?"

"Davida's a key witness in the murder of a white policeman. She'll be put through the wringer. In court. In the newspapers. The dirt will stick to her for the rest of her life. Do you really think she'll go to university?"

"I didn't think that far ahead," Winston muttered. "I didn't think about it."

"You didn't have to," Emmanuel said. "You're a white man. Remember?"

Emmanuel sat down next to Shabalala and considered the health of the case. Sick but not fatal. He had a written statement from Davida for the docket and a five-sentence lie from Winston claiming to be in Lourenço Marques buying supplies on the night Captain Pretorius was murdered. No confession, but enough to haul Winston in for formal questioning in the near future. That was the end of the good news.

"A couple of miles along the main road?" Emmanuel repeated the information the Zulu constable had given him, hoping he'd got some part of it wrong. The men from the Security Branch were smack between them and Mooihoek.

"*Yebo*. A car and two men are at the roadblock, waiting."

"Any chance of getting by them?"

"Across many farms and through many fences, but not at night. Not in the dark."

The police van was now parked in the circular driveway in front of King's homestead. Van Niekerk didn't have the power to call off a Security Branch roadblock and Emmanuel wasn't inclined to let the major know about the mess he was in.

"They won't let us through without searching the vehicle," Emmanuel said. "We'll have to spend the night here and check the roads at dawn."

"What shall we do with him? The young one?"

"King's icehouse out beyond the back *stoep*. Zweigman said that's the best place for him."

"Home," Shabalala said. "That is the only place for him."

"Not much of a home after the lies his father told."

"To live in this country a man, he must be a liar. You tell the truth —" Shabalala clapped his hands together to make a hard sound. "They break you."

CHAPTER
TWENTY-ONE

He fell through the sky, and his body twisted and arched in the air like a leaf on the wind. He smelled wild sage grass and heard the sweet, high voice of Louis Pretorius singing an Afrikaans hymn. A tree branch snapped and he continued to drop at incredible speed towards the hard crust of the earth. He called out for help and felt a gust of cold wind tear across his face as he plummeted without stopping.

Emmanuel sat up gasping for breath in the darkness. He felt around him; his fingers brushed a blanket and the hard edges of a wrought-iron bedstead. He had no idea where he was. No memory of lying down in a wide bed with soft sheets in a room that smelled of fresh thatch and mud.

To the right of the bed he found a box of matches and in the weak light cast by the flame found an unused candle with a fresh wick. He lit the candle and tried slowing his breath to normal. The naive tribal designs painted onto the bare concrete floor helped place him. He knew where he was. A just-completed guest bedroom attached to the back of Elliott King's homestead.

424

The quiet rustle of the reed mat at the foot of the bed alerted him to her presence and he held up the candle to cast light further into the room. She sat on the floor with her chin on her drawn-up knees like a pensive child.

"Did your father send you?" he asked. "Or your brother?"

"Were you dreaming about the mountain?" She shuffled forwards and placed her elbows on the mattress. He was sweat-stained and shaky, but she showed no fear of him.

"Yes." Emmanuel saw no point in lying and it was a relief to tell the truth to someone who had been there. "I was."

"Was he in the dream?"

"Just his voice. Singing," Emmanuel said. "I fell off the side of the mountain and went down like a stone. You?"

"He was washing me under the waterfall and when I looked down, the skin on my arms was torn to ribbons. I saw the white of my bones through the flesh."

"He's gone. The dreams will stop but it might take a while," Emmanuel said. After the ordeal on the mountain, he knew he represented a safe haven from all the terrible things Louis had done to her in the name of purity. All victims of war and violence felt a bond with those who saved them. The bond was fragile, however, and should not be encouraged. Now was the time to tell her to disconnect. Life would resume and they would be strangers to each other again. That was as it should be.

She moved closer and Emmanuel didn't stop her.

"Do you think I'm a bad person?" she asked.

"Why would I think that?"

"Because of the captain and what I did with him."

"You had good reasons for everything you did," he said and realised, with a sense of discomfort, that this was the first personal conversation he'd held with a non-white person since his return from Europe. Interviews, witness statements, formal and informal questioning: he came into contact with every race group in the course of his work, but this was different. She was talking with him. One human being to another. Her skin shone velvet brown in the candlelight.

"Do you think God knows everything?"

"If there is a God, he'll understand the position you were put in. That's as close to philosophy as I come in the middle of the night."

"Hmm."

The sound was low and thoughtful. She tasted the idea of an understanding God. She reached out and touched the scar on his shoulder. He glimpsed sanctuary in her eyes and felt the warmth of her skin and her breath. Easy now, Emmanuel told himself. This is a police operation: a murder investigation in which she figures centrally. This was no time to give in like a vice cop at the end of the shift.

"You're hurt," she said.

The sleeve of her nightdress fell back to her elbow and he touched the long red scars along her arm.

"So are you."

She leaned forwards and kissed him. Her mouth felt lush and warm and yielded to his. Her tongue tasted him. She climbed onto the bed and slid herself between his legs, then rested her hands on his knees as the kiss continued, an endless dance.

He pulled back. Not far enough to convince himself or her of his intention to disengage.

"Why are you doing this?" he asked.

"I want to be in charge this time." Her hands slid over his thighs to his wrists, which she held in place with a firm grip. "Will you let me be in charge, Detective Sergeant Emmanuel Cooper?"

She gave him power and asked for it back in the same breath. It was exciting and shaming: that raw appeal to his rank.

"Yes," he said.

Sleep pulled him under, past riptides and eddies to a place of safety. He slept like the dead but the dead did not bother him. He was in the burned-out cellar of his dreams with the woman curled against his back for warmth.

"*Get up!*" The command was barked loud and clear into his ear. "*That is an order, soldier!*"

Emmanuel pushed his face deep into the pillow. He wasn't ready to leave the cocoon. The war could go on without him.

"*Up. Now!*" the sergeant major said. "*Put your shorts on. You don't want them to find you bare-arsed, laddie.*"

The bottle of white pills, still almost half-full, stood next to the spent candle stub. Emmanuel reached for it and saw, through half-opened eyes, the pale pre-dawn light that crept through the curtains.

"*Forget the pills,*" the sergeant major said. "*Shorts first and then wash your face, for God's sake. You smell like a Frenchman.*"

Emmanuel sat up, alert to the rumble of voices on the other side of the bedroom door. He reached for his shorts and pulled them on, then touched Davida on the shoulder.

"Get up," he whispered. "Put your nightgown on."

"Why?" She was sleepy and warm, the crumpled sheets wrapped around her body.

"Company," he said and lifted her up by her shoulders so he could drop her cotton shift over her head.

"Whatever happens, stay low and don't say anything." She was now wide awake and alert to the footsteps outside the door. She slid off the bed and sprang into the corner like a cat.

Outside, King's voice was raised in protest. "There's no need for this —"

Emmanuel stood up and the door smashed inward. Silver hinges flew into the air and Dickie and Piet appeared as solid black silhouettes against the grey dawn light in the open doorway.

"Down! Down!" Piet's handgun was drawn, hammer cocked, finger on the trigger. "Get down."

Emmanuel sat on the edge of the bed, conscious of Davida hidden in the dark corner behind him. She was

428

low to the ground and silent, but it was inevitable that Piet and his partner would find her.

"Get the curtains, Dickie."

Two more Security Branch men pushed King back towards the main rooms of the house.

"That's my property!" King fumed. The Security Branch officers pressed him into the kitchen. One of the men remained on guard in the corridor while the other returned to the destroyed doorway. Piet and Dickie had come with backup. Thank God the mad Scottish sergeant had woken him up. He had his shorts on and Davida had her nightdress on. That was something.

"You're in a world of trouble," Piet said. "The Pretorius brothers are opening the icehouse now. What are they going to find, Cooper?"

Emmanuel tried to get a handle on that information. Did Shabalala leave his lonely vigil outside the icehouse and walk to Jacob's Rest with the news? No. Shabalala would never leave Louis alone, not for a second.

The sound, half scream, half howl, was terrible to hear. The Pretorius boys had found their baby brother lying cold and blue amongst the bottles of fizzy soft drinks and ice cube trays. Emmanuel got to his feet, thinking of Shabalala facing the rage of the grieving Pretorius family alone.

"Sit down." Piet clipped his gun back into the holster and began to walk a slow circuit of the room. He kicked a pile of discarded clothing with his foot and randomly lifted artifacts and books. He stopped at the foot of the bed and peered into the corner.

"Well, well, Cooper," he said, "this explains why this room smells like a whorehouse."

A cold finger of fear touched Emmanuel's spine. He had to get Piet away from Davida, even if it spared her only a few minutes of his special attentions.

"Is that the only place you get to be with a woman?" Emmanuel said. "In a whorehouse? Makes sense with a face like yours. I hope you leave a decent tip."

"Secure this package, Dickie." Piet indicated Davida's hiding place and lurched towards the bed where Emmanuel remained standing.

"You are in my world now, Detective Sergeant Cooper." Piet was unnaturally calm. "You should show some respect."

In Piet's world, fear and respect were the same and Emmanuel wasn't going to show either without a fight. Davida cowered in Dickie's shadow and he went on the offensive.

"What are you doing here?" he asked. There were rules about how white policemen dealt with each other and Piet was walking a thin line.

"I was invited." Piet fumbled in his grubby jacket and pulled out a fresh pack of cigarettes. The stench of stale beer, sweat, and blood wafted from him. "King sent one of his kaffirs to the police station to ask for our help. A hell of a thing, the old kaffir making it there on a bicycle in the dark."

"Why would King need you?" He already knew the answer. Why wait for a team of Hebrew lawyers to get to work when it was possible to play one branch of the police force against the other and muddy the waters even further? King had smelled his separation from the main task force and used it against him: basic warfare tactics. There was only one flaw in the plan. The rich Englishman hadn't planned on the Security Branch finding Davida in the room with him and against all reason Emmanuel found he was glad of the knowledge. Davida had come to him of her own accord.

Piet lit a cigarette and inhaled.

"We got a confession last night," Piet said. "The colonel is on his way from Pretoria to pose for photos. It's going to be a big case. Everyone wants a piece of the action."

"He signed?" Emmanuel asked. Nobody, but nobody in government, was going to look too closely at the confession of a known communist, least of all van Niekerk, whose ambition was to rise on the political tide. Piet and Dickie were bulletproof and Emmanuel himself was half naked.

"Of course," Piet said. "So you can imagine my surprise when I heard you had someone else in line for the murder. A murder that I have a written and signed confession for."

If he dropped it now and said he made a mistake about Winston King's involvement, then apologised for the inconvenience he'd caused, maybe he'd get to fight another day. The Security Branch had outmanoeuvred him and now a black man from Fort Bennington College was going to hang for crossing the river on a Wednesday instead of a Saturday.

Piet smoked the rest of his cigarette in silence and blew smoke rings into the air schoolboy style. A bad sign. He walked over to the pile of clothes, picked up Emmanuel's discarded jacket, and rifled through the pockets until he found what he was looking for.

He held up Davida's statement between thumb and forefinger.

"Your evidence?" he said.

"A statement." Emmanuel didn't give him any more. Nothing was going to stop Lieutenant Lapping from reading over the long list of damning allegations levelled at Captain Pretorius: adultery, manufacture of pornography, physical assault, and criminal misconduct as defined under the Immorality Act.

Piet unfolded the paper and read the handwritten statement. He finished and looked to the corner where Davida huddled at Dickie's feet.

"You write this?" he asked.

Davida pressed deeper into the corner, afraid to look up, afraid to answer. Dickie reached down and slapped her across the face with an open hand, drawing blood from the corner of her mouth. Fear kept her silent.

"Answer," Dickie said.

"Yes." She pressed her hand against her throbbing cheek.

"Look —" Emmanuel got Piet's attention. "You have your confession. This is nothing compared to what's going on at the station."

Piet smiled. "I'll leave after you have been punished for disobeying orders and for getting on my fucking nerves and not a moment before, Cooper."

The pockmarked lieutenant stepped away to reveal Henrick and Paul Pretorius standing side by side in the

432

smashed doorway. He held the piece of paper up for them to see.

"Know what this is?" Piet asked. "It's a statement claiming that your father was a deviant and a liar who defiled himself by blood mixing. What do you have to say to that?"

The Pretorius brothers moved towards Emmanuel in a rage. He blocked a punch from Paul and ducked under Henrick's sledgehammer blow before a jab to the stomach sent him reeling back onto the bed. The wooden beams of the ceiling tilted at a crazy angle above him. Paul breathed down on him.

"You're going to pay," he said. "For Louis and for the lies you're telling about my pa."

"Every word, true," Emmanuel said and tried not to tense when the punches hit him from every direction. He tasted bile and blood and heard the wet smack of his flesh yielding to fists. So, this is what Donny Rooke felt like out on the kaffir path: a punching bag in the Pretorius family's private gymnasium.

"Stop, stop, stop," Piet ordered. "You can't take it out of him all at once like that. It's dangerous. You have to slow down. Consider where you're delivering the message and how."

Emmanuel struggled to sit up. If Piet was calling the shots he was in deep, deep trouble. The Security Branch officer could keep him alive and in pain for days. Piet took off his jacket and rolled his sleeves up to the bicep.

"Henrick. Hold him down and keep him down," Piet instructed.

"I'm a police officer," Emmanuel groaned. "What you're doing is against the law."

"I'm not doing anything," Piet said. "This is a private beating carried out by two men whose brother you killed and hid in an icehouse."

That did sound bad. Inaccurate, but a jury would think twice about punishing the Pretorius boys for taking out their anger on the man who Louis had said tried to molest him.

"Now," Piet continued. "Start with a slap. Open-handed. Not soft and not hard. Just enough to get his attention."

"You have my attention," Emmanuel said and Paul delivered a stinging hit across his cheek. Not too hard and not soft either. The tin soldier was a natural.

"Good." Piet was impressed. "Now pose a question and wait for the answer."

"Why did you tell those lies about my pa?"

"No lies," Emmanuel said. "Your pa liked to fuck dark girls. Outdoors and from behind."

Paul hit him hard across the face and sent the blood and spit flying from his mouth. The skin above his left eye burned and he focused on the enraged Paul Pretorius, who was struggling against Piet Lapping's hold.

"Calm down," Piet said. "That was too hard too early."

"He said —"

"The detective sergeant is testing you," Piet pointed out with a scholarly fussiness. "The stronger prisoners will do that. Your job is to remain calm."

"I almost forgot —" Emmanuel blinked away the blood that ran from a cut in his eyebrow. "Louis was the one molesting those coloured women last year. Your pa sent him off to a crazy farm. Check if you don't believe me."

"*For Christ's sake, shut up,*" the sergeant major whispered as Henrick rose off the bed and hammered his fists indiscriminately into whatever patch of flesh he could find. Piet's little talk on remaining calm clearly had no impact on Henrick.

"Get him off," Piet instucted Paul. "We don't want a dead policeman on our hands."

Henrick's weight lifted off him, but the pain remained and surged in waves from his toes to his cranium. His mouth was puffed and cut, which made taunting the Pretorius boys a linguistic challenge. He heard his own breath, ragged and defeated. An hour more and he'd be sausage meat.

"You understand now, don't you?" Piet said. "You are in shit up to your elbows."

Emmanuel shrugged. He knew he was in trouble: he could feel it in his face, his chest, and his stomach.

"Bring the girl," Piet instructed his partner and Emmanuel sat up straight. He was scared: for himself and for Davida, who appeared slight and nymphlike in her white cotton nightdress. This morning was going to be bad for everyone. What was Mrs Ellis going through, knowing her girl was locked away with armed and violent men? Even King must know that he'd opened his door to a force he could not control.

"Don't be frightened," Piet said to Emmanuel when Davida was pushed roughly around the foot of the bed. "The physical work is done and now we move to a longer-term punishment. One that you have kindly handed to me in the form of this girl."

Emmanuel tried to stand but Henrick slammed him down. Davida's face was streaked with tears, but she didn't make a sound.

"Was she worth it?" Piet asked. "I hope so, because you're going to spend the next couple of years in jail wondering why you flushed your life and your career down the toilet for one night between the sheets."

Emmanuel worked his swollen tongue against the roof of his mouth until a semblance of feeling returned. He wanted Davida out of the room and out of harm's way even if it meant going against van Niekerk's orders about keeping the past hidden.

"No law broken." Emmanuel managed to get the three words out, slurred but recognisable.

Dickie sniggered. "Have you forgotten what country you're in? You've been caught with a non-white. You're going to jail."

"Not white," Emmanuel said, even as he thought about van Niekerk's response to what he was doing.

"I know she's not white," Piet said. "That's why you're going *down*."

"Not white," Emmanuel repeated.

Piet stared at him dumbfounded. "Fuck off." He grabbed his hand and checked the skin underneath Emmanuel's fingernails for dark pigment. It was an old wives' skin colour test passing as science. He dropped the hand with a grunt. "You're as white as me and Dickie here."

436

Emmanuel reached down and lifted one of his leather shoes onto his knee. He slid a finger under the inner sole and pulled out a single piece of paper.

"The missing intelligence report . . ." Piet smiled. Most interrogations were intensely boring: the repetitive questions, the strangled denials, the hour-long beatings. There were no real surprises left on the job anymore.

Piet opened the page and whistled low in response to the information.

"Little Emmanuel Kuyper," he muttered. "I remember the photographs of you in the newspaper. You and your little sister. You had the whole country crying."

"What are you talking about?" Dickie tried to keep up with the conversation. He didn't read much, not even the lowbrow daily papers that carried more pictures than print.

"Emmanuel Kuyper. That was his name before he changed it; probably to avoid the connection with his famous parents," Piet explained. "Cooper here is the boy whose father was acquitted of manslaughter after the jury found he had good reason to believe a half-caste shopkeeper had fathered his children. A part-Malay, if I remember."

"Bullshit," Dickie said. "There's not a drop of Malay blood in him. Look at him. He's white, white."

"That's what caused the scandal." Piet lit up again, lost in memory. "Half the country thought the father's story was a pack of lies while the other half thought the mother was a whore. During the trial, the father's side of the family put the children up for adoption. An Afrikaner family who didn't want them turned over to a coloured orphanage took in Cooper and his sister. You were brought up in a proper Afrikaner home till you left school, hey, Cooper? Probably threw a torch onto the bonfire with all the other Voortrekker Scouts at the Great Trek celebration."

The feeling in Emmanuel's mouth returned. He was going to burn a couple of bridges in the next few moments, but he didn't care about the consequences. So long as Davida walked out unharmed and he could follow her.

Piet squinted hard and flicked the intelligence report to the floor. "Your mother may have been fucking the Malay," he said, "but there's not a drop of brown blood in you."

"Prove it," Emmanuel said.

There was a pause while Lapping examined the problem from every angle.

"Interesting," he said. "We can't charge you under the Immorality Act if you're mixed race but that doesn't mean your life isn't about to go down the drain if I pursue this claim and get you reclassified."

"Go ahead," Emmanuel said.

"You'll lose your job," Paul Pretorius joined in. "You'll lose your home and your friends. Everything."

"He's going to lose all that anyway once he's charged under the act." Lieutenant Lapping circled Davida, thinking aloud all the while. "This way he saves himself and the girl from a public court appearance and makes them both innocent parties as they've committed no offence. Clever."

438

"He's trying to weasel out of it." Dickie was furious. "He's changing the rules on us. Look at him. He's white."

"I think he is," Piet said mildly. "But there's no way to prove it, which is why the detective sergeant has chosen to give us this report. Claiming to be non-white is his easiest way out. No prison term and as much black snatch as he can poke. Right, Cooper?"

Emmanuel shrugged. His life was spinning down the drain while Piet imagined him living it up in a shebeen full of black women. It didn't surprise him. Blacks and coloureds laughed louder and longer . . . or so it seemed to whites. He was going to miss the job, his sister, and his life.

"He gets to walk away." Paul Pretorius couldn't believe it. "Reclassification isn't enough to pay him back for Louis."

Piet ground his cigarette butt under his heel and immediately lit another, as if it were oxygen and not nicotine that was poisoning his bloodstream. He sucked deep until the tip of the cigarette glowed hot and red.

"Cooper is forgetting that a non-white man has little protection from the law." The lieutenant handed the cigarette to Paul. "We will now be forced to make the punishment for what happened to Louis immediate and physical in the extreme."

Shit, Emmanuel thought. Was there no way out of Piet Lapping's carnival of perpetual pain? The Security Branch officer in the doorway swung around and faced into the house, hand on his gun holster.

"Speak —" The officer barked the command down the corridor.

"Lieutenant Lapping?" Mrs Ellis's voice, sharp with fear, called out from the sitting room. "Lieutenant Lapping?"

"Mummy —" Davida whispered before Dickie cupped his hand over her mouth.

"*Ja?*" Piet pursed his bulbous lips. The sound of a female voice put a damper on the high he experienced during physical questioning: like having your mother walk in on you just before the climax.

"Phone call," the housekeeper said quickly, aware on a base, instinctual level that the men in the room were unused to a woman interrupting their dark business.

"What?" Piet moved to the destroyed doorway and listened. He was ready to leap and strangle the housekeeper if she made a wrong move.

"There's a man on the phone. He asked to talk to a Lieutenant Lapping right away."

"The colonel?" Dickie asked.

"No," Piet said and unrolled his sleeves and buttoned them, careful of appearances outside the room. "He doesn't know we're here."

So — Emmanuel's brain formed the thought with sluggish determination — Piet was keeping this excursion secret. He was determined to clear any obstacles that could throw doubts over the confession he'd extracted from the communist last night.

"Put the cigarette out and don't do anything until I get back," Piet said and left the room to answer the phone.

440

"Take a break." Dickie stepped into the boss's shoes and found them quite comfortable. "Cooper and his friend aren't going anywhere."

The Pretorius brothers retreated to the window and fell into a whispered conversation while Dickie pushed Davida into a chair and stood over her. Emmanuel sank his throbbing head into his hands. It was his fault that Davida was here, in this room with men who stank of violence and hate. Their pleasure had come at a high price.

"Look up." Piet Lapping was back in the bedroom and he was not calm. "Look at me, Cooper."

Piet paced back and forth in front of the bed, his fingers flicking the flame of his cigarette lighter off and on like a lighthouse beacon. Something had set him off and destroyed the mystic calm he insisted was a mainstay of the "work".

"You're really something," Piet said through tight lips. "You and your sissy friend van Niekerk."

Emmanuel had no idea what he was talking about. Van Niekerk was in Jo'burg and unaware of the disaster with Louis or that the Security Branch interrogation was taking place at Elliott King's game ranch. How the hell had van Niekerk tracked him down?

"What happened?" Dickie asked.

Piet ignored him and bent down in front of Emmanuel, his pebble eyes wet with rage.

"Mozambique. That's where you got them. Am I right?"

Emmanuel lifted an eyebrow in response. Piet could go fish.

"What?" Dickie walked to his partner's side but kept plenty of space between them in case he needed to duck out of the way in a hurry. Lieutenant Lapping was unpredictable when he was angry and he was rarely this angry.

"I should have known," Piet mused aloud. "That day you left for Lourenço Marques to question the underwear salesman. I smelled something was wrong . . ."

"What underwear salesman?" Dickie was trying his best to get involved and be a genuine partner, not just a muscleman.

"Shut up, Dickie," Piet said. "I need to get this straight so we don't do anything foolish. I need to think."

Piet flicked the lighter on and off, the sound of it like gunfire in the tense atmosphere. A muscle jumped in the cratered skin of his cheek and Emmanuel held his breath.

"He's going to release the photos if we touch another hair on your pretty head," Piet said after a long while. "He wants you to call him in ten minutes to verify that you're safe, like a fucking virgin at her first dance."

Emmanuel stood up, his body stiff from the beating he'd taken. He didn't care what the Security Branch threw at him. Van Niekerk had the photos and their power couldn't be pissed away by slinging childish insults. He glanced over at Davida and saw that she understood. They were going to walk out of the room and then they were going to run.

"You're going to let him go?" Paul Pretorius pointed an accusing finger at the pockmarked lieutenant. "You promised us he'd get what was coming to him."

442

Piet caught Paul's finger and twisted hard until the finger snapped out of its socket.

"Agghh —" Paul Pretorius groaned and sweat broke out on his forehead.

"We are letting him go because your pa couldn't keep his pants buttoned up and that slippery fuck van Niekerk has proof of it."

"That's a lie." Paul was red-faced with pain. "He's lying."

Piet let go of Paul's dislocated finger and said, "I did consider the possibility that he was lying, but he has something, this van Niekerk. It was in his voice. I could hear it: the pleasure he takes in having power over us. Over me."

Dickie marshalled a decent thought and threw it into the ring. "Maybe he's just a good liar."

"Consider the facts," Piet said patiently. "Van Niekerk knows my fucking name, he knows where I am when even the colonel has no idea. This is not someone to be taken lightly and that is why I cannot take the risk that he is just playing with us."

Emmanuel limped past the bickering Security Branch men and held out his hand to Davida, who was perched at the edge of her chair, ready to make a run for it.

"Let's go," he said.

She stood up and took his hand. Her fingers curled around his and squeezed tight. Emmanuel turned to the door and noticed pockmarked Piet staring at them with evil intent. Not good. Emmanuel started walking. Please, God. The shattered doorway was so close now. Just four more steps.

"So sweet," Piet muttered. "The way you looked at her just then. It's as if you actually like her."

Davida's fingers slipped from his and Piet pulled her back into the room with a yank. He held her in the tight band of his arms. Davida twisted and kicked but remained imprisoned against the foul-smelling white man with the cratered face.

"Don't do this." Emmanuel heard the pleading tone in his voice and tried again, stronger this time. "Let her go, Lieutenant."

"The deal," Piet said, "was for your release. We keep her."

"No!" Davida arched her back and tried to wriggle free but she was no match for Piet's bullish strength coupled with his experience in subduing troublesome prisoners. "Let me go!"

Piet lifted her in the air, as easily as he'd lift an empty laundry basket, and threw her back on the bed. The springs groaned. He straddled her in one quick move and pinned her arms above her head.

Emmanuel was close behind. His battered body found a sputter of speed from a reserve located behind his damaged kidneys. He smacked Piet hard in the side of the head and got no reaction. He went in for a second hit and connected with air. Dickie and Paul pulled him back and threw him into the chair. The dark fear from the dream consumed him and grew stronger.

"Good," Piet said as Davida's body strained and pressed against his inner thighs. "I like spirit in a woman: a bit of fight."

444

"You have everything you want," Emmanuel said. "She's of no use to you."

"I want the photos. The photos for the girl, that's the trade."

"If van Niekerk won't give them up?" Emmanuel asked. That was a real possibility. "What then?"

"Well . . ." Piet pressed a thumb against Davida's mouth and forced her lips apart. "You can fuck off out of here or you can stay and watch me work on her. Your choice, Cooper."

"No." Emmanuel struggled against the mother lode of Boer muscle holding him in the chair but couldn't break free. "Don't do this."

"You cannot imagine —" Piet's breath was coming hard as the body underneath him continued to buck and grind "— how beautiful my work can be. I will get to know this woman in ways that are beyond you. I will break her open and touch her soul."

"Please —" Davida arched away from the evil man leaning close to her. "Emmanuel, help me —"

"Wait," Emmanuel said. He needed Piet to stop and listen. "Wait. I'll talk to van Niekerk and try to make a deal."

"The girl for the photos. That's the only deal I'm interested in. I'm not going to let your major hang onto evidence that might spoil my case further down the track."

"Okay," Emmanuel said. "Let her off the bed and sit her in the chair. I'll make the call."

Piet shifted his weight and considered the request. He was reluctant to break away from the bruising and intimate tango that prisoner and interrogator danced together in the dark of the holding cells. He lifted his body and let the girl wriggle from under him. If he didn't get the photos, he had this to look forward to. The task of breaking the woman to his will.

Emmanuel sat Davida down in the chair and let her feel his touch, gentle and unforced. It hurt to look in her eyes and see the stark terror flickering in the dark circle of her pupils.

"Don't leave me," she whispered. "Please don't go."

"I have to," he said. "I'll come back in a few minutes. I promise."

"You promise?"

"Yes." He didn't know if he was coming back with the keys to her release or with nothing at all. He had to roll the dice.

"Go with him," Piet said to Dickie. "Make sure he doesn't start trouble."

"I'm going alone," Emmanuel said. "Van Niekerk won't talk if someone else is listening in. Or is that what you're hoping for, Lieutenant? A no from van Niekerk so you can get back to work on the girl?"

"Piss off," Piet said and fumbled for his cigarettes. "You have ten minutes."

"Fifteen," Emmanuel said and shuffled out of the room past the guard in the hallway.

He made slow progress towards the office, his bruised muscles twitching with five different kinds of pain. The cut on his eyebrow had opened again and he stopped to wipe away the trickle of blood obscuring his vision.

446

Through the red haze he saw Mrs Ellis standing in the doorway to the kitchen, neat and trim.

"My God . . . my God . . ." she whispered. "Did they do this to you?"

Emmanuel nodded. He was still in his undershorts: a sorry, beaten man with skin pulsing red, yellow and bright purple.

"My baby —" Mrs Ellis gave voice to her worst fears. "My baby is alone with those men?"

"Yes," Emmanuel said and limped to the office. He had fifteen, twenty minutes tops to turn things around. "I'm trying to get her out."

"Trying?" Elliott King appeared in front of him, his face pinched tight with impotent rage. "You lured her into that room. It's your fault she's in this position."

Emmanuel slammed Elliott King hard in the chest and sent him flying back into a wall. He leaned to within an inch of King's suntanned face. "Your daughter came of her own accord and she would have left of her own accord but for you and your half-baked attempt to manipulate events. This has been your doing right from the start."

"I sent for the police, not a gang of Afrikaner thugs. I should have known not to trust the Dutch."

"You entrusted Davida, body and soul, to a Dutchman in exchange for a piece of land," Emmanuel said. "Now you're not even in charge of your own house. How does it feel, Mr King?" Emmanuel turned his back on him and limped to the office.

Winston King was inside with the phone to his ear and a crossed-out list of names balanced on his knees.

447

He hung up and rubbed the flat of his palms over his eyes.

"No takers," Winston said. "Botha will try to contact the commissioner of police in an hour or so to see what can be done. No promises, though. Nobody wants to mess with these Security Branch fuckers. For once, the size of your donations isn't big enough."

"The commissioner won't take the call," Emmanuel said. "A member of the Communist Party confessed to Captain Pretorius's murder last night. The Security Branch has a signed confession. Nobody is going to go up against them."

"Shit." Winston looked sick. "Fucking hell."

"I'll take that as an expression of genuine regret for your actions," Emmanuel said and signalled him out of the office. "It comes a little too late for the poor bastard who was beaten into a confession and it comes too late for Davida. Two other people are going to pay the price for you, but you're used to that, aren't you, Winston? Someone else picking up the bill."

"Davida doesn't mean anything to those men," Winston protested. "Why hold her?"

"She's currency," Emmanuel said. "They want to exchange her for a piece of evidence that could derail their case in the future."

"I'll tell them —" Winston's face was ashen. "I'll confess to everything if they let Davida go. I'll put it in writing."

"Wait —" King said from the doorway. "I'll give them a good price to walk away. How much do you think they'll take?"

"This might be hard for you to understand," Emmanuel said and sank into the office chair. "But this situation is above money. Those men believe they are guarding the future of South Africa. Your cash means nothing to them. Not with a communist ready for trial."

"No-one is above money," King stated with certainty.

"Fine." Emmanuel lifted the phone. "You and Winston go in and offer them a bribe, see what happens."

The King men eyed the blood dripping off his chin onto the beaten flesh of his torso.

"You'll make the deal for her?" Winston blushed at his own cowardice.

"I'll try," Emmanuel said and placed the phone to his ear. "Now get out. Both of you."

Emmanuel pushed the casement window up und leaned out to take a deep breath of fresh air. The sun was over the horizon and a golden light shone onto the meandering river and squat hills. It was going to be another fine day, full of wildflowers and newborn springbok. The office door opened behind him but he didn't turn around. He didn't have the heart or the stomach to face anyone right now.

"He won't exchange the evidence for my girl, will he?" Mrs Ellis said.

"No," Emmanuel replied. "He won't."

Van Niekerk had been blunt to the point of insult. There was nothing in the proposal for him. No reason to exchange the ultimate blackmail tool for a frightened

449

girl. He already had a maid and a cook. He had no use for another non-white female.

"They're not going to kill her." The major had been brutal in his summation. "I've seen the photographs and there's nothing those men can do to her that hasn't already been done. Disengage and walk away, for Christ's sake."

He could imagine van Niekerk doing just that. Walking away from a helpless human being without a second thought. That was his strength, and it would take him to the very top.

"What can I do?" The housekeeper was humble in her powerlessness. "What must I do to help my baby?"

Emmanuel heard the clink of cutlery and smelled the freshly brewed coffee. He checked his watch: 6:50 am. He had three minutes left to make a decision. Go with van Niekerk and rise to the top of the pyramid of evil. Or stay here and go down fighting in defence of what was right.

He turned to Mrs Ellis. She'd brought him a mug of coffee and a buttered ham sandwich cut on the diagonal. It was enough to light a spark.

"What's in the pantry?" he asked.

"Everything," she said. "We're very well stocked. Mr King insists on it."

God bless the greedy rich, Emmanuel thought as the spark struggled to become a workable idea.

"Meat?" he asked.

"Bacon. *Boerewors* sausages and wild game steaks."

"Sweet things?"

450

"I have some jam biscuits made up and a sponge cake for afternoon tea. Also some dried fruit and store-bought sweets."

"Is Constable Hepple still here?"

"He's out on the veranda waiting for you. He told Johannes and Shabalala that he couldn't go back to town with them. He couldn't desert his post."

"Bring Hansie, Elliott King and Winston in here," he said. "We have to move fast."

Emmanuel limped back to the spare bedroom with the mug of coffee in one hand and a half-eaten sandwich in the other. He stood in the doorway and sipped at the drink. The hot liquid singed the cut inside his mouth, slid over the lump in his throat, and continued down to the aching knot of fear in his stomach.

Sunlight filtered into the room but the Security Branch officers and the Pretorius brothers retained a greyish cast, the result of too little sleep, too little food, and too much beer.

"Well?" Piet was lounging on the bed, no doubt keeping the space warm in preparation for the woman's return. Cigarette butts littered the floor around him.

Emmanuel forced more coffee into his bruised mouth and went to check on Davida: scared stiff, but holding up. He handed her the coffee which she drank down in a few thirsty gulps. She reached for the sandwich but he kept that firmly in his hand. It was a long shot. Relying on a plain ham sandwich to save Davida's skin. He saw Dickie out of the corner of his

451

eye. The big man was looking at the sandwich and at nothing else.

"Major van Niekerk wants more time to think about it. He's going to call back in half an hour with an answer." Emmanuel took a bite of the homemade bread and chewed it before continuing. "Can you wait that long?"

Piet stood up and flicked ash from his pants. "The answer is yes or no."

"What do you want most, Lieutenant? The photographs or the chance to drop your pants for your country?"

Piet flushed. "And what the fuck are we supposed to do while your major prances around?"

Emmanuel shrugged and checked his watch. Any minute now Mrs Ellis was going to fire the opening salvo of the battle. He took a bite of the sandwich and felt the hungry gazes of Dickie and the Pretorius brothers follow the movement of his hands. He licked butter from his fingers.

"Where did you get that food?" Dickie blurted. "And the coffee?"

"This?" Emmanuel held the sandwich up. "Housekeeper gave it to me from the *braai* plate."

"What *braai*?" Dickie said and sniffed the air like a hound dog. The smell of woodsmoke began to rise and mix with the aroma of bacon, onions and fried sausage.

"That bastard, King." Emmanuel shook his head. "He's got enough food in the kitchen to feed an army. Although I never had anything like that when I was marching through France. No *boerewors* or sponge cake in my ration pack."

Dickie's stomach gurgled and the Pretorius brothers stepped towards the smashed doorway. The sizzle of oil and meat called all men.

"Wait," Piet ordered. "This is a set-up. Why would anyone light a *braai* at this time of morning?"

The lieutenant was a pure freak of nature, always on the lookout for danger. He didn't need food or sleep so long as the "work" remained unfinished.

"Practice . . ." Davida leaned forwards in the chair with the empty coffee mug held close to her chest. "Mr King is going to have a breakfast *braai* for the guests when the lodge opens. He likes to test the food and pick what he wants."

"What happens to the food he doesn't eat?" Dickie asked.

"He gives it to the workers," Davida said. "The ones building the huts."

Dickie groaned at the thought of all that white man's food going into the mouths of black workmen who were happy with a cob of roast corn and a piece of dried bread twice a day. He sniffed and thought he smelled brewed coffee amid the aroma of roast meat.

"Lieutenant . . ." Dickie begged. He was a big man. He liked six-egg breakfasts wiped up with a loaf of bread and washed down with a pot of black coffee. His stomach started to eat itself from inside. "Please . . ."

Piet eyed his men and saw the beginning of mutiny stirring. He'd been negligent; they hadn't had a real meal in forty-eight hours. He pulled the woman over to the bed and secured her to the frame with his handcuffs.

"Half an hour," Piet said.

Emmanuel handed Hansie a plate piled high with three kinds of meat and a fat slice of bread on top. The Security Branch crew hoed into the feast served up by Mrs Ellis and King himself, who'd donned a servant's apron for the occasion. Winston served coffee and tea with the oily charm that melted the knickers off English girls and made men dig deeper into their pockets for a tip.

"Take this to the man guarding the bedroom," Emmanuel told Hansie. "Tell him the lieutenant said to eat it in the kitchen while you stand guard."

Hansie went off and Emmanuel waited. Everything was going according to plan, but for Piet's restlessness. He ate and drank with his men but stopped every few minutes to check his watch and scan the area.

Emmanuel waited until Piet did his security check, then slipped into the house and bolted for the bedroom. He estimated he had two minutes. He pulled a set of keys out of his wrinkled pants and handed them to Hansie, who now stood guard outside the bedroom.

"You know what to do?"

"Of course," Hansie said and grabbed the keys.

"Good . . ." Emmanuel checked the corridor. Empty. "Remember, don't stop until you get to Mozambique."

"Yes, Sarge." Hansie took off; the car keys jangled happily in his hands.

454

Emmanuel unlocked Davida's cuffs and set her free. Her wrists were marked with blood, but that was child's play compared to what Piet Lapping would take out of her if she was still here when he got back.

"We have to be quick. Go out the window and run straight to the night watchman's hut. Fast as you can."

She had to be out of the room and sprinting before Hansie fired up the sports car and drew the men to the front of the house. The window creaked open and Emmanuel lifted her in his arms.

"You?" she said.

"I'll be fine." He slid her out of the window. "Run," he said.

She bolted across a patch of bush in her white cotton shift. She ran hard and did not look back. A memory surfaced as her form flew away from the house . . .

Emmanuel's little sister ran fast down the alley, barefoot in her nightgown with the blue forget-me-nots embroidered on the collar. Emmanuel ran alongside her. He smelled wood fires in the air as they raced towards the light of the hotel on the corner. Fear blocked out the cold of the winter night. Anger burned in him at not being strong enough to stop the blade. When he was older, bigger, he'd stand and fight. Behind them, the screams of their dying mother chased them farther and farther into the darkness . . .

The sports car fired up with a roar and a spray of loose gravel as Hansie sped out onto the road.

Emmanuel imagined the grin on Hansie's face as he revved the sleek Jag across the veldt. He heard the blast of a horn, then footsteps and voices raised in surprise. The Security Branch was taking the bait. Car engines turned over and wheels spun. The pursuit had begun.

He listened for Davida, but with luck she'd made it to the night watchman's hut and escape. The plan was to transport her to a safe place known only to King and his faithful servants.

Emmanuel turned to leave. By all conventional standards, this case was a failure. The wrong man beaten into a confession, the Security Branch triumphant, and van Niekerk set to blackmail his way up the ladder. Rescuing Davida would have to be the saving grace. It would have to be enough for him.

"You think you know pain?" Piet stood in the doorway, calm as a cobra eyeing a field mouse. "A bullet wound and a few bruises? They are nothing. The scribbling of a child on your body."

Emmanuel swivelled and jumped for the open window. He was getting out with his liver, lungs and spleen intact. Iron hands pulled him back into the room and Lieutenant Piet Lapping began the lesson in earnest.

Emmanuel tasted blood. It was dark. It was painful to breathe. He drifted in and out of consciousness on a tide controlled by pockmarked Piet. His blurred outline hovered over him and he thought: the Pretorius boys know nothing about administering a proper beating. Piet is right to give lessons.

456